Praise for the novels of Debra Webb

"The twists and turns in this dark, taut drama make it both creepy and compelling, multiplying the enjoyment. It's hard-edged and emotional, ensnaring the reader in a world perfectly imagined. I bid a grand welcome to a new voice in the thriller world."
—*New York Times* bestselling author Steve Berry on *The Longest Silence*

"Webb weaves incredible twists and turns and a mind-blowing conclusion with multiple villainous perpetrators."
—*RT Book Reviews* on *The Longest Silence*

"This psychological thriller is rife with tension that begins on page one and doesn't let up. It's a race against the clock that had me whispering to the pair of flawed, desperate protagonists, 'Hurry, hurry.' A gripping read."
—#1 *New York Times* bestselling author Sandra Brown on *The Longest Silence*

"A dark, twisted game of cat and mouse! Debra Webb mines our innermost fears as a police detective takes on a serial killer with help from an unexpected ally—or is he the bigger threat? You will fly through the pages of this action-packed thriller!"
—*New York Times* bestselling author Lisa Gardner on *No Darker Place*

"A steamy, provocative novel with deep, deadly secrets guaranteed to be worthy of your time."
—*Fresh Fiction* on *Traceless*

"Interspersed with fine-tuned suspense...the cliffhanger conclusion will leave readers eagerly anticipating future installments."
—*Publishers Weekly* on *Obsession*

DEBRA WEBB

THE SECRETS WE BURY

mira

mira

ISBN-13: 978-0-7783-0830-0

Recycling programs
for this product may
not exist in your area.

The Secrets We Bury

CONTENTS

This book is dedicated to Donna England Boyd.
Thank you for being a dear, dear friend
and for being the sister of my heart. It's you who will
always make me call Huntland my second home.
May your life forever be filled with love and music and
your heart always rise to the next dance. Love you!

THE SECRETS WE BURY

RIP
Geneva Phillips
Beloved Wife and Mother
June 2, 1946–May 5, 2019

Geneva Phillips was born in Winchester, Tennessee, on June 2, 1946. She was a loving wife and mother, a consummate homemaker and a treasured member of the Ladies Civic Club, as well as a talented musician and a member of the choir at the Second Avenue Methodist Church. She died at home on Sunday, May 5, 2019. Geneva was predeceased by her beloved husband, Howard, and her only sibling, a brother, Gerald. She is survived by two daughters, Patricia Patterson of Winchester and Jennifer Brinkley of Louisville, Kentucky, and three grandchildren.

The family will receive friends on Tuesday, May 7, 5:00 to 7:00 p.m., at the DuPont Funeral Home.

One

Mothers shouldn't die this close to Mother's Day.

Especially mothers whose daughters, despite being grown and having families of their own, still considered Mom to be their best friend. Rowan DuPont had spent the better part of last night consoling the daughters of Geneva Phillips. Geneva had failed to show at church on Sunday morning, and later that same afternoon she wasn't answering her cell. Her younger daughter entered her mother's home to check on her and found Geneva deceased in the bathtub.

Now the seventy-two-year-old woman's body waited in refrigeration for Rowan to begin the preparations for her final journey. The viewing wasn't until tomorrow evening, so there was no particular rush. The husband of one of the daughters was away on business in London and wouldn't arrive back home until late today. There was time for a short break, which turned into a morning drive that had taken Rowan across town and to a place she hadn't visited in better than two decades.

Like death, some things were inevitable. Coming back to this place was one of those things. Perhaps it was the hours spent with the sisters last night that had prompted memories of Rowan's own sister. She and her twin had once been inseparable. Wasn't that generally the way with identical twins?

The breeze shifted, lifting a wisp of hair across her face. Rowan swiped it away and stared out over Tims Ford Lake. The dark, murky waters spread like sprawling arms some thirty-odd miles upstream from the nearby dam, enveloping the treacherous Elk River in its embrace. The water was deep and unforgiving. Even standing on the bank, at least ten feet from the edge, a chill crept up Rowan's spine. She hated this place. Hated the water. The ripples that broke the shadowy surface...the smell of fish and rotting plant life. She hated every little thing about it.

This was the spot where her sister's body had been found.

July 6, twenty-seven years ago. Rowan and Raven had turned twelve years old the previous fall. Rowan's gaze lingered on the decaying tree trunk and the cluster of newer branches and overgrowth stretching from the bank into the hungry water where her sister's lifeless body had snagged. The current had dragged her pale, thin body a good distance before depositing her at this spot. It had taken eight hours and twenty-three minutes for the search teams to find her.

Rowan had known her sister was dead before the call had come that Raven had gone missing. Her parents had rushed to help with the search, leaving a neighbor with

Rowan. She had stood at her bedroom window watching for their return. The house had felt completely empty and Rowan had understood that her life would never be the same after that day.

No matter that nearly three decades has passed since that sultry summer day, she could still recall the horrifying feel of the final tug, and then the ominous release of her sister's physical presence.

She shifted her gaze from the water to the sky. Last night the temperature had taken an unseasonable plunge. Blackberry winter, the locals called it. Whether it held some glimmer of basis in botany or was merely rooted in folklore, blackberry bushes all over the county were in full bloom. Rowan pulled her sweater tight around her. Though today was the first time she had come to this place since returning home from Nashville, the dark water was never far from her thoughts. How could it be? The lake swelled and withdrew around Winchester like the rhythmic breath of a sleeping giant, at once harmless and menacing.

Rowan had sneaked away to this spot dozens of times after her sister was buried. Other times she had ridden her bike to the cemetery and visited her there or simply sat in Raven's room and stared at the bed where she had once laid her head. But Rowan felt closest to her sister here, near the water that had snatched her life away like the merciless talons of a hawk descending on a fleeing field mouse.

"You should have stayed home," Rowan murmured to herself. The ache, no matter the many years that had passed, twisted in her chest.

She had begged Raven not to go to the party. Her sister had been convinced that Rowan's behavior was nothing more than jealousy since she hadn't been invited. The suggestion hadn't been entirely unjustified, but mostly Rowan had felt a smothering dread, a panic that had bordered on hysteria. She had needed her sister to stay home. Every adolescent instinct she possessed had been screaming and restless with that looming sense of trepidation.

But Raven had ignored her sister's pleas and attended the big barbecue and swim party with her best friend, Tessa Cardwell. Raven DuPont died that day, and Rowan had spent all the years since wondering what she could have done differently to change that outcome.

Nothing. She could not rewrite history any more than she was able to change her sister's mind.

Rowan exhaled a beleaguered breath. At moments like this she felt exactly as if her life was moving backward. She'd enjoyed a fulfilling career with the Metropolitan Nashville Police Department as an adviser for the Special Crimes Unit. As a psychiatrist, she had found her work immensely satisfying, and she had helped to solve numerous homicide cases. But then, not quite two months ago, everything had changed. The one case that Rowan didn't recognize had been happening right in front of her, shattering her life…and sending everything spiraling out of control.

The life she had built in Nashville had been comfortable, with enough intellectual challenge in her career to make it uniquely interesting. Though she had not possessed a gold shield, the detectives in the Special Crimes Unit had valued her opinion and treated her as if she was as much a member of the team as any of them. But that was before…*before* the man she admired and trusted proved to be a serial killer—a killer who'd murdered her father and an MNPD officer as well as more than a hundred other victims over the past several decades.

A mere one month, twenty-two days and about fourteen hours ago, esteemed psychiatrist Dr. Julian Addington emerged from his cloak of secrecy and changed the way the world viewed serial killers. He was the first of his kind: incredibly prolific, cognitively brilliant and innately chameleonlike—able to change his MO at will. Far too clever to hunt among his own patients or social set, he had chosen his victims carefully, always ensuring he or she could never be traced back to him or his life.

Julian had fooled Rowan for the past two decades and then he'd taken her father, her only remaining family, from her. He'd devastated and humiliated her both personally and professionally.

Anger and loathing churned inside her. He wanted her to suffer. He wanted her to be defeated…to give up. But she would not. Determination solidified inside her. She would not allow him that victory or that level of control over her.

Her gaze drifted out over the water once more. Since her father's death and moving back to Winchester, people had asked her dozens of times why she'd returned to take over the funeral home after all these years. She always gave the same answer: *I'm a DuPont, it's what we do.*

Her father, of course, had always hoped Rowan would do so. It was the DuPont way. The funeral home had been in the family for a 150 years. The legacy had been passed from one generation to the next time and time again. When she'd graduated from college and chosen to go to medical school and become a psychiatrist rather than to return home and take over the family business, Edward DuPont had been devastated. For more than a year after that decision, she and her father had been estranged. Now she mourned that lost year with an ache that was soul-deep.

They had reconciled, she reminded herself, and other than the perpetual guilt she felt over not visiting often enough, things had been good between her and her father. Like all else in her life until recently, their relationship had been comfortable. They'd spoken by phone regularly. She missed those chats. He kept her up to speed on who married or moved or passed, and she would tell him as much as she could about her latest case. He had loved hearing about her work with Metro. As much as he'd wanted her to take over the family legacy, he had wanted her to be happy more than anything else.

"I miss you, Daddy," she murmured.

Looking back, Rowan deeply regretted having allowed Julian to become a part of her life all those years ago. She had shared her deepest, darkest secrets with him, including her previously strained relationship with her father. She had purged years of pent-up frustrations and anxieties to the bastard, first as his patient and then, later, as a colleague and friend.

Though logic told her otherwise, a part of her would always feel the weight of responsibility for her father's murder.

Due to her inability to see what Julian was, she could not possibly return to Metro, though they had assured her there would always be a place for her in the department. How could she dare to pretend some knowledge or insight the detectives themselves did not possess when she had unknowingly been a close friend to one of the most prolific serial killers the world had ever known?

She could not. *This* was her life now.

Would taking over the family business completely assuage the guilt she felt for letting her father down all those years ago? Certainly not. Never. But it was what she had to do. It was her destiny. In truth, she had started to regret her career decision well before her father's murder. Perhaps it was the approaching age milestone of forty or simply a midlife crisis. She had found herself pondering what might have been different if she'd made that choice and regretting, frankly, that she hadn't.

Since she and Raven were old enough to follow the simplest directions, they had been trained to prepare a body for its final journey. By the time they were twelve, they could carry out the necessary steps nearly as well as their father with little or no direction.

Growing up surrounded by death had, of course, left its mark. Her hyperawareness of death and all its ripples and aftershocks made putting so much stock into a relationship with another human being a less than attractive proposal. Why go out of her way to risk that level of pain in the event that person was lost? And with life came loss. To that end, she would likely never marry or have children. But she had her work and, like her father, she intended to do her very best. Both of them had always been workaholics. Taking care of the dead was a somber albeit important task, particularly for those left behind. The families of the loved ones who passed through the DuPont doors looked to her for support and guidance during their time of sorrow and emotional turmoil.

Speaking of which, she pulled her cell from her pocket and checked the time. She should get back to the funeral home. Mrs. Phillips was waiting. Rowan turned away from the part of her past that still felt fresh despite the passage of time.

Along this part of the shore, the landscape was thickly wooded and dense with undergrowth, which was the reason she'd worn her rubber boots and was slowly picking her way back to the road. As she attempted to slide her phone back into her hip pocket, a limb snagged her hair. Instinctively, she reached up to pull it loose, dropping her cell phone in the process.

"Damn it." Rowan reached down and felt through the thatch beneath the underbrush. More of her long blond strands caught in the brush. She should have taken the time to pull her hair back in a ponytail as she usually did. She tugged the hair loose, bundled the thick mass into her left hand and then crouched down to dig around with her right in search of her phone. Like most people, she felt utterly lost without the damn thing.

Where the hell had it fallen?

She would have left it in the car except that she never wanted a family member to call the funeral home and reach a machine. With that in mind, she forwarded calls to her cell when she was away. Eventually she hoped to trust her father's new assistant director enough to allow him to handle all incoming calls. Wouldn't have helped this morning, though, since he was on vacation.

New assistant director? She almost laughed at the idea. Woody Holder had been with her father for two years, but Herman Carter had been with him a lifetime before that. She supposed in comparison, *new* was a reasonable way of looking at Woody's tenure thus far. Her father had still referred to him as the new guy. Maybe it was his lackadaisical attitude. At forty-five, Woody appeared to possess absolutely no ambition and very little motivation. Rowan really should consider finding a new, more dependable assistant director and letting Woody go.

Her fingers raked through the leaves and decaying ground cover until she encountered something cool and hard but not metal or plastic. Definitely not her phone. She stilled, frowned in concentration as her sense of touch attempted to identify the object she couldn't see without sticking her head into the bushes. Not happening. She might have chalked the object up to being a limb or a rock if not for the familiar, tingling sensation rushing along every single nerve ending in her body. Her instincts were humming fiercely.

Assuredly not a rock.

Holding her breath, she reached back to the same spot and touched the object again. Her fingers dug into the soft earth around the object and curled instinctively.

Long. Narrow. Cylindrical.

She pulled it from the rich, soft dirt, the thriving moss and the tangle of rotting leaves.

Bone.

She frowned, studied it closely. *Human* bone.

Her pulse tripped into a faster rhythm. She placed the bone aside, reached back in with both hands and carefully scratched away more of the leaves.

Another bone…and then another. Bones that, judging by their condition, had been here for a very long time.

Meticulously sifting through the layers of leaves and plant life, she discovered that her cell phone had fallen into the rib cage. The *human* rib cage. Her mind racing with questions and conclusions, she cautiously fished out the phone. She took a breath, hit her contacts list and tapped the name of Winchester's chief of police.

When he picked up, rather than hello, she said, "I'm at the lake. There's something here you need to see and it can't wait. Better call Burt and send him in this direction, as well." Burt Johnston was a local veterinarian who had served as the county coroner for as long as Rowan could remember.

Chief of Police William "Billy" Brannigan's first response was, "Are *you* okay?"

Billy and Rowan had been friends since grade school. He had made her transition back to life in Winchester so much more bearable. And there was Herman. He was more like an uncle than a mere friend of the family. Eventually, she hoped the two of them would stop worrying so about her. She wasn't that fragile young girl who had left Winchester twenty-odd years ago. Recent events had rocked her, that was true, but she was completely capable of taking care of herself. She would never again allow herself to be vulnerable to anyone.

"I'm fine, but someone's not. You should stop worrying about me and get over here, Billy."

"I'm on my way."

She ended the call. There had been no need for her to tell him precisely where she was at the lake. He would know. Rowan DuPont didn't swim; she never came near the lake unless it was to visit her sister, and she hadn't done that in a very, very long time.

Strange, all those times Rowan had come to visit Raven, she'd never realized there was someone else here, too.

Barely fifteen minutes passed before Chief of Police Billy—Bill to those who hadn't grown up with him—Brannigan was tearing nosily through the woods. Rowan pushed away from the tree she'd been leaning against and waved. He spotted her and altered his course.

"Burt's on his way." Billy stopped next to her and

pushed his brown Stetson up his forehead. "You sure you're okay?" He looked her up and down, his gaze pausing on the boots she wore. Pink, dotted with blue-and-yellow flowers. They were as old as dirt but she loved them. She'd had them since she was a teenager. Frankly, she couldn't believe her father had kept them all those years.

Billy's lips spread into a grin. "I like the boots."

She rolled her eyes. "Thanks. And, yes, for the second time, I'm okay." She pointed to the throng of bushes where she'd dropped her phone. "But the female hidden under those bushes is definitely not okay."

He moved in the direction she indicated and crouched down to take a closer look. "You sure this is a female?"

Rowan squatted next to him. "You can see the pelvis." She pointed to the exposed bones that were more or less in a pile. "Definitely female. I can't determine the age—probably over fourteen. I tried not to disturb the positioning of the bones—other than the couple I pulled up before I recognized they were human remains." She leaned in, studying the remains as best she could. "From what I see, it doesn't appear the bones have been damaged by any larger animals."

She indicated the smooth surfaces. "No visible teeth marks. Judging by the positioning, I'd say she was dumped here exactly the way you see. On her left side, knees bent toward her chest, arms flung forward. As tissue deteriorated, the bones settled into a sort of pile and the plant life swallowed them up."

Billy held out his arms in front of him. "Like she was carried to this spot, one arm behind her back, one under her legs—the way a man might carry a woman—and dumped or placed on the ground in that same position."

"That's the way it looks," Rowan agreed.

"You think she was dead when she was left here?"

She made a face, scrutinized what she could see of the skull. "It's difficult to say. There's no obvious indication of cause of death. No visible fractures to the skull or missing pieces, but there's a lot of it I can't see without disturbing the scene."

He hummed a note of indecision. "How long you think she's been here?"

"A while. Years." Rowan shrugged. "Maybe decades. There's a total lack of tissue. The bones I picked up are dry, almost flaky. If there was any clothing, it's gone. To disappear so completely, it would certainly have had to be an organic material of some sort. Maybe when they dig around they'll find a zipper or buttons—something to suggest what she was wearing." She looked to her old friend. "But I'm no medical examiner or anthropologist. I'm merely speculating based on a small amount of knowledge and a very preliminary examination."

"I appreciate your insights." Billy shook his head. "Damn. I can't believe she's been here that long and no one discovered her before now."

"It's a remote, overgrown area." Rowan looked around. "No reason for anyone to come through here." She kept the *except me* to herself. "I suppose it's a good thing I dropped my phone."

When she'd left the funeral home this morning, she'd tucked her phone into the pocket of her jeans. She hadn't bothered with her purse or even her driver's license. Just her phone and, of course, the pepper spray she carried everywhere. The drive to the lake was only a few miles. She had a handgun but she hadn't bothered with it this morning—not for coming here.

But then, she hadn't expected to stumble upon human remains.

In fact, she hadn't expected to see anyone. If she'd had any idea she would be running into Billy and the half a dozen other official folks who would now descend on what was in all likelihood a crime scene, she would have dressed more appropriately. She spent most of her free time in jeans and Ts nowadays. The cotton material was breathable. Perfect for wearing under all that protective gear when working in the mortuary room and easy to launder afterward. She wouldn't be winning any awards for her fashion sense, but she was comfortable.

When working with the dead, it was always better to be as comfortable as possible.

Most of her time on the job in Nashville had been spent in heels and business suits. It was a nice perk not to have to dress up anymore. Since taking over the family business, she'd discovered that she preferred a ponytail to a French twist or a chignon any day of the week. And sneakers rather than heels were always a good thing.

Or maybe she'd grown lazy since returning home. She gave herself grace since she was still adjusting to the loss of her father. Of course, she dressed suitably for meeting the families of lost loved ones, for the viewings and the services. The business suits from her years with Metro came in handy for just those purposes. As her father always said, there were certain expectations when overseeing such a somber occasion.

"I'll need an official statement from you." Billy stood and offered his hand. "I can come by the funeral home later and take care of the statement if that works better for you."

She took his hand and pushed to her feet. "That would

be my preference, yes." She glanced toward the road. "Does that mean I can go?" Rowan really did not want to be here when the media showed up. And the media would show up. As soon as word about finding human remains spread through the police department, someone would give the local newspaper a heads-up. It was the natural course of things. The possibility of a homicide was a secret hardly anyone could keep. Rowan had endured enough of the spotlight after the release of her book, *The Language of Death*, and then the very public unmasking of her friend and colleague, Julian Addington, as a new breed of prolific serial killer.

Not to mention this was the second set of human bones to be found in Winchester in as many months. The other bones had been identified and the old case solved. Still, a steady stream of homicide cases was never a good thing for the chief of police.

He glanced around. "I don't see any reason for you to stay." He studied her a moment, those dark brown eyes of his searching hers. "If you're sure you're okay?"

Billy Brannigan was a true hometown hero, always had been. First on the football field and in the local charity rodeo circuit, then for more than a decade and a half as a cop and eventually as the chief of police in Winchester. Folks swore Billy was born wearing a Stetson and cowboy boots. He was a year older than Rowan and he'd made it his mission to take her under his wing after her sister's death. Rowan had been totally lost without her twin, and at twelve she'd had enough insanity in her life with adolescence anyway. Billy had watched over her, threatened to pound anyone who wasn't nice to her. And when her mother died only a few months after her sister, Billy had taken care of Rowan again. He was the only other person on the planet who knew her deepest, darkest secrets.

He and the bastard who'd murdered her father.

"I'm fine. Really. I'll see you later." The sound of traffic on the road warned that she needed to get moving.

"Hey." His fingers curled around her upper arm when she would have walked past him. "Next time you come out here, bring that big old dog of yours and your handgun or ask me to come. You shouldn't be in a remote area like this alone. We both know *he* is still out there."

He. Rowan pushed the image of Julian from her head. She patted her other pocket. "I have my pepper spray." She glanced around again. "And somewhere nearby there might even be a special agent from the FBI's special joint task force keeping an eye on me to make sure I don't aid and abet Julian."

Though at this point the FBI had stopped surveilling her, the very idea made her feel ill. But the Bureau had its reasons in the beginning for suspecting her—all of which were circumstantial and utterly misleading—but nothing she said or did was going to change their minds completely. Her name and the possibilities of her involvement with Julian on a sexual level as well as the suggestion that she might have been part of his extracurricular activities had been smeared across every news channel, every newspaper and online news source. How could she be so close to the man and not see what he was? Particularly considering her formal education and training?

The taint of suspicion would likely follow her the rest of her life. This ugly reality no doubt pleased Julian immensely. At least the folks in her hometown had ignored the rampant rumors for the most part. Business hadn't dropped off and no one looked at her any differently than they ever had. Then again, she'd always been considered strange.

Basically, not much had changed.

Billy nodded, a sad smile on his lips—lips she had fantasized about kissing when she was fourteen years old. So very long ago. A sigh slipped from her. Life would never again be that simple.

"The pepper spray is good, but you should bring your weapon next time," he said, "and Freud, okay?"

She drew in a big breath and let it out dramatically to show him that she was indulging his protective instincts. "*Okay*, Billy, I will not go to any other remote locations alone and without my dog and my handgun. No matter that I'm a grown woman and completely capable of taking care of myself."

For the past six weeks she had worked diligently at honing her self-defense skills. For the first time in her life she owned a handgun and, more important, she knew how to use it. Billy had insisted on giving her lessons. Maybe she was a fool, but she was not afraid of running into Julian. She was prepared for that encounter… looked forward to it, actually. Killing him wasn't her goal—at least not at first. She wanted answers. Then she wanted him to spend the rest of his days in solitary confinement being prodded and poked and tested by forensic psychiatrists.

Billy dipped his head in acknowledgment. "I'm aware, but do it for me."

She rolled her eyes. "For you. Okay."

She gave him a salute, then moved cautiously through the dense bushes until she reached the road, where she'd left her car. In truth, rather than acquiesce to his wishes, she would have loved to tell Billy he was overreacting, being overprotective. Overdoing the big brother thing. But that would be a lie. Julian had murdered all those people, some in ways so heinous that it shocked even seasoned homicide detectives. He had promised Rowan that before he was done, she would want to end the agony of living with all the guilt.

He wasn't the sort of man to make idle threats.

But Rowan intended to see that *he* was the one who wanted the agony to end. She wasn't the only one who had shared secrets during their lengthy friendship. It was true that she hadn't suspected for a moment that he was a killer, but she did know many, many of his most personal thoughts. He had worries just like any other person. He had hopes and dreams. Obviously it was possible he had made up much of what he had told her. Psychopaths oftentimes lied when the truth would serve them better. Still, he was a mere human with human frailties.

She climbed into her car, started the engine. Let him come.

The sooner, the better.

She was ready to show him all she'd learned.

Two

Rowan had washed, disinfected and moisturized Geneva Phillips's body. Generally she would leave that step to her assistant, Woody. As was the usual protocol, upon taking possession of a body and then again before starting the process of embalming, she carefully checked for vital signs to ensure the deceased was indeed deceased. No pulse in either the carotid or radial artery. Obvious lividity, clouded corneas and, of course, rigor mortis. All indications that life was no longer present were apparent.

There was no question that Geneva Phillips had passed.

Everyone had heard the stories about people waking up in funeral homes. Some were mere folk tales but others were not. All the more reason for the second vitals check just before starting the embalming process. There was no going back after that step.

Now Mrs. Phillips lay on her back on the preparation table, her head resting on the head block. After massaging and moving her limbs to relieve the remaining rigor, which helped with drainage and distribution of the embalming fluid, Rowan sealed her eyes and capped them, locked her jaw into position with wire and sealed her lips. Her face was set in a natural-looking expression. Rowan was ready to begin embalming.

With the necessary incisions made and the tubes inserted, Rowan would turn on the pump, which would drain the blood vessels and pump preserving chemicals into those same veins and arteries. The dyes and additives in the embalming fluid would help the body to take on a more florid appearance. This step took a bit of time. As she reached for the switch, Rowan hesitated. She studied the body once more, then stepped back from the table. She removed her protective gloves and set them aside on the instrument table, then reached for the face shield she wore, placing it there, as well. For a long moment she scrutinized the body, walked all the way around the table to confirm what she had only just now noticed.

The lividity suggested Mrs. Phillips had died on her back, similar to the way she lay right now, and had stayed in that position for several hours, more than six in all probability. Burt had told Rowan that the elderly woman died in a slip and fall in the bathtub, probable skull fracture based on the indention on the lower portion at the back of her head.

This scenario was quite possible; however, the lividity did not bear out the theory.

Not unless Mrs. Phillips had a very long bathtub. The lady was about Rowan's height, five foot six, which would require a tub considerably longer than the standard size to allow her to lie completely flat so that the blood would settle along the sides of her body from her head to her heels as if she had been lying flat on her back when her heart stopped beating.

Before Rowan went any further with the embalming,

she needed to be certain. She tugged her gloves back on, removed the drain and arterial tubes from the body and closed with tape the insertion points she had made in the carotid artery and the internal jugular. She then wheeled the table carrying Mrs. Phillips back into refrigeration until she was ready to resume the embalming.

Rowan glanced at the coffin already in refrigeration. Ronald Whitt's viewing was tonight. It was after 11:00 a.m. now. She would need to check on this bathtub situation and return to the funeral home as quickly as possible to prepare. She removed her gloves and apron and then grabbed the items she would need—her keys, cell phone and a tape measure—and locked up. As she made her way to her car, she fished out her cell and tapped the contact to put through the necessary call.

Cause and manner of death were no longer a part of her work as they had been in Nashville. Whatever happened to Mrs. Phillips wasn't actually within the scope of her responsibility. Certainly she didn't want to step on any toes, particularly those of friends like Burt, the duly elected coroner.

But this was far too obvious to ignore.

Billy accepted her call, made a comment to whoever was with him and then asked, "Hey, Ro, what's up?"

"Anything on the bones yet?" It was too early, she knew, but the need to ask would not be ignored. How had the remains lain in those woods all these years only yards from where Raven had been found? Rowan had gone to that particular spot numerous times before leaving for college. Certainly it was possible the remains had been there long before Raven's death. Determining the age of the bones was well outside Rowan's expertise.

"Nothing yet. Burt's sending the remains to the lab

in Nashville. We most likely won't hear anything for a while."

She really hadn't expected any other answer. Pushing the troubling thoughts aside, she asked the more pressing question. "Do you have a minute to meet me at the house where Geneva Phillips lived? Her older daughter is staying there while she's in town for the funeral, but I don't want to show up at her door without you."

"Sure. I can break away for a few minutes. You mind telling me why we're going to her house?"

A reasonable question, yet not so easy to answer. "I'm not entirely sure. I just need to look at her bathtub."

There was a distinct pause. "Well, all righty then. I'll be there in five minutes."

Rowan appreciated her friend's trust. He hadn't pressed for an answer on her reasoning. She hoped she wasn't wasting his time or her own.

The trip from First Avenue to Woodlawn took only a few minutes. A quick detour around the courthouse square, a short drive along Dinah Shore Boulevard and a left at the drugstore onto Woodlawn.

Billy was there already. He climbed out of his truck and met her on the sidewalk. "Looks like Jennifer's home."

The car with the Kentucky plates sat in the driveway. Mrs. Phillips's older daughter had driven from Louisville to Winchester early last evening. "We should tell her that you need another look at the bathroom to finish up your final report. I really don't want to upset her if I'm wrong about *this*."

Billy's brow furrowed. "I don't usually do reports on this sort of thing. That would fall under Burt's purview."

Rowan grimaced. "I know. I'm hoping Jennifer isn't

familiar with the standard operating procedures related to the chief of police responding to a 911 call."

He cocked his head and studied her. "Care to let me in on why we need to do this at all?"

"I'd rather wait until I've had a look at the tub." Her face pinched into another of those grimaces. She should just tell him. But then if she was wrong... Since learning the shocking truth about Julian, she didn't trust her instincts the way she once had. "If that's okay with you."

He shrugged. Glanced at the house. "Sure. I trust that whatever you've got on your mind is important. So how about we knock on the door and get to it?"

"Thanks, Billy. I really appreciate you indulging me this way."

As they moved up the sidewalk, he said, "Burt mentioned you were right about the remains being female. He thinks maybe they've been in those woods at least two decades, maybe three. He and a couple of his coroner buddies from surrounding counties went to a seminar at the Body Farm last summer."

The Body Farm was actually a research facility for studying the decomposition of human remains. Rowan had visited once, many years ago.

Rowan nodded. Burt's estimation was slightly longer than hers, but the way the vegetation had wrapped around the remains, it would have been difficult to make an accurate conclusion without a closer examination, even for someone trained in the field. She pushed the doorbell. "Any unresolved disappearances from that time frame?"

Rowan didn't recall any missing person cases in the Winchester area from when she was a kid. But unless it was someone she knew or the circumstances were particularly gruesome or shocking, she might not, especially if it was around the same time as Raven's death. The final six months of that year had been especially devastating for her and her father.

Billy shook his head. "I can't recall any, but I've got one of my detectives looking back over the case logs beginning thirty years ago. Hopefully he'll have something for me before the day is done."

It was always possible the location where the remains were found was nothing more than a dump site. The actual murder might not have happened in Winchester or even in Franklin County, for that matter. Before she could stop her mind from taking that path, the images from all those souvenirs Julian had curated from his many, many victims streamed through her brain.

Jennifer Brinkley opened the door, banishing the images from Rowan's thoughts. The grieving woman's eyes were red and puffy from crying. Understandable. Her daughter, Kelley, who had done the driving from Louisville, stood beside her. Kelley was a senior in college. Her father was the one who was traveling back from London today. It suddenly occurred to Rowan that Jennifer and Patty's father had died around the same time as Rowan's. Which made their mother's death all the more painful.

"I'm sorry to bother you, ma'am," Billy said, "but I was hoping to have one last look in the bathroom in order to finish up my final report. I failed to take a few measurements."

Sounded like a reasonable excuse to Rowan. Unless the other woman had recently experienced the death of a family member that required the involvement of the police, the average person wouldn't have a clue what sorts of reports needed to be submitted. Particularly a death considered anything other than natural causes.

Jennifer looked confused for a moment, but then she apparently dismissed her questions and nodded. "Of course, Chief. Whatever you need to do."

When she looked to Rowan, Rowan said, "We met last night and went over the final arrangements for your mother."

The other woman nodded. "Of course. You're the undertaker's daughter—I mean the undertaker." A weary smile tugged at her lips. "I remember you from high school. I was a senior when you were a freshman, so you probably don't remember me. But everyone knew you."

Rowan mustered up a smile. Folks in Winchester had called her the undertaker's daughter her whole life. Somewhere in the back of her mind she wondered if that would change now that *she* was the undertaker. "I don't remember you, but I remember your mother. She was extra kind to me after my mother died."

Jennifer nodded as more tears welled in her eyes. "She always tried to be kind to anyone having a difficult time."

"She did," Rowan agreed. "Chief Brannigan thought you might feel more comfortable if I came along with him."

"Please come in." Jennifer and her daughter stepped back, opened the door wider. "You know the way," she said to the chief. "We've been using the downstairs bathroom. We really don't want to go in…that one."

"I understand," Billy assured her. "We'll only be a minute."

Billy nodded toward the stairs, and Rowan headed in that direction. The house was the only historic home left on the street. Most of the others were traditional ranch-style homes built after the former century-old homes either burned or were torn down for one reason or another. This one still had the original heart-of-pine wood floors and the charm and character of late-nineteenth-century architecture.

The bedrooms were upstairs, as was the bathroom the owner had used. A typical layout with the added luxury of an upstairs bath, probably a former bedroom or part of one. Extra bedrooms were often cannibalized for the sake of an added bath or a larger closet.

"Last door on the left," Billy said as Rowan reached the second-story landing.

She followed the narrow hall and opened the door. For a long moment she stood in the doorway and took in the small room. On her way home from the old high school that had been torn down a few years back, Rowan had driven along this street many times as a teenager. The bathroom looked exactly how she had imagined one in this old house would. No more than six feet wide with a vintage pedestal sink to her immediate left, a toilet—a newer model—and then an original-to-the-era claw-foot tub. Above the tub was a window.

Rowan reached into the pocket of her jeans and retrieved the small tape measure she'd brought with her. She extended the measuring tape along the length of the tub to confirm what she suspected.

"I must be getting better at this mind-reading thing," Billy noted. "You never mentioned measuring anything, and I told Jennifer I needed a few more measurements."

Focused on the task, Rowan recognized he was speaking to her, so she hummed an *mmm-hmm*, but her mind was fixed on playing out the sequence of events that ended in the elderly woman's death. Any way she played it, the numbers didn't add up.

"Did Mrs. Phillips fall out of the tub?"

Even as she asked the question, Rowan didn't see how Mrs. Phillips could have landed in a way that would have allowed her to stretch out fully on her back. There was about seven feet of tiled floor between the tub and the door. Chances were she would have fallen onto her side or in a crumpled position. The toilet was in the way of any other scenario.

"She was right there in the tub." Billy moved closer, his body against Rowan's so that he could direct her attention as he spoke. He pointed to the end of the tub away from the spout. "Her head was lying against that rim and her feet were down at this end." He gestured to the drain.

"Her knees were bent?" She had no doubt, but Rowan asked the question anyway.

"That's right."

He eyed her a moment, his face close enough for her to smell the aftershave he wore. It was the same one he'd worn back in high school. Classic. Male. Subtle. She breathed it in now, grateful for the familiarity. With her life so upside down of late, she couldn't help clinging to any semblance of normalcy.

"What's going on in that head of yours, Ro?"

"Something is off with the way she died. The lividity of the body tells us that Mrs. Phillips died lying flat on her back, legs straight. She remained in that position long enough for the lividity to become fixed. At least six or more hours." Rowan looked back at the tub. "If she had fallen in the tub and stayed in the position in which she was found, the lividity would have been in her buttocks, ankles and feet. Not along her back, thighs and calves."

"Are you suggesting—" he glanced over his shoulder at the open door, then lowered his voice before continuing "—that someone placed her in the tub *after* she died?"

Rowan moved her head from side to side. "I'm not suggesting anything, Billy."

He stared at her, waiting for the rest.

"I am telling you that she couldn't possibly have died in that position and remained so until she was found yesterday. You said Burt put time of death approximately ten hours before she was found, right?"

Billy nodded, his gaze narrowed in concentration. "So, you believe someone came back—after at least six hours—and moved her into the tub."

"It's the only conceivable explanation." Rowan exhaled a big breath. "It wouldn't have been an easy task, either, considering her state of rigor by that point."

He stared at the tub, then stepped back to survey the room as a whole. "Well, damn. If that's the case, we're trampling all over a homicide scene."

Rowan glanced at the door to ensure they were still alone. "You should talk to the younger daughter, Patricia, and find out if her mother had any enemies or if there's anything missing from the house."

He nodded his agreement with her suggestion. Rowan bit her tongue at the idea that she'd just told the chief of police how to do his job. She had no right to doubt his skill as an investigator and certainly no authority to order him around. "Sorry," she offered. "Old habits die hard."

"No problem. I was thinking the same thing." He stared at the tub and blew out a breath. "I'll have Burt come by the funeral home for a second look at the body—Mrs. Phillips." He shook his head. "I don't see how he missed this."

"He had no reason to suspect foul play," Rowan reminded Billy. The last thing she wanted to do was make the man who had served as county coroner for forty-some-odd years look bad. "The situation appeared straightforward. We humans have a habit of seeing what we expect to see."

Billy frowned. "But you noticed."

"Not until I had her on the table." She gestured to the small room around them. "The lighting in here is poor and her body was folded into that tub. I had the luxury of good lighting and plenty of time without a distraught family member hovering nearby. I'm certain he did the best he could under the circumstances."

Billy acknowledged her litany of excuses with a nod. "I'm just glad you noticed something was off."

"Looks like I'm the bearer of bad news a second time today." So much for keeping a low profile until the gossip about her personal tragedy in Nashville died down.

He nodded, a weary smile on his lips. "I'm just glad you're home, Ro."

Sometimes she had a hard time being glad about that, but at the moment she was reasonably happy to be here. Billy made the concept of fitting back into the community considerably easier. Not that she expected easy when it came to her life in this small town. Winchester was a charming, genteel place. But there had never been anything charming and genteel about her life. Her face and name were and always would be associated with death.

Being connected to a now infamous serial killer wasn't helping.

"We should keep this quiet until we see what Burt has to say," Billy cautioned.

The warning was the right call, not a suggestion of his doubt regarding her deductions about Mrs. Phillips. Until there was some concrete conclusion about manner of death, there was no reason to upset the family. "I won't say anything to anyone until you give me the go-ahead."

Rowan's gaze landed on the pink bar of soap and the folded pink towel on the closed toilet lid. From all appearances, Mrs. Phillips had been preparing for a bath or shower. Since she hadn't shown up for church, whoever had entered her home and killed her had caught her readying for Sunday services.

"I'll call Burt, and we'll meet you at the funeral home as quickly as I can get him moving."

Anticipation trickled into Rowan's veins. She hadn't expected to ever be involved—even remotely—in another potential homicide investigation. Now suddenly she was in the middle of not one but two.

Rowan nodded. "I'll be there."

By the time Billy and the coroner arrived, Rowan had moved Mrs. Phillips back into the embalming room. She'd positioned the lights on the areas of fixed lividity. The better lighting would help Burt tremendously. He was, after all, well into his seventies. Rowan was extremely thankful for the contacts she wore. Dealing with a face shield was so much easier with contacts than with glasses. Frankly, she doubted Burt's vision was any worse than her own. She'd worn glasses since she was ten years old. The need for corrective lenses had been another of the few differences between Rowan and her twin sister. With her sister's ever-burgeoning social life,

Rowan couldn't help wondering what other differences would have developed between them. Would Raven have been married and have had children by now? Would she have stayed and worked with their father? Or would she have left as Rowan did?

Maybe if Raven and their mother had lived, Rowan would have stayed, too.

Just more of those things Rowan would never know.

Billy sat on a stool next to the whiteboard Rowan used to keep track of the steps completed for each new client, the chemicals used and requests from family members related to preparation. There was a high, narrow desk—an old plantation desk—as well. Her father had kept peppermint candy in the top right-hand drawer. He always said nothing went better with the smell of the dead than peppermint.

"You didn't notice any other marks on her body when you bathed her and did that massage thing you do?" Billy asked.

Rowan stood beside him, too anxious to sit. They had been watching Burt for approximately fifteen minutes now. Though to her knowledge, Billy had never been present during the steps of preparing the recently deceased for internment, he'd insisted she talk him through it back in high school. He'd wanted to tour the embalming room and to know every step of the process. She had been seventeen and he'd been eighteen. He'd just broken up with his latest girlfriend, and she was pretty sure he'd sneaked a couple of his dad's beers before coming over. He'd wanted to talk, to distract himself from his misery. She'd ended up making him spend the night. He was the only other person who had ever slept in her dead sister's room.

Her mind had played that night numerous times over the years. Him collapsing onto the twin-size bed. Her tugging at first one boot and then the other. She'd carefully placed his trademark hat on the nightstand and the boots next to that. He'd gone to sleep almost immediately. Looking back, she decided he had passed out. In fact, she was reasonably confident he was more inebriated by that point than he had been when he first arrived. Maybe he'd stashed several beers in his truck. She distinctly recalled him running back out to his truck more than once.

"I didn't notice any other injuries or abnormalities," she explained, "and I looked closely once I noticed the contradicting lividity."

Since Burt began his examination, it had occurred to Rowan that it was not a good thing she had washed the body, shampooed the hair, rinsed away the dried blood... as well as any potential evidence. Particularly since there would need to be a vaginal swab to ensure no sexual assault had occurred and a check for tissue beneath the deceased's fingernails in the event she fought her attacker during the final moments of her life. Although there was no visible indication such as bruising on her thighs, at this point they couldn't risk overlooking any evidence. Thankfully, Rowan had not reached the step in her preparations where she cleansed and filled the body cavities.

"The scalp was broken and there was some blood," she went on, "but the most significant aspect of the injury was the fairly deep compression at the base of the skull." Blunt trauma to that area could cause basilar skull fractures, which would have set off a chain of events like intracranial bleeding. In Rowan's opinion this was most likely the type of injury that had ended the elderly woman's life. "Depending on the severity, death would have been quick."

"What about the size of the compressed area?"

Rowan understood that he was attempting to conclude the type of object used to cause the trauma. "Two to three inches. Curved." She thought of the rim on the tub. "Not unlike the rim of that tub where her body was found. Or perhaps a baseball bat."

Billy watched the coroner's movements. "So we can't rule out the idea that she fell in the tub."

Rowan shrugged. "I can't rule out that possibility, no, but I can tell you that if she did, someone moved her onto the floor or someplace where she lay flat on her back for the next half-dozen hours or so."

"Or she managed to get up after the initial fall and then fell onto her back on the floor," he countered with a dubious look in her direction. He was reaching for any sort of explanation that didn't include murder. "But then she wouldn't have been able to climb back into the tub six or so hours after her heart stopped beating." He blew out a disgusted breath.

Rowan had had this same conversation with herself on the drive back to the funeral home and again as she waited for Billy and the coroner to arrive. "If she fell twice, where are the other bruises?"

Admittedly, if any bruising had occurred on her backside, it was obscured by the lividity. Another thought occurred to Rowan. "Where's the blood on the floor? Unless your people cleaned it up or the daughter did, there would be blood from the damage to the scalp. And, of course, there's the issue of how she ended up back in the tub."

Billy shook his head. "There was no blood on the

floor when we arrived. Patty was very upset. I'm pretty confident she hadn't cleaned the floor. In fact, she was sitting on the floor next to the bathtub when we arrived."

"You didn't see any blood on the floor or on her clothes?" Burt asked as he glanced over his shoulder, joining the attempt to narrow down the possible scenarios to something besides murder.

Billy shook his head. "Nope, but I will be asking Patty if she saw any when she arrived and found her mother."

Another question bobbed to the surface of the river of unknowns in Rowan's churning mind. "Where were her clothes? Her nightgown? Whatever she had on before she got into the tub?" This was assuming Mrs. Phillips was still breathing when she ended up in that tub.

Not likely, Rowan.

"I walked through the upstairs area—as a formality." Billy's forehead furrowed in thought. "I noticed a nightgown on the bed."

"Was the bed made?" Rowan didn't know Geneva Phillips particularly well, but she wouldn't have taken her for a woman who walked around naked, even in the privacy of her own home.

"It was."

Rowan was impressed with his attention to detail. He was the chief of police, she reminded herself. She had to stop seeing him as her old friend, the popular guy in school and beloved high school football hero. Billy was a highly trained, experienced law enforcement officer. He possessed a master's degree in criminal justice, and he had worked a decade and a half with the Winchester Police Department, including serving as the top cop. He was no amateur by any means. His place on the Addington joint task force was not his first foray with a multi-agency task force, either, though she suspected the agent in charge had selected Billy as much for his longtime friendship with Rowan as for anything else.

Billy's face lined in thought. "Patty said the front door was locked when she arrived. I asked her that specifically even though I had no reason to suspect foul play." He shrugged. "Habit, I guess."

Patricia Phillips, now Patterson, had been called Patty for as long as Rowan could recall. She was two years older than Rowan. She remembered her more than her older sister, Jennifer.

"What about the back door?" Rowan asked. If she came in the front and found her mother dead, she likely hadn't bothered checking the back door.

Billy's eyebrows went up his forehead. "Good question." He withdrew his cell phone and made a call. When the person on the other end answered, he said, "Jennifer, I hate to bother you again, but have you or your sister gone out the back door since you arrived?" He listened for a moment. "Do you mind checking to see if it's locked?"

Several seconds passed and Rowan couldn't help holding her breath.

Billy frowned again. "As far as you know, has anyone gone in or out that door?" He listened for another moment before thanking her and ending the call. "The back door was unlocked." He shook his head. "Damn it all to hell. I should have checked that, but the situation looked cut-and-dried. I didn't see any reason to look beyond what appeared to be the obvious." He turned his hands up. "To be perfectly honest, it wasn't the sort of situation that triggered my instincts."

Rowan felt his pain. No law enforcement officer liked

to realize that he'd missed something at a potential crime scene. But like he said, this one had seemed completely unambiguous. She opened her mouth to say something reassuring when Burt turned away from the body he'd been examining and removed his glasses.

Billy stood. Rowan held her breath again.

"Welp—" the older man peeled off his gloves "—I am ashamed to say that I screwed up on this one." He glanced back at the deceased woman and exhaled a weary breath. "Really screwed up." He faced Billy and Rowan once more. "There is way she died in that bathtub. Whatever happened, whether it was an accident or a homicide, someone picked her up long hours after the blow to the back of her head occurred and placed her in that tub."

Hands on his hips, Billy grimaced. "As grateful as I am that I'll have the opportunity to find the person who did this terrible thing, I hate like hell to deliver that news to the family."

"It's my mistake," Burt said. "I'll go with you to talk to the family."

Billy shook his head. "You don't need to that, Burt. But thank you for the offer."

Rowan thought of the bones she'd stumbled upon at the lake. Now Billy had two possible murders to investigate.

Even as the thought crossed her mind, he turned to her. "I know you put homicide investigations behind you when you left Nashville, but I could use your help, Ro. Fresh eyes, fresh perspective."

She nodded. "Whatever you need."

Rowan had been taking care of the dead in one fashion or another most of her life. No need to allow her one monumental mistake of failing to recognize a murderer right under her nose to change the path fate had set for her.

On some level she might have been subconsciously waiting since the day she arrived back in Winchester for Billy to ask this very question.

Death had always been more a part of her life than living.

Three

"Patty, I'm really sorry to bother you right now." Billy dropped his head for a moment. He hated like hell to dredge up the possibility of murder. He took a breath, raised his head and met her gaze once more. "But these questions have to be asked. If you'll bear with me, I'll make this interview as quick and forthright as possible."

The woman staring at him in total confusion was a year his senior, but he remembered her from school. Unlike her older sister, who had been the star of the girls' basketball team, Patty had been a cheerleader. Head cheerleader, if he recalled correctly. She cheered at every game he played his freshman through junior years. Both the Phillips girls had been popular and had grown up to be great mothers and successful career women. Jennifer was an economic adviser for a Fortune 500 company in Louisville and Patty was principal at the elementary school right here in Winchester.

She finally blinked. "Okay. I understand you have to do what you have to do. What kind of questions?"

"First, I want you to walk me through yesterday afternoon from the moment you arrived at your mother's house until I showed up. You pulled into the driveway and you can start right there."

Lines marred her brow. "I already did that. Last night." She hugged her arms around herself. "You asked me a million questions while Mr. Johnston was…" She shook her head. "I thought I understood the need for all these extra questions, but I don't. Not really. I'm heartbroken and confused and this is frightening me. Why are you asking me these questions again, Billy?"

He acknowledged her confusion with a nod, gave her a sad smile. "I understand this is difficult and I certainly don't want to frighten you, but it's really important that we have the clearest picture possible of the minutes before you called me."

She blinked once, twice. He hoped like hell she wasn't about to point out how he'd dodged the question entirely. These women were reeling. Their father had passed away just two months ago, and now their mother. And worse, their mother might have been murdered.

What was he thinking? Obviously she had been murdered. He supposed there was a scant outside chance the whole thing was some sort of bizarre accident, but he doubted it. Seriously doubted it.

Patty looked away and exhaled a mighty breath. "I parked in the driveway. I was really worried because I kept calling her—house phone and cell—and she wasn't answering. Momma always answers…*answered* her phone."

He dipped his head. His own momma was the same. She kept that cell phone close. As proud of Billy as she was, she worried about him. Every time a policeman anywhere in the country was shot, she called to remind him to be extra careful out there.

"Did you notice anyone—maybe a neighbor—outside?" Two of his officers were interviewing the neighbors along Woodlawn. If he was lucky, someone had seen an unfamiliar vehicle or person in the neighborhood on Sunday. He desperately needed a starting place on this one. Geneva Phillips was the kind of woman who didn't have any enemies. Never been in trouble. Never caused any trouble. Just a nice lady who lived a kind and quiet life.

"Not that I noticed." She lifted her shoulders and let them fall. "I was really worried, so when I got out of my car I hurried to the door and banged over and over. When she didn't answer I unlocked the front door with my key. Both my sister and I have keys. Momma wanted it that way. Said if we ever needed anything just to go in and get it." Her lips trembled. "But I always knocked first anyway."

He smiled, hated to see the fresh glimmer of tears in her eyes. "My momma says the same thing. I don't think they ever stop wanting to take care of us."

She managed a faint smile. "I aspire to be that kind of momma."

Patty had two boys in elementary school. From what he'd seen, they were a bit on the rowdy side, but she was always patient with them. "You already are," he assured her. "Every time I ran into Mrs. Phillips, she bragged about you and Jenn. Always talked about her grandkids. She was very proud of you both."

Patty blinked back more tears and moistened her lips. "Anyway, I started calling for her as soon as I walked through the door. The house was eerily quiet." She frowned. "You know what I mean? Like the spirit of

the house was gone or something. Like there was nothing left…"

Billy nodded. "An emptiness." He'd sensed the same
the first time he'd walked into his grandmother's house
after she'd passed. The vibrant, sweet lady was gone and
that gracious spirit of hers had vanished, too. The house
was nothing but four walls then. She had been the es-
sence of that home.

"Yes. Emptiness." Another big sigh hissed past her
lips. "So I went to the kitchen. It was her favorite place.
She wasn't in the kitchen, so I went upstairs. The whole
time I was calling for her."

"But you didn't go to the back door?"

She hesitated. Shook her head. "I looked out the window over the sink just to make sure she wasn't on the
back porch, but no, I didn't go near the door." Another
of those deep frowns furrowed her brow. "Jenn said you
asked her about the back door. What's going on, Chief?"

"Before we talk about that," he hedged, "let's finish
with what you did when you went upstairs."

Her face still reflecting confusion, she continued, "I
went into her bedroom. It's that first room on the right.
The windows face out over the street. She loved looking out in the mornings when she got up. This street's
so quiet and she could see the flowers in the yards of the
other houses. She loved flowers, you know."

She hesitated one, two, three seconds before going
on. "She wasn't in her room, so I went to the bathroom.
She was in the tub." She covered her trembling lips with
the fingers of one hand, then cleared her throat. "Her
eyes were open but she wasn't breathing, and her body
was cold and hard, like…" Her emotions got the better
of her then.

Billy gave her a moment to collect herself. She dabbed at her eyes with a tissue. This was about the worst time in the world to have to ask more questions, but there was no help for it.

"Think a moment, Patty," he said. "Was the bathroom door open or closed?"

She frowned as if trying to recall. "Open."

"When you looked in, did you notice any blood on the floor? Did you see any blood at all?"

There had been one smear of blood where Mrs. Phillips's head had lain. Billy had noticed it when she was removed from the tub. He had gone over and over the time he and Burt had spent in that bathroom. If there was blood anywhere else, he had not seen it and Burt hadn't, either. The evidence techs would need to check for any indications of blood that had been cleaned up anywhere else in the house.

She thought for a long moment, and then finally, she said, "No. Only what was in her hair."

His pulse rate picked up. "And what about her clothes? Her nightgown was on the bed. Was it her habit to go into the bathroom for her shower or bath without any clothes on and without taking what she planned to put on afterward?"

Patty's eyes rounded as if she'd only just considered the idea. "I can't imagine Momma ever walking around in the house without clothes on. Not ever. Not for any reason. And she always took whatever she intended to wear into the bathroom with her. Even though she lived alone, she was a very modest person." She smiled and just as quickly that smile crumpled into tears. "She told us a million times to always wear clean drawers and to never be caught with them off. 'You never know when you'll be in an accident,' she'd say." She scrubbed at her eyes with the backs of her hands. "There is no way she would have walked out of her bedroom without a stitch on." Her watery gaze captured Billy's. "What are you thinking happened?"

"Right now, I'm not entirely certain. Of course, there's always the chance she just plain forgot or decided it was time she did things differently," Billy offered, but he had a bad feeling that was not the case. "Whatever happened, we have to rule out all the possibilities."

"What kind of possibilities?" She seemed to shrink into herself as she asked the question.

"Have you and your sister had a chance to go through the house to ensure nothing is missing?"

Her breath caught. "You think someone hurt Momma?"

He held up his hands and spoke as calmly and gently as possible. "That's one of the possibilities we have to consider."

"We haven't really looked for anything that might be missing, but we can, if that's important."

"If you wouldn't mind," he urged, "it would be very helpful."

She nodded her agreement.

"Patty, I'm aware how highly thought of your momma was in this community, but I have to ask this next question."

"Okay." The single word was spoken in such a small voice that he wouldn't have realized she'd spoken at all if he hadn't been looking directly at her.

Billy ached for having to cause her this additional pain. "Is there anyone who might have felt ill will to-

ward your momma? Anyone who had some sort of griev-
ance with her?"

Patty shook her head adamantly. "Everybody loved
Momma. She didn't have any enemies, Chief. If what
you're suggesting is true, it had to be a robbery. Somebody who didn't know her. Maybe they were passing
through town. Followed her home from the Piggly Wiggly. Or some crazed addict on some awful drug. No one
in their right mind who knew her would have hurt her."

He nodded. Geneva Phillips had that kind of reputation. But there were bad people in this world who did bad
things and sometimes they went unnoticed, like the son
of a bitch who'd killed Ro's father. Money, drugs, jealousy—there was no shortage of motives for those who
committed violent crimes, given the right circumstances.

"All right. As I mentioned before, my evidence techs
are preparing to go through the house and check for any
prints and additional forensic evidence. I've asked Jenn
to step out for the day. As soon as the techs are finished,
I need you and your sister to go through the house very
carefully. As best you can, determine if anything at all
is missing. Check her bank account. We want to ensure
that all valuables in general or items that might have
some value to another person are where they should be."

She nodded. "We can do that. I can check her bank
account online. My name is on the account, too."

"That's good. You and Jenn talk about this and see
if you can come up with anyone who might have held a
grudge against your momma related to some misunderstanding, recent or in the past." He stood. "I'll give you
a call as soon as it's okay to return to the house. We can
compare notes once you've had a chance to complete
your inventory."

She walked him to the door, her arms tight around her body. "Thanks for being so thorough, Chief. The thought of someone hurting Momma is nearly more than I can bear. I…I hope it was just an accident."

"I hope so, too."

But it was too late to hold out any real hope. The evidence was pretty damn clear. Someone had slammed Geneva Phillips in the back of the head with something like a baseball bat, and then he'd left her to die naked and alone in her bathroom.

When Billy found the bastard, he would pay.

City hall was just off the courthouse square on the south side. Billy parked in his designated slot and got out of his truck. He surveyed the folks walking along the sidewalk and the shops open for business. The downtown had gone through some tough times, but a major revitalization the past couple of years had turned things around. Local artists and craftsmen had opened up the closed shops. The state of Tennessee had provided the city with the funding to revamp the whole area.

Things were good…except for the fact that Julian Addington was still on the loose, which meant Rowan wasn't safe no matter how she pretended not to worry. Billy was a member of the joint task force based in Nashville overseeing the investigation of the Addington case. Though he suspected the only reason he'd been asked to be a part of the task force was because Rowan was here—in his jurisdiction. Special Agent Josh Dressler and the others always started the daily briefings off with a *How's Dr. DuPont?*

She was at the center of this case, no matter that she was as innocent as any of the victims who had died by

Addington's hand. She had been drugged just like the others in Nashville, only the bastard hadn't given her a lethal dose. His reasoning was clear. The son of a bitch still had plans for Rowan.

Fury blazed hot in Billy's gut. Dressler needn't remind him to keep a close eye on her, yet he did at the end of every single briefing. Billy had every intention of keeping her safe. The others hoped she would be the reason Addington surfaced again. If he showed up in Billy's jurisdiction, he wouldn't walk away so easily.

With the investigation expanding with each passing day, he damned sure didn't need another two unsolved murders hanging over his head—particularly one that had gone cold so long ago. He'd just been through this. Back in February, human remains had been discovered buried in the basement of the *Winchester Gazette*. As it turned out, twenty-four years prior, Mary Jo Anderson had killed a man in self-defense and then buried him in the basement of her husband's newspaper building. Since the man had been affiliated with organized crime out of Chicago, no one had reported him missing or come looking for him. It wasn't until a broken water main had required the digging up of the newspaper's basement that the remains had been discovered.

Now Billy had another decades-old mystery on his hands. With a weary sigh, he climbed the steps and entered the building. He placed his sidearm and badge as well as the keys and the change in his pocket in the tray and passed through the metal detector.

"Afternoon, Chief," Officer James Wiley said.

"Wiley." Billy gave him a nod as he gathered his belongings, reholstered his weapon and put the rest away.

There had been a time when an officer of the law

wouldn't have had to go through the screening procedures, but now it was a necessary evil for every person who walked through the doors. When Billy had taken the highest position in the Winchester Police Department, he had been told he wasn't required to remove his weapon like everyone else. But Billy wasn't about to do anything different than any other officer in his department.

He walked down the corridor, bypassed the bull pen most of his officers and detectives called home, and went on to his office. As soon as he reached the small lobby, Cindy Farris, his assistant, perked up.

"Afternoon, Chief." She thrust a wad of messages at him. "Detective Lincoln needs to see you ASAP."

"Thanks, Cindy. Send him my way."

In his office, he tossed the dozen or so messages onto this desk and hung his hat on the tree in the corner. He'd no more than sat down when Cindy walked in with a steaming cup of coffee.

"Thought you might need a little pick-me-up." She placed the black brew on his desk and flashed him a smile.

"You are an angel, Cindy." He returned her smile and reached for the mug.

Cindy and his momma were best friends, had been for most of their lives. Cindy would turn seventy next month, but she refused to retire. Billy had a feeling the lady wouldn't retire until she had no choice. She liked being active and productive. He teased her that she mostly liked being able to keep tabs on him for his momma. Either way, he didn't mind. She was a damned good assistant and had the details on everyone in town, and she baked him a chocolate cake at least twice a month.

Cindy walked out, and Detective Clarence Lincoln

walked in. His shirt was wrinkled and there was a speck of what looked like mustard on his tie. The man had likely been hunkered over his computer or a file cabinet since Billy called him about looking for any unresolved missing person cases over the past three decades. He'd probably eaten his lunch while doing the same.

Lincoln collapsed into a chair in front of Billy's desk. "I finally found her."

Billy dropped his head back and groaned. Not at all what he'd wanted to hear. "We have an unsolved missing person case?"

He, like the chief before him and the one before that, prided himself on keeping a clear record on cases. They all got solved or his people kept investigating. Winchester was a small town with a reasonably low crime rate, so they were lucky to have that ability. He couldn't believe a case had fallen through the cracks.

What the hell was he saying? He had watched the removal of those bones from the basement of the newspaper building back in February. It happened. Granted, that was a crime no one knew had been committed. A department couldn't investigate criminal activity it didn't know about.

Still, it had been a doozy of a surprise to discover.

"Technically—" the detective pushed his glasses up his nose "—*we* don't have a missing person. This girl was from Los Angeles—as in California. After finding out from one of the girl's friends that she'd taken a bus to Winchester, her mother called looking for her, and Chief Holcomb opened a file."

Luther Holcomb was the former chief of police. Billy had known him his entire life. He'd recruited Billy into the force all those years ago and then he'd urged him to accept his position when he retired.

"The mother," Lincoln went on, "faxed Holcomb a photo. He made some calls, questioned some folks. A couple of people had seen her around, but none knew her or had any idea what happened to her. She seemed to show up and then disappear in a matter of a few days. End of story. Closed file."

"How old was she, and what was she doing in Winchester without her parents' permission?"

Lincoln glanced at the file in his hand. "Seventeen. Lived in Los Angeles with her mother until she disappeared. Ran away in late June of that year. She had a pen pal here in Winchester, so her mother thought her cross-country trip came as a result of that relationship. A detective called and followed up with Holcomb. According to his report, Holcomb told the detective that a girl matching her description had been spotted in the Winchester area but that no one had seen her since the initial sightings. One person mentioned seeing her at the old bus station that used to be right off the boulevard. I guess Holcomb figured she left town. There was no further activity on the file and it was closed that same year."

Billy scrubbed a hand across his jaw. "Call Los Angeles PD and see if the girl was ever found."

"Already done. She is still listed as missing. No updates since the call to Holcomb twenty-seven years ago."

Damn. "Well, then we're going to need a copy of her dental records."

"I'll make the request now. Oh, and Norton Cates, a tech at the lab, sent me this." He passed Billy his cell, a photo on the screen. "That necklace was found with the remains."

Billy studied the silver necklace with its sun and moon pendant. "Okay. Touch base with Holcomb. See if he remembers anything relevant that's not in his report. Find out if that detective in LA can confirm the necklace belonged to the missing girl."

"Will do."

Well, damn. Bones were popping up all over the place. He hoped this wasn't an indication of things to come.

"Wait." Billy frowned. "What's the missing girl's name?" Lincoln hadn't mentioned her name. If he had, Billy had missed it entirely.

His detective grimaced. "I was going to tell you that part after we did the identification with the dental records." He shrugged. "Just to be sure. No need to get everyone all out of sorts until we know."

Another of those bad feelings knotted in Billy's gut. "The name, please."

"Alisha Addington." Lincoln expelled a big breath. "Seventeen-year-old daughter of Anna and Julian Addington."

Billy sagged back in his chair. "Oh hell."

Four

By five o'clock, Ronald Whitt's body had been properly arranged in his casket and transported from the basement refrigeration unit via the elevator to the viewing room designated as Parlor Three on the first floor. Since the family had wanted a full casket view, Rowan had tucked him carefully into position, ensuring his facial expression was pleasant enough, the buttons of his shirt, the collar and the tie were just so and even the hem of his trousers and his socks were smooth and perfectly in place. She'd polished the leather uppers and checked the bottoms of the shoes the family had dropped off and ended up adding a layer of black paint so that the dark soles appeared pristine.

The flowers had been arranged tastefully around the casket. The registration podium stood ready just outside the door with the guest book. Music selected by the family, a classic track of uplifting hymns, played softly in the background. The family had arrived and was gathered around Mr. Whitt. For the next hour they would spend private time with their lost loved one. From six to eight thirty, visitors would pay their respects. Rowan had spoken with the deceased's wife and son to see if there was anything they needed. From now until the last family member departed she would be standing by.

Her cell phone vibrated with an incoming call, and Rowan stepped into the corridor outside the parlor. She reached into the pocket of her dove-gray suit jacket and checked the screen. *Billy.* Moving toward the lobby so as not to disturb the mourners, she answered. "Hey."

"Hey yourself."

She smiled, thankful for the reprieve of a friendly voice. Grief was immensely draining. Growing up, her father had always warned her to maintain a certain mental distance, but she had always found doing so difficult. Her education in psychiatry as well as her residency in the field and a two-year fellowship in forensic psychiatry had helped her to develop those emotional boundaries of which her father had spoken. Unfortunately, recent events had caused an undeniable crack in her carefully constructed facade and a noticeable failure in her hard-earned confidence. She still felt off balance.

But she was determined to find her footing once more. It would take time, but she refused to play the part of victim to Julian Addington. Not anymore, at least. She dismissed the thought and said, "I hope your day has gone more smoothly than mine."

Rowan had been at full speed since he and Burt left the funeral home today. Though she had her doubts as to whether his afternoon could have gone any better than hers, considering he had two unsolved potential murder cases staring him in the face. Never a good place to be.

"I wish," he said with a weary chuckle. "Look, I was wondering if maybe you'd have some time after the

Whitt viewing. I can help you close up. Maybe we can have a beer and talk, like old times."

Closing up entailed readying Mr. Whitt to go back into refrigeration and putting away his flowers. "Sure." She could use the company. After so many years away, she'd forgotten how lonely this old house could be at the end of the day. "Is there some news on the remains or about Mrs. Phillips?"

"We're still processing the Phillips home and gathering information on the remains. Mainly, I just wanted to talk."

Rowan had known Billy Brannigan her whole life. She recognized every nuance of his deep voice. He wasn't being entirely honest with her right now. The front entrance opened and a cluster of well-dressed visitors entered the lobby, reminding her she needed to get back to work.

"I have to go now," she said, wishing she had a few more moments to explore what she'd heard in his voice. "I'll see you at nine."

"I'll be there."

Rowan put her phone away and smiled for the newcomers. "Good evening. Are you here for the Whitt family?"

Heads bobbed and a flurry of positive responses rumbled through the group. His church friends, she decided. Rowan could always tell the ones who attended church with the deceased. They dressed for the visitation as if they were heading to a regularly scheduled church service.

"This way." Rowan gestured to the corridor and then led the way to Parlor Three. "If you'd like to sign the guest register," she suggested, "I'm sure the family will appreciate it."

A few moments were required for the seven new arrivals to sign in and wander into the parlor. Rowan stood by, smile plastered in place. When the final guest, a woman, had penned her signature, she hesitated before joining the others.

"You don't remember me, do you?"

The woman looked vaguely familiar. Tall, brunette, brown eyes. Thin, with the muscle tone of a woman dedicated to working out. Her sleeveless black sheath hit a few inches above her knees and showed off her nicely sculpted arms and legs. She looked to be about Rowan's age.

"I'm afraid I don't. Did we attend school together?"

"No, I went to Huntland." She tucked her clutch under her arm and extended her hand. "Sherry Lusk. I remember you because you're the reason Billy Brannigan dropped me like a rock."

Surprised and more than a little puzzled, Rowan gave her hand a quick shake and released it. Now she remembered. Sherry was the one Billy had bemoaned the night he'd had to stay over at Rowan's house.

"Yes, of course, Sherry. I remember the name."

Actually, Rowan hadn't really known Sherry at all. She'd only heard Billy mention her now and then. Usually because the two were fighting or had broken up again. As far as Rowan could recall, all the couple ever did was fight.

"He was always infatuated with you." Sherry shook her head as if she didn't understand the appeal. "No other woman had a shred of hope. Even after you left, he never really looked at anyone else seriously."

A tight laugh burst out of Rowan. "I'm afraid you must have me confused with someone else. Billy and I were never anything but friends. We're still friends."

Sherry smirked as if she knew something Rowan didn't. "Maybe from your perspective, but trust me, you were all he ever talked about. Ro this and Ro that." She rolled her eyes. "I imagine now that you're back, he'll try to make sure you don't get away again."

Somehow Rowan kept her smile in place. The thing about working with the public was that sometimes you just had to let the most ridiculous comments go. Having your say just wasn't worth the bad press.

Sherry started toward the parlor but then hesitated. "I was sorry to hear about your father. He was a true pillar of this community. I can't tell you how helpful he was to Mother and me when my father died. He'll be greatly missed."

Rowan thanked her and watched as she disappeared into the small crowd gathered around Mr. Whitt's casket.

She didn't doubt the woman's comments about her father. Kind and helpful was his way. As for the other, it never ceased to amaze her how folks twisted things around and created their own versions of the truth.

The very idea. Rowan shook her head. When she was a kid, she'd had a secret crush on Billy, that was true, but neither he nor anyone else ever knew. It was Rowan's secret and she intended to keep it that way for the rest of her days.

Billy deserved someone with far less baggage than the heavy load she carried. Besides, they were friends. She didn't want to risk losing or damaging that relationship.

The lobby door opened once more and a straggler arrived. Rowan didn't recognize him at first. He was tall and distinguished looking and wore an elegant suit that wouldn't be found on the rack in a typical department store. He turned and his profile pinged a memory. Jared Knowles. *Dr.* Jared Knowles. He was the same age as Billy. Like his father before him, Knowles had gone to medical school. He and his father had the only orthopedic practice in the area.

"Rowan." Jared smiled, diverted his set path to the viewing room and started her way instead. He gave her one of those quick hugs that really wasn't a hug—didn't really mean anything on an emotional level. "I apologize for not being at your father's funeral. I had an emergency at the hospital, and by the time I was finished, the service was over." He sighed. "He was an amazing man. I've been meaning to drop by, but you know how time gets away."

Rowan forced her smile to stay in place as she nodded. "Thank you. How are you? You look well." He did look great, though she suspected he'd had a touch of work done around the eyes and mouth. No one who'd passed the forty-year mark had skin that smooth and flawless.

"I'm great." One of those fake smiles she recognized from those who considered themselves superior to the person to whom they were speaking appeared on his unlined face. "The practice is thriving, and when I'm not working I travel. Life couldn't be better."

Oh yes, she remembered Jared Knowles. An arrogant braggart, that was what he had always been. His father had been the town's only orthopedist until Jared followed in his footsteps.

"It's so nice to see you," Rowan said, hoping he'd take the cue and move on.

Jared reached for her hand, gave it a squeeze. "We

should have dinner sometime. It would be very nice to converse with someone equally intellectually interesting. It's quite a challenge in this small town."

Somehow Rowan managed to keep the smile on her lips but she refused to say a word and chance him considering her response an agreement. What an arrogant man!

When he'd finally melded into the crowd of visitors, she wandered into the parlor and took her position. Within the next half hour the room filled to capacity. The overflow stood in small groups in the corridor, chatting, while some huddled together in the lobby, but all eventually made their way through the parlor and shared their condolences with the family.

A few minutes before visitation was scheduled to end, the crowd remained good-sized, at least forty or forty-five guests. Mr. Whitt had operated Whitt's Barber Shop for forty years. Everyone in and around Winchester knew him. She imagined there would be a full chapel tomorrow for his service and a large crowd at Franklin Memorial Gardens for the burial. She would need to go over the instructions with the pallbearers ahead of time. She'd arranged a police escort for the procession. Charlotte Kinsley, a part-time funeral assistant, would be taking care of the music and overseeing the loading of the flowers. Herman would be filling in for Woody.

A man walked into the parlor and made his way up the center aisle to the receiving line at the casket. Rowan might not have paid attention to him as he passed her position near the door except for his aftershave. There was something familiar about it. Not that his scent was relevant. Most brands of aftershave could be purchased and worn by anyone. He stood at the open casket for a moment, his head bowed in silent reflection, and then he nodded to the family and moved away, taking a position on the other side of the room. His attention came to rest on Rowan.

Rowan looked away, and focused on the family. Several minutes later she still felt the man watching her. She mulled over his physical appearance. Black hair peppered with gray. He was medium height, with broad shoulders. Maybe sixty-five. Unlike most of those who had paid their respects to Mr. Whitt tonight, this man's suit was not an off-the-rack mass-produced label. She reminded herself she had not lived in Winchester in twenty-one years. He could be a new resident. Maybe he had known her father and was considering walking over and speaking to Rowan. Either way, this certainly wasn't the first time she had been the object of curious stares since her return to Winchester. The DuPont girls had always been objects of curiosity. Whatever else Rowan had done, growing up in a funeral home guaranteed labels like *odd* and *strange*.

Worst-case scenario, he could be an investigative reporter from any of the larger media outlets. God knew she had endured more than her share in the past two months. The media was determined to paint her as some sort of accessory or coconspirator in Julian's handiwork rather than the victim she was.

Victim. Fury tightened in her belly. She hated Julian for what he'd done. Hated every minute of every hour she'd spent with him…hated that she had trusted him so completely. Foremost, she despised that she had even once looked up to him in a fatherly way.

The minutes passed and the stranger stayed right where he was and continued watching her almost as if he wanted her to recognize he was doing so.

Had the task force decided to send in someone new to make sure she was not in contact with Julian? For the first few weeks after her return to Winchester, an FBI agent had followed her around. Eventually, he'd stopped appearing around every corner. Of course that didn't mean he or another one wouldn't show up again.

She looked away. Julian had stolen her father and left a black mark on the career she had worked so hard to build. He had torn her apart, personally and professionally.

If it took the rest of her life, she intended to see that he paid for his depraved crimes.

Ten minutes before visitation was scheduled to end, Rowan moved up the aisle and sat down near Mr. Whitt's son, Lance, another barber who would be taking over the family business. Most of the family was seated now, weary of the production of the receiving line. Mrs. Whitt sat in the front row with her sister.

"I just wanted to let you know that we have about ten minutes left." Rowan patted Lance on the arm. "If you need longer, let me know."

He tried to smile, couldn't quite manage the feat. "We'll be ready to go." He glanced at his wife, who sat on the other end of the pew. "The babies are asleep, and the last thing we want to do is have them wake up and start crying."

Lance was taking his father's death particularly hard. The two had worked together every day since Lance graduated high school. Now he had to go back into that barbershop and work without the man who had taught him everything he needed to know about good barbering. He had told Rowan his father's life story when he made the funeral arrangements. His mother had been far too distraught.

"The most difficult thing about coming back to Winchester," Rowan said quietly, "was knowing my father wouldn't be here. Walking into this house, taking up the work that he taught me as a child—it was really challenging those first couple of weeks." He turned to her and she smiled. "But it gets easier, I promise."

He nodded. "Thank you. I'll keep that in mind. I know customers are expecting me back by Friday and I don't want to let them down."

"I remind myself," she said, "that this is what my father wanted, and that gives me great comfort."

Lance actually smiled then. "My dad always said he was building a future for me and my kids." He shrugged. "And he did. I can't let him down. Not after all his hard work."

"Exactly." Rowan gave his arm another pat and stood. "Whenever you're ready."

As she moved back toward the door, she felt the stranger's gaze on her again. He'd no doubt been watching while she spoke to Lance Whitt. She wanted to know who he was and why he continued to stare at her. His relentless stare made her uneasy. But she wouldn't confront him with the family still gathered. If he lingered as they began to leave, she would question him then.

By quarter to nine, the family had moved to the lobby and was making the final preparations to go. Thank goodness Jared Knowles had received a call and hurried away. She made a mental note to avoid the man in the future. Mrs. Whitt had thanked Rowan repeatedly for the great job she did readying her husband. Rowan reminded Lance that the family could arrive an hour before tomorrow's funeral to spend some private time with Mr. Whitt.

The stranger hung back, lingering in the fringes of the close family members. While Rowan had Lance off to one side, she asked, "Is that man in the charcoal suit a member of your family or just a close friend?"

He glanced at the man who watched without turning away. "No, ma'am. I don't know him."

"Maybe he was one of your father's customers."

Lance shook his head. "I've never seen him before. Would you like me to stay until he leaves?"

Rowan smiled. "That's very kind of you, but you should go on. Chief Brannigan will be here in a few minutes. I'm sure I'll be fine until then."

Lance urged her to reconsider, but she insisted he go on with his family. As he walked out and she prepared to confront the man, a woman walked through the entrance and directly toward Rowan.

Rowan resisted the urge to tell her that the funeral home was closing. She wanted to question this man and close up for the night, but deep down she was grateful for the buffer. When she would have greeted the woman, she abruptly recognized her.

Audrey Anderson from the *Gazette*, Winchester's newspaper.

The idea that some breaking news had occurred during the visitation was Rowan's first thought. Maybe Billy wouldn't make it at nine, after all. She couldn't help wondering if there was an update about the bones or maybe if Billy had found Mrs. Phillips's killer.

"Rowan." Audrey glanced at the man loitering a dozen or so feet away before settling her full attention on Rowan.

"Audrey." Rowan gave her a nod and a polite smile.

Three years younger, she hadn't been friends with Rowan in school. In fact, Rowan only knew her because of the friendship of their fathers, and that had been a very long time ago. She remembered Audrey's father's death, and she had wondered at the time what she would do if she lost her father, since he was all she'd had left by then.

Now she knew.

The Anderson name had been big news a couple of months ago. The discovery of decades-old remains in the basement of the newspaper building had made national headlines. With her find at the lake today, Rowan couldn't help wondering how many other bodies were hidden around Winchester. Strange how such a small town could have people go missing and no one notice. She supposed the bones she had found this morning would likely prove to be an outsider's just as those found in the newspaper basement had been.

"Do you have a couple of minutes to talk?"

Rowan instinctively braced. "What's this about? Business or a personal matter?"

If Audrey had questions about Geneva Phillips or the bones Rowan had stumbled upon, she couldn't help her.

"Actually, it's about *you*."

Ah, Rowan got it now. Audrey wanted an exclusive about the woman—the psychiatrist who had worked with Metro Nashville PD for more than six years—who hadn't recognized a serial killer when she saw one. Not just any serial killer, mind you, but the serial killer who had been her mentor and friend for years. The same one who had murdered her father and over a hundred other people.

"I'm afraid I don't have time for an interview tonight, Audrey." She shook her head, hoped her expression showed some level of regret no matter that she felt none. "I have to attend to Mr. Whitt and close the funeral home for the night. Perhaps another time."

"Actually—" she glanced again at the man determined to linger "—I don't think this can wait, Rowan. Otherwise, I would gladly schedule something for the morning."

So maybe there was some sort of news Rowan had missed. "Give me a moment," she said.

Rowan had reached the end of her patience with this guy watching every move she made. She marched over to him, crossed her arms over her chest and looked him straight in the eyes. "May I help you, sir?"

He shifted his jacket. Rowan tensed but then she saw the badge clipped to his belt. "I'm Detective Cash Barton, ma'am, Los Angeles PD. I need to ask you a few questions."

First, Rowan had no idea why Los Angeles PD would want to ask her anything. The vague notion that Julian had likely murdered someone there filtered through her mind. He had victims all over the country. Second, badges could be purchased on the internet, and this man's wardrobe suggested he did not live on a cop's salary. "Let's see your official ID, Detective Barton."

He pulled out his credentials case and flipped it open for her to view.

"Would you remove it from the case, please?"

With an impatient sigh, he removed the identification from the case and handed it to her. Rowan examined it carefully and then passed it back to him.

Satisfied, she asked, "How can I help you, Detective?"

Barton glanced at Audrey. "We need to speak privately, ma'am."

Rowan nodded. "Well, make yourself comfortable." She gestured to the two sofas facing each other with a coffee table in between. "Have a cup of coffee—you'll find it in the lounge around the corner—and I'll be right with you."

With that she turned on her heel and walked back to where Audrey waited. "You don't mind if I prepare Mr. Whitt for refrigeration while we talk?"

Audrey's face visibly paled. "Whatever works for you."

They walked back to Parlor Three. Rowan reached beneath Mr. Whitt's shoulders and lowered the portion of the casket bed that allowed his head and upper torso to be slightly elevated during the visitation. She would prepare his body in the casket in the same manner for the funeral tomorrow. The family had requested a casket with this feature. Once he was lying flat, she adjusted the small flowers left in the casket by the grandchildren and closed the full-length lid. Most families requested only a half viewing casket, but some, like the Whitts, wanted a full view.

Audrey didn't speak until Rowan had closed the lid. She seemed to release the breath she'd been holding. "I heard about the bones you discovered out by the lake."

Rowan hoped the conversation stayed focused on the present and not the recent past. "I'm afraid you'll have to speak to Chief Brannigan about that, Audrey. I really can't discuss anything about what I did or did not find."

She nodded. "I know. But what I wanted to ask you is why you were at that particular spot this morning. Do you still visit the place where Raven's body was found?"

Rowan stared at her for a long moment. Then she

lifted the skirt and released the brakes of the cart supporting the casket. "Walk with me."

The flowers could wait, but she needed to get Mr. Whitt into refrigeration. Bodies deteriorated rapidly at room temperature—even a chilly room temperature—despite the chemicals involved in the embalming process. Some things were inevitable and decomposition was one of them.

Audrey followed along, opening the side door marked Staff Only that led into a private corridor. At the elevator, Rowan said, "Push the down button, please."

Although the celebrated reporter hesitated, she did as Rowan asked. Once they were loaded onto the elevator with Mr. Whitt, the car bumped into movement, sliding slowly downward until it bounced to a stop at the basement level. Rowan pushed the cart past the dark mortuary room and toward the refrigeration unit. Audrey opened the door and Rowan rolled Mr. Whitt inside. The newspaperwoman, on the other hand, waited in the corridor.

When Rowan closed up the refrigeration unit, Audrey said, "Can we talk upstairs?"

Rowan smiled, couldn't help herself. "Certainly."

This time they climbed the stairs. Audrey seemed inordinately relieved they didn't take the cargo elevator made especially for transporting caskets.

Rowan snagged the flatbed cart en route back to the parlor. The cart was for moving the flowers from one location to another or to the van for transporting to the cemetery. It was long and flat, the loading surface only a few inches off the floor, and yet the handle for maneuvering it stood at waist level. This cart made life considerably easier. Rowan remembered well moving flowers from the parlors to the walk-in coolers and back again.

The task had been assigned to her and her sister from the time they were ten years old.

Rowan had loaded the most delicate flower arrangements onto the cart before she spoke. "I haven't been back to that place since I was eighteen." She paused in her work. "When I was a teenager I went fairly often." She didn't know why she felt compelled to share that information with this woman, but she did anyway. "We were identical twins. I felt it was my obligation to visit her there and at the cemetery."

Audrey picked up an arrangement. "Have you been to the cemetery?"

"That one can stay," Rowan said, nodding to the arrangement Audrey held, then pointing to another. "That one should go."

Audrey placed the arrangement back where it had been and reached for the one Rowan had indicated.

"I visited her when we laid my father to rest."

When Rowan prepared to push the cart out of the room, Audrey asked, "There's just one more question I wanted to ask."

Took her long enough to get to the point of her visit. Rowan doubted her showing up tonight had anything to do with when or how often she visited her dead sister.

Rowan shrugged. "Ask away. I reserve the right not to answer if I don't feel comfortable doing so."

Audrey turned her hands up. "Fair enough. Do you think the bones you discovered have anything to do with your sister's death?"

The bold statement was the last thing Rowan would have considered the ambitious reporter might ask. It was a concept that, frankly, had not crossed her mind. She'd been too busy all afternoon and evening to ponder the find. She had not considered any sort of connection.

"No." She shook her head. "My sister drowned a good distance from where her body was discovered tangled in those branches. I can't see how one would have had anything to do with the other. In fact, I'm not sure they know how or when those bones came to be in that particular spot as of yet."

Audrey canted her head and studied Rowan a moment. "Quite the coincidence, wouldn't you say?"

Before she could respond, the detective from Los Angeles walked in. "I really need to speak to you, Dr. DuPont."

Rowan looked to Audrey. "I'm sorry. I honestly can't answer that question since I have no idea of the circumstances involved."

Audrey nodded. "Very well. If you want to talk about things, call me. I have a number of handy resources. I'd like to make sure this story gets reported properly. The truth is important to me, Rowan. I'll do the story right whether anyone else does or not."

"Thank you. I'll keep that in mind."

When Audrey had left the room, Rowan turned to Barton. "So, how can I help you, Detective?"

"I'd like to talk to you about the remains you found."

Big surprise. Apparently the whole world now knew about the bones. Although she had no idea why a detective from Los Angeles would be involved. "As I told Ms. Anderson, that's a subject you'll need to discuss with Chief Brannigan." She glanced at the clock on the wall. "He should be here any minute. I'm certain he can address any questions you have."

"Ma'am, we have reason to believe the victim was

a young girl we've been trying to find for nearly thirty years."

Rowan frowned. Apparently there had been some breaking news. "Again, I'm sorry I can't help you. I have no idea to whom those remains belong. I've been here all evening and I haven't heard any news. If there's been a breaking development in the find, I'm not aware of it."

"You know Dr. Julian Addington," he countered. "Quite well, I believe."

She wanted to snap a response at him for being so insensitive, but she had a feeling his statement had nothing to do with insensitivity and everything to do with some fact of which she was unaware.

"I'm certain *you* are well aware of my relationship with Julian Addington." She refused to respect the bastard who had killed her father by using the title Doctor.

"Were you aware he had a wife and a daughter in Los Angeles?"

Surprise flashed on Rowan's face before she could school the reaction. "I am under the impression he has never been married."

"Well, he did and he was until his former wife divorced him twenty-five years ago," Barton assured her, "and he had a daughter. She disappeared when she was seventeen years old."

Inside, where this stranger couldn't see, Rowan stilled, went oddly quiet as if the very blood in her body had ceased to move. "Disappeared?"

He nodded. "She's been missing for twenty-seven years. Since about the same time your sister died."

"You think those bones belong to her?" Rowan's head spun. How was that possible? Why in all those years she and Julian were so close had he never told her about his family? She had shared everything about hers with him.

"I think maybe you need to sit down, Dr. DuPont."

Rowan thought maybe he was right.

Five

Rowan watched through the front windows as Billy and the detective from Los Angeles argued in the parking lot. Billy had walked in just after Barton made his big, stunning announcement.

Julian Addington had been married.

He'd had a daughter.

Rowan reminded herself to breathe. It wasn't that this notion was too far-fetched or even that it sounded unreasonable. It was the idea that he had bemoaned the sacrifice of a personal life to his career with such seemingly genuine regret. He always reminded Rowan that the two of them had this sad state in common. There had never been the proper time for devotion to spouse and family.

"Of course there wasn't, you son of a bitch, you were too busy murdering people."

Next to her, Freud, her German shepherd, rubbed against her leg. Rowan shook herself and turned away from the window. She rubbed his head. "It's okay, boy." Freud wagged his tail but didn't look any more convinced than she felt. He could sense her uneasiness.

Billy had practically dragged the detective out of the

lobby. In a sort of shock, Rowan had wandered back to the parlor and finished storing Mr. Whitt's delicate flowers. Once she was satisfied the family hadn't left anything behind, she had closed up the parlor. Housekeeping would come through first thing in the morning to clean and to prepare the chapel for the afternoon service.

When she was finished, rather than go outside to join whatever discussion was going on between the West Coast detective and the Winchester chief of police, she came upstairs to wait for Billy. She preferred to hear this theory about Julian's family from him. It was a protective instinct. Rowan understood the involuntary coping mechanism.

Frustration and the slightest inkling of anger stirred inside her. As much as she preferred to hear the whole story from a trusted friend, she also intended to tell him exactly how she felt about his having kept this information from her for several hours. He should have told her when he called rather than put it off until he could tell her face-to-face as if she were too fragile to hear the news over the phone.

Yes, it was true that her life had been devastated with the murder of her father and the stunning secrets Julian had been harboring. But she was a grown woman. A highly trained psychiatrist. She understood how these things worked and was certainly capable of handling the news.

She shook her head, attempted to tamp down the irritation.

While she'd waited she had taken Freud down the back stairs that led to the private corridor beyond the viewing parlors. After he'd run around the backyard for a few minutes, they'd made their way up the stairs once more.

Rowan still found the news hard to believe. *The monster had a daughter.* Before Billy had arrived and hauled the detective outside, Barton had explained that Alisha Addington had been seventeen years old when she'd disappeared. What in the world was she doing running away from home and coming here? It made no sense whatsoever. Rowan and her sister certainly hadn't known her; they were only twelve at the time. She remembered vividly introducing her father to Julian when she was a sophomore in college. The two men had never met before; they had not known each other at all.

The idea that Raven had somehow known Alisha was ludicrous.

Movement in the parking lot below drew Rowan's attention there once more. Detective Barton strode to his car and drove away. Rowan wanted to feel relieved, but somehow she didn't. A few seconds later Billy bounded up the stairs and knocked on the front door of the living quarters. She took her time making her way there.

While the funeral home's preparatory work took place in the basement and the formal services on the first floor, the second and third floors were home. The third floor was actually not that large: two bedrooms and a Jack and Jill bath. The second floor, however, was quite expansive with a family room, kitchen and dining room as well as another bedroom and two more baths, one nothing more than a powder room. This had been home for the first eighteen years of Rowan's life.

And here she was again. Freud had adjusted well. He was only too happy to remain curled up near the sofa while she attended to viewings and funerals downstairs. He seemed to understand that barking was off-limits during those times. He was a good dog and she had never been more grateful for his companionship.

She hesitated a moment at the door, then opened it. "Is it true?"

"Can I come in?"

Billy looked tired. Rowan should have been ashamed for making him ask. He'd had a long day, too. But she was frustrated with him for not telling her the whole story when they spoke on the phone earlier. Clearly, this was what he'd wanted to stop by and speak with her about, only Audrey Anderson and Detective Barton had beaten him to the punch.

"You couldn't have warned me when you called?" She stood her ground in the doorway.

Hat in hand, he shrugged. "I wanted to tell you in person. I wasn't trying to keep anything from you, Ro."

She sighed. "Come in." She opened the door wider and then closed it behind him. "Would you still like that beer?"

He laughed. "I might need several after the way this day has gone." Freud rushed over to greet him and Billy scratched him behind the ears. "Hey, buddy."

"Have a seat. I'll grab a cold one." Rowan moved the jacket she had discarded from the back of the sofa and grabbed the heels she'd kicked off. "Then I expect the whole story," she warned.

"You got it."

She draped her jacket across the banister of the staircase leading up to the third level, and set her heels on the bottom step. She could take them up when she went to bed. Right now she was simply too tired. Two beers were sounding better all the time. Billy's company was always good, current circumstances notwithstanding.

As she opened the fridge, the light pooled around her. She grabbed two longneck bottles and nudged the door closed with her hip. She blinked, considered the kitchen in the near darkness. It looked better this way. Her father had never renovated any part of the living quarters. The kitchen was very early seventies or maybe late sixties. Either way, she needed to tackle this project.

It would keep her mind off the manhunt for Julian and the questions about their relationship still making the rounds in the media. And now there was a daughter. A *dead* daughter.

She trudged back into the family room, which was just another word for living room with a cased opening at one end that featured the dining room. This part of the house was old, old and in need of updating. Her father hadn't noticed all the little things that screamed for a touch of TLC. He had been the sort of man who could be happy in a cave as long as he had a sleeping bag and the means to prepare a hot meal. Freud sat next to Billy as if he sensed the chief of police needed his allegiance and protection more than Rowan.

"Tell me everything." Rowan handed one of the sweating bottles to Billy. She sat down on the sofa facing him. He'd taken her father's favorite chair. Her dad wouldn't have minded and she certainly didn't.

"Lincoln, one of my detectives—"

"Do you mean Clarence Lincoln?"

Billy nodded. "Besides me, he was the best quarterback in this part of the state." He grinned. "The only one who ever kicked my butt, but then, I was having a bad night."

Rowan remembered that night and the other star quarterback. "He went to Moore County, right?"

"He did. The *Gazette* ran a feature article on the two of us back in the day. One of us usually dominated the headlines anyway." He shook his head. "Some people tried to make it about race, but it wasn't. Clarence and I never looked at each other that way. Still don't. We're cops. Color has nothing to do with it."

"Clarence is Herman's nephew," she reminded Billy. "He used to come to the funeral home and play with me and Raven sometimes when we were really little kids. Then his daddy died and he never came again. Bad memories, I guess."

This was off subject, but her nerves could stand the momentary reprieve. Besides, she was still a little annoyed that Billy hadn't told her this news hours ago. As a matter of fact, a dig at his history would make her feel loads better.

"This must be the day for old friends from other schools." She sipped her beer. "Another of yours dropped by the Whitt visitation tonight."

"Oh yeah?" Unlike her, Billy didn't sip. He guzzled a long swallow.

"Sherry Lusk."

He coughed, almost spewed beer across the coffee table. "Sherry?"

Rowan nodded. "She said I was the reason you and she never worked out. Imagine my surprise." Taking another sip of beer kept the smile tugging at her lips from appearing.

Billy wiped his mouth with the back of his hand. "I guess blaming you was easier than facing her own faults."

Rowan had no intention of following up on that statement. "So tell me." She leaned forward, placed her bottle of beer on the coffee table and clasped her hands in her lap. As much as she wanted to pretend that nothing Julian had done in his life, besides killing her father and all those other people, mattered to her one way or another, that wasn't possible. Somehow he had made this missing, possibly murdered daughter about her and her family. The motive was what Rowan could not fathom.

"I asked Lincoln to look for any missing person cases that had not resolved during the past thirty years, but there was only one and it really wasn't our case. Twenty-seven years ago…"

She flinched at the time frame. The same year her sister had died.

"In late June," he went on, "the mother called Chief Holcomb looking for her daughter. She claimed her daughter had run away to visit a pen pal here in Winchester—a pen pal named Raven DuPont."

Another wave of shock quaked through Rowan. "A pen pal?"

Billy nodded. "According to Holcomb's notes, he stopped by the funeral home and talked to your father. Both Edward and Raven insisted there was no pen pal and that they hadn't seen the girl whose picture Holcomb was flashing around."

Rowan took a moment to absorb this information. It was possible her father hadn't associated that long-ago visit by Holcomb with Julian when Rowan first introduced them. Neither her father nor her sister had ever mentioned the incident to her. Of course, at that time, Raven wouldn't have. She had loved her secrets, especially those she kept from her mirror image.

She shrugged. "I can only assume my father forgot about the incident. I'm sure there's a lot from that year he didn't recall." God knew she had tried to block out as much of it as possible.

"Understandable," Billy agreed. "A week or so later there was a follow-up call from Detective Barton and that was the end of it. Since this was the only case on our books that wasn't solved, Lincoln called LAPD to see if the girl had been found, and the next thing we knew, Barton was here. Only he didn't tell us he was coming. He just showed up at your door. I chewed him out but good for that, Ro. I can assure you he won't bother you again without going through me first."

As much as she appreciated his determination to shield her from the unpleasantness of all this, it was simply not something he could do. She had to be involved. Had to know how this related to her family. Why would Julian lie to her about his family for all those years?

He was a psychopath! She had to remember that point.

Whatever his motives, Rowan needed the truth and she intended to find it.

"How long will it be before the medical examiner releases Mrs. Phillips's body?" Rowan considered that Woody would be back on Monday. As long as she had taken care of Mrs. Phillips by then, Rowan would feel comfortable leaving for a couple of days. A quick trip to the West Coast and maybe she would find some part of the truth that would help solve this puzzle.

"Now, wait a minute, Ro." Billy held up his hands, apparently recognizing where she was going with the question. "I know what you're thinking."

"I can fly out to LA one day and fly back the next." All she needed was the name and address for Julian's former wife. Rowan had questions for the woman. Starting with, had she been fooled by Julian for all those years, as well?

"You can't just go flying across the country and demanding answers from a total stranger—one whose husband murdered your father."

Rowan squared her shoulders. "She might not answer, but there is nothing stopping me from asking."

He shook his head. "You worked with Metro long enough to realize this has to be handled by the book, step by step. The task force is already involved. I briefed Dressler right before I called you."

This was another facet of this case that blew her mind. How could the FBI not know about Julian's ex-wife and daughter? If anyone could have ferreted out that secret, the task force should have been able to do so. "You called Dressler first."

It wasn't really a question. Obviously he had.

"I did. Dressler flew out to LA this afternoon to interview her. I'm sure I don't have to remind you that anything you do might in some way hamper the investigation."

God, he was right. Rowan slumped back against the couch. She didn't know what she had been thinking. Any family Julian had would be questioned, perhaps even put under surveillance once the task force became aware they existed. They damned sure kept tabs on Rowan. Josh Dressler himself had questioned her mercilessly and repeatedly. She didn't mind doing all within her power to help the task force find Julian, but she did mind being made to feel like the bastard's accomplice or that she knew one or more of his vile secrets.

Why had he never taken trips to the West Coast? "In all those years that we were friends, he never once mentioned having any sort of connection to California." She shook her head. "Was Addington even his real name?"

"So far there haven't been any aliases found connected to him. From what Dressler told me, Addington never lived in California. That's where his wife was from originally, so when they separated, she took their daughter and returned."

Rowan's gaze met his. "I'm still reeling at the concept that he was married and had a daughter. How could I not know that?"

Billy shrugged. "I don't know the details, but Barton said they were divorced."

She nodded. "He mentioned that they had divorced twenty-five years ago." This made no sense whatsoever. Rowan tried not to read too much into the idea that the divorce occurred only a few years before she and Julian met. "I'm stunned."

Billy leaned forward, propped his forearms on his knees. "Ro, that detective claims Mrs. Addington believes her daughter came here looking for your family— for Raven. Is there any way your father might have been unaware that Raven was writing to her?"

Rowan frowned. "What?" She shook her head before he could answer. "I don't think so. But then, Raven had changed so much that year. She kept lots of secrets from me. I can't be certain of all she did or didn't do. She probably kept secrets from our parents, too."

"Is it possible your mother or father knew the Addingtons?"

"You know that's not possible," Rowan argued. "Mother died not long after Raven, and I introduced my father to Julian many years later."

"You're right." Billy reached for his beer, drained it. "This makes no sense at all."

"How old is she? His wife, I mean?"

"According to the DMV, she's sixty-five." Billy set his empty bottle on the coffee table.

He didn't have to say that she was about the same age Rowan's mother would be if she were still alive. "Did Barton mention what she's saying about Julian? I assume she claims not to have any idea where he is."

"That's the story Barton gave me. Dressler will pass along whatever he learns in his visit with the wife."

Rowan and Dressler had worked together on a few cases when she was in Nashville.

Billy turned up his hands. "Barton claims they haven't seen each other since their daughter's disappearance, and as far as the ex-wife is concerned, Addington was dead to her before that."

"Is there a financial connection?" Julian's family had been quite wealthy. There would be alimony of some kind unless the split was so ugly his wife wanted nothing more from him.

Of course it got ugly, Ro. He was a depraved killer. But he'd always seemed so normal. So gentle and kind. What a fool she had been.

How was any of this possible?

More important, how could she not have seen it?

Eventually she had to stop asking herself that pointless question. Had to stop beating herself up for not seeing what no one else appeared to have seen, either.

"I asked that same question," Billy confirmed. "Evidently, the ex-wife comes from a wealthy family of her own. So I guess she didn't need anything from him."

Rowan shook her head. This was simply too much.

"I'm just supposed to wait for someone to tell me what's going on?"

She had thought she could do this but she'd been wrong. Sitting back and waiting for someone else—the task force—to figure out this bizarre mystery was something she simply could not do.

Rowan understood that now.

Billy shrugged. "I don't think anyone knows what's going on."

His conclusion was likely true to some extent. If Mrs. Addington had reason to withhold information, it would be difficult to prove without evidence. If there was evidence, she would already be a part of the case.

Another fact struck Rowan as odd. "There wasn't a single connection to a wife, much less a daughter, found at his home in Nashville or the retreat in Hendersonville. Nothing. Not even a photograph."

There were, on the other hand, several photos of Rowan. Deep inside where Billy wouldn't see, she shuddered.

"Ro, I understand that nothing I say will make you feel any better about how you're seemingly connected to all this, but for now the best thing you can do is go on with your life. Agent Dressler will call if there's something you need to know. I'll keep my finger on the pulse of this thing, you have my word. And I'll keep you informed. I won't let you down."

Billy had never let her down. "I have no doubt that you'll do all within your power to keep me in the loop and to help get to the bottom of this…" She shook her head. "Whatever it is."

He drew in a long breath, let it go as if trying to relax the tension visible in his posture. "I know you too well,

Ro. You'll never wait for anyone else—not even me—to figure this out. I just don't want you getting hurt in the process. If I can't convince you to stay out of this investigation, at least include me in your plans."

"This is not seventh grade, Billy. You don't have to protect me anymore."

He grinned. "I am well aware I don't have to protect you, Ro, but I want to. Your daddy would want me to, as well. I'm thinking it's time for you to break down and get a security system installed."

"You're playing dirty now, bringing Daddy into this." But he was right. She knew this, too. "As for the security system, I've been thinking about having one installed."

"Good. You take care of that and let me do my job. I'll need your help, for sure, but don't get ahead of me on this thing, okay?"

As much as she wanted to make him feel more comfortable she couldn't make him a promise like that one. "I can't guarantee you I won't get ahead of you, Billy. You have a lot of cases—like the Geneva Phillips case—and I don't. But I will keep you informed. You have my word on that."

"Close enough, I guess." He smiled, then frowned. "When they pulled all the vines and leaves away from the bones by the lake, they did find one thing." He pulled out his cell and tapped the screen a few times before passing it to Rowan.

She studied the photo on the screen. A silver necklace with a sun and moon charm. The inside of the sun was a dark stone, amber maybe. "Was there anything else?" She passed the phone back to him.

He shook his head. "The evidence techs said the same thing you did about her clothes having disintegrated.

They haven't found anything so far, but it's possible they could find something else in tomorrow's sweep."

Rowan searched her memory banks for any recollection of a necklace like the one found with the remains. Nothing. It looked vaguely familiar, but jewelry with the sun and the moon was commonplace. She could have seen something like it anywhere. "Nothing on cause of death yet?"

He shook his head. "We're hoping to have more tomorrow."

"What about the Phillips case? Anything new there?"

"None of the neighbors saw a stranger in the neighborhood on the day of her death. The daughters haven't found anything missing so far and everyone says the same thing: Geneva wouldn't hurt a fly and she definitely didn't have any enemies."

"And yet, someone killed her."

Billy couldn't argue the assessment. "So, how about that other beer?"

"I could use one myself."

If they were having a second beer, particularly since Billy had to drive home, they needed to eat. Rowan pulled a pizza from the freezer and popped it into the oven. They talked about their school days and his failed relationships and pretty much everything else…except the Addington case.

Nearly two hours later, when she watched from her family room window as he drove away, she felt more alone than ever, even with Freud waiting at her side. She let the curtain fall back over the window and turned away. She had to find a way to feel comfortable in this house again. Since coming home she'd dreamed of either her sister or her mother every night. Not happy dreams, either. Always ones about their deaths and a few about her own. Whether it was all that had happened the past few weeks or adjusting to the change in her life circumstances, she seemed off her stride. She kept forgetting things, misplacing things and just feeling off balance.

She reminded herself that her life would settle down in time but it certainly didn't feel as if that was happening. In fact, it felt like things were deteriorating.

Putting the worries out of her head, she glanced around. "We could both use a distraction, couldn't we, boy?" She scrubbed at Freud's back.

Her gaze shifted toward the kitchen. Maybe that renovation would do the trick. When all this insanity was behind her, she could call a few contractors and get some estimates. With Mrs. Phillips's visitation postponed, she didn't have anything on tomorrow's schedule except the funeral for Mr. Whitt. But death rarely took a day off. Chances were an intake would end up at the basement entrance before the day was through.

Rowan locked the door. Billy had promised to lock the lobby entrance as he left. She turned out the lights and headed up to the third floor, grabbing her heels and jacket as she went. Freud trailed behind her, his nails clicking on the hardwood. The third floor had been her and Raven's private space. The bathroom at the end of the hall had a door from each bedroom. Rowan's bedroom was on the right, facing the front yard. Raven's was on the left, overlooking the backyard.

Rowan stared for a long moment at the closed door. She never went into her sister's room. Not since she'd left for college anyway. She hadn't been in there since she'd come home, either. Freud whimpered as if he, too, sensed the painful memories hidden beyond that door.

Goose bumps shivered over her skin, but Rowan shook off the foolish reaction. She went into her room, hung up her jacket and put away the heels. The navy suit would be best for tomorrow's funeral. She removed the suit and the matching heels from the closet and hung the suit on the wall hook next to the full-length mirror. She'd gone through that phase as a teenager where she'd needed to really scrutinize her appearance before leaving the house each morning, so her father had installed a big mirror. She sighed. Strange, when she looked in that mirror right now she still saw glimpses of that lonely little girl she'd been back then.

But she was not that little girl anymore. Lifting her chin in defiance of the self-pity, she headed for the shower. Freud followed and curled up on the cool tile floor. It had been a long day. She turned on the water, shucked her skirt and blouse and then her underthings. With a towel on the counter and her contacts removed, she stepped beneath the hot spray of water. She skimmed the soap over her body and for the next few minutes she forgot everything else.

When she stepped out of the shower and toweled off she felt completely relaxed. A few more minutes were required to dry her hair. Freud waited patiently. She pulled on clean panties and dragged on her nightshirt as she walked to the bed. Hopefully she would sleep like the dead tonight.

She rolled her eyes. No pun intended. After all, poor Mr. Whitt was only a few floors below her. She climbed into the bed and sank into her pillows with a sigh. Freud curled up in his own bed next to hers.

When she reached up to turn off the bedside table lamp, something in her peripheral vision stalled her.

She blinked. Looked again. The navy suit was not hanging on the hook by the mirror.

After throwing back the covers, she stood and walked into the closet. Her fingers trailed along the fabric until they came to rest on the navy suit. Hadn't she hung it out for tomorrow before she took her shower? Her pulse skittered, but then she reminded herself that it had been a long day, culminating in a shocking revelation from Detective Barton, and then she'd had a couple of beers.

She hung it on the hook next to the mirror. Again… *maybe*. Freud lifted his head and watched her every move.

Then she went to bed. Her faithful pet lowered his head once more. Rowan pulled the covers up around her shoulders and closed her eyes. The forgetfulness was getting old. It seemed as if she misplaced something or forgot something every day.

Unless it was not her at all.

Could someone have come into the house and gotten into her room while she was in the shower?

Julian?

She opened her eyes. No. The door was locked. Though Herman and Woody as well as the cleaning team had keys to the funeral home, no one had a key to the living quarters. Besides, Freud would have barked or growled and gone into attack mode if he'd heard a sound and certainly if he'd picked up the scent of a stranger.

Except Julian wasn't a stranger to him. Freud loved Julian.

Rowan forced herself to look at the situation rationally. Why on earth would anyone come into her room unless it was to harm or to rob her? Certainly no one would gain anything from moving her suit. The idea was beyond ridiculous.

Unless it was Julian playing one of his sick games. The idea didn't seem completely plausible. Why would Julian risk his freedom and perhaps his life to toy with her in such a simplistic, childish fashion?

Besides, it wouldn't be the first time she'd forgotten something or thought she'd taken care of something and later discovered that she had not. It happened to everyone now and again. No matter how organized she tried to be, it was easy to overlook something or make a mistake after a day like today. With all that had happened, she had reason not to be at her best.

Still, considering she remembered so vividly hanging the suit next to the mirror…it felt *odd*. Felt…wrong.

"Just do it." She flung back the covers once more and climbed out of bed. She fumbled for her glasses on the bedside table, grabbed the weapon she kept in the drawer of her bedside table and went downstairs, with Freud at her side. On the second floor, the door that separated the living quarters from the rest of the house was locked. She unlocked it and moved into the corridor.

The long corridor before reaching the main landing above the lobby was dark. The cool air whispering from the registers sent a chill over her skin. She shivered and rubbed at the goose bumps with her left hand. The fingers of her right hand instinctively tightened on the butt of the handgun she carried.

She would feel utterly foolish when she confirmed all the doors were locked.

When she reached the main landing, moonlight filtered in through the towering stained glass with its angels ascending to heaven. She turned her back to the images and reached for the railing. She stalled on the first step, stared at the banister from which her mother's lifeless body had hung.

For a second she was suddenly twelve years old again and standing at the front door, staring up at the grotesque image.

Momma?

Her twelve-year-old voice echoed around Rowan, resurrecting the devastation and terror from that day so long ago.

Anger bolted through her and she shoved the memories away. No loving mother would do that to her child.

Focused on the task at hand, she descended the stairs and checked the front door. *Locked.* Billy would not have failed to do so. Before going back upstairs, she checked the side entrances at the portico and the chapel. Locked. Then, Freud still on her heels, she padded to the corridor leading beyond the parlors and to the back of the house. The back door was locked, as well. She scanned the moonlit yard. No fleeing figures, no odd shadows... just the dark night. The double doors used for receiving were bolted. They were never unlocked except for the intake of new arrivals.

She sighed. So foolish. "Let's go back upstairs, boy." She gestured to the rear staircase, the one the family had always used for privacy, and Freud bounded upward. Rowan readied to follow and then she stilled. The hair on the back of her neck stood on end. The undeniable sensation that someone was watching her crawled over her skin.

Clutching her weapon more tightly, she slowly turned around. Her free hand reached for the switch on the wall. Her heart thundered in her chest. With her fingers on their destination, she flipped the switch and light filled the room.

She was alone.

"Pull yourself together, Ro," she muttered.

Frustrated with herself for overreacting, she shut off the light and climbed the stairs. Freud waited for her at the top. She unlocked the rear door to the living quarters and then locked it once more behind them. She did the same at the main entry. Silently railing at herself for getting spooked, she climbed the final set of stairs to the third floor and went back to bed. She placed her glasses and her weapon on the bedside table, and for the second time tonight she sank into the pillows. She told her mind to shut off.

It refused.

She doubted she would be sleeping much tonight.

Something else she had done very little of since coming home. As much as she wanted to blame her inability to get some shut-eye on the funeral home, she recognized it was primarily about Julian.

He was out there. Possibly watching her and plotting his next move.

Six

Last night's dreams had followed Rowan from her fitful sleep, lingering as the sunlight speared through the kitchen windows, heralding a new day. She poured a second cup of coffee and decided to take a walk in the gardens. Maybe the fresh air would help cleanse the haunting memories of the past from her mind.

On the second story landing, she hesitated. Freud did the same. He stared up at his mistress, waiting for some indication of what to do next. Her attention settled on the oak banister to which her mother had secured the rope she'd used to hang herself. Rowan's chest tightened at the memory. It was only days before Christmas. They had all still been grieving the loss of Raven. As painful as it was for a parent to lose a child, only an identical twin understood the enormity of losing the other half of her- or himself. Rowan felt as if a part of her had died in that lake.

On some level she still felt her sister—they had started out as one, after all. For years after Raven died, Rowan talked to her reflection as if she were speaking to her sister. Particularly after their mother died. Norah DuPont hadn't just died; she had killed herself. To this day the thought remained like a dagger to Rowan's chest. She had needed the comfort of her sister. Her father had done all that he could. He had tried to spend more time with Rowan, but the dead didn't wait for the grieving. Her father had to work. Over and over he had told Rowan that the funeral home was her legacy, too. It was her future.

But all she had felt after that awful year was *alone*. No matter that she'd had her father and Billy. Deep inside, she had been empty.

She turned from the staircase and that ominous banister and studied the large stained-glass window that overlooked the landing and the first floor lobby below. Her mother had painstakingly restored the beautiful artwork that depicted angels ascending toward a perfect blue sky, leaving the earthly meadows below far behind.

Rowan had stopped believing in angels the day she came home from school and found her mother hanging from that railing. She had never prayed again after that moment, either. She'd gone to church on Sunday mornings with her father because that was what he expected, but she had never believed again.

In her adolescent mind, God and the angels had not protected her family. If they had really existed, surely they would have.

Rowan pushed away the thoughts and descended the stairs. Freud trailed her. Besides the *tick, tick* of Freud's nails clacking on the hardwood, it was so quiet she could almost hear the house breathing. It had stood for 150 years. Had witnessed the preparation of thousands of those who had passed in the community and the grief of those left behind. Certainly a sigh was in order. Her father and his family had carried on the family legacy all that time. She had made up her mind after his death that she would not be the one to drop the ball. Since she had no children, it was very likely that the family legacy would end with her.

Beyond the door marked Staff Only, the corridor led to the rear exit. Rowan walked outside into the crisp spring morning. Freud trotted ahead of her to do his business. She breathed deeply of the fresh air and the azalea blooms. In addition to fancying herself a writer, her mother had adored gardening. Her father had struggled to keep the gardens going after her death. He'd managed a fair job. The sheer number of flowers and shrubs was daunting. Rowan wasn't entirely sure she could handle the magnitude of caretaking the gardens would require. Rather than risk being the one who killed her mother's flowers, she had hired a landscaper for maintenance, at least for now. Tuesdays and Thursdays were his days to come by. He would be here this afternoon.

Herman was coming at eleven to help with the Whitt funeral preparations. The service wasn't until one, but there was a great deal to do before deeming the chapel ready. The cleaning team would arrive soon, though they wouldn't need Rowan to supervise their work. She considered going back to the lake, to the place where she'd found the bones.

In all likelihood the area was cordoned off as a crime scene. She wandered over to the three small crosses that her father had painstakingly made on the far side of the backyard. This was the family's pet cemetery. She and her sister had had three pets over the years, two dogs and a cat. After Raven died, Rowan decided she couldn't bear to lose anything else, so there had been no more pets until she bought her place in Nashville. She watched Freud sniff around the fenced perimeter of the yard. She was glad she'd made that decision. She loved him like mad.

Her father had always told her there were other pets buried in the backyard. In the South it was common practice for folks to bury a beloved pet in the backyard. Rowan had never found any markers. Maybe they had been removed over the years.

Rowan smiled, though the memories had sadness streaming through her. "I miss you, Daddy." Her father had been a good man and a great dad. She wasn't always the best daughter, but she had made him proud no matter that she'd chosen a different route for her career in the beginning.

Walking back into the house, through the corridor and into the lobby, she decided she might have some breakfast, after all. She hadn't really felt like eating when she first woke up. The dreams had been too fresh, too strong and disturbing. Her chest had felt tight and her pulse had been racing. The fresh air had been exactly what she needed.

As she reached the lobby staircase, a key turned in the lock of the front entrance. Freud growled. Beyond the glass in the double doors, she spotted Herman. He waved a paper sack at her. She smiled. It looked as if breakfast was already here. Freud whimpered as he, too, recognized Herman.

"Good morning, sunshine," he called as he walked in. He glanced at Freud. "Mr. Furry."

Freud trotted over to him for the snack Herman always brought in his pocket. He dug out the treat and

Freud took it gently from his fingers. "There you go, boy." Herman gave him a scratch between the ears.

Rowan smiled. Herman was the most cheerful man she had ever known. "I hope that's breakfast for two I smell in that bag."

"Bagels and cream cheese." He shook the bag. "Strawberry fruit spread."

Even after all these years he hadn't forgotten her favorites. Whenever she had visited, her father had always picked up bagels at the bakery on the town square. Rowan could already taste the tang of the sourdough bagels and the smooth cream cheese, not to mention the sweet and tart strawberries.

"We should take this party upstairs." The cleaning crew would be here any moment and she felt confident there were not enough bagels in that small bag to share. Not to mention, Freud wasn't fond of vacuum cleaners.

They climbed the stairs side by side, Freud bringing up the rear. Herman chatted on and on about the weather and how he intended to go fishing later that afternoon. On the second-floor landing, Rowan couldn't help glancing at that railing once more. But she exiled the memories that attempted to intrude and led the way into her kitchen.

Her kitchen.

This was the first time since she'd returned that she had officially considered the kitchen or any other part of the place hers.

"You still drinking decaf?"

Herman placed the bag on the counter. "Only when I'm with my wife." He grinned. "The rest of the time I do as I please."

Rowan would just bet he did as he pleased. "Decaf

it is, then." He made a face and Rowan added, "I'm not going to have Estelle asking me if you've been behaving and be forced to tell her you haven't."

He sighed and sat down on one of the two stools at the counter. "I swear, getting old is hell."

Her father always said the same thing. The two men had been so close, they were like brothers. "Well, in my expert opinion—" she shoved the basket of decaf coffee grounds into place and pressed the brew button "—it's far better than the alternative."

They both laughed. You learned to have a few jokes handy when working with the dead. It was part of staying sane, her father had advised when she and Raven were working alongside him. Every DuPont for four generations had passed down this funeral home to their son or sons. Until Edward DuPont had a set of twin girls and no other children. Rowan was the fifth generation DuPont to serve as undertaker.

The aroma of the rich, dark blend filled the room as she poured, refilling her own cup and another for Herman. She asked, "How is Estelle?"

Her father had mentioned Herman's wife was battling cancer. But that had been nearly two years ago. Shamefully, since returning home, Rowan had been too busy to think to ask how Estelle was doing. She really, really needed to stop allowing the investigation into Julian's history and whereabouts to interfere with her life. She understood the need to be careful but she also had to move on.

It was time she started looking forward rather than back.

"She's doing great." Herman nodded as he opened the bag. "We were really lucky to find the right doctor and treatments that could keep her healthy. I want her with me as long as possible."

Rowan reached over and squeezed his hand. "I'm glad to hear it."

"Me, too, darling. Me, too." Herman placed the bagels on bread plates and doled out the packets of cream cheese and fruit spread. "Since we couldn't have any children of our own, she's all I've got."

His comment spurred a thought she'd long ago tucked away. Rowan frowned. "Why didn't my parents ever have more children?" She'd always wondered but never asked the question. They might have ended up with a boy if they'd gone for a round two.

Herman made a face. "I don't recall either one of them ever mentioning why. I know your momma was traveling a lot for her writing after you girls were born. Maybe she didn't want another pregnancy to interfere with her work."

Rowan tried not to laugh at the idea. "Do you think she was serious about her writing? I mean, I know she spent a lot of time working at it, but she never published anything."

He chewed for a moment, washed down the bite of bagel with the freshly brewed coffee. "Mostly I think she just liked the distraction. You know, she was from a family of farmers. They cultivated the land, grew things. Living in this house and spending so much time surrounded by the dead, it was tough on a soul not accustomed to such darkness."

"It is a macabre profession," Rowan agreed. Kids in school had been ruthless with their teasing. Raven had lashed out at anyone who made a smart remark. Rowan had hung her head and pretended not to hear. She had never liked controversy. Still didn't.

"Or maybe your momma and daddy just decided not to mess with perfection when it came to their kids."

Rowan did laugh then.

After a couple of bites of bagel, she asked, "Did my parents get along well enough?"

Herman shrugged. "They had their ups and downs like most married couples. Your father was so serious and committed to the business. Your mother was different. She was a free spirit. She spoke her mind whether anyone wanted to hear it or not. Wouldn't join any of the clubs the other ladies in town joined and never attended church as I recall. Most considered her a rebel, I expect."

Rowan hadn't remembered her mother being so outspoken. She did recall that she always seemed to be deep into a story on Sunday mornings and never had time to go to the services with them.

There was one more thing she had to ask. "But they loved each other?"

Herman sat down his coffee cup and studied her, surprise evident on his face. "Well, of course they did. Why would you ask?"

"My mother has been dead for more than twenty-six years, almost twenty-seven, and I had never once dreamed of her until right before Daddy was…died." She shrugged, cradled her cup with both hands. "Now I dream of her nearly every night and it's almost always the same. I hear her arguing with someone. A man. Daddy, I assume."

"Well, now, they had some arguments rightly enough. Your daddy didn't agree with her going off on all those trips and leaving you girls to fend for yourselves. He thought y'all needed your momma around more."

Seemed a reasonable expectation to Rowan. "But she didn't see it that way."

Herman shook his head adamantly. "Not at all. She said just because she had children didn't mean she was giving up her life. She'd already given up a whole lot just marrying an undertaker."

Rowan winced. "That must have been a painful admission for my father to hear."

The older man, who had always been a big part of her family, made one of those faces that said, *not so much.* "He took her eccentricities in stride. Never complained unless she planned too many trips too close together."

Rowan thought about the other questions she wanted to ask. "Did you notice that Raven seemed to change toward me the year she died?"

Rowan had always felt as if their relationship had gone through a inexorable shift that year. Raven was suddenly popular and running with the who's who at school while Rowan still lurked in the shadows. Billy had been her only friend and he'd been so busy with football and the charity rodeo, he really hadn't been around much. That year, it felt like everything changed. Her mother was gone more often than ever. It was as if something had happened to disrupt the algorithms of their lives and then they were both gone. Rowan had often wondered if her mother had loved her more, would she have stayed instead of following her favorite daughter into death? Her father had insisted that her mother had loved her just as much and would have done the same if Rowan had been the one to drown...but deep down she still felt that wasn't the case.

As a psychiatrist she understood it wasn't that simple. Unfortunately she would likely never understand why her mother had taken her life, leaving a child who needed her so much.

"No, girl, you are worrying yourself for nothing. Adolescence is a tough time. All siblings have difficulty during those years. You know that."

She did understand, yes, but like most girls on the verge of being a teenager who have siblings, it had felt exactly as if her sister had started to hate her. Looking back, she recognized that her emotions had been exaggerated.

Apparently sensing the conversation needed to be changed, Herman said, "Was that Billy's truck I saw here last night after Mr. Whitt's visitation? I was going to come by to see if you needed a hand, but I thought maybe you were *busy*."

Rowan rolled her eyes. "You are as bad as Daddy was. Trust me, it was official police business."

"About those bones you found? Or about Geneva?"

"He's still investigating both. As of last night there was nothing new on Mrs. Phillips, but it turns out there's a strong possibility that the remains I found are those of Julian Addington's daughter."

Surprise claimed the older man's face. "You can't be serious? Your daddy always worried that Addington wanted you all to himself. That he would one day try talking you into marrying him. Guess he already had a significant other."

Now Rowan was the one surprised. "Daddy thought Addington and I were more than friends?"

"No, no, now, don't take this the wrong way." He held up his hands and moved them from side to side in emphasis. "He knew you only looked at the man as a friend and a mentor, but he figured Addington wanted more. Something about the way he looked at you, he told me."

"He never said a word to me." Rowan was a bit shocked.

"I guess he didn't want you to think he was being overprotective or nosing into your personal business."

Rowan recalled a number of particularly ugly arguments she and her father had during her college years. Especially after what she had done. Instinctively, she tugged at the sleeves of her blouse to ensure they covered the scars on her wrists. Though there were no physical scars related to her second attempt—she'd used sleeping pills that time—she had come far closer to success.

"I hurt him. I regret that more than you can know."

Herman nodded sagely. "You did, but the two of you got past those painful times. You can take my word for it, Ro, he did not harbor any ill feelings about those days. He didn't even talk about them, ever. He treated the situation like it never happened."

On some level, that knowledge comforted her, but on another, she would give anything for one more day with her father to make sure he understood how very much she had always loved him. "You know, there are parts of my childhood that are blank. I've tried to fill in all the spaces but it's like some things are missing."

"Wait until you get to my age," Herman said, "and then you'll be trying to recall what you did yesterday or an hour ago."

Rowan laughed, couldn't help herself. "Professionally speaking, I recognize the blank spaces are normal. All children have traumatic or hurtful moments that they block. You could ask six children who lived through a particular event to describe what happened and you would most likely come away with six different versions. Still, I wonder."

"If it makes you feel any better, I was here most of the time, working with your daddy. If anything too awful to remember besides your sister's and your momma's deaths happened, I don't have any recollection of it, either."

"Thanks, Herman, that makes me feel better." Still, there were those damned dreams. They were coming from somewhere.

He stared into his coffee cup a moment before meeting her gaze once more. "You still dream of your sister?"

"More often now than when I was in Nashville, but with being home and doing the work we once helped my father do, that's to be expected." At least that was what Rowan told herself every morning when she woke from a fretful sleep and disturbing dreams of Raven and their mother still lingered.

"I suppose so." He finished his coffee. "I should get on my way. I'll be back in a couple of hours to help." He stood and carried his cup to the sink and his napkin and paper to the trash. "You canceled Mrs. Phillips's visitation?"

"No choice. There has to be an autopsy." The procedure made the death even more painful for her daughters. But it couldn't be avoided. Geneva Phillips deserved justice. Until they understood what happened to her, it was difficult to build a profile of the person who had killed her. Rowan hoped it didn't take long.

"Let me know if you need me to pick up any supplies. I'm happy to do it."

"We're good," Rowan assured him. "I had Woody restock everything before he started his vacation."

Rowan and Freud walked Herman down the stairs and to the front door. She waved as she watched him drive away.

Maybe there was a way she could fill in the blank places in her memory. She could dig through the mass of journals and notes her mother had kept and perhaps find some insights. She had started to once, years ago, but preparing for medical school had distracted her, and she'd never gotten back to the task. She had a couple of hours before Mr. Whitt's funeral. Now was as good a time as any to dig around.

Maybe she would discover some big secret that explained everything.

Rowan stilled. She wasn't entirely certain she was ready for *everything*.

Seven

Rowan hadn't gone into her parents' bedroom since the day she and Billy selected the suit for her father's funeral. Standing in their room now felt like an invasion of their privacy. She turned on the light and crossed the room. Norah DuPont had created a writing nook in the big bay window. Rowan wasn't sure the window was original to the house, but it had been here for as long as she could remember. Knowing her father, he probably had it installed just for his wife. He'd gone out of his way to cater to her needs.

Norah had been a beautiful woman and, as Herman said, a free spirit. Rowan was sure her father—the undertaker—had been overly grateful to have her as his wife. But Norah was the one who should have been grateful. A burst of anger fired in Rowan's chest. As much as she had loved both her parents, she could not help but resent her mother's selfishness.

She sat down at the small writing desk her mother had used. The most painful part was that Rowan had done the same thing to her father. Seven months after her sister and her mother were dead and gone, Rowan had tried taking her own life. The only thing she had accomplished was to leave ugly scars on her wrists and to hurt her father. She'd been thinking only of herself at the time. Her twin had left her, her mother had left her and rather than see the loving father who had not, she'd selfishly decided she wanted to die, too.

Thinking of how badly she had hurt him still twisted her heart. So very, very selfish of her. He had found her and stopped the bleeding, stitched her foolish work and nursed her so that no one would ever have to know what she had done. He'd wanted to protect her from what others would say. Only Billy and Herman had known. Rowan was immensely grateful that she and her father had discussed that hurtful past while he was in Nashville visiting her right before his…death. Any lingering doubt as to whether he had forgiven her had been dispelled. And though she would always regret her adolescent decisions, deep in her heart she knew he had forgiven her.

Rowan opened the journal in which her mother had made her last entry.

This place—this house—has drained the joy and the life from me. I cannot go on.

"Thanks, Mom," Rowan muttered.

What kind of mother did that to her child? Of course Rowan was aware of the classic textbook explanations, but none of those assuaged the emptiness, hurt and resentment left by her mother's decision. She closed the journal. Frankly, until all these recent dreams, she had rarely thought of her mother. Irrationally she thought, *Why should I?* Clearly her mother had not been thinking of her. Even though Rowan knew as an adult and a doctor that her reactionary thoughts were also selfish.

A framed photograph of Norah and her daughters

sat on the desk. It was taken perhaps two months before Raven had died. The azaleas in the yard had already started to bloom. Rowan and Raven had the same blond hair and blue eyes as their mother. As Rowan grew older, her father had often remarked that she was the spitting image of her mother. And Rowan had always resented that fact. She would have much preferred to look like her father.

She stared at her reflection in the window. And just like her mother, she had hurt her father deeply not once, but twice. As a freshman in college, the dreams of Raven had overwhelmed her again. Being thrust into a new environment at college and once again finding herself isolated without any friends, she had grown depressed. Rather than seek help she swallowed a handful of her roommate's sleeping pills. Rowan sighed. That time her father was not there to intervene and she ended up at the hospital with a mandatory stay in a psych unit.

Dr. Julian Addington had been the psychiatrist to evaluate her. He had taken a special interest in Rowan. It was all so obvious now. He had been watching her and made sure he was the one to evaluate her and then to continue as her therapist all through her undergraduate years. By the time he announced that she no longer required his services, they were close friends. If only their association had ended there. Instead, they had become colleagues as well as friends.

Then he murdered her father for no other reason than to hurt her.

Her decision to stay in Nashville after her education and residency and to follow in Julian's footsteps to some degree had catered to his massive ego. When her book, *The Language of Death*, was released, Julian had not been so pleased, apparently, to find it was dedicated to her father. After having bared so much of her soul within the pages of that book, she had eventually confessed her long-kept secret to her father and to Julian—she had made the wrong choice. As satisfying as her career in Nashville was, deep down she wished she'd followed in her father's footsteps.

In his demented mind, Julian had taken her admission as an insult. His extreme emotional reaction had caused the killer who had murdered more than a hundred people without leaving so much as a trace to make his first mistake.

He had become emotionally attached to Rowan and she had been his downfall.

She stared out the window. Except he was still out there. Whoever died next by his hand was on her, just as her father's death was.

"Get on with it, already." Rowan shook off the thoughts and opened the center desk drawer. Inside was a small tin of candies. A smile tugged at her lips at the memory of her mother's cinnamon-scented breath. The image of her smile filled Rowan's mind. Norah had loved braiding their hair. She would often braid her own as well and say they were triplets. *We all have matching pink ribbons...*

A warm sensation whispered through Rowan. How had Rowan forgotten? Her brain wouldn't allow those sweet and tender memories beyond the hurtful ones of her mother's suicide—a self-protective mechanism. But now, with all the questions about their history, she needed to push through those defenses and remember everything. Somewhere amid all those tucked-away memories were answers that she desperately needed.

Her gaze wandered back to the window looking out over the backyard. The three of them had spent endless hours picnicking in the summer. On a quilt her mother had hand-stitched…surrounded by the flowers of her garden.

Rowan's heart beat faster as the moments played like a long forgotten video in her head. Funny how those things had completely slipped her mind. Just more of those painful places and moments that were easier to block than to touch. The painful images—her mother hanging from that second floor banister, Raven's gray and bloated body—bored into her brain.

Rowan's breath caught, and she forced the recollections away and began picking through the papers and completely random items in the desk drawers. She moved to the small two-drawer file cabinet that sat next to the desk. The journals were filed by year. Rowan pulled out the one for the final year of Norah's life. She started with January. Month by month she skimmed through her mother's writing. The best Rowan could determine, she took a short trip each month. Two of the trips that year were in Colorado but not as far west as California. And certainly none to Nashville were noted.

She mentioned Rowan and Raven, and her garden occasionally. Each day of writing began with where she was and her mood. She spoke of sitting at this window and watching her daughters play. Two or three pages of ramblings about her stories filled each day that she worked. Rowan was surprised she didn't write every day. In Rowan's memory she had always been bent over this desk.

The words she wrote were consistently related to her most recent travels. There were so many beginnings but only a few had endings. Hardly any had middles. The journals actually appeared more like notes and ideas that had inspired her but not real stories. Parts flowed like narrative but very little actually went anywhere.

Strange, Rowan decided. Surely she hadn't sent something this incomplete to a publisher and expected anything other than a rejection.

An entry for September of that final year seemed familiar to Rowan, but she couldn't be sure. Twenty-seven years was a very long time ago. Perhaps she had heard her mother speak of the story idea. Rowan frowned. Probably not. Norah had been very private about her stories.

Rowan wondered if her father had ever read any of the notes. He had never mentioned it if he had. Like her, he might have found the mere thought too painful.

Closing the drawer, she stood. It was time she prepared for the funeral. The cleaners were likely finished downstairs and the chapel preparations would be nearly complete.

Freud's deep, throaty barks echoed in the air. Rowan walked around to the backside of the desk and peered out the window. He stood on the far side of the yard, the hair on his back standing on end, his posture one of attack readiness. She didn't see anyone in the yard or near the fence. Beyond the six-foot privacy fence she could see that there was no one in the alley on the other side. Maybe a squirrel or cat she couldn't see from here was taunting Freud.

She crossed the room but hesitated at the door. The closet door was open a crack. Had she forgotten to close it two months ago when she and Billy had selected the suit her father would wear?

Rowan walked to the closet and reached to close the door, but something on the floor prevented it from closing. She bent down and picked up the black cloth. A jacket. One of her father's jackets. Flipping on the light in the walk-in closet, she gasped. Two more jackets and a pair of trousers were strewn on the floor.

Had she left this mess? She didn't recall leaving anything on the floor. She did remember looking through the various suits with Billy until she'd found the charcoal one she wanted. Frankly, the days around her father's funeral had been like walking through a fog. Perhaps some of his things had slipped off the hangers and she hadn't noticed. Frustrated with herself, she picked up each jacket, shook the wrinkles from it and hung it back on the lone wooden rod. As she picked up the trousers, she spotted a slip of paper on the floor beneath them. When the trousers were back on a hanger, she retrieved the paper and opened it. It was a cocktail napkin from the Night Owl. No note or phone number written on it.

She wasn't familiar with the establishment but apparently it was a club or bar. Perhaps her father had gone with a friend. She would ask Herman. The napkin must have been in his pocket and fallen out when she was rifling through the hangers for the proper burial suit. She shouldn't have been so careless.

Once she'd set the closet to rights, she turned off the light and closed the door. Her mother's closet was next to her father's. The master bedroom had once been two bedrooms. The second bedroom had been divided into closets when her parents married. Her father had said that Norah's one condition for moving into the funeral home was that she had a larger closet.

Funny, Rowan had wished for the same. As much

as she would like to have more room, she could never use her parents' room. It just wouldn't feel right. Plus, she would have to pack and store all their things. For now, she simply couldn't do that. Her father had left her mother's things just as they were. She supposed she would do the same…for now.

She turned on the light and checked her mother's closet, as well. The closed-up room still smelled like her—the subtle fragrance of flowers. Her mother had loved roses and peonies and lavender. Actually, there wasn't a blooming plant she could think of that her mother hadn't liked. Rowan hadn't come into this closet since leaving for college. She wondered now if her father had.

A partially opened drawer revealed the end of a night-shirt that had been tugged out of place. Rowan opened the drawer and looked at the array of cotton shirts. Her mother always slept in nightshirts. No silky lingerie or pajamas for her. Plain old cotton nightshirts and thick socks. This was something they had in common. There was another drawer full of socks. Rowan was a fan of comfy socks, too.

Rowan touched the fabric of her mother's dresses. Mostly natural fabrics. Her mother preferred organic materials and foods. Unlike Rowan, Norah had gone for the ankle-length skirts and tank tops rather than jeans. Even in the winter she simply changed out her flip-flops for boots and added a sweater or coat to her flimsy tank top or T. Her father had called her a flower child.

Norah hadn't been much of a jewelry fan, either. A string of pearls and a silver chain lay in a vintage bone china bowl that served as a tray on the built-in drawer set. Another penchant the two of them shared. Rowan thought of the suits and heels she'd worn in her former career. Norah would not have approved. Too stuffy, she would have said. Too fake.

"What about you, Mother?" Rowan's fingers trailed along the fabrics. "What were you hiding behind all this simplicity?"

Rather than risk answering herself, Rowan turned off the light and left her parents' space. The sound of Freud still carrying on outside drew her down the rear stairs and to the back door. The area had two access points. The double doors designed for the delivery of the bodies, which were always bolted and locked. Then, near the staircase that went up to the living quarters was a single back door that led out onto a porch with wide steps down to the yard.

As she reached the steps, her cell vibrated. Rowan was so focused on the dog she jumped at the unexpected intrusion of her cell.

It was probably Billy or Herman. She answered without checking the screen. "Hey."

Rather than the *Hey yourself* she expected from Billy or the *I'm headed your way* from Herman, there was only the sharp sound of a quickly indrawn breath.

"Hello?" Frowning, she drew the phone away from her ear and checked the screen. Unknown Number.

"Hello?" Probably a telemarketer. "Thanks for calling," she muttered. "I'm hanging up now."

"Rowan."

Another sharply indrawn breath…only this time it was hers.

Julian Addington.

Fury fired through her. "What do you want?" Asking

him where he was would be pointless. He wasn't going to tell her the truth if he told her anything at all.

"I've missed you, Rowan."

The urge to vomit sent a bitter taste into her mouth. "I wish I could say the same, but obviously that isn't possible, you son of a bitch." Anger snatched away her control. "You murdered my father."

"I did. But rest assured that I did so quite mercifully. He never saw it coming. I had no desire for him to suffer. It was *you* I wanted to feel the pain of loss."

She struggled to conquer her emotions. "I hope you're enjoying your victory." She hesitated. "But wait, your decision to murder my father and that police officer took a great deal from you, as well. The life you knew with all the money and prestige is gone. Over. Everyone knows what an impostor you are. A liar and a murderer. A pathetic excuse for a human being."

"We can't all be so ingenious," he tossed back. "I'm certain my name will echo through history, as will yours, but for entirely different reasons. You are nothing without me, Rowan. I saved your life. I gave you purpose. I made you what you are. A little gratitude wouldn't kill you."

"The only thing I feel for you, Julian, is sheer hatred. I want you to die screaming in agony. I would love nothing better than to see you staked to the ground and torn apart by ravenous animals." She took a breath, struggled to regain control of her emotions. "Is that enough gratitude for you?"

He laughed. The sound was like salt in her wounds. How had she ever considered this man brilliant and charming, much less a trusted friend?

"How far you've fallen, Rowan. You're already returned to your roots. The small-town girl with no hope of anything except playing with dead things and marrying some boot-wearing former small-time football star who is about as complex as a stone. Will you have his babies, too? I hear older women are doing all sorts of things to prime their aging uteri for childbirth. I thought I taught you better, Rowan. You are worth so much more than a sperm bag and human incubator."

"Goodbye, Julian. Good luck evading all those law enforcement agencies on your trail even as we speak."

"I understand you've found Alisha."

The words stopped Rowan cold. It wasn't a question. He knew. How could he know? Her name had not been released.

His ex-wife.

Of course.

"Who is Alisha?" Rowan refused to give him any information. He already knew too much. There were many other things she should be saying, asking, but none of those things would launch from her brain to her tongue.

"You don't remember?"

Rowan felt a prick of dread in the pit of her stomach. "Aren't you afraid the FBI is tracing your call, Julian? Really, I thought you were supposed to be some amazingly intelligent killer. Perhaps the police have overestimated your skill."

This was one thing she understood about Julian. He was immensely competitive and did not take assaults on his reputation or intelligence level well.

He laughed. "You know me inside and out, Rowan."

Silence thickened between them. Rowan's heart pumped harder and harder.

"Think, Rowan. You will remember. Like many painful memories of your childhood, you have suppressed this one, as well. You will remember."

The dread needling at her evolved into a sense of rising panic. "I'm afraid you're wrong again, Julian, just as you are about our relationship. You have been wrong about so many things. My father made me who I am. He instilled his strength and determination in me. He is the man I loved, admired and respected above all others. Not you. It was never you."

"I've left you a gift, Rowan. Something to help you remember. Watch your step, you are closer to death than you know."

The call ended.

Rowan resisted the urge to throw the phone. But the damned thing was far too pivotal to her work. And it was a connection to *him*… If serving as the bait that helped lure him in was necessary, she was happy to oblige. She took a breath, let it out slowly. Then another and another. His final words to her echoed over and over in her head. Well, of course she was close to death. She lived and worked in a funeral home.

The silence around her suddenly demanded her attention. Her gaze sought and found Freud. Sitting beneath the tree, he was watching her as if he, too, understood the call had been from a monster. At least he'd stopped his infernal barking. She drew in another deep, cleansing breath, steadied the tiny tremor quaking through her limbs and reached for calm.

"Come on, boy," she called. She had work to do. Mr. Whitt's funeral was at one. The family would be here soon. She needed to appear presentable even if she was shaking inside.

Freud ignored her, turned his attention back to the

tulip tree that stood next to the fence and started to bark once more. What on earth was he barking at?

Rowan stalked across the yard and peered up into the tree. Pinkish-purple blooms would open soon from the thousands of buds weighing down the limbs. She couldn't see a squirrel or a bird or one damned thing that would make him bark.

"Freud," she repeated in a stern voice, "come."

He glanced at her, then back at the tree.

Rowan shook her head. His fur and his stance warned he was ready to attack. The question was, attack what?

"What is it you see, boy?" She put her hand up to block the sun and scrutinized the tree limb by limb.

Finally, she saw the culprit. A small leather pouch. Like a tiny purse. It appeared beaded, like one of those crafted by hand found at local artisan shops.

How long had it been hanging in this tree?

She had to put a foot between the V of two thick limbs to boost herself up far enough to reach the bag. It didn't appear weatherworn. It couldn't have been out here all that long. She thought of the neighborhood on the street that ran beyond the alley behind the funeral home. It was possible some of the children who lived nearby sneaked onto the property from time to time. Kids loved to tempt the unknown and the mysterious. There was nothing more ghoulish than a funeral home. The small bag closed with strings. She untied it and loosened the opening to see if there was anything inside. The smell of leather emanated from the bag.

I've left you a gift...

Julian's words echoed in her brain.

A small, thin object was deep inside. Rowan reached in with two fingers and tugged the object out.

A wallet-size photograph.

She turned it over and stared at the image. The air in her lungs evacuated.

Long blond hair and bright blue eyes stared out from the photo. The teenage girl wore a short skirt and a tight-fitting T with UCLA on it. Around her neck was a silver chain. Rowan peered closely at the necklace, saw the amber…the silver sun and moon.

Alisha Addington.

Eight

Billy couldn't shake the idea that Rowan had sounded odd when he spoke to her as he left city hall. The Whitt funeral was in a couple of hours. Maybe she was just busy. He probably shouldn't have asked her to go with him to talk to Mrs. Phillips's daughters. But they had started this together and he felt she needed to be there. She had a way of talking to folks that put them at ease.

He pulled into the parking lot at the funeral home and got out of his truck. Halfway up the steps the door opened and Charlotte Kinsley walked out.

"Morning, Chief."

"Morning, Charlotte."

She hitched her head toward the door. "Ro's in the chapel making sure everything is just right."

"Thanks." Billy walked through the door, turned left and walked past the three visitation parlors.

DuPonts had built the house as a funeral home and residence. It had never been anything else. Rowan's grandfather had added the chapel on the west side of the main floor. On the opposite side he'd added the large portico where the hearse waited during a funeral service.

Behind the hearse the vehicles of the family members would line up for the procession to the cemetery.

Over the past 150 years, modern conveniences, like the elevator and the small first-floor walk-in cooler for the flowers, had been added. But more important than any of that, this funeral home was a family-owned-and-operated business. A family who cared about the people in the community. Rowan, like her daddy, was an important asset to Winchester. Billy wanted her to be happy with her life here. If she wasn't happy, she might decide to leave again. He hoped that wouldn't happen.

Addington, the son of a bitch, wasn't making anything about her life easy right now. Billy's conversation with Dressler after the briefing this morning had gone over the same damned ground they covered each time. Was there any possibility Rowan was communicating with Addington? Could she have any idea where he was hiding? Did Billy have any reason to believe Addington was in his jurisdiction?

Each time Billy set the guy straight. Rowan would never hide anything that might help find her father's killer. And if the bastard showed up in Winchester, Billy intended to see that he didn't get away.

He paused at the door to the chapel and watched as Rowan walked the aisles, scanning the rows of benches, ensuring all was as it should be. She wore one of her big-city business suits, this one an elegant navy. Her hair was up and arranged in some sort of sophisticated twist. She looked serene and beautiful. But he liked her best in those plain old T-shirts and jeans she wore when she was relaxing or doing her work downstairs. He wondered if she had any idea how much she looked like her mother. He remembered Norah DuPont. She'd watched him closely as if she had known even back then that he had a sweet spot for her younger daughter. Raven had liked reminding Rowan that she was the oldest. Rowan would always plant her hands on her hips and protest that her sister was only older by ten minutes. Norah had laughed and said that Rowan had made up for that ten minutes by crying the loudest. Billy had loved every minute of it, and Norah had noticed.

Something else Rowan and her mother had in common: Norah had read people with surprising accuracy. Even back then, Billy had a thing for details. He had watched Norah, too. What teenage boy wouldn't have? She had been a pretty lady. He wouldn't have expected her to do what she did. Seemed out of character. He never talked about it to Rowan. She didn't need his adolescent analysis of her mother. Rowan was more than qualified to make her own evaluation, then and now. Edward had mentioned once that Norah had fooled him. Billy wished he had followed up on the comment.

Now it was too late.

Rowan turned around as if she'd sensed his presence. Her automatic smile had him grinning, too. "You ready?"

She nodded. "I'll need to be back before one to greet the family."

"I promise I'll have you back before one. This shouldn't take more than a few minutes."

She adjusted her jacket. Checked for her cell in the pocket. "I'm ready, then."

He followed her along the corridor, back to the lobby and out the door. Before she could, he reached for the passenger-side door of his truck and opened it. When she had settled in the seat, he closed the door and strode around to the driver's side.

"Any news on the remains?" she asked as he started the engine.

"I just got the call before I headed over here. The dental records confirm the remains are Alisha Addington's."

"Wow."

Her voice told him the news still shocked her even though she'd resigned herself to the reality that Addington had lied to her on yet another level. Billy gave her a moment to get right with that news before he said the rest.

"The medical examiner in Nashville completed her preliminary exam. She concluded cause of death as asphyxiation by strangulation."

Rowan searched his eyes and face. "She must have found hyoid bone fractures. That's about all that was left to suggest the conclusion of strangulation."

Billy nodded. "That's what the report she faxed me says."

"It's official then," Rowan said, her voice resigned. "She was murdered."

"Yeah." All these old murders suddenly surfacing was creepy as hell. "I'm hoping we won't be finding any more old bones for a while."

Rowan laughed, a soft, weary sound. "Me, too."

He braked for the red light at the intersection of Second and High. "You have something on your mind, Ro?" He decided it would be in his best interest not to mention that she looked tired.

"Just the usual." She glanced at him, smiled, but it didn't reach her eyes. "I'm not sleeping so well. I suppose I'm still acclimating to being back home."

The light changed and he rolled forward. "You've been gone a long time. It'll take time to adjust. Besides, sleeping in a funeral home is an acquired thing, you know." He flashed her a grin, hoping to lighten the moment. "I can't imagine it's easy to lie down and sleep knowing there's a body stored below."

She laughed, the real McCoy this time. "I did consider last night that as tired as I was, I should sleep like the dead."

"You certainly wouldn't have been alone."

They both laughed. It wasn't really funny but they both needed to grab hold of the lighthearted moment.

"You are the only person in the world who could make a joke about the dead."

He frowned, glanced at her. "I'm hoping that's a compliment." He parked in front of the Phillips home.

"Don't worry. It is." She reached for her seat belt.

He looked at her then, really looked. "Anytime you need me to stay with you, Ro, you know I will. I've slept across the hall from you before."

The sadness that claimed her expression then made him regret the words.

"Thank you, Billy. I'll keep that in mind."

He mentally kicked himself about a dozen times as they walked to the front door. The one thing he did not want—ever—was for her to think he was hitting on her.

"It's okay," she said, looking up at him after he'd rung the bell. "I know you made the offer because you care."

The frustration gripping his chest loosened. He nodded. "You're my best friend, Ro. I want to help in whatever way you need."

Before she could respond, the door opened and Patty looked from him to Rowan and back, then said, "Come on in."

They followed her into the living room. Jenn and her

daughter, Kelley, were already seated. Billy waited for Rowan to settle on the sofa, and then he sat beside her. Beyond having to tell a family that someone they loved was dead, this was the part of his job that he disliked most.

"Did your husband make it home from London?" Billy asked. He'd heard that Mr. Brinkley had, but asking might help break the tension and set the daughters at ease.

"He did," Jenn said. "Thank you for asking."

"You have news for us, Chief?" Patty asked, getting straight to the point.

"We'd like to have Mother's funeral," Jenn said with a glance at Rowan.

"The ME's office called," Billy said. "They should be releasing your mother's body by the end of the week."

The two women exchanged a look. "What else did the medical examiner say?" Patty wanted to know.

"She did confirm," Billy went on, "blunt force trauma to the back of the head as cause of death." Their eyes widened and clouded with tears. "She's listing manner of death as homicide."

"So she was murdered?" This from Jenn.

Billy nodded. "No question. This is why it's so important that we learn of anyone who might have had a grudge against her. Anyone who may have wanted to hurt her for any reason."

She moved her head from side to side. "There is no one. I'm telling you, Chief. Mother did not have enemies. No one would have wanted to hurt her. We've been over this already."

"But someone did hurt her. And the only way we're

going to find that person is if we talk about the possibilities."

"You didn't find any fingerprints that don't belong?" Jenn asked as she dabbed at her eyes.

This was a difficult part to explain. "We found dozens of fingerprints. We've ruled out both of yours and your mother's. But there are dozens more, and unless they pop up in a database we're not likely to know who they belong to."

They stared at him, confused and frustrated and maybe a little angry. He was the chief of police. He was supposed to have protected their mother, and he sure as hell was supposed to be able to find out who killed her.

"But," Rowan put in, "if a suspect is found, the prints could help confirm that he was in the house. It's a long and arduous task, but it's one that may help in the future even if not right now."

Both women nodded despite the confusion cluttering their faces.

"I talked to her closest neighbors again," Patty said. "No one saw anything out of the ordinary on Sunday. No one saw company at Mom's house."

"But many of them were gone to church for a couple of hours that morning," Jenn reminded her sister. "Whoever did this could have come then."

Billy's investigation had found the same when the neighbors were interviewed. "You mentioned that you haven't noticed anything missing?" Billy needed somewhere to start and right now he had nothing. Not one damned thing that would point him in a direction.

Patty shook her head. "Nothing. She had a stash of petty cash in a coffee can in the kitchen and even it's still there."

"Tell us what's been going on in your mother's life the past few months." Rowan glanced at Billy before continuing, "I'm aware your father died around the same time as mine. I'm sure that was a very difficult time for your mother."

"It was." Jenn stared at her hands a moment before going on. "Dad had surgery on his shoulder a couple of months before he died. He just never seemed to get back on his feet after that. You know, he didn't bounce back the way Dr. Knowles thought he would. The physical therapy really took everything out of him. And then the heart attack." She looked away. "I guess it was all too much for him."

"He was midsixties?" Rowan asked.

"He'd just turned sixty-five," Patty answered. "He said he never thought he'd see the day he'd be happy to be sixty-five, but he was looking forward to having Medicare."

"Had he been diagnosed with any heart issues?" Billy asked.

She nodded. "He'd had some blockages taken care of year before last, but there were more. He needed surgery again but he was waiting until he recovered from the shoulder surgery first. I guess he waited too long."

"Had your mother suffered any lingering depression that you noticed?" Rowan asked. "Was she seeing anyone for counseling?"

"No," Jenn said. "She prayed a lot and spent a lot of time reading her Bible, but she didn't seem depressed. We talked on the phone two or three times a week." She looked to her sister. "What do you think?"

"There was something wrong after the funeral." Patty's forehead lined as if she were trying to recall a particular memory. "She seemed upset or angry about something but she wouldn't say what."

"Was she upset by someone who attended the funeral?" Billy hadn't been at Mr. Phillips's funeral and he hadn't heard about any trouble having occurred, but those things happened from time to time, especially in a small town where everyone knew everyone else.

"I don't think so. She just said something about it being wrong, but she wouldn't say what. She told me it was nothing; she would take care of it."

Jenn sighed. "Mother worried too much about us. She always tried to take care of everything herself so she didn't have to trouble us with whatever it was."

"We told her," Patty put in, "that we wanted to help with whatever she and Daddy needed, but she wouldn't listen."

"Most won't," Billy agreed. His own parents were the same way.

"Did the service go as she'd expected?" Rowan wanted to know.

"The service was beautiful," Jenn assured her. "And the visitation. We couldn't have been more pleased."

Rowan nodded. "That's good to hear. Perhaps someone said something that upset Mrs. Phillips. People can be oblivious to seemingly harmless statements made at a bad time."

Rowan was on the same wavelength as Billy. He had reached the same conclusion.

Both women nodded again. This news had shaken them. Jenn's daughter, Kelley, hadn't said a word. Being the first grandchild, she had likely been particularly close to her grandmother.

"Please let me know if you discover anything at all

you feel might be relevant to the investigation. Anything at all," Billy urged. "You never know what might make a difference."

"We sure will," Patty promised.

"We'll get out of your way, then." Billy stood, and Rowan did the same. "I'll keep you posted as the investigation moves along."

The daughters walked them to the door. He sure as hell wished he'd had better news for them. Nothing about murder was ever pleasant, but to have not one piece of evidence as a starting point was particularly frustrating.

Billy had pulled away from the curb when Rowan spoke. "What do you know about the Night Owl?"

The question surprised him. Talk about coming out of left field. "It's a club over in Decherd." He glanced at her. "Why do you ask?" He supposed someone could have invited her to go out for a drink.

"I was looking in my parents' closets and I found a cocktail napkin from the Night Owl with one of my father's trousers."

Now there was a surprise. "You think he went to the Owl for a drink with a friend?"

She looked at him, and he met her gaze for a moment before shifting his attention back to the street. Whatever the case, she was unsettled by the idea.

"I have no clue. He never mentioned it. I'll ask Herman. He's helping with Mr. Whitt's funeral. It's just surprising, that's all."

"Well, it's not exactly a shady place. I think the owner tried to fashion it after a jazz bar he visited in Nashville. There's music and a bar, a few tables, but no dance floor or anything like that. Not exactly a classy place but trendy, I guess."

She was silent for the rest of the drive. When he parked in front of the funeral home, he shut off the engine and looked at her until she was ready to say whatever she had to say. He knew her well enough to know she had something on her mind.

"I've been forgetting things," she said quietly.

He considered the statement for a moment. "You've been overwhelmed."

A trusted friend had murdered her father and that friend turned out to be not only a fraud but also a serial killer. Add to that the fact that the FBI saw her as a significant person of interest to the case and she had a right to be overwhelmed.

"This is true."

There was not a lick of conviction in her statement. "But?"

"I walk into a room and things are moved or misplaced." She shrugged. "Different from the way I remember leaving them."

Unease nudged him. "Has this happened often?"

She nodded, her gaze still focused beyond the windshield at the parking lot or the trees or nothing at all. "There's something every day."

"Who has keys?"

"Herman, Charlotte, the cleaning team and Woody." She turned to him then. "But no one except me has a key to the living quarters."

Damn. "So this is happening in your private space?"

She nodded again. "Last night I hung my suit out before I got into the shower. When I came out of the bathroom it wasn't there. It was back in the closet."

His unease mounted. "Freud was in the room?"

"He was curled up on the rug in the bathroom. The door

was closed but I can't believe he wouldn't bark if someone came into my room and moved something." She exhaled a big breath. "That leaves only one explanation—me. I think I do something but I don't or I do it and I don't remember. Either way, it's not a good thing." She shrugged. "My mother committed suicide. As a psychiatrist, I've wondered if there were issues that went undiagnosed." Her gaze sought his. "Issues I may have inherited."

"Ro." He put his hand on hers, gave it a squeeze. "You are not losing your mind and your mother was not suffering from any issues I ever noticed beyond the tragic loss of your sister. You've got a lot going on with just having buried your father and all this crap with Addington. Then there's taking over the funeral home. Jesus, who wouldn't be forgetting things?"

She was silent for a moment, and then she said, "I even considered that it was *him*. I checked every lock in the house and they were all secure." She released a big breath. "It couldn't be him."

"The task force is doing everything possible to find him." The words weren't enough, but Billy needed to say something. If he could find the son of a bitch…

"He called me this morning."

The words stopped Billy cold. He swallowed. "Who called you?" He knew. He did. But he wanted to hope for another two or three seconds that he was wrong.

"Julian. He called to tell me how disappointed he was in me and how I'd regressed to my roots." She laughed but the sound held no humor. "He wanted me to know that he's watching."

Fury punched Billy in the gut. He held it back, had to act like a cop. "Did he say anything else?"

"He knows about the bones. He said something about

me finding Alisha. So he's close. Close enough to know what's going on around me. Or he has someone feeding him information."

Holy shit. "Do you believe he's here? Would he take that kind of risk just to be close to you?"

Billy had a feeling her father had been more right than Rowan realized. Addington was obsessed with her. He'd gone over the edge and murdered her father. He'd killed a cop, too. Not to mention about four other people just to get Rowan's attention. None of which counted the more than a hundred other victims he'd murdered over the years. Then he'd drugged Rowan and made his escape, but leaving her alive. If he'd wanted her dead, he would have killed her. But he either couldn't bring himself to do it or he still had plans for her.

Billy's money was on the latter.

He could be anywhere, doing anything. The bastard had endless resources…and yet he was staying close, it seemed, in an attempt to be nearer to Rowan.

When she didn't answer, Billy asked again, "Do you think he's close? Maybe even here in Winchester?"

She turned to Billy. "I know he's here—or he has someone here. He left me a gift."

They stared at each other for a moment before Billy responded. "What kind of gift?"

"A small leather bag. Beaded, with a drawstring tie. The kind teenage girls were crazy about when we were kids."

"Where did he leave this bag?"

"It was hanging in the tulip tree in the backyard."

The son of a bitch dared to set foot in Winchester? In her damned yard? "When did you find this?"

Instead of answering his question, she said, "There

was a photo inside. A picture of Alisha. She was wearing the necklace. The one found with her remains."

That part wasn't really a surprise. Detective Barton had confirmed that the necklace belonged to Alisha Addington. "You know what I have to do."

She nodded. "I know."

The funeral home had just become a crime scene. Something else to add to the joint task force's assessment of Rowan's connection to Julian.

Nine

An hour later, Rowan stood outside the chapel while the family visited with Mr. Whitt privately for the last time before the funeral service. She had turned over the small beaded purse and the photo to Billy. He and his two-man evidence team were in the backyard. She'd given him permission to request her cell phone records in an effort to learn from where Julian had called. He had already called Dressler and brought him up to speed.

All those efforts would be a waste of time. Julian was far too smart to allow something as simple as a cell phone or a photo to trace back to his location. No. He had been murdering people for, as best the FBI could determine, around forty years. He was not going to be caught using a traceable cell phone or leaving any other sort of clues.

But she understood that Billy had to try. As the chief of police he was obligated to protect her and he took his job very seriously. On top of that, they were friends.

Rowan sighed. Now Agent Dressler would be driving down from Nashville to interview her *again*. She couldn't wait. She'd been made to feel like a criminal already. What else could they do to her?

She decided she really didn't want to know the answer to that question.

Charlotte had helped Rowan prepare Mr. Whitt for the service and arrange the flowers in the chapel. The memorial pamphlets were stacked on a table on either side of the chapel entrance. The family had been well pleased with the tri-fold full-color page that focused on the celebration of their loved one's life. This was more of Charlotte's handiwork.

If only she would agree to learn the embalming steps, Rowan would love to have her as an assistant director full-time. A twinge of guilt followed the thought. She really should give Woody more of a chance to prove himself before looking for a replacement. However, his absence this week only magnified her need for a qualified and self-motivated assistant, particularly given that Billy had asked her to help with his homicide investigations.

Rowan noted the first arrivals entering the lobby. She walked in that direction to welcome them. Another part of her work was to make the family and friends feel comfortable during the process of bidding farewell to the deceased. Then there was the little detail of ensuring no one who arrived for visitation or for the funeral had provoking trouble on his or her mind.

As if the thought had summoned him, Cash Barton stood among those gathered. Irritation crackled inside Rowan. This was neither the time nor the place for his intrusion.

"Good afternoon," Rowan announced. "We still have a few minutes before the chapel will be open for you to take your seats. Please feel free to visit the lounge for coffee or water while you wait."

She kept her smile pinned in place as some followed her suggestion and headed for the lounge. Others settled into the available seating in the lobby.

Her gaze swung to Barton. "May I help you, sir?"

"I'm just here to pay my respects like everyone else," he said, his cocky West Coast attitude making an appearance.

"Why don't we talk in my office?" Rowan didn't wait for his answer. She made a sharp left and strode down the hall, beyond the lounge, to her office—the one where she met with families to make arrangements.

No need for her to look back, Barton followed. She could almost feel his gaze burning a hole in her back.

She had a few minutes since Charlotte was with the family. What she didn't have was the patience for this sort of behavior. Barton was a police detective with decades of experience. He was well aware how inappropriate his behavior in this instance was. He had no right to intrude during such a somber time for the family of the dead man lying in the chapel. Apparently the detective had chosen to ignore Billy's warning.

Billy would not be happy when he found out and since he was in the backyard at this very moment, he would know soon enough.

Rowan crossed her office and rounded the desk. Before sitting down, she gestured to the chairs on the other side of the mahogany desk that had belonged to her father and his father before him and his grandfather and great-grandfather before that. "Sit, Detective Barton, and let's get this out of the way. I have a funeral about to begin."

"After you." He remained standing until she'd taken her seat, then he settled into a wingback.

There were several things Rowan wanted to say to the man. Instead, she waited for him to begin. He was the one who wanted to ask questions. Why help him along? Anything she might say would be coming from an emotional place. Never a good thing at a time like this.

"I heard a rumor that Addington paid you a visit."

"Rumors are immensely unreliable, Detective. I suggest you verify your sources before assuming everything you hear is accurate."

His lips formed a grim line as he shifted in his chair. The man was clearly tense, impatient and frustrated. *Welcome to the club.*

"Are you stating, for the record, that you've had no interaction with Julian Addington since returning to Winchester?"

He really was pulling out all the stops. "Am I on the record?" she demanded. "Is this an official interview, Detective Barton? I don't recall being informed of my rights. I haven't been given the opportunity to call my attorney."

Now he was angry. The set of his jaw, the rigidity of his posture. Oh yes, very angry. "You think that cowboy chief of police will be able to keep me from finding out what I need to know?" He moved his head firmly from side to side. "I've been a detective almost as long as the two of you have been alive. I know what I'm doing and I won't be ignored by two yokels determined to play power games."

Surprise flashed in his eyes before he schooled his expression. Too late he recognized he'd said entirely too much. A good detective never allowed a person of interest or a suspect to take control of his emotions or to lead the interview.

Rowan smiled. "Detective, I'm sure your inability to remain emotionally detached from this case was not something you intended to show anyone—especially me. Let me guess, you and Mrs. Addington are friends. *Good* friends."

Resignation claimed his face. "I apologize, Dr. Du-Pont. I crossed the line. Over the years this case has become personal for me. I've been looking for this little girl for a very long time. To have my search end like this is not exactly what I'd hoped for."

Rowan relaxed into her chair. They were on even ground now. She, too, was emotionally involved in this situation. She wanted Julian Addington to be caught. She wanted him to pay for what he had done. She was tired of the fear and the uncertainty. The bastard or someone working for him had been in her backyard…right outside her door.

"I understand. No one wants to learn the person they've been searching for is dead. But frankly, I don't see how I can help you with your quest for answers. If Alisha came to Winchester, I never met her. I did not know she existed. I had no idea Julian had ever been married."

Confusion or something of that order lined his face. "I find it difficult to believe that you were friends for so many years and you had no idea about his family or his…*proclivities*."

"Are you suggesting that I somehow shielded his secret or ignored his murderous behavior?" Rowan understood that there would be those who believed she must have known. Certainly the FBI had suggested as much.

She should have expected the scrutiny.

She had no excuse. He had blinded her. Made her believe in him at a very vulnerable time in her life.

"I'm not suggesting anything, Doctor. I'm stating a fact. Your work with the police department in Nashville—your stellar record of helping to find countless murderers. How do you explain being so close to the man and not recognizing what he was? The two of you published papers on serial killers and murder. What am I supposed to believe?"

Rowan tamped down her emotions. "Yes. We were close, and yes, we discussed murder and serial killers at length, and yes, I was trained to recognize a killer. But I didn't see beyond the mask he showed me." She squared her shoulders and demanded, "What about his wife? How long was she married to him? Slept with him? Had a child with him? Did she know? What about you, Detective Barton? You've been involved with his ex-wife all these years. Have been searching for his daughter… How did you not recognize such a prolific serial killer?"

Silence stood between them like a block of ice for five seconds.

"I guess we were both fooled by a monster disguised as a genius."

Rowan laughed. "It pains me to say as much, but the genius part is no disguise. Julian is brilliant. He won't be caught easily. Not by you or me or anyone else. He will kill at his leisure. He fears nothing. And he won't stop until someone stops him."

These things she understood with complete certainty.

The detective's complexion paled. "Then how in God's name are we going to stop him?"

For a long moment she considered stating that she

had no idea, but her every instinct urged her to trust this man—this weary detective who wanted the same things she did...justice, closure...peace.

"He has some fascination with me. I believe this is why he went to such lengths to hide his true self from me. He showed me the man he wanted to be. The father figure who could make up for his failings with his own daughter by being a shining example in that role with me. And he almost succeeded." The conclusions rushed through Rowan with such force that she almost lost her breath. "But he failed to remember one basic human factor—there is no changing a person's deepest, most ingrained core beliefs. I loved my father, even when we weren't on good terms. He was my father, a good father, and I was never going to abandon him or stop loving him. I was never going to allow Julian to take his place."

"You are his one mistake," Barton offered.

A single misstep rooted in emotion. Somehow she and her family were a part of an elemental desire or regret Julian felt compelled to conquer or to rectify. Otherwise he would not continue toying with her when he was one of the most wanted fugitives on the planet. None of that, of course, meant that he was actually in Winchester. In her opinion he would be a fool to take such a risk.

But the shockingly prolific and unprofileable psychopathic serial killer was, after all, human. He was not completely immune to emotion.

"At the very least I am some part of a mistake he deeply regrets." Her part was not completely clear to her as of yet.

"I would like you to help me find him."

This was Barton's first naked confession to her. His search for the Addingtons' long-lost daughter was not merely a black mark on the detective's professional re-cord. This was personal. He needed to find the truth.

"I would like to find him as well, Detective. He mur-dered my father."

"I'm only asking that you be honest with me. Share whatever you know so I can be at the front of this inves-tigation rather than bringing up the rear."

Before she could answer, Billy rapped on the door and walked into her office. If the look on his face was any indication, he was livid.

"Detective Barton, we need to have a word." Billy's voice was low and hot with fury.

Rowan stood. "Gentlemen, I'm afraid I'll have to leave the two of you to work this out. I have a funeral to oversee."

"I'd like you to hear this, Ro," Billy countered. "It won't take long."

She glanced at the clock on the wall. "I have five min-utes."

"Plenty of time," Billy said, his teeth practically grinding on the words.

"Detective Barton, your lieutenant tells me you were taken off this case about ten years ago. You have no ju-risdiction here and you damned well aren't representing your department." Billy pushed the sides of his jacket away and braced his hands on his hips. "Now, I can't prevent you from visiting our town, assuming you don't break any laws. But you are to stay away from Dr. Du-Pont and this investigation. Are we clear on that?"

The older man nodded. "Crystal."

"Then I suggest you be on your way, sir."

For the first time since she'd met the detective from

LA, Rowan felt a little sorry for him. Still, she was not going to undermine Billy's authority.

Barton glanced at her. "Think about what I said." He removed a business card from his pocket and laid it on her desk. "Call me if you decide you want to talk."

Billy looked ready to grab him by the shirtfront and drag him out of the funeral home. Not exactly good for business.

"Good day, Detective. I appreciate your concern."

The two men stared at each other for a few more seconds and then Barton left.

When his footfalls had faded in the distance, Billy turned to her.

She braced for a dose of his frustration.

"Ro, I don't want you talking to that guy. He's hanging on to his job by the skin of his teeth. He's due to retire at the end of the year and the impression I got from his superior officer was that they were trying to overlook his fixation with the Addington case until he walks away with his pension."

Rowan recognized a cold hard fact about Barton then. Julian hadn't murdered a loved one of his as he had Rowan and the families of so many other victims, but he had certainly stolen the man's life just the same.

"I have no intention of talking to him unless doing so serves our mutual purpose."

"Good." He frowned. "I think."

"You sent the purse and the photo to the lab?" Of course he had, but asking the question shifted the subject and hopefully would serve to diffuse his frustration.

He nodded. Dropped his hands to his sides and exhaled a big breath. "The gate at the side of the house doesn't have a lock. Anyone can come into your backyard. I'll pick up a lock and take care of that today. If you've got someone doing lawn service, you can give them a key."

She shrugged. "Whatever you think is best."

"I'm assigning a protection detail for a few days, just to be on the safe side."

"Do you really think that's necessary? We can't be sure it was actually him, and I don't want you to waste resources." He had people to whom he answered in the local political hierarchy as well as the community. Sparing resources on her protection when she was perfectly capable of protecting herself was not smart.

"If it wasn't him," Billy argued, "it was someone acting on his behalf. Don't fight me on this one, Ro. You know what he's capable of."

Billy was right. She knew all too well.

Ten

Rowan awoke from a dead sleep.

She opened her eyes and blinked at the darkness.

What had awakened her? For the first time since her father was murdered she'd been sleeping deeply and without the usual array of bizarre dreams.

Whimpering echoed through the darkness.

Freud.

Adrenaline seared through her veins. She sat upright and threw the covers back. Reaching in the darkness, she felt for her glasses, tucked them into place. "C'mere, boy."

His whimpers grew louder. Rowan reached out, twisted the switch on the bedside lamp and then blinked at the harsh glare of light in the darkness. Freud sat at the door, his paws and nose against the crack where the door met the frame.

Maybe he needed to go out. She had sent him out before going to bed last night. Perhaps he hadn't done his business. It was possible someone had given him a snack that didn't agree with him. People did that sometimes. They didn't stop to think that the candy bar they had decided not to finish might not be good for a dog.

Rowan got up, slid her feet into her sandals and headed for the door. On second thought, she turned back to the bedside table and picked up her weapon. As much as she didn't want to need it, she wasn't taking the risk.

Usually Freud stayed on the second floor during visitations and funerals. In the beginning she had occasionally allowed him downstairs, but then a guest had given him a piece of candy from the vending machine in the lounge. Rowan hated the idea of locking him in the living quarters during those long hours when there were back-to-back services, but she might have no other choice.

She opened the door and he bolted from the room, his nails clicking on the stairs as he rushed down to the second floor. Rowan followed considerably slower. She turned on the light in the living room. Freud pawed at the door.

"Okay, okay." She reached to unlock it. Her fingers stalled on the latch. The door wasn't locked.

A jolt of uncertainty radiated through her. Had she forgotten to lock the door? She tried to remember, but couldn't quite recall. Locking up was one of those instinctive, mindless things she did by rote.

She opened the door and once more Freud took off, the rapid succession of *click-click-clicks* like a bag of coins scattered across the wood floor as he rushed downward. Slowly, Rowan descended the main staircase. "You have to wait for me to open the back door anyway," she called after the eager animal.

At the bottom of the stairs she turned on a light, and then another in the rear hall. But Freud wasn't waiting for her at the back door as she'd expected. In fact, that door wasn't locked, either.

It wasn't even closed.

Her heart rocketed into her throat as she stared at the open door, the darkness from outside crowding against the lights she had just turned on.

Her fingers tightened around the weapon as she lifted it so that the barrel pointed outward. She stood perfectly still and listened. The large grandfather clock in the lobby *ticked*…the sound growing louder and louder in time with the trepidation building inside her.

Outside in the farthest recesses of the fenced yard, Freud barked and barked. She thought of the small purse and the photo that had been left in the tulip tree. Was the deliverer of that message out there again?

Her pulse skittered. Drawing in a deep breath was nearly impossible.

One thing at a time, Ro.

First, there was absolutely no possibility that she had left this door unlocked, much less open. Whether she vividly remembered the steps of closing and locking it, she had done so. She would never have gone upstairs without checking it first. Absolutely no way.

Her first instinct was to hurry to the front windows and see if the Winchester PD cruiser was out there, but that would mean taking her eyes off the door. Her second impulse was to search the house.

Instead of following either of those reflexes, she walked to the door, dread strumming through her with every beat of her heart, and flipped the switch that turned on the outdoor lights. Bright beams of gold streamed across the yard, highlighting Freud pacing around the tulip tree like a soldier on guard duty.

Had Julian or one of his minions left her something else to ponder? Some other clue in his debauched game? Why would he risk getting so close again? He had to know she would turn the evidence over to the police. An official vehicle was sitting right outside her house.

The challenge. Oh yes. He liked the challenge.

Her weapon held at the ready, she walked out onto the porch and stared as far as the light would allow her to see. Freud sniffed and barked and trotted back and forth near the tree. It was too dark, and at this hour she was certainly not going out there to see what had been left for her—if anything—this time.

"Freud! Come!"

For a moment he ignored her, his own instincts over-riding his training.

"Freud…come!" she repeated more sternly.

This time his head swung toward her and he trotted back to the house. She quickly closed the door and locked it, this time double-checking her work before feeling comfortable. After giving Freud a scratch on the head, she headed back to the lobby. She wanted to see that the city cruiser was still in the parking lot. Had the officer heard Freud barking?

She glanced around the room, peered up the stairs that went to the living quarters, thought of the door that had been unlocked on the second floor. Maybe she did forget to lock one door, but both?

Not a chance.

A chill raced over her skin. Someone could be in the house at this very moment. She glanced down at Freud. But if that was the case, why wasn't he barking?

Because whoever was here or had been here was

someone he knew…a scent he recognized. There was no other explanation.

And if the officer was still parked out front, why hadn't he looked to see what was going on with Freud barking frantically at his hour? She glanced at the clock in the corridor between the receiving area and the lobby. 2:30 a.m.

An ungodly hour for a dog to be outside barking like mad under any circumstances. As she started forward once more, her gaze landed on the door to the walk-in cooler. It was ajar.

A mixture of fresh alarm and frustration arced inside her. How had she done something so stupid? There were no flowers in the cooler tonight, but having it run all night could damage the compressor.

Maybe the person who had unlocked her back door had done this, too.

Keeping her weapon leveled for firing, she walked toward the door. There were far too many coincidences to brush one or all off so easily. She took a breath, opened the door and flipped on the light. The room was empty save for a couple of petals from one of the arrangements with roses. When she would have closed the door, she spotted a flat object on one of the shelves.

With Freud on her heels, she moved across the refrigerated box, keeping an eye over her shoulder. The rows of shelves were empty other than the single object that she now recognized as a mirror. It lay glass side down, and the intricate metal case on the back was one she recognized. Her mother's, the one that had lain on her dressing table for as long as Rowan could remember. She picked it up and turned it mirror side up. Her heart stumbled. Words were written in what looked like black permanent marker.

We're waiting for you, Rowan.

She almost dropped the mirror. Carefully, she placed it back on the shelf, turned and stormed out of the cooler, closing the door behind her. From there she didn't stop until she reached the front entrance in the lobby.

The cruiser sat in the middle of the parking lot just as it had been when she went to bed. The funeral home's front lights, including the streetlights, were on, sending a pale glow over the parking area from the front entrance all the way to the street. Obviously whoever had come into her house had entered through the back door. She wanted to search the place from bottom to top and back, but she did not want to do it alone.

Rowan hated, hated, hated feeling out of control and... *afraid*.

"Don't be stupid." She was not going to pretend she didn't need help. Julian was a killer, the worst kind. She would be a fool not to be afraid of him.

Taking a breath, she unlocked the door and walked out. She patted her thigh so Freud would follow. She didn't generally allow him to exit through the front entrance. She worried about him getting hit by a car in the parking lot or ending up on the main street that ran in front of the funeral home. It was best if he believed the front entrance was for people only.

But tonight—this morning actually—was different. She needed him at her side.

She approached the passenger side of the cruiser, her weapon aimed at the ground. She could vaguely make out the officer's profile behind the wheel in the dark vehicle. She waved just in case he glanced up and saw her coming his way. If he had dozed off, she certainly didn't want to startle him and end up getting shot.

Leaning down, she peered in through the passenger window and raised her free hand to rap on the glass. Air trapped in her throat and her gasp echoed in the darkness. The front of his uniform was awash in blood. His head had fallen awkwardly forward, but the ugly gash around his neck was visible even in the near-total darkness.

Blood had spewed onto the steering wheel, soaked into his shirtfront and pooled in his lap and on the gray interior.

A scream rent the air.

It wasn't until Rowan stumbled backward and landed on her butt that she realized the sound had come from her.

She instinctively grabbed at her waist in search of a pocket. No pocket. No phone. Her cell phone was still upstairs where she'd left it.

Freud whimpered in concern.

She stared at him. Tried to collect herself to think what to do.

Make sure the man is not alive. She scrambled to her feet, rushed to the vehicle and reached for the door handle.

No.

Don't touch it.

She didn't want to obscure any prints the killer might have left…but she had to be sure. She used the tail of her nightshirt and two fingers to lift up on the handle. The door opened. Blood had oozed down the inside of it. Carefully, she checked his carotid artery. No pulse. Skin was cool.

Defeat sank into her bones. He was dead.

Then she ran. Her bare feet slapping against the asphalt, her fingers locked around her weapon. There was a courtesy phone in the lobby. She rushed to it, couldn't remember Billy's cell phone number, so she called 911.

Then she went back outside and stood in the middle of the parking lot, near the fallen officer's cruiser, and waited. Freud waited next to her.

She wasn't going back inside until the house had been searched.

She closed her eyes and wished away the horrific picture in front of her.

Billy's truck was the third vehicle to arrive at the scene. A couple of police officers who had been only a few blocks away outside the courthouse were the first to arrive. Then the ambulance. And finally, Billy.

Burt was on his way. Yellow tape stretched around the parking lot. Local reporter Audrey Anderson was already on the sidewalk in front of the funeral home. Rowan stood in the lobby, Billy's jacket around her, another officer standing a few feet away. She had surrendered her weapon to the first officers who had arrived but Billy had returned it to her shortly after his arrival.

Billy and yet another officer were searching the house and backyard. He'd instructed her not to move, and for the first time in her adult life she had obeyed a command that went against her certainty that she could handle anything. She had no desire to walk about the house or to look in all the dark corners for fear of what she might find.

As she watched out the window, Burt arrived, followed almost immediately by the crime scene van and then two other police cruisers. Her knees went weak, and Rowan somehow managed to get her bottom into a nearby chair. She didn't know the officer who had been murdered personally, but she knew his family. The entire town would mourn this tragic loss. She had brought this horror to Winchester.

This was Addington. She felt certain of it. She sensed it in the deepest recesses of her soul. Fifteen years ago he had slit the throats of five victims while they sat in their cars. His slasher phase, the FBI had concluded. Quantico's esteemed Behavioral Analysis Unit had completed endless reports on the man and he still remained an enigma. He could not be placed into a particular category...could not be profiled in the usual way.

Bastard.

She hoped she had the opportunity to watch him die by lethal injection. If she had ever wanted anything more she had no memory of it just now.

Billy appeared through the Staff Only door and walked over to where she sat. Looking completely exhausted himself, he collapsed into a chair beside her.

She drew in a breath and asked, "Did you find anything?"

He shook his head. "Only the mirror. The evidence techs will take it in for analyzing. I'll make sure they're really careful with it, Ro."

Her head bobbed up and down. She wanted to thank him but she didn't trust her voice. Feeling weak or overwhelmed and afraid was not the norm for her. But then, nothing had been the norm since her father was murdered. She felt out of sorts, out of place...and so alone. Billy had tried hard to make her feel at home and to be a good friend, but somehow she couldn't seem to get herself together.

"What about the tree?" She had explained how Freud had behaved as if there had been something or someone in or near the tree.

"Nothing." He shook his head. "It's possible he was picking up the lingering scent of whoever left the bag and photo for you."

She hadn't considered that possibility. "I guess so."

But someone had been here and that someone had murdered a Winchester police officer. The reality made her sick all over again.

"I put in a call to a locksmith to change all the locks. I can't find any indication the locks have been tampered with, so I'm going to assume Addington somehow got a copy of the key."

Another deep breath. Maybe he was right. Maybe she wasn't losing her mind and Julian had done all of this...but why kill the officer and not her? "I had one in my desk drawer at home in Nashville. Daddy made me keep one. I suppose he could have taken it when he was over for dinner."

The idea churned mercilessly in her belly.

"He could have made himself a copy weeks or months ago," Billy suggested.

She nodded, fought the uncharacteristic tears. She was generally far stronger than this. "I'm so sorry about Officer Miller."

Another person was dead, and she was responsible. Logic told her it wasn't her fault but that didn't prevent her from feeling the guilt. She was the one who had allowed Julian into her life. Now he'd followed her to her hometown.

"I am, too." Billy's arm went around her. "But his murder is not your fault, Ro, and I won't have you taking this on your shoulders."

"My door was unlocked." She took a moment to compose herself. "I wish he had come into my room and confronted me…instead of doing this." She pressed her fingers to her lips to hide their trembling, feeling heart-sick.

"Come on." He stood and pulled her to her feet. "You need to pack a few things. You're staying with me for a while."

She shook her head. "I can't do that. I have work to do here. Mrs. Phillips will be back at the end of the week and… I have to be *here*."

He shrugged. "Then I'm staying with you."

The mere concept hit her like a punch to the gut. "No." She shook her head. The last thing she needed was more fodder for the gossip mill, but more important, she did not want him ending up like her father…like Officer Miller. "You are not staying here."

He stared at her, his eyes too knowing. "I understand you're afraid something will happen to me—the way it did your daddy and the officer who was protecting him and now Officer Miller. I really do get it. But I can't leave you alone, Ro. Not after all this. Even if we weren't friends, I have an obligation as chief of police to provide protection in situations like this."

No way. No way. No way. She shook her head again. "No, and unless you need anything else from me, I'm going upstairs. I need… I need…" She shook her head again. "I just need not to see or talk about this anymore."

"Rowan DuPont, you are being unreasonable."

She ignored him, kept walking.

Unreasonable or not, she refused to be responsible for anyone else dying.

When she reached the second floor landing, she couldn't help but stare at the banister from which her mother had been dangling all those years ago when she came home from school.

Julian had known about Rowan's dreams. She had shared with him how in the dreams her sister would plead for her to come into the water…to please come, she was waiting for her.

He was using all the secrets she had shared against her now. Putting her off balance, making her second-guess herself. He was a master manipulator. He had studied the human psyche…had worked with patients for decades. He not only knew all the buttons to push, but also understood how to amplify the reaction.

She turned away from the banister and marched to the living quarters that were her home. Freud trotted along beside her. At least now she understood why he hadn't barked at the person who had come into her house.

Because Freud had recognized the scent of the monster who had once been his master's close friend.

Eleven

Sleep had eluded Rowan the rest of the night. Every time she drifted off she would see that poor man's face and his slashed throat. At some point in the wee hours before dawn, she'd done an internet search on him and learned that he had left a wife and parents behind. Over and over she had reminded herself of Billy's words. This was not her fault, and on an intellectual level she understood as much, but in her heart where intellect did not rule, she felt tremendous regret and guilt for his death.

She wondered if Billy had been able to tell himself it wasn't her fault when he was making the notification to the man's family?

Unable to sleep, she'd gone down to the basement storeroom and worn herself out on the boxing bag she'd had delivered less than a week after she'd moved in. Until Julian's betrayal she had never once felt the need to be expertly prepared to defend herself. Since then, she'd taken every available self-defense class in the area and learned to defeat the stress and anxiety on the punch-

ing bag. Billy had taught her how to use the .38 she'd
bought. She might not be an expert marksman just yet,
but she could hit a paper torso from a reasonable distance with no trouble. Billy had advised her not to worry
so much about where she hit her target. If the first shot
didn't stop him, then she was to keep shooting until he
stopped moving.

She was as prepared as she could be and somehow
she still felt helpless.

After standing in the shower until the hot water was
depleted, she had rallied the wherewithal to pop her contacts into her raw eyes, drink coffee and throw a load of
laundry into the machine. She had been ignoring laundry for a few days now. If she didn't pull herself together
soon she'd have nothing to wear.

Her fingers felt cold even clasped around the hot mug
as she thought of her mother's mirror and the message
that had been left for her. If Julian or someone working for him had come into her house and moved things
around and left messages, that likely meant he was close.
Close enough to enjoy the results of his efforts. No matter that she despised the idea of feeling afraid, she would
be grateful when the locksmith arrived to change the
locks. As brave as she wanted to be, she was not going
to be foolish just to prove a point.

She couldn't help wondering if Julian had killed Geneva Phillips. Would he start killing people in her hometown simply to toy with her? She couldn't see how he
would have known the Phillips family would choose
DuPont Funeral Home. Officer Damon Miller's family
certainly had not. Was Julian merely trying to make her
feel uncomfortable in Winchester? Or maybe he wanted
to turn the community against her. Make them fear her

presence and simultaneously brand her the outcast she'd felt like as a child. Being the undertaker's daughter had not been helpful when it came to making friends or being accepted. No matter that she was an adult now and reality had not changed. No one wanted to be friends with the woman who ripped the final remnants of humanity from a body. No one except Billy. And Herman.

The realization of just how important to her both men were terrified Rowan more than anything else. Julian would understand this, too. She had often spoken of Billy having been her only real friend as a child. Whatever Julian's intent, she had to stop him. People were dying and she would not stand idly by and allow Billy or Herman to become another of his victims.

Rowan tugged her cell from the pocket of her jeans. Since at this point she had no work in the mortuary to do today, she intended to spend some more time going through her mother's journals and through family albums—particularly from the last year of Raven's and Norah's lives—to see if there was anything that would prompt a memory of Alisha Addington from that summer.

Julian insisted she would remember.

She gritted her teeth as she tapped her contact for April Jones. Lieutenant Jones was the detective in charge of the Special Crimes Unit at Metro where Rowan had worked. Jones was also assigned to the joint task force with the FBI to find Julian. The bastard had murdered four people in Nashville in an attempt to show Rowan exactly what he was capable of—and show her, he did. Then he'd murdered her father and the police officer watching him...the same way he'd murdered Officer Miller last night.

She shuddered and pushed the painful memories away. "Dr. DuPont, how are you?"

Rowan summoned her steadiest voice. "I'm good. How are you?"

After a few moments catching up, she listened to her former colleague and friend's summary of how the SCU was doing without Rowan. They missed her. It wasn't the same, and so on. Rowan appreciated the sentiments but she could never return. No matter that the unit as well as Metro's chief insisted they would love to have her back, her name and reputation were far too tarnished now. The shadow of doubt would likely never lift completely. In truth, she wasn't sure she would ever trust herself to analyze a killer on that level again. Perhaps in time.

"Anything new on the search for Addington?" It wasn't necessary for Rowan to tell her what had been happening down here. Jones would know. As members of the same joint task force assigned to find Julian, Billy was in contact with both Lieutenant Jones and Agent Dressler. He had a responsibility to keep them informed of all related events.

"He's a ghost." The lieutenant's tone reflected the frustration she felt with that admission as well as with the investigation. "It's as if he vanished. I think he followed you to Winchester and is hiding out somewhere down there in those hills on the outskirts of town."

Rowan laughed despite the troubling idea, and relaxed the slightest bit. "Unfortunately, you may be more right than you know."

"Agent Dressler called this morning," Jones went on. "He's headed your way. Apparently that police chief of yours is convinced Addington is there. Particularly after the discovery of the bones. I can't believe no one knew he'd been married. Even the FBI was surprised by that one. From the paper trail, it looks as if he and Anna Prentice were married in Mexico, which is why there was no marriage license here. They never even filed taxes together. A very odd couple, let me tell you. Dressler has interviewed her and she is one strange bird."

Rowan couldn't fathom how Julian had kept all his twisted lies completely separate and totally secret. Or straight, for that matter. And there would be more to come, Rowan felt certain. "He called me. I suppose you heard about that."

"I did. He's determined to haunt you, Dr. DuPont. And then he'll likely kill you if he gets a chance."

"It certainly appears my destruction and demise are his ultimate goal," Rowan admitted. "I've been trying to find some connection between my family and his daughter, Alisha, whose remains were found. According to Mrs. Addington and a couple of local witnesses, Alisha was in Winchester looking for my family." Rowan rubbed at her temple with her free hand. "I still can't wrap my head around the idea that Julian was acquainted with my family before he and I met, which wasn't until I was in college. It's unnerving. I feel as if there's this big mystery about my life and I was there but I had no idea it was happening all around me."

"Makes you wonder if you really ever know anyone." Jones sighed. "Surely your father would have mentioned knowing Addington. Particularly since he had reservations about the man's intentions."

So Billy had passed along his and Herman's thoughts on the subject to the task force, as well. Rowan wanted to be annoyed by the idea, but he was right to do whatever necessary to aid in the search for Julian.

"I'm certain he would have," Rowan agreed. "He wasn't exactly a fan of Julian's."

"Maybe your mother, then."

"If there is a connection," Rowan confessed, "that has to be the case. It must have been through her. But good grief, where do I begin? I've been going through her writing journals and photographs. It'll take some time and I still may not find what I'm looking for. Her writings are scattered, sometimes fiction, sometimes whatever was happening in her life at the time. There's no consistency."

"You sound worried, Rowan."

The only time the lieutenant called Rowan by her first name was when *she* was worried. "The police officer on my protection detail was murdered last night right under my nose. I am worried. I don't want anyone else to die."

A moment of silence passed. "I feel you. You are in a very difficult situation. But his murder is not on you. It's on Addington. You know this better than anyone."

Rowan did know it, but knowing it and feeling it were two very different things. "I'll try harder to bear that in mind."

They spoke for a few minutes more and finally Jones urged, "Call me anytime. I'm here if you need me."

Rowan thanked her and they ended the call. She squared her shoulders and put the subject away for a bit. She should have breakfast and get on with this blind stumble down memory lane as written by her mother. She slid her phone into her back pocket and headed for the kitchen. Most people wanted to remember their mothers.

It wasn't precisely that Rowan didn't want to remember her. It was more that she didn't feel comfortable re-

membering her. Norah had been a good mother, to the
best of Rowan's recall, but she was never as involved
with her and Raven's lives as their father had been.
Norah was always off on some adventure or shut away
in her room at her writing desk. There were moments, of
course. Rowan had flashes of memory with her mother.
Picnics in the backyard. Walks in the woods. But none
of the usual ones like birthday parties, holidays or school
events. Sundays in church. Her father was always front
and center at those events. Strange.

She reached into the fridge for a cup of yogurt. No
matter how she distracted herself, she couldn't stop
thinking about the officer last night and how she should
have fought Billy on the issue of assigning a protection
detail. One cop in a car was not going to stop Julian Addington. Now there would be two cops assigned, twice
the potential victims.

Though her appetite was nonexistent, she forced a
spoonful of yogurt. The oddly sour taste spurred her
gag reflex. She spit the yogurt in the sink and washed
it away. Then she checked the date on the container. It
had expired two weeks ago.

"What?" Hadn't she just picked this up on Sunday
morning? Since she didn't attend church services, popping into the market while everyone else was at church
made for a less crowded and faster shopping experience. Fewer prying eyes and not so many tongues wagging behind hands.

Rowan would have to make it a point to check the ex-
piration dates in the future. How irresponsible of a store
to sell dairy products expired for nearly two weeks. She
opted for fruit instead. After poking her head into the
fridge once more, she came away with molded raspber-

ries…molded blueberries. Strawberries that were more brown than red.

What in the world?

Tossing each container into the trash, she was taken aback by finding two more items had gone bad. They had looked perfectly fine when she bought them earlier in the week. Finally, frustrated, she reached for an apple. Her thumb sank into the mushy piece of fruit. She stared at the brown that gushed out.

The apple was spoiled, too. For heaven's sake.

She checked the rest in the bowl on the counter. All of them were rotten.

Okay, this was too much. She trashed the apples and washed her hands. If she'd had no appetite before, she felt completely ill now.

Maybe she'd just have another cup of coffee, check the laundry and then get on with what she had planned for the day. In the undertaking business you never knew when a walk-in would appear at the door or a call from the hospital would come. It was imperative that she took advantage of every available opportunity to search her family's past. The sooner she uncovered this secret past Julian seemed to want her to find, maybe the sooner she would find him.

He had to be stopped…even if she had to kill him herself.

The idea had her going still, a hand on the carafe. She'd never been forced to kill anyone or thing. She wasn't sure she could. But it was no longer because she didn't know how or didn't possess the necessary equipment. She had trained extensively with the .38 that usually stayed in her bedside table. The self-defense classes had taught her how to disable a person with nothing more than her hands and feet. She was as prepared as she could physically be. It was the emotional part that lagged, but she was working on that aspect, as well.

If she had been at home when Julian murdered her father…she could have killed him with whatever weapon her hands found first. Not the slightest doubt rose to counter the conclusion. The bastard had murdered her father.

Rage swelled inside her even now. She felt fairly confident she could do it now or tomorrow or on whatever occasion presented itself. No matter that at her very core she wanted to help others—compassion had always been her primary focus—a man like Julian didn't deserve understanding or compassion.

He deserved what he so cavalierly dished out.

He deserved death.

She shuddered and banished the uncertainty that attempted to creep into her bones.

Her mug refilled, she walked into the small laundry room off the kitchen and abruptly slipped on the damp floor, almost falling. She barely caught herself and hot coffee splashed on the floor amid the mounds of bubbles. Luckily her hand was spared the steaming hot liquid.

"What in the world?"

Bubbles had overflowed the lid, streamed down the front of the washing machine and spread across the floor.

She turned the washing machine off, grabbed towels from the next load she'd intended to wash and started mopping up the mess. Now she needed to add having the washing machine repaired to her list of things to do.

Once the floor was dried, she hung up the towels. She couldn't wash them until she had the machine checked out. Maybe it was the detergent she'd used. She opened the cabinet over the washing machine and grabbed the detergent bottle. Reading the label, her mouth gapped.

It wasn't laundry detergent; it was dish detergent. No wonder bubbles had overflowed. How could she have mistaken dish detergent for laundry detergent? She plopped the bottle onto the closed lid of the washing machine and shook her head in frustration.

"What is wrong with you?"

This was something she certainly knew better than to do. She and Raven had done this very thing when they were kids. They'd wanted to help their dad since their mother was away. Unable to find any laundry detergent in the house, in their ten-year-old minds dish detergent should have worked just as well. Bubbles had ended up all over the kitchen as well as the laundry room floor.

Like now.

The bell for the entrance door of the funeral home chimed, and Rowan shook off the frustration. Her attention had been elsewhere and she'd made a mistake. She'd been doing a lot of that lately. And maybe she hadn't gone to the market earlier this week. Maybe it had been the week before.

Or maybe she was losing her mind.

Some sort of mental instability ran in the family, didn't it? After all, a mentally sound mother wouldn't have hanged herself for her twelve-year-old daughter to come home and find her dangling body, would she?

Perhaps Norah DuPont hadn't been an aspiring writer. Maybe she'd been suffering from some undiagnosed condition and the writing had been her way of releasing the demons in her head. Rowan regretted the thought no sooner than it formed. Her mother had lost a child. Obviously, she couldn't bear the pain. But being the child left behind, Rowan couldn't help seeing the act as selfish and unstable.

After taking the elastic hairband from around her wrist, Rowan fashioned the long strands into a ponytail as she descended the stairs. She took a big breath and checked out the window before opening the door. Though she doubted Julian would appear and ring the bell, particularly with daylight and a Winchester PD cruiser sitting outside, no need to take chances. Billy and another man—this one in a khaki-colored uniform and carrying a toolbox—waited.

The locksmith, she presumed.

She unlocked and opened the door. "Good morning." It actually hadn't been good, but pretending all was well proved considerably more appealing than confessing that she felt as if she'd slipped over some ledge and couldn't quite climb back up. Besides, the more uncertainty she shared with Billy, the more overprotective he became.

Billy removed his hat and gave her a nod. "Morning. This is Houston Smith. He's here to change the locks for you."

A locksmith with the name Smith. "Thank you for coming so quickly, Mr. Smith."

"Happy to do it, ma'am. Mr. DuPont took care of my daddy when he passed. He was a fine man."

Rowan managed a smile as she stepped back for the two to enter. It wasn't until Billy was inside that she got a clear view of the parking lot and street. Several commercial vehicles were scattered about. She spotted one from the *Tullahoma Telegraph* and another from the *Winchester Gazette* as well as the *Tennessean*.

Billy ushered her back and closed the door. "I should

have sent you a text and warned you about the crowd outside."

"How long have they been out there?" She hadn't looked out front this morning. She'd been too busy throwing away spoiled food and cleaning up those damned bubbles.

He ran his fingers through his hair. "The first one showed up about three this morning."

His answer gave Rowan pause. How would he know that unless... "I told you I didn't want you hanging around playing protector, Billy Brannigan!"

The locksmith cleared his throat and stared at the floor.

Rowan didn't care. She was not going to allow Billy to get away with going directly against her wishes. Damn it!

He gestured to the second-floor landing. "Why don't you start with the private residence, Houston? There are two doors. You can key those alike, and then she'll need another keyed-alike set for the four doors down here."

"I'll get to it, Chief." Houston nodded to Rowan and hustled up the stairs.

When he had disappeared from view, Rowan turned back to the man staring down at her with resignation written all over his face. "I appreciate that you want to keep me safe, Billy. I really do. But I will not have anyone else dying on my account. I can take care of myself! You know this. I can hit a target well enough to get the job done—you said so yourself, and I've put you down on the floor a couple of times with my defensive moves."

She'd been so pleased with the new techniques she'd learned, she'd wanted to show them off. Billy had smiled through it all no matter that he'd walked with a bit of a hitch for a day or two.

"I'm certain you can, Ro, but I don't want you getting yourself hurt or worse because you're too hardheaded to listen to reason. Besides, how well you can fire your weapon is only relevant if you're carrying it."

She opened her mouth to give him a piece of her mind, but then snapped it shut. How could she argue with his logic? Didn't matter. This wasn't about what he wanted, or what he felt was best. This was about what she understood with complete certainty. Her worries weren't about a protection detail per se, it was the fact that her and Billy's friendship would make Julian want to hurt *him* in particular.

But that argument wouldn't change Billy's mind; it would only make him more determined. Rather than pursue the debate, she squared her shoulders and announced, "I should see if Mr. Smith needs any assistance." She gave him her back and headed for the stairs.

"I'm not going to change my mind, Ro." Billy followed her. "Like I said, I have an obligation to protect the citizens of this town whether they have sense enough to recognize they need protecting or not. It's my sworn duty, so don't waste your time trying to persuade me to see this any other way."

Rowan didn't waste her breath arguing with him. He had a valid point. In her experience, it was best to table the issue and move on.

By the time the locksmith had installed new locks, including dead bolts on both the private residence doors and the same but with different keys on the first-floor entries, Billy's patience had run out.

Rowan paid Mr. Smith and he left, none too soon for his liking judging by his uncomfortable expression. Most folks were uneasy working in a funeral home.

"Have a nice day, Billy." Rowan headed for the front door, ready to see her old friend out as well before he could relaunch the debate regarding her protection.

"Not so fast, Ro." He flattened a hand on the door and leaned against it. "We're going to settle this right now."

She moved her head from side to side. "It's already settled. There is nothing else to discuss."

He drew in a big breath. "You are the—"

Whatever he planned to say was cut off by the sound of his cell phone. Reluctantly, he answered it. "Brannigan," he growled.

As he listened, Rowan turned and headed back to the stairs. She had things to do. She could argue with Billy another time. Not that she intended to be swayed into changing her mind. His protection was as important to her as hers was to him.

"Be right there."

She didn't look back. He could lock the door behind him.

"Juanita Wilburn found her brother's body in his yard. I'd like you to go with me to have a look, Ro."

She hesitated. She'd almost made it to the landing. "Burt's your coroner. Not me." Billy didn't need her to go. He wanted her to go so he could continue trying to change her mind. And so he could keep an eye on her. She recognized the pattern.

"I know Burt's the coroner," he said, his voice softer now. "But after what happened with Mrs. Phillips, I feel like I need a second set of eyes on any bodies that turn up under unusual circumstances."

She still didn't turn around. "What happened to Mr. Wilburn?" If she was thinking of the right man, he wasn't much older than her. Appeared physically fit the last time she saw him, but there was always the chance he had a heart attack or maybe a stroke. Could have been cancer or an accident of some sort. Life was just full of unpleasant and deadly surprises.

"The dispatcher wasn't sure. Juanita was pretty upset. She kept talking about his right arm being chewed off."

Rowan frowned, turned back to look at Billy despite her best intentions. "When was the last time you had a bear mauling?" Or maybe it was a coyote. They were far more prevalent in the area than bears and they could do serious damage under the right circumstances.

Billy thought about her question for a second. "Not since we were in middle school and Teddy Winger's daddy had his leg chewed on by that black bear with the cub."

Rowan descended the stairs. She had her cell. She didn't really need her purse or anything more than the key. "I guess we'll know when we've had a look."

He gave her a nod. "I'll pull out of the parking lot and then sneak in around back so you don't have to deal with the folks out front."

She paused at the bottom of the stairs. "Thanks."

He slipped on his hat and smiled. "Thank *you*. I appreciate the help."

Twelve

Logan Wilburn's farm was on Lynchburg Road only a few miles outside Winchester proper but still within the city limits. He was forty-five, had been married once to a woman he met while he was in the military, but had no children. His ex-wife had moved back to Kansas after the divorce. His only sibling, a sister named Juanita, was in the house with the officer taking her report. She had stated over and over that if she'd told him once, she'd told him a thousand times to be careful with that damned commercial-sized chipper. It was too big and too dangerous, in her opinion.

Rowan didn't really know Logan but his sister was another story. Juanita was on the cleaning team that took care of the funeral home. She was one of the newer members of the team but she'd worked for Rowan's father for two or three years if Rowan recalled accurately. Most of the others had been on the team since she was a child. Like her father always said, working at a funeral home provided a certain level of job security. People appreciated the safety net of knowing they weren't likely to be laid off.

Wilburn's body lay near the barn, right next to the
large wood chipping machine Juanita blamed for her
brother's death. According to his sister's statement, the
victim had gathered up all the fallen limbs from last
week's wind and rainstorms and decided he would run
them through the machine, turning them into mulch.
Based on the lividity and advanced stage of rigor mortis, Burt and Rowan had agreed that he likely died late
yesterday evening, obviously before dark. Surely no one
in his right mind would have been operating a piece of
equipment like this one at night. Rowan hadn't noticed
any exterior lighting that would have allowed otherwise.

"Based on what I'm seeing," Burt said, standing back
and looking at the scene once more, "he put in a limb
and for some reason his hand went with it and the pull
of the damned thing dragged him on into the machine."
He shook his head. "Probably kept grinding and gnaw-
ing away at his shoulder until his whole arm was just
gone. Pure adrenaline probably propelled his body up
and back, and then he collapsed right where his sister
found him."

Rowan crouched down and studied the way the body
was crumpled and where his head lay on the handful of
bricks piled on the ground. His prone position had required that the coroner turn him over to get a better look
at any other injuries. Beyond the raw flesh and raggedly
sheared off muscles and tendons where his arm had once
been, there was a gash on his forehead where he'd hit the
bricks. Next to the bricks was a larger mound of rocks.
Since he had placed bricks and rocks around his trees
to hold the mulch he'd spread previously, she assumed
these were for that same purpose.

"But he doesn't appear to have rolled or flopped when

he fell and hit the brick. It seems to me his body would have rolled or seized rather than just fallen onto one spot and stayed put," Rowan countered.

"Fair point," Burt allowed. "There most likely would have been some twitching and jerking."

She scanned the ground, already covered in a thick carpet of grass, for any signs of a struggle or any other suggestion that something was amiss. Much of the blood was in and around the machine, covering a small scattering of freshly shredded mulch. A good deal more had leaked onto the grass from the hole left by his missing arm. There were no obvious indications of a struggle anywhere near the body. Maybe she was working too hard to make this about murder rather than a simple, unfortunate accident. She had worked homicides for half a dozen years. Seeing the worst one human could do to another had a tendency to make one skeptical.

Billy squatted next to her. "What feels off to me is that he set this thing up in the grass rather than in that hard packed dirt over there closer to the barn. I would think having it next to the barn would have made for an easier cleanup after the chipping was done." He surveyed the bloody area around the machine. "I can't see him bothering with the few limbs that would have generated this small scattering of mulch, and I sure don't see a larger pile those few came from."

"I wondered about that, too," Burt agreed. He scratched at his head and peered at the positioning of the gas-operated machine and the lack of fallen limbs ready to feed into it. "Doesn't seem too practical and Logan was a practical man. He was always one to plan things out to accomplish the most work in the least amount of time."

Rowan had considered this, as well. Not that she knew Wilburn the way the others did, but the scene just didn't make sense from a practical standpoint. Wilburn's lawn suggested he took pride in maintaining it. Setting up a piece of gas-burning equipment on that lush, green lawn seemed wrong. She picked up one of the rocks. The grass was nonexistent beneath it and the dirt had indented from its weight. She did the same with a brick. Obviously the bricks had been in the spot for quite some time, as well. Maybe for a future landscaping project.

She took a breath and bit the bullet. "Let's assume for a moment that someone hit him on the head with one of these bricks."

"I'm thinking it would have taken a hell of a blow to kill him with that brick considering the skin is barely broken and the strike was on the top of the forehead, one of the hardest parts of the skull."

Rowan nodded. "I can't disagree with you there, Burt." Then she played devil's advocate. "It's possible he fell, bumped his head and when he got back up to finish his work, he felt dizzy and fell into the chipper."

Billy was the one shaking his head then. "Unless he was unconscious or completely disabled, he would have tried to yank his arm back, right?"

The coroner pushed his glasses up his nose and studied the position of the chipping machine. "And he would have flopped around, trying to get loose. His movements would have made the machine move or maybe even turn over. Surely there would be grass flattened down or rutted out from his movements."

"Unless he was already unconscious," Rowan said, drawing them to the conclusion she had reached, "that's exactly what he would have done."

Billy stared at her for a moment. "You're saying you're convinced this wasn't an accident?"

"I'm saying let's walk around a little more and see if we find anything that suggests one way or the other."

"Like wood chips from where he's done this before?" Burt offered.

"Or a pile of limbs he'd gathered," Billy suggested.

Rowan smiled. "Exactly. And beer cans or bottles that might imply he had been drinking and accidentally fell into the chipper." Of course, blood tests would rule out or confirm that possibility, but this entire scene felt wrong to her. It spoke of staging rather than a simple accident.

They spread out and walked about the yard, paying extra attention to the area inside and around the barn. Burt was the one to find the signs of a previous chipping endeavor on the far side of the barn.

Lucky Ledbetter, Burt's assistant, along with the second of the two officers who answered the 911 call, whose name Rowan did not know, stood by and watched curiously while the three of them went about this exercise. They found no other signs of foul play or of a struggle. And no waiting pile of limbs.

"If the blow to his head was enough to rattle him," Billy began when they had returned to where the body and the chipper waited, "then maybe while he was rattled or unconscious the perp rolled that machine over here, fired it up and stuck his arm into it to finish him off and make it look like an accident." Before Burt could protest, Billy added, "If the blow to his head didn't do the job, he may have forced him at gunpoint."

"But why would anyone want to do that?" Burt asked with a shake of his head. "Logan didn't have money lying around. He used the same bank I do. We often talked about the dropping interest rates. And as far as I know he's never been in any sort of trouble."

Rowan folded her arms over her chest and looked from one to the other. "Maybe he had an insurance policy? He may have been murdered for the farm or over some sort of dispute. Or for a piece of information he possessed that mattered to the person who killed him."

Billy pushed his hat up his forehead, a classic tell that he was having a hard time swallowing her theory. "Do you have a suspect in mind? Like maybe his sister who's in there all torn up over finding her brother dead?"

He knew she didn't have a specific suspect. Rowan had been gone for years. She had no idea if Logan Wilburn had any enemies and she certainly had no way of knowing whether or not he and his sister were on good terms. But the story was the same in Winchester as it was in Nashville: desperate people did desperate things and there was always a motive. They only had to find it.

"I do." Rowan jerked her head toward the actual murder weapon—the chipper. "Your killer is the person who shut this thing off once the man was dead." She shrugged. "This is a big, commercial-grade machine. Unless it was shut off—and we know Logan Wilburn didn't turn it off—it would have continued running until the gas tank was empty. The gas tank is not empty. I checked."

Billy's gaze narrowed. For about five seconds it was so quiet Rowan could hear the old barn groaning in the slight breeze.

Burt was the first of the two to lean forward and check the gas level in the tank. "I'll be damned." He turned to Billy. "She's right."

Half an hour later Burt and Lucky had taken the body

away, crime scene techs had begun collecting evidence and Juanita Wilburn, confused and shaken, had been questioned again and then driven home to await news.

The drive back into Winchester was quiet. Rowan imagined Billy was working on his speech for persuading her to allow him to stay close, particularly at night.

Finally, she saved him the effort. "I do not want you sleeping outside the funeral home again tonight."

More of that silence lingered for a few blocks.

"Ro, you need to let me do my job. Let me make the decisions where the safety of the citizens of my town, including you, is concerned. Addington's determination to get to you isn't only affecting you."

How could she argue with that point? A man was dead—Officer Damon Miller had died for no other reason than the fact that he was assigned to protect her. "I'm okay with a protection detail. But you cannot be a part of it and it would be better if they tried to stay out of sight. Julian won't get close if the risk to his continued freedom is too great."

Billy glanced at her. "You want him to get close?"

Rowan bit her lips together until the frustrated response she wanted to hurl at him passed. "I want him close enough to catch. Yes. If that means putting myself at some measure of risk, then that's what I'm going to do."

The announcement was obviously not what Billy wanted to hear.

Before he could launch a rebuttal they were back at the funeral home. Thankfully the reporters were gone but there was one dark sedan in the lot and a man waiting at the entrance.

"This day just gets better and better," Billy grumbled.

Rowan sighed. Billy was right. FBI Agent Josh Dressler. She was still furious at him for allowing the agent from Quantico, Ike Lancaster, to give her such a hard time.

"I thought he was coming to my office this afternoon." Billy parked, renewed frustration evident in his movements.

"Maybe your office told him you were here."

"Maybe." Billy got out of his truck. He came around to open her door.

Rowan climbed out and suddenly felt underdressed. During her years at the Metro Nashville Police Department, Dressler had always been the liaison between MNPD and the FBI's field office there. She had never attended a meeting with him while wearing jeans and a T. She elbowed aside the thought and made a decision that she would not allow her manner of dress to put her at a disadvantage.

"Dr. DuPont." Dressler's smile was as charming as ever. He removed his sunglasses and tucked them into his jacket pocket.

"I'm sorry you had to wait, Josh." She joined him at the door and shoved the key into the lock. "You should have told us what time you were arriving."

He gave her a wink. "Then you might have had an excuse for being unavailable."

She laughed and opened the lobby door, then hitched her head toward the man standing on the other side of her. "Perhaps you can have your meeting with Chief Brannigan at the same time as the one with me. After all, transparency is crucial in this case, wouldn't you say?"

"Of course. Of course." The two shook hands and followed her inside.

"Would you like water or coffee?" It was past lunchtime. Maybe she should order something to be delivered. God knew everything in her fridge had proved inedible. She really would have to go shopping again soon.

"No, thanks. I had lunch at a little place in Tullahoma." Dressler smiled.

Rowan had forgotten how blinding his smile could be. The man would be the perfect model for toothpaste commercials. "This way," she said. "We can talk in my office."

When she'd settled behind her desk and the two men had taken seats on the other side, she turned to the agent. "How is the search for Addington going? Did his wife have any earth-shattering insights?"

He studied her a moment, his expression closed. "She stands by her assertion that she's had no contact with her ex-husband since their daughter disappeared."

Rowan had her doubts on the matter.

"As for the search, there is nothing new beyond his possible appearance here, in your charming little town."

Rowan had her doubts about that, too. She waffled a bit on the idea, but she couldn't see Julian taking that level of risk just to be near her.

"We've set up a second special task force," Dressler went on. "This one is working specifically to tie all the murders to the souvenirs we found in his home in Hendersonville. Then, of course, we have the one focused solely on finding him and bringing him in, to which Chief Brannigan and I are both are assigned."

"So you actually have nothing as of yet," Rowan surmised. Whenever someone evaded the question by providing detailed answers to other aspects of the subject, then he had nothing relevant to share.

Dressler gave a quick nod. "We have nothing beyond his call to you and the gift he left you."

"He's here or he's been here." Billy was adamant on the matter.

"We believe so, as well," Dressler granted, "but we can't confirm his movements. We have a lot of theories about where he might be and what he's doing but we have no—zero—proof of any of it. We're learning he has a history of using puppets."

Outrage flashed inside her when his gaze rested on Rowan as he said the last. The words made her want to launch a protest, but the agent already knew how she felt. Initiating that debate with him wouldn't accomplish anything. More likely it would expose her emotions to him. Julian had not used her to harm anyone. Not until the past two months, anyway, and then he hadn't used her for an aspect of his kills. She had only been the motive.

Which was bad enough.

"He has considerable resources," she reminded the agent. "If he wanted to disappear and never be found, he could."

"Which is exactly why we believe he's still close," Dressler said. "It's clear he isn't finished taunting you, Dr. DuPont. This is why your cooperation and protection are essential."

Before Billy could grab that ball and run with it, Rowan asked, "What about this ex-wife who has suddenly stepped into the picture? Are you really going to accept her word that the two of them have had no contact?" She still couldn't get right with the idea that Julian had never once mentioned a wife or a daughter.

Then again, he didn't tell you about all the people he had murdered, either.

"We can't find a single connection between the two of them beyond the marriage license they obtained in Mexico and the subsequent divorce. We've checked cell phone records, computer histories, friends, colleagues, neighbors. According to his wife they had a difference of opinion on raising their daughter and when she disappeared, that ended any connection between them."

Rowan tried hard to imagine Alisha as part of her and her family's past, but she could not dig up a single memory.

"So what now?" she asked. "Where are your vast powers of analysis leading you at this point, considering his call to me and the message left on my mother's mirror?"

"To some finale with you," Dressler said bluntly. "We believe you are the answer to finding him."

Finally, someone who agreed with her.

"I don't like the sound of that, Agent Dressler," Billy argued.

"Dr. DuPont is familiar with the tactic," he assured Billy, which would not make him feel the slightest bit better. "She has served on numerous joint task forces in the past."

Billy turned to the man then. "Playing a role on a task force and putting herself in the crosshairs of a killer as bait are two very different things."

"We have a new plan, Chief," Dressler stated, not put off at all by Billy's distrust. "We have reason to believe Dr. DuPont is not someone Addington is willing to leave behind. If Dr. DuPont will cooperate, I am confident we will catch him."

"Have you found evidence to confirm that conclusion?" Rowan watched his face for tells. He certainly sounded sure of himself but he would, without question, inflate the truth if it served his purpose. The end justified the means.

Dressler nodded. "We have. We found videos of *you* going back to the first time he saw you as a patient."

"That's no surprise." Rowan didn't see this revelation as a game changer at all. The sessions of patients were often recorded.

"There are others," Dressler went on. "Videos that are obviously from well before you were in college. He's been watching you for a very long time, Rowan. The man is and has been utterly obsessed with you for longer than you know."

"What sort of videos?"

The agent shrugged. "Videos of you walking to school when you were a teenager, maybe fifteen or sixteen Standing outside the school gym on prom night when you were a senior. Dozens of candid moments in your life."

His words sliced through Rowan. Somehow she had hoped whatever news the agent had would help solve the mystery of Julian Addington, but all he'd done so far was add another cryptic layer to a history of which she had no recall.

Still, considering this new evidence, Rowan could no longer deny the facts. Julian had been somehow connected to her family well before she'd met him.

Thirteen

Billy stood in an exam room in the ER, his hands on his hips, shaking his head. "Do we know what the hell happened?"

Juanita Wilburn lay on the exam table, her skin gray, eyes open and her mouth slack.

Officer Lebron White shrugged. "Dr. Walker said they're running a tox screen to confirm what's in her system, but he's guessing, based on her medical records and the blood pressure medication she was prescribed—I think he called it a beta-blocker—that she swallowed, like, a whole prescription of the pills. The empty bottle was lying next to her. They tried real hard to save her but they couldn't get her heart to start beating again."

Damn it all to hell. He'd had more questions for Juanita but he'd wanted to give her time to pull herself together. "Are the evidence techs at her home?"

White nodded. "Soon as I saw the words on her wall, I called them." He held up a plastic evidence bag. "And the folks working to resuscitate her found this in her throat. The note's inside a plastic sandwich baggy and I placed the whole thing in this bag to preserve any possible trace evidence."

Billy took the evidence bag and read the note through the layers of plastic.

You should have watched this one more closely, Rowan.

"This is what's written on her wall." White held up his cell phone.

On the screen was an image of the woman lying in her bed, words painted in red—maybe blood, according to White—scrawled across the wall above her: *They're all going to know what you did.*

Billy heaved a sigh. "All right. Go back to her place and make sure they don't miss anything. I want to know if the blood on her wall is her brother's. I'll call Burt. We'll need to send both her and her brother to the state lab for autopsies."

"Yes, sir."

Billy made the necessary call and headed out to his truck as he listened to three rings. One of the techs at the vet clinic answered, and Billy heard dogs barking in the background as he waited for Burt to pick up. Burt didn't actually handle the patients at his two veterinarian clinics anymore; he mostly oversaw the operations. After all, the man was pushing eighty.

"I take it we're going to need autopsies," the older man said in lieu of a greeting. "Louis Walker told me about the note they found."

"Yep," Billy confirmed. "We'll need one on the brother and the sister."

"All right, well, I'm about to make your day a little worse."

Billy started his truck. "I'm listening."

"After I heard about the note, I took another look at Damon Miller. He had a note tucked into his throat, too. Damned thing was in there so deep I didn't see it the first time."

Son of a bitch. It wasn't that the identity of his officer's murderer was news to Billy. He'd known it was Addington. But to hear that the bastard used him, as he had Juanita Wilburn, as a messenger made Billy sick and mad as hell at the same time. Son of a bitch!

"Can you read it to me?"

"Sure. Sure. Hold on a minute." Burt fumbled around on his desk and then said, "'Who's going to protect you, Rowan, while he sleeps?'"

Fury ignited anew inside Billy. "Thanks, Burt. Don't let anyone else see or touch it. I'll get a tech over there ASAP."

Billy tossed his phone onto the seat and reached for the gearshift. Maybe he'd just go by Burt's office and pick up that note himself. As he shifted into Drive, a gurney being rolled out the doors distracted him. The patient had been bagged and was being carted toward the waiting van with Gardner's Funeral Home emblazoned across the side. He might not have paid much attention except the man pushing the gurney was Woody Holder. The Woody Holder who was employed by DuPont's. The same one who was supposed to be on vacation this week.

Billy decided not to say anything to the guy but he would damned sure be letting Rowan know. If Woody was picking up extra work here and there, she might not mind, but if he'd quit and just hadn't told her, that was a whole other story.

Before the day was done he wanted to ensure the protection detail he'd assigned was in place. From now on, the detail would work in pairs. He wasn't giving Addington a chance to murder another of his officers. And he intended to have a very long talk with Rowan about anything else Addington might have said to her. It wasn't that he didn't trust her to tell him everything—wait, no that was wrong. He did *not* trust her to tell him what she didn't want him to know. She had his best interest at heart. The trouble was she wasn't thinking of her own. Dressler had warned Billy that he'd better be keeping an eye on her. Billy had figured Dressler was more concerned about the case than Rowan's welfare, but the way the agent had looked at her today, Billy wasn't so sure.

He'd first met Dressler after Rowan's father was murdered. At the time Billy had been too worried about her to notice much about the man, but there was no missing the fact that the agent in the high-end suit had a thing for her. As hard as Billy tried to dismiss the idea as none of his business, he wondered if the two had been an item at one time. She'd lived in Nashville for more than twenty years. He couldn't expect that she'd had no relationships. But whenever she visited she never mentioned a boyfriend, and her father had never said anything about one, so he'd assumed there were no serious relationships in her life. He'd concluded that she was like him, too busy to bother with a real relationship.

"None of my business," he muttered aloud this time in hopes the words would actually sink in.

Bottom line, she was finally home again and he wasn't exactly happy about the idea that someone might swoop in and try to lure her away.

Including this insane serial killer who had been her good friend all those years.

Frustrated now, as much at himself as anyone else,

he drove across town. The town and the people strolling along the sidewalks all looked exactly as they had a month ago or a year ago. And yet, somehow, everything had changed. Billy had been chief of police for four years now. He'd served the department for more than a decade before that. Not once in all that time had so many bizarre cases suddenly cropped up.

First it was the bones in the basement of the *Gazette* building. Then it was the bones out by the lake. Add to that the unsolved murder of Geneva Phillips, and the macabre killings of Damon Miller and the Wilburns, and things were getting a whole lot crazier.

The very strong possibility that a serial killer was responsible for at least three of those murders just made bad matters worse. One of the things Dressler had mentioned to Billy before leaving was another press conference to warn the community about Addington. Billy was all for that. He'd put out the word on his own when Rowan's father was murdered. But they had proof now that Addington had either been here or had someone in the area watching Rowan and presenting a danger to the community at large. He had Audrey Anderson over at the *Gazette* as well as Christina Cortland from Channel Fourteen working on messages for the community that would start running on the evening news tonight.

As for Rowan, however much she protested, Billy wasn't letting that guy get close to her, and the only way to ensure that did not happen was to keep her under watch—whether she liked it or not.

He parked in front of the funeral home and climbed out of his truck. When he reached the door he was pleased to find it locked. The front entrance generally stayed unlocked but he'd warned Rowan not to leave it that way anymore. With her working in the basement it was far too easy for someone to come in and trap her down there. He pushed the doorbell. It rang in the living quarters and in the basement so it wasn't as if she was going to miss a visit by anyone needing her service.

A minute or so later she appeared at the door and unlocked it. As soon as it was open she frowned at him. "This is annoying. You have a key. Why didn't you just come on in?"

He removed his hat, stepped inside and locked the door behind him. "Get used to it or I'll post a protection detail in the lobby, too."

She rolled her eyes and walked away.

He followed.

"If you want to talk we'll have to do it while I work. Charlie Hall's family wants to do a viewing tomorrow at two and then the funeral over at the Baptist church. They're interring him in the cemetery next to the church and apparently he asked to be buried at sundown. With no one but me here, I have to stay ahead of things."

"Charlie Hall died?" Billy followed her past the elevator to the stairs at the end of the corridor. The basement stairs were right under the rear stairs leading up to the living quarters. "How did I not know this?"

"Heart attack." Rowan glanced over her shoulder. "I guess you've been a little busy."

"Damn." Billy frowned. "I suppose that's not so bad since he was ninety-two."

"His daughter said he was working in his garden when it happened. He sat down on a bench under a shade tree to rest, fell asleep and never got up again." Rowan rounded the rear staircase and headed down to the basement.

Billy did the same, ducking his head as they descended into the basement area. The stairs were narrow and cramped. Frankly, he preferred the elevator, but he could see how having the stairs would be good if the power went out or the elevator broke down.

"Well, if you've gotta go, that's the way to do it. Doing something he loved and then taking a nap."

Rowan pulled on an apron, gloves and then a face shield. "We all have to go sometime. There are certainly better ways than others."

He gave a nod, not exactly a pleasant thought. Old Charlie lay on the table as naked as the day he was born—except for the white sheet lying across his privates—and considerably more wrinkled.

Billy walked around to the other side of the mortuary table so he could see her responses. He kept his gaze on her face as she reached for an instrument on the tray. He had never watched this process and wasn't sure he actually wanted to. She'd already set Charlie's face. When they were teenagers she'd told him about that part. He spotted the photo provided by the family on the instrument tray. His jaw would have been wired shut, his lips sealed with glue or sutures, and then some sort of adhesive was used to make his smile look like the one in the photo as best possible. His eyes were sealed closed.

As he watched, Rowan used a scalpel to make an incision in the carotid artery and then the jugular vein. He clenched his jaw as she inserted the arterial tubes.

Finally, she looked up at him. "I'm guessing Dressler reiterated that I should be very careful and report any contact to you so that you can report directly to him."

Billy nodded, his gaze on her face again rather than the corpse on the table. "I have reservations about where his loyalties lie. We all want to stop Addington, but there are some risks I'm not willing to take."

"His loyalties lie with closing the case." She shook her head. "You know as well as I do that you can't track a killer who doesn't leave a trail. Dressler is well aware. He has an obligation to avoid collateral damage— particularly that of civilians—but, more than anything, he wants to close the case. He needs me to do it."

Billy gritted his teeth for a moment to restrain what he had to say about what Dressler wanted. "All the more reason for me to make sure you're kept safe. We know what Addington is capable of. Why pretend baiting him isn't a risk? It is. A big one. We need to keep that in mind, Ro."

"I'm about to turn on the pump," she said, changing the subject. "Why don't you go up and let Freud out for me. We can talk over a late lunch when I'm finished here."

"I'll do that." Billy gave the dead man a nod and walked out of the room. He'd just as soon break the news about Juanita Wilburn and the messages from Addington when Rowan wasn't standing over a corpse. Or maybe it was because he'd rather not stand over one and have the conversation. He was all the way on the second floor via the stairs before he'd cleared the smell of embalming chemicals from his lungs.

The door to the living quarters was unlocked. He frowned. "Damn it, Ro." Freud wasn't waiting for him on the other side of the door as Billy had expected.

"Freud! Hey, boy, where are you?"

The dog whimpered. Worry stirring, Billy followed the sound. The door to Edward's bedroom stood open. Billy had been in Rowan's parents' bedroom a couple of times over the years, most recently when he helped her pick out the suit for her father's funeral.

At the door he spotted Freud stretched out on his belly on the floor, his nose pointed at the writing desk in the bay window.

"What's up, boy?"

When Billy entered the room, Freud got to his feet and trotted toward the window. He sat down next to the desk. Billy followed him. Rowan had been going through her mother's journals and some old photos. He smiled and picked up one of her as a child. Raven sat next to her. They couldn't have been older than seven or eight. Pigtails and pink dresses.

Billy put down the picture and scratched Freud on the head. "Come on, boy. I'm supposed to be letting you out to do your business."

As if he'd understood exactly what Billy said, the dog trotted out of the room. Billy followed him. He closed the door, decided not to lock it just in case Rowan didn't have her key. Downstairs, he opened the back door and Freud raced out into the yard.

Billy sat on the back porch and made follow-up calls for the next hour. He checked in with Detective Lincoln. Lincoln hadn't been able to catch Luther. The former chief was on a fishing trip. Since he'd retired, the man refused to carry a cell phone. According to the note on his door, he would be back on Thursday. Talking to him would be a priority for Billy tomorrow.

The notes to Rowan confirmed the Wilburn and Miller cases were connected to Addington. Billy had viewed enough of Julian Addington's handwriting in the mounds of evidence related to his case to recognize the man's scrawl when he saw it. Rowan could confirm, but he was pretty damned certain already. As soon as he had gone over the details with Rowan he would fax a copy to the task force and one directly to Dressler.

Four murders, all somehow related to Addington.

Finally, Rowan appeared, without the apron, gloves and face shield.

"You left the door upstairs unlocked," he scolded her.

She frowned. "I thought I locked it."

He shook his head. "You did not."

Rowan shrugged. "I've been forgetting a lot lately."

"You have a damned good excuse to be forgetful these days," he reminded her as he stood. She looked tired and he would bet she hadn't taken the time to eat breakfast. "Are we going up for lunch?"

"We are. Freud can stay out for a while. He likes chasing the rabbits and the birds."

Billy locked the back door and followed her upstairs and into the kitchen that could have been a kitchen in any other old house. He peered out the window over the sink and watched Freud frolic. One would never know that Mr. Charlie Hall was wearing nothing but a sheet and chilling in the basement.

"Peanut butter sandwich okay with you? I haven't had a chance to do any shopping."

He turned back to her. "Sure. It's the mainstay of my diet."

She smiled. "We certainly ate our share growing up."

Rowan's mother had not exactly been a gourmet cook. She'd loved the idea of gourmet cooking so she'd purchased lots of cookbooks but she usually ended up throwing out what she prepared. Pizza and peanut butter sandwiches were generally on the menu.

"You finally started going through your mom's journals."

She glanced up from spreading peanut butter on the bread. "I did." She frowned then. "Did I tell you that already?"

"You said you were going to and then I saw things out." He gestured toward the other end of the second floor. "I found Freud in your parents' bedroom."

She reached for the refrigerator door but paused. "The door was open and Freud was in there? How strange. I thought I put everything away and closed the door."

"A couple of journals and a few photos were lying on her desk."

Rowan poured the iced tea. "I swear, I don't know where my head is." She pushed a plate across the counter toward him and then a glass of iced tea. "And the dreams." She shook her head again and scooted up onto a bar stool. "The dreams are worse than ever."

"You still dreaming of Raven?" He took the second of the two stools. Set his hat on the counter and picked up his sandwich.

"I am." She chewed for a while. "It's really weird. Now I'm dreaming about Norah, too. Right before Daddy died was the first time I ever dreamed about her."

Billy sipped his tea. "Anything specific about the dreams?"

She shrugged and reached for her sweating glass. "Nothing a good shrink couldn't turn into a reason to commit me."

Billy laughed. "Well, in that case, I think it's best if you don't tell any shrinks. But you can always tell me, Ro."

She stared at him for a long moment, her eyes weary

with uncertainty. "I know and that means a great deal to me."

They ate in silence for a few minutes. He was not looking forward to telling her the latest bad news. Maybe it could wait a few minutes more.

"So—" he tore off another bite of his sandwich "—you and Dressler have a thing?"

Rowan laughed, whether from the question or from him eating while he talked, he couldn't be sure. Either way it was good to hear her laugh. She'd had very little reason to do so lately.

"Dressler and I have never had a *thing*," she said. "Not for his lack of trying, but because I have always been focused on work. I just never had the time to devote to a personal relationship that complicated."

Billy wanted to be glad about her reasoning but he also felt sad. "You were in Nashville for a really long time, Ro. Surely there was someone."

"I dated off and on but no one I cared to see more than once or twice. I was always so busy. Hyperfocused on work. You know me." She finished off her sandwich.

He did know her and chances were she was telling it like it was. Rowan had never focused on her own needs. She was far too engrossed in what everyone else needed.

"We have to change that, Ro. You should start taking time for you."

She raised her eyebrows at him. "You mean the way you do."

Okay, so they were both guilty of the same offense. "Touché."

Billy took his plate and glass to the sink. He couldn't put off what had to be done any longer. "I have some news and an update."

Rowan put her plate atop his and looked at him expectantly. "All right, let's hear it."

Her tone warned that she was braced for the worst. "Juanita Wilburn is dead."

She made a face. "What happened?"

"She swallowed a bottle full of her meds, but I'm fairly confident it wasn't because she wanted to. There's a message, *They're all going to know what you did*, written in what we believe is blood on the wall above her bed." He drew in a big breath. "There was a note tucked into a sandwich bag and left in her throat, as well."

He reached into his shirt pocket and removed the folded evidence bag. She took it and read the note, *You should have watched this one more closely, Rowan*, before meeting his gaze once more. "This is definitely his handwriting."

She didn't have to clarify who she meant. Billy nodded. "You said Juanita was part of the cleaning team that takes care of the funeral home."

Rowan nodded. "For about three years now."

"Does the team clean the living quarters, as well?"

"No, but my keys are usually lying on the table near the door. She could have made a copy."

"Juanita had access to the new keys?"

"The whole team does if you consider that I rarely locked my door until now. I never had any reason to worry."

"So we'll change the locks again." Billy refolded the bag and tucked it back into his pocket. "I'd like to talk to the cleaning team, if that's okay with you."

She nodded. "Sure."

"No prints other than yours were found on the mirror," he went on. He might as well get the rest of this said. "The writing on the mirror wasn't a match for Addington's."

"It wasn't his," she agreed. "I guess that means he has at least one person working with him."

"Looks that way." Billy pressed his lips together for a moment before passing along the final bit of news on the case. "I guess Miller had fallen asleep."

Rowan's blue gaze searched his, hers full of regret.

"They found a note in his throat, too. *Who's going to protect you, Rowan, while he sleeps?*"

She looked away.

Enough was enough, but, oh hell, he'd almost forgotten about the other. "One more thing."

Her attention swung to him once more. "Tell me it doesn't get worse."

"Not worse," he promised. He wished there was something he could say to make some aspect of this a little easier, but there were no words. "I saw Woody today."

Rowan frowned. "I thought he was in Panama City or someplace beachy and touristy like that."

"So did I, but he was over at the hospital when I was leaving after checking on the Juanita Wilburn situation."

"Is he ill? Maybe his mother is sick."

Billy shook his head. "Neither of the above. He was wheeling a body out to load into a Gardner's Funeral Home van."

"Is that a fact?" Rowan placed her glass in the sink and then crossed her arms over her chest. "Well, I guess I won't need an excuse to be rid of him, after all."

"Maybe he's in a financial bind and picking up extra work?" Billy shrugged. "There could be an explanation."

"When I ask him I guess I'll know."

Fourteen

Once Mr. Hall was rolled into refrigeration and the remaining list of to-do's for his visitation were done, Rowan decided she would call Woody and see what he had to say for himself before she cleaned up. From the moment Billy told her about seeing her assistant at the hospital, she'd been seething. Where was the man's sense of professionalism?

Since she'd been in the mortuary room for hours, it was time to give Freud another break. As the call went through she walked up the stairs. She never allowed Freud into the mortuary room with her since he had a terrible habit of licking at anything she dropped on the floor. Though she tried hard not to drip or drop anything, it did happen occasionally. Thank goodness for the floor drain that allowed her to hose out the room after each service.

About the same time she opened the door to her living room and Freud strolled out with a wag of his tail, Woody answered the phone.

"I hope you're enjoying your vacation at the beach."

She couldn't help herself. She had to know if he would lie to her a second time.

A huge breath whistled across the line. "I guess I should just tell you the truth and get it over with."

She started back down the stairs, Freud trotting ahead of her. "Oh my, this sounds serious."

"I was offered a director's position at Gardner's. I couldn't turn it down, and after what's happened to you recently, I didn't have the heart to tell you. I've actually been working part-time as an assistant for them since before I hired on with your father. He knew about it and was cool with it. I wanted to give you time to find someone else so I thought I'd try to handle both for as long as you needed me to."

She rolled her eyes and opened the back door to allow Freud outside. He shot out like a bullet—as if Billy hadn't let him out a mere three hours ago. "That's great, Woody, really great. So I'll cut your final paycheck for this vacation week and you can pick it up at your convenience. I'm sure Herman can help me out until I find someone else."

He stuttered, looking for the right response, but Rowan ended the call. She had no interest in anything else he had to say. Her father had put up with him too long. She had no intention of continuing that management style. Her father had gotten a little soft in his later years. Rowan smiled as she headed back down the stairs to the mortuary. It would be nice to have Herman around more often for a while.

Seeing instruments spread over the mortuary table stopped her. When she'd walked out of the room, all the instruments she'd used on Mr. Hall had been stacked on the tray, ready for sterilizing. Her gloves and apron had already been cleaned and put away. But now, they lay across the table as if she'd only just taken them off.

She scrubbed at her forehead. *Okay, think, Rowan.* Did she actually pile the instruments onto the tray or had she just intended to? Her head hurt with confusion. In medical school she'd gone through a time when she felt as if she couldn't rely on her memory. She had been so overwhelmed that she'd often forgotten what she had done two minutes before.

The past few weeks had been traumatizing. It was more than possible that she simply needed to slow down and stop fixating on Julian and her father's death. She couldn't change any of what had happened in the past. But she could keep moving forward. She owed it to herself to do so. Still, this didn't feel like just her forgetting. This felt exactly like someone trying to make her believe she couldn't remember her own actions.

But what was the point? If Julian or his cohort were going to all the trouble to break into her home, why not take her or try to kill her? Why the games?

Was this part of the agony he wanted her to feel?

When the locks were changed again, she would know. This time she intended to ensure the few people who had the keys were ones she trusted completely.

Frustrated, she began the cleanup. Sterilizing and scrubbing, draining and cleaning the pump. Wiping down the equipment and tables. The task was a good forty-five-minute physical workout.

When the cleansing task was complete, she climbed the narrow stairs to the first floor. She should drag Freud in and head upstairs for a shower and dinner. She was spent. There was pizza left over from the one she'd ordered last night. A glass or two of wine would be nice.

At the top of the stairs she stalled.

The back door stood open.

Fear whipped through her. Her hand went instinctively into her pocket, her fingers wrapping around her cell phone.

Had she locked the door? Had she even closed it?

Maybe she'd only pushed it and the latch didn't catch, allowing the breeze to send it swinging open.

Freud suddenly appeared from the lobby end of the corridor.

"Jesus, boy, you scared the hell out of me." She understood now. It was possible she had failed to push the door hard enough for the latch to catch and Freud had pushed it open when he was ready to come inside. Okay. Okay. No problem. She exhaled a big breath.

Considering the Miller and Wilburn murders, she chose not to just let it go. She'd done that several times already. Instead, she walked out front and found the first of the two officers on protection detail. She explained the situation and the two were quick to do a thorough search of the building and yards, front and back. Since one of the two completed a full walk around the property every half hour, it was reasonable to assume if anyone had come into her house it would have been right after the last security check. He'd likely used her decision to come outside and talk to the officers as the perfect time to escape out the back.

Someone knew her every move.

Billy arrived in the midst of the fray. The locksmith, Houston Smith, was in tow.

Rowan stood in the lobby while the locksmith did his work and Billy and the two officers had another look around. All the windows were checked and every single entry into the building was scrutinized for any indication of tampering. Rowan called an emergency meeting with the staff: Herman, Charlotte Kinsley and Rhonda Mc-Cord, the head of the cleaning team. Everyone received new keys and Billy reminded them of their security obligations, particularly under the circumstances. Rowan ordered Asian food from a local favorite restaurant on the boulevard and had dinner delivered for everyone, including the locksmith.

By the time the funeral home had cleared save Billy, Rowan was dead on her feet.

"The company will be here tomorrow to install the security system," she promised him. Her father had always waved off the idea of having a security system. Rowan had one in Nashville, but she hadn't felt the need here... until now. Now there was no ignoring the pressing necessity. She should have done it days ago.

"Good." Billy nodded. "Call me if you need me."

"Thanks for everything, Billy. I'm certain I don't say that often enough."

He searched her eyes for a long moment before he moved. When he did, his arms went around her and he hugged her close. Warmth spread through her and she rested against him, felt protected and cared for.

"I just want you safe, Ro."

She hugged him back. "I know. Thank you for being a good friend."

When he was gone, she closed and locked the door and turned out the lights as she and Freud made their way up the stairs. "Come on, boy."

She climbed the stairs to the second floor. Freud's nails clicked along behind her. Upstairs, she took a quick shower and poured herself a glass of wine. She placed the wine on the coffee table and decided to dig around in her mother's things again. When she reached her parents' bedroom, Rowan frowned. The photos and journals Billy had noticed were spread over the desk.

Hadn't she put those away?

Beyond the idea that something was going wrong inside her head, it was time to stop with the denial and to admit that someone—possibly Julian himself—had been toying with her, up close and personal. She could not pretend any longer that this was mere forgetfulness.

"Not any more, you bastard." New locks, new rules and a two-man protection detail.

With a weary sigh, she gathered another journal and another box of photos. Her mother never bothered with albums except for special occasions. She preferred the shoebox organization system. The year or years the photos were taken were marked on the box. Tonight Rowan had selected the year Raven and their mother died as well as the year before.

The journal was more of her random musings about story ideas and brainstorming. Rowan turned a page and read a different style of entry. This one was written in block print, not her mother's airy, flamboyant style. The emotion in the words was evidenced by the way the pen had furrowed into the paper, leaving vivid indentations. This wasn't about a research trip or a story she was considering. This was an event that occurred at home.

Edward took me off the bank account today. Took my credit cards. Warned me that if I left again there would be consequences. Does he think he can keep me here forever? I do not belong to him.

The forcefully written entry floored Rowan. Her parents had never argued in front of her. In her dreams her mother seemed to be arguing with someone but those might or might not have been actual memories. Yet, this was proof that her parents weren't on the same page—at least not at the moment these words were written.

"What were you doing that Daddy had felt the need to rein you in?" The one thing Rowan knew with complete certainty was that her father had never been unkind or overbearing. Never. Whatever had been happening, he must have had a reason for acting in such a controlling manner.

Rowan flipped through the pages and found no additional entries such as that one. She moved on to the photos. Most were just random shots of Rowan and her sister playing in the house or outside. There were a few of them in the mortuary room with their father. Rowan shuffled back through the photos for the last year of Raven's life. She had begun to dress completely different from Rowan. The change had hurt her feelings in the beginning. She remembered that now. Their whole lives they had dressed in matching clothes or at least coordinating clothes, but that came to a halt that last year.

How had Rowan forgotten those details? Perhaps *forgotten* was the wrong word. *Repressed.* So much about that summer was far too painful to touch, so Rowan had locked it away. But the photos had her remembering. Raven had grown more and more uninhibited and her wardrobe reflected that mood. She swore with every breath and ran with the popular kids who were known for their mean girl attitudes and arrogance.

Rowan went back a few months and studied the photos of her sister before that evolution. "What happened to make you want to be someone else?"

She pulled out another handful of photographs. One by one she went through them. Fewer and fewer showed her and Raven together. Most were either of Rowan alone or Raven with her friends. When those friends came to their house—which was rare—they snubbed Rowan as if she didn't exist.

Had you ever wished your sister dead?

The words shook Rowan. Julian had asked her that during a therapy session not long after her second suicide attempt.

Had you ever wished your sister dead?

The question was about Rowan's extreme guilt that her sister had died and she had not. Resentment that her mother had preferred to follow Raven into death than to live with Rowan.

As an adult trained in psychiatry, Rowan understood how she had taken on that blame as a child. Now, she recognized those feelings were not founded in any sort of reality. Her mother had loved her, her father had assured her of as much over and over. She recalled the loving moments they had shared. Her sister had loved her, as well. Adolescence was difficult for all children. Throw being a twin in the mix and it was doubly complicated. Independence was uppermost in the mind of most adolescent girls. It was difficult to be independent from your mirror image.

More photos pinged Rowan's memory banks, reminding her of the good as well as the bad. The next photo she picked up was taken the day Raven went to the party at the lake without Rowan. The air in her lungs deserted her.

In the photo her sister was wearing her new bikini beneath the wrap Rowan suspected she stripped off once she'd gotten past their father. But there was something else. A necklace. Rowan held the photograph close to her face, squinted in an effort to make out the design. Her heart had already started to pound. The size and shape were right.

What she needed was a magnifying glass.

She rushed to the small desk that sat beneath the front windows and searched through the drawers. Finally, she found what she needed. She peered through the magnifying glass and studied the necklace.

Sun...moon...silver...and amber.

Her heart surged into her throat. It was the necklace they had found with the remains. The remains belonging to Alisha Addington. If it wasn't the same necklace, it was one exactly like it.

Rowan rushed back to the coffee table and grabbed her cell. She tapped the contact for Billy. As soon as he answered she blurted, "I found the necklace."

"What? Ro? Has something happened?" Billy's voice was thick with sleep.

Unsure of her rubbery legs and sudden weak knees, she sank onto the sofa. "No. No, nothing has happened."

He yawned. "What about the necklace?"

"The one found with Alisha Addington's remains. I found it."

"I thought the necklace was at the lab with her bones."

Rowan shook herself. She wasn't making sense. "No, I mean, I found the necklace in a photograph."

"What photograph?"

She had his attention now. He sounded wide-awake. She should just tell him to come over and see for himself. She glanced at the clock. But it was late. She was tired. He was tired.

It was better if they did this on the phone.

"I found a photo of Raven, taken the day she drowned. She was ready for the party and Mom took a photo. She's wearing the necklace, Billy. The one found with Alisha's remains. This could very well be proof the two were in contact at some point prior to their deaths."

Had her sister run into Julian's daughter at the mall or some other popular hangout of the day?

Had they met again the day of the big party at the lake house?

The photograph slipped from Rowan's fingers and fluttered to the floor.

Had her sister killed Alisha Addington and then drowned trying to get away without being caught?

Or was Raven a victim of Alisha?

Fifteen

The doorbell in the lobby rang at 8:01. Rowan peeked out the living room window on the second floor and spotted the car belonging to Audrey Anderson. Rowan cringed. She had hoped it was Herman.

"Stay, boy," she said to Freud, running her fingers across his back.

A faithful friend, he did as she asked and watched as she walked out the door. On second thought, maybe if she took Freud, Audrey would be ready to leave. Rowan liked Audrey, but she was a reporter. Rowan had faced enough questions from determined reporters to last her a lifetime. That said, Audrey had mentioned having resources. Maybe it was a worth a listen to whatever she had to say.

Despite her reservations, Rowan patted her thigh and headed down to the first floor. Freud trotted after her. She tried to keep last night's dream from rolling through her mind as she walked along this corridor, but it was impossible. In the dream she had come home early from school and found her mother standing on the landing adjusting the noose around her neck. Rowan had called out to her and for a moment they had stared at each other. Then her mother jumped over the railing.

Goose bumps rose on her skin even now, but Rowan pushed the thought aside and crossed the lobby to the main entrance. Freud sniffed at the door.

"Sit." When he obeyed, she said, "Good boy." Rowan unlocked the dead bolt and opened the door. She produced a smile for her unexpected visitor.

Audrey waved a small paper sack from the local coffee shop. "A mutual friend told me you love bagels, cream cheese and strawberry spread." She held up the drink tray with two cups of coffee. "And a nice Colombian dark roast."

Rowan's stomach signaled that she had better say yes. "Good morning. Come in."

Freud eyed the other woman, then sniffed her leg. She grimaced but didn't jump away. Rowan guessed the hotshot reporter had faced bigger worries than a German shepherd wanting to get to know her better.

Rowan glanced outside, then closed the door and locked it. True to his word, Billy had ensured his protection detail was out of sight. As long as that continued to be the case, she could deal with it. If she couldn't see them, hopefully Julian wouldn't be able to, either. She did not want anyone else being killed because of her.

"Why don't we sit?" Rowan suggested.

"Perfect." Audrey smiled.

When they had settled into one of the seating areas, Rowan said, "Audrey, I wanted to thank you for the lovely tribute your paper did for Officer Miller. I'm certain his family was grateful."

"I appreciate you saying so. We've tried to keep the *Gazette* a community newspaper. We want that small-town feel to continue as a mainstay of our publishing platform."

With that out of the way, Rowan asked, "So, what can I do for you this morning?"

Audrey passed her a coffee container and then started laying out the goodies from her bag. "I've been thinking about this Alisha Addington." She hesitated a moment to spread cream cheese on her bagel. "She attended high school at Beverly Hills High. I've discovered that she wasn't a very good student."

While she added strawberry spread to her bagel, Rowan watched her. Audrey had said she had contacts and resources. Perhaps they were even better than Rowan had suspected. "How do you mean?"

"Her attendance record was terrible. Her mother was summoned to the school on numerous occasions. There were rumors of drug abuse among her group of friends. And she was one of those 'mean girl' types, according to the people my contact interviewed."

Rowan added the cream cheese to her own bagel. "Were there documented episodes of bullying?"

"Oh yes." Audrey bit into her bagel and nodded adamantly.

Rowan went for the strawberry spread next. "I'm not going to ask how you obtained this information."

The reporter dabbed at her lips with a napkin. "I have a friend who has a friend." She shrugged. "You know."

Rowan nodded. "How severe were these episodes?"

"One victim—a thirteen-year-old girl—committed suicide. There was a lawsuit but it was dropped. As it turns out the mother is loaded. She probably paid the family off. She spared no expense keeping her only child in designer clothes and out of as much trouble as possible."

Rowan drew in a sharp breath. She thought of the necklace in the photo her sister had been wearing and then the one found with Alisha's remains...and around her neck in the photo Julian had left in the tulip tree.

And she still had no confirmed answer for what Alisha was doing in Winchester anyway. "I appreciate the information, but I can't see how that helps in determining how she ended up murdered here."

"She had to have spoken to someone when she showed up in Winchester. The internet was in its infancy back then. Whatever she was looking for, she began her search somewhere. All I have to do is find the person or persons who gave her directions or advice or whatever. Chief Brannigan said he would take any help he could get. We all know he wants this case solved as quickly as possible, particularly with the connection to Dr. Julian Addington."

Rowan wasn't touching that statement. "Where do you intend to begin? Assuming you haven't already begun."

"There was only one motel, a bed-and-breakfast, and the Antebellum Inn in town at the time. She wasn't a guest at the inn, according to Donna England, and she's been running that place for thirty years. She knows everyone. So we can mark that one off the list. I've spoken to the owner of the Lake Winds Motel, and he says she didn't stay at his motel. He remembered when Chief Holcomb came around asking about her right after the detective from LA called."

Lucy's B and B was closed now and Lucy was in the

assisted living home over by the hospital—more of Herman's updates. "Have you spoken to Lucy yet?"

"Not yet, but I'm having tea with her this afternoon after I have lunch with my mother. Lucy is like my mother—her memories are leaving her but the few she has are more likely to be from back then than yesterday."

"How is your mother?" Rowan felt embarrassed she hadn't thought to ask already.

"She's doing as well as can be expected. A little better now that the past has been laid to rest."

Rowan wondered how many more old secrets were going to be exhumed before this ripple in time or twist of fate was finished with her and her hometown. The bones discovered in the newspaper basement had been put there by Audrey and her mother when Audrey was just a kid.

There was something the two of them had in common—a devastating trauma during adolescence.

"We have a lot in common, Rowan," the other woman said, echoing Rowan's thought. "And I'm not just talking about the bones in our pasts."

Rowan laughed. She couldn't deny the allegation. "We all have secrets. It's only a matter of how powerful they are whether or not they find their way back to the surface." Her fingers tugged instinctively at the sleeves of the old sweatshirt she wore today. It was her favorite. Cotton and at least fifteen years old. She wore the pale pink thing around the house when she was chilly or whenever she wanted to hide the scars on her wrists.

The reporter didn't miss the move. "Kudos for having the guts to talk about that in your book."

Most days Rowan wished she hadn't. "Speaking of which, I overheard someone at the diner say you were being courted with a book deal."

Audrey looked heavenward. "Please. Like I'm going to allow some publisher to drag my mother's name through the mud. There is not enough money in the world to make me do it."

Rowan had a little experience in the publishing world. "Watch your step or they'll have someone else writing it and then you have no control."

Audrey tilted her head. "I hadn't considered that possibility. I suppose I should revisit the offer."

"Imagine all the upgrades you could do to the newspaper."

"Are you glad you wrote *The Language of Death*?"

"For the most part. I regret that I was so brutally honest. You might want to keep that in mind." Rowan shook her head. "You're a reporter. I'm certain you know exactly where to take your story."

"Reporting on other people's lives is vastly different than reporting on your own."

Truer words had never been spoken. Rowan finished off her bagel, then sipped her coffee. Audrey did the same.

"You know," Rowan said after dabbing her lips with the paper napkin, "my sister drifted toward the mean girl crowd the final year of her life. Maybe some of those girls saw Alisha. I'm sure Raven and her friends hung out in the nearest malls and cool hangouts. Maybe they ran into Alisha there. I wouldn't know because I was never invited."

"Good idea. You have any names?" Audrey readied her phone for taking notes.

Rowan listed off the three girls, two of them older, with whom Raven had become involved. Tessa Cardwell, her sister's closest friend, Hilary Thomas and Kristy

Singleton. "Herman tells me they still live in the area. Who knows? One or more may have seen Alisha, particularly if she was looking for my sister. Billy is trying to arrange interview appointments with all three but so far none have happened."

Audrey grinned. "Unlike the chief, I won't give them the opportunity to show up on their own."

All the more reason Rowan had decided to give her the names. Giving Billy grace, he'd had his hands full the past few days and he was hampered by the boundaries of the law.

"But you didn't see her?" Audrey looked Rowan straight in the eyes as she asked the question.

"I did not. Not only did I not see her, but also chances are she didn't see me. I was the wallflower no one saw."

Audrey added a few more notes, then gave Rowan a nod. "I should be on my way. I have a few mean girls to call on." She reached for the napkins and sandwich wrap.

"I'll take care of that. Thank you for breakfast, by the way."

"It was my pleasure, really."

Rowan followed her to the door. Audrey turned back to her. "I'll keep you up to speed on what I find out from the ladies on the list you gave me."

For a moment Rowan wondered if she really wanted to know. The things she had newly remembered and discovered about Raven's final months weren't pleasant. Did she really want to know if her sister was so evil that she would harm another person? But Raven had only been twelve. Surely she couldn't have killed a girl five years her senior. Case after case of child murderers rolled through Rowan's brain, contradicting her assessment.

The entire scenario made no sense. Not to mention

the notion that her mother or father had known Julian all those years ago still felt ludicrous.

Rowan stood at the door and watched Audrey drive away. Maybe she had made her first new friend.

Another car, this one a dark sedan with tinted windows, rolled into the parking lot. It was too early for any of the Hall family. Rowan wasn't really dressed for meeting potential clients. Her comfy jeans, sweatshirt and flip-flops were about as unbusinesslike as could be.

Freud stuck his head between her legs and the door frame. He issued a low growl. "Go," Rowan ordered him. "Go on."

His head hanging low, he lumbered across the lobby and plopped down on the rug. Rowan stepped outside and closed the door behind her to prevent him from popping his head out for a hello sniff.

The driver emerged and opened the rear passenger-side door. A woman arose from the back seat. Her designer suit fit against her body as perfectly as her own skin. The deep blue fabric highlighted her gray eyes and made her pale skin look like porcelain.

Anna Prentice Addington. Rowan had done a Google search on the lady. She was tall and thin and carried herself like an elegant swan. This was a woman accustomed to having things her way. All Rowan needed now was for Detective Barton to show up.

"May I help you?" Rowan asked as if she had not recognized the woman.

Anna crossed the few feet that separated them and didn't stop until she stood very nearly in Rowan's personal space. "You are every bit as beautiful as your mother was."

Rowan endured the way her gaze roamed her face

and then the rest of her before she spoke again. "And you are…?"

She had no desire for the woman to believe she had bothered to learn what she looked like. There was no reason to give her any ammunition. She was already way ahead in this complex and mysterious game.

"Anna Prentice Addington."

Rowan would have dropped the Addington part decades ago. "How can I help you, Mrs. Addington?"

She flinched as if it pained her to be referred to in that way. "I believe what we have to talk about would be best discussed with some measure of privacy."

"Of course." Rowan opened the door and led the way into the lobby of the funeral home. She quickly gathered the trash from her and Audrey's shared breakfast. "Would you like coffee or tea?"

"Water would be lovely."

"Please, have a seat. I'll get the water."

Freud followed Rowan to the lounge. She tossed the trash and grabbed two bottles of water from the fridge. She returned to the lobby, and Anna was seated and waiting. She passed a bottle to the woman and then took her own seat.

"What is it you've come here to say, Mrs. Addington? I've already told your associate, Detective Barton, all I know—which is nothing—about your daughter. My deepest sympathies for your loss."

"Thank you." She took a sip of her water.

Rowan waited for the other shoe to drop.

"He was in love with your mother first," the lady announced before taking another sip of water. "His total obsession with her was very hurtful to me and to our daughter."

Rowan opted not to launch her rebuttal until she heard the rest of what her unexpected visitor had to say, assuming there was more.

"When Norah was gone, he became obsessed with you. He watched you every chance he had. It was truly pathetic."

Rowan took a moment to gather her thoughts, then she began. "How did my mother and Julian meet?"

One finely arched brow rose a notch higher than the other. "Why, she was his patient. I thought you knew. Your mother was seeing him for multiple personality disorder—they call it dissociative identity disorder these days."

Now there was a surprise. To Rowan's knowledge, her mother had never been diagnosed with any sort of disorder. Though after reading a good many of her writings, Rowan felt confident there was something not quite as it should be.

"DID is rare," Rowan argued. "And generally misdiagnosed. There are no medical records to support your assertion. Besides, how would you have had access to your husband's medical files?"

Anna smiled. "Oh, I did my research, my dear. When Julian was away, I made myself at home in his office. I saw her files. I'm certain the FBI has found them by now. Perhaps they simply haven't shared the information with you."

"If my mother was his patient as you suggest, and he pursued a personal relationship with her, then he took advantage of her. She was another of his victims." If this was true, Rowan wondered if he was medicating her mother, and if so, perhaps the medication prompted her suicide. Anticipation had her heart beating faster.

"Aren't we all his victims?"

The regret and sympathy in her eyes forced Rowan to look away for a moment.

When she had steadied her composure, Rowan asked, "How would my mother have become his patient? She wasn't the type to run to the doctor for every little ache." In fact, she couldn't recall a single instance of her mother being ill.

"Perhaps your father felt the truth would be too painful for you," the woman suggested. "He sent Norah to Nashville for treatment after a particularly intense episode. It was a private hospital. Obviously he didn't want his wife's health issues to become common knowledge in your quaint little town."

"What hospital?" Outrage simmered inside Rowan. None of this could be true.

"Serenity," she responded without missing a beat. "Unfortunately it closed many years ago, so there's no way to find the records. I can only tell you what was in my husband's files."

This was nonsense. Rowan's father would never have kept that kind of secret from her. "Why did your daughter come here? None of us knew about her. Or you or Julian, for that matter—unless my mother did."

"She was curious about the woman he loved more than me, more than her."

Rowan shook her head. This entire scenario grew more ludicrous by the second. "How do you know all these things when you had no idea he was killing people?"

She stared at Rowan for a long moment. "Did you?"

"But I wasn't married to him."

"You might as well have been. Think about the past

ten or so years, Rowan. You were very much like an old married couple without the physical intimacy."

Rowan refused to view her and Julian's relationship that way. They were friends and colleagues. Nothing more. "You've been divorced for more than two decades. How would you know anything about me or my relationship with Julian?"

"I've had someone watching him, Rowan, and you for all these years."

Rowan nodded. She understood now. "Detective Barton." At least she now knew why his aftershave had smelled familiar. She had likely been close to him on numerous occasions without realizing he wasn't just another stranger in the crowd. "Once you were divorced, why would you care?"

Rather than answer the question, Anna's gaze drifted to the railing where Rowan's mother had taken her life. "Is it true that you were the one to find her?"

Rowan's mouth parched. She moistened her lips. "I did not know your daughter. My mother and sister did not know your daughter. I understand you're seeking answers, but you won't find them here."

The older woman nodded. "I'm aware. You see, he wants *you* to find the answers. No one else. You are the one thing in this world that matters to him. He will show you everything, and then he will destroy you as he has everything else in his life."

"He doesn't appear to have destroyed you." In fact, she appeared to be doing particularly well, and if Rowan was right, she and her longtime friend Detective Barton were far more than mere friends.

Anna stood then. "I pity you, Rowan DuPont. He won't stop until he has what he wants. I am so very grateful that he stopped wanting me years ago—after he'd destroyed me by causing my daughter's death."

Rowan studied her another moment. "You believe his alleged affair with my mother destroyed your daughter?"

Anna gathered her purse and her bottle of water. "You'll see. I'll be here, in Winchester, waiting."

She was at the door before Rowan stopped mulling over her statement and caught up with her. "Waiting for what?"

"For the truth about who murdered my daughter. One of you DuPonts did it and I intend to know which one it was."

With that ominous announcement, she left.

Rowan went to the window and watched her drive away.

Was it possible her mother or her sister had killed Alisha Addington?

Impossible. They were her family—granted, a little eccentric, but not murderers.

Rowan thought of the necklace. She had the sudden urgent feeling that she needed to find the answer before Anna Addington.

After all, Rowan hadn't suspected for a moment that Julian Addington was a murderer.

Who knew what his ex-wife might be capable of…

Sixteen

Billy climbed out of his truck and glanced around the parking lot of the Antebellum Inn. The place was built in 1890 and only had five guest rooms. But it was the only place he suspected a woman like Anna Prentice Addington would care to stay in their small town.

The black sedan that had been chauffeuring her around town was parked in the lot. Billy climbed the steps, removed his hat and crossed the porch. Inside was cool and dimly lit. The lights in these old houses left something to be desired. A gentleman in a dark suit sat in one of the parlor chairs. Billy nodded to him and approached the desk.

"Good afternoon, Chief. What can I do for you today?" Donna England smiled and propped her arms on the counter. She had gone to school with his mother, though she was several years younger. He had yet to encounter Donna without her inquiring after his mother. She was a nice lady.

"Afternoon, Mrs. England. I'm here to visit one of your guests, Anna Addington."

"She's in room three, second door on the right up the stairs, Chief."

"Thank you, ma'am." He gave her a nod.

"How's your momma? I hear she's pining for some grandbabies. I think you better find yourself a wife, Chief."

Billy chuckled. "How can I find a wife when the girl who stole my heart is already married?" He gave her a wink and headed for the stairs.

Her giggles followed him, as did the man in the dark suit. When Billy reached room number three he turned to the man. "Is there something I can do for you, friend?"

Hands hanging loosely at his sides as if he might be prepared to draw, the man studied Billy a moment. "I highly doubt it, cowboy."

Billy smiled and then leaned forward, close enough to whisper in the man's ear. "Then I suggest you get the hell out of my face before I lose my patience."

The man withdrew a step when Billy pulled back just far enough to stare him straight in the eyes.

The door behind him opened and a female voice said, "It's all right, Garrett. I've been expecting Chief Brannigan."

Without taking his eyes from Billy's, Garrett said, "Whatever you say, ma'am."

He executed a military-style about-face and walked away. Billy watched until he had descended the stairs. Then he turned to the lady.

"Afternoon, ma'am. I'm Chief William Brannigan. I'd like a few minutes of your time." The lady had evidently known he would come calling after her visit to the funeral home.

"Come in, Chief."

Billy followed her inside and took one of the two seats she offered on either side of the table near the bay windows.

When they were both seated, he started the conversation with, "I apologize for the unannounced visit, but as you can imagine, I'm deeply involved in several homicides I believe were committed by your former husband. I would greatly appreciate any insights you might be willing to share."

She stared at him a moment and then she laughed. "I'm certain your friend Rowan has warned you that no one has true insights into Julian. He is a complete enigma. The FBI's illustrious task force will never find him, of that you can rest assured."

"Then perhaps you can share with me your conclusions about his fascination with Dr. DuPont."

She shrugged. "That one is easy. She is a clone of her mother. Julian was obsessed, madly in love with Norah. He would have done anything for her. With her and Raven's deaths, that only leaves Rowan. He will go to his grave attempting to resurrect what he had with Norah."

"This is why you separated and eventually divorced?"

She shrugged, her bejeweled earrings dangling with the move. "We lived separate lives for many years before the divorce. I had what I wanted from him—a daughter. If I had never seen him again it would have been too soon. My ex-husband was an arrogant man, Chief. He loved making me feel as if I were nothing. He turned our daughter into the same sort of uncaring soul he is. I tried to salvage her but I fear my efforts were too little too late. The damage was done. She turned out just like him."

Billy braced for an explosion. She was not going to like his next question. "Was she also a killer like him?"

The woman sighed, stared a moment at the many rings on her fingers before she met his gaze once more. "I suspect she would have been had she not been murdered herself."

Billy held her gaze, the tension rising between them faster than the swampy muck of the lowlands drawing a calf into its dangerous depths. "Did she come here to hurt Norah DuPont and her family?"

For a single second Billy thought she was going to answer, but then the raw emotion in her eyes vanished and her expression closed. "I have no idea, Chief. She was seventeen years old. I think she was merely curious about the whore who stole her father away."

"Or maybe what you really want," he countered, "is to learn whether your ex-husband murdered your daughter."

"Actually," she protested, "what I really want to know is when can I claim my daughter's remains so that I may put this tragedy and this tragic place behind me once and for all."

The conversation went downhill from there.

Billy waved to Donna and exchanged a look with Garrett as he passed through the lobby on his way out. No matter that Anna Addington had shut down on him, he'd gotten what he wanted.

Her daughter had come to Winchester with an agenda. She was hurting because of her father's betrayal and, like most teenagers, she wanted to hurt someone back. And Alisha hadn't been just any teenager—she had been the daughter of a serial killer. A daughter whose own mother feared she had tendencies similar to her father's.

From the inn, Billy drove to Decherd to the Night Owl. En route he received the news he'd been expecting: the blood on Juanita Wilburn's wall was the same type as her brother's. DNA would confirm it was his but Billy didn't need an in-depth analysis to know that Addington or his underling had used the man's blood to warn his sister that she was next.

"Son of a bitch."

Billy parked at the Night Owl. It was too early for the place to be open but he knew the owner, Gus Cagle. He was always there by lunch to prep for the evening.

"Hey, Billy," Cagle shouted as he strode through the front entrance. He laughed. "I'd offer you a beer but I'll bet you're on duty."

"That I am." Billy slid onto a stool and watched as Gus put away freshly washed glasses.

"What can I do you for?" Cagle asked as he dried another glass.

"Do you recall Edward DuPont ever coming in for a beer or a drink with a friend?"

Cagle made a face. "The undertaker?" He shook his head, then stopped midshake. "Wait a minute. I take that back. He was in here back in January." He frowned in concentration. "Right after New Year's. Early January. I can't recall the exact date."

Billy nodded. "That's okay. I don't need the exact date. Was he with someone?" Edward's visit to the Night Owl could have been nothing more than a man having a drink with friends, but it was unusual for Edward Du-Pont. In Billy's opinion, anything out of the ordinary was worth investigating.

"I don't think so." Cagle shrugged. "I mean, he was sitting at the bar and there were other people filling the rest of the stools, like always. But I think he came in alone."

"Was he a fairly regular customer?"

Cagle laughed. "No way. I'd never seen him anywhere outside the funeral home. I'm pretty sure he didn't get out much."

Billy considered his next move for a bit, then he asked, "Who else was sitting at the bar that night? Maybe someone he spoke to, even briefly." He realized his desperation was showing, but he needed to know what had brought Edward to this place when he'd didn't generally solicit the local bars and taverns.

Cagle crossed one arm over his chest and propped the other there so he could stroke his beard while he concentrated.

It would be damned nice to tie up this loose end. He hadn't learned one thing relevant from Raven's friends. All three had been more than happy to talk but nothing a single one of them said helped. Tessa claimed that she and Raven hadn't been speaking due to an argument over some boy. Adolescent kids. He shook his head. That was one part of his youth he had no desire to ever relive.

"Yeah." Cagle nodded, his hands falling back to their work of drying glasses. "He did talk to one guy. I didn't know the dude. Gray hair—maybe it was white. Older. Kind of distinguished looking. He and DuPont chatted for a few minutes. If I remember right, he bought the drinks." He nodded again. "Yeah, that's right. He paid the tab with a hundred-dollar bill and left his change. I remember that tip." He grinned. "The waitstaff like big tippers."

Adrenaline firing through his veins, Billy reached for his cell phone and pulled up a photo. "Was the older, distinguished guy this man?"

Cagle studied the photo for a moment, then nodded. "Yeah, yeah, that's him. Definitely." His eyes suddenly rounded like saucers. "Oh hell, that's the serial killer guy. The one from Nashville."

Julian Addington.

Oh hell was right.

Seventeen

Rowan watched from her living room window as Billy climbed out of his truck. She'd given him keys so he could let himself in. She had a few minutes before setting up the viewing parlor for Mr. Hall's visitation. Herman was coming by to help. He had agreed to fill in until she found a new assistant director. He even had a few suggestions.

Rowan would be glad to have someone else trained. This was not a one-person operation. More important, she was relieved that Billy was finally here. She'd been waiting for hours to hear how his interview with the former Mrs. Addington had gone.

She opened the door when she heard Billy's footfalls in the hall heading her way. "What took you so long?"

He reached up to remove his hat, his face lined with far too much concern. Her heart surged into her throat. "Now I'm not sure I want to know," she confessed.

He held her gaze a moment, his hat in his hands. "We should sit down."

Rowan grabbed him by the arm and dragged him inside. She closed the door and motioned toward the sofa.

"We have to hurry. I don't have a lot of time." Damn Woody Holder for leaving her in this position.

"I'll make it as fast as I can." Billy took a seat. He glanced around. "What happened to the security system? I thought they were coming today to install."

"They were backed up this morning with one of the technicians out sick so they couldn't come until this afternoon." She turned her hands up. "That wasn't possible because of the service, so they rescheduled for Monday."

Billy shook his head. "I'll call and see what I can do."

She waved him off. "I don't have time to worry about that." She reached into her pocket and pulled out the photo of her sister wearing the necklace. Maybe not *the* necklace but one like it. She handed it to Billy. "You should enter this into evidence, I guess."

He nodded and accepted the photo, studied it closely. She didn't miss the slight hitch in his respiration. "Sure looks like the same necklace."

She shrugged. "It does. Like I told you before, that photo—" she nodded toward his hand "—was taken the day she died. Just before she left for the party at the Vining home." This was not stacking up for a good outcome. Her chest ached at all the malice that seemed to be rising to the surface.

Billy stared at the photo for a long moment, then tucked it into his shirt pocket. "The necklace was discovered only a few yards from where Raven's body was found, nearly three decades apart."

Rowan nodded. The scenario forming in her head was far too bizarre to even consider.

"I keep asking myself," he said with a shake of his head, "how the rescuers tromped around in that area and didn't see the Addington girl's body. I need to track down the ones who discovered Raven's body and get a blow-by-blow account—as best anyone can give nearly thirty years later—of exactly what happened that evening."

Rowan's heart began to beat faster. "Boat number two of the rescue teams on the water that day was the one to find her. Then the paramedics and police moved in via ground. Which meant all or part of the group had to have walked through those woods." Right past where Alisha had lain.

"But by the time they went into the area, they were focused on recovering the body of a missing girl—a local—someone everyone in the community knew." Billy's forehead furrowed in concentration. "They weren't looking for anyone else. If the underbrush was thick enough, and it probably was, and most likely it was too early after Alisha's murder for an odor, the rescue team would have had no reason to look around. They were locked onto their mission."

Rowan thought of the necklace and the proximity of the two bodies. "No matter how this looks, my sister could not have been involved in what happened to Alisha. The reports have all suggested that Raven drowned somewhere close to the Vining home and then the water carried her to where she was found."

Billy held her gaze for a moment before responding, "Did she?"

His question echoed in the silence that followed.

When she said nothing, he went on, "Based on the reports from that day, no one actually saw her go into the water."

Rowan hadn't considered the possibility that her sister had not gone into the water somewhere beyond the Vining's backyard. All these years, she had believed Raven got into trouble in the water and was swept away without anyone noticing until it was too late. She had just assumed, as everyone else did, that was the sequence of tragic events.

"I'll talk to Holcomb and get the names of the folks who did the actual recovery."

Rowan licked her lips, wished her mouth didn't feel so parched. "What are you thinking?"

"I'm thinking Raven was lured away by this older girl and murdered, then dragged down to the water to make it look as if she'd drowned."

Rowan flinched at the image of Alisha holding Raven under the water.

"Sorry." He stared at the hat in his hands for a moment. "Her own mother suspected she had tendencies like her father."

"She actually made that statement to you—an officer of the law assigned to the task force hunting her ex-husband?"

Billy nodded. "She did."

"Considering the mother's admission, the scenario you suggested is certainly a valid one. Raven was adventurous and completely fearless." Cold seeped into Rowan's bones. "The idea of some older girl from a place like Los Angeles wanting to talk to her—she would definitely have gone along. If we go with the theory that Alisha was out for revenge against the people she saw as responsible for taking her father, then who killed Alisha?"

Billy opened his mouth to respond but hesitated.

"What?" she demanded. This was not the time to withhold his thoughts even if whatever he had on his mind was something she didn't want to hear.

"If we go down this road, that opens up your parents—

and you—to scrutiny. The people closest to Raven are the ones who would have the most motive to retaliate for her murder."

As always, he had a very good point. "First, I know it wasn't me."

Billy smiled sadly. "That's good to hear. But it won't stop the investigation from targeting you. This is a dead girl from California who happens to be the daughter of a wanted serial killer. The feds are already all over it. This could turn into a media frenzy."

Rowan couldn't focus on where the investigation would go or how the media would react to it. With her entire being she resisted any possible connection. "It couldn't have been my father. He was preparing the body of Caroline Rutherford's mother. She died the night before, remember? They wanted to have her visitation that same evening but couldn't because my sister had died."

Billy nodded slowly. "Yeah. I remember."

"So that only leaves Norah." Rowan felt a twinge of guilt for automatically wanting to point a finger at her mother. But the truth was, if it was one of them, it had to be her. Anna's words about Norah having dissociative identity disorder nudged at Rowan. The diagnosis was not confirmed. Rowan had made several calls, and the hospital she had named was indeed closed—extremely convenient. Rowan wasn't going down that path without evidence.

But it would explain so much…

Worry gnawed at her. Her inability to remember so many things recently, the sleeplessness and the bizarre dreams. Could those be signs she was headed down that same path?

"You stayed home that day. Do you have any idea what your mother did?"

Billy's question drew her from the disturbing thoughts. Rowan had racked her brain trying to recall where Norah was the day Raven died and so far nothing had come to her. "She wasn't home. I remember thinking that she should have taken me along with her since I wasn't invited to the party Raven was attending."

Her mother never took either of them on her research trips. No matter how Rowan tried to see it, something was wrong with that scenario. Her mother had either been having an affair as Anna Addington asserted or was up to something else that was no good. Rowan's instincts had been telling her that her whole life, but she hadn't wanted to own it.

It was past time she faced the fact that Norah Du-Pont had never really been a good mother—she'd had her moments, but mostly she had not done so well. She clearly hadn't been a very good wife, either. Certainly not a traditional one. Why had her father stayed in the relationship?

Anger sparked in Rowan's chest, but along with the anger came culpability and doubt. She was condemning her mother without knowing all the facts and she had no idea if her conclusions held any real merit. All she had was the word of a bitter woman.

Rowan looked to her friend. "Tell me the rest of what she said to you."

Billy exhaled a big breath. "She believes Addington and your mother were having an affair. She said he was obsessed with her. She is certain her daughter came here out of curiosity because she learned about her father's fascination with Norah."

Rowan understood that he was making this easy on her. "I have a feeling there was more."

He shook his head. "She believes he sees you as his other Norah. He's obsessed with you. I think she's just hanging around to see what happens next. Like an episode of some housewives' reality show."

Not once had Rowan ever felt like the object of his obsession…at least, not until recently. He'd hidden all those heinous aspects of his personality from her.

"Ro, is there something else bothering you? If he's contacted you again—"

"No." She shook her head, hadn't meant to get distracted. "This is unnerving, but we need to know what happened. The only way to do that is to dig until we find it." She took a big breath. "Did you have any luck with the other interviews?"

"I talked to all three of your sister's friends. None of them had seen Alisha. They were all at the party but don't remember seeing Raven leave or go into the water."

"What about her behavior that day? Her mental state?" Rowan had so many questions. And yet she wasn't sure she wanted all the answers…but she *needed* the answers.

"Nothing out of the ordinary beyond a dispute with Cardwell over a boy." He shrugged. "No offense to your sister's choice in friends, but as airheaded as those three were back then, I doubt they remember their own mental states, much less anyone else's."

Unfortunately, he was correct on that assessment.

"So we have no concrete evidence of anything?" Her shoulders drooped. All they had were more questions.

"There is one thing we now know for sure."

His tone told her it wasn't good. "At this point I'll take anything."

"Your dad did go to the Night Owl the first part of January, right after New Year's. He met someone there. They talked for a few minutes and then he left."

Worry swept through her. "Who?"

"Julian Addington."

Rowan adjusted Charlie Hall's tie and stood back to make sure she was happy with how he looked lying in his casket. Though the light blue suit was from the eighties, it was in pristine condition. His oldest daughter had delivered it for her dad. She'd forgotten a tie so Rowan had selected a navy one from the stockroom. Mr. Hall was a World War II veteran so a flag had been placed atop his casket.

"He looks good," Herman said. "You haven't lost your touch, Ro."

She laughed. "I'm a little rusty."

She smoothed down a wisp of the dead man's hair. "Herman, do you think my mother was having an affair or affairs with all that traveling?"

They both turned from the casket and walked through the parlor to ensure all was ready for the visitation. The family would be here any moment. Rowan had changed into a lavender suit and matching heels. She wasn't one to throw money away except when it came to shoes. She had a pair to match every suit and dress she owned.

"I suppose it's possible, Ro, but your daddy never mentioned any such worry. Where are you getting this idea?"

She told him about Anna Addington's visit and the possibility that the daughter, Alisha, had been involved with Raven somehow. She kept the idea of Raven's death being a murder to herself. She would need far more in terms of evidence to make such a statement even to a longtime family friend like Herman.

"I don't know why I keep dreaming of them arguing." She shook her head. Every single night she dreamed of Raven calling to her. *Come into the water, Rowan. I miss you.* She shuddered inwardly. And every night there were the dreams of Norah. Those dreams were completely random and disconnected. Norah was digging in the flowers or making a mess in the kitchen, but there was always the arguing. Rowan could hear her mother arguing with a man but she couldn't make out who the man was. In the dream Rowan inched closer and closer to the door of the room where they were arguing but couldn't bring herself to look. Her training told her that this was because she did in fact recognize the voice and seeing him would force her to face the truth—a truth she clearly had suppressed.

Sadly, this was in all probability true.

At the door she and Herman stood back and viewed the room as a whole. The flowers were arranged symmetrically around the deceased. Charlotte and Herman would see that Mr. Hall and all his flowers were moved to the church when the visitation was over, and then to the cemetery. With the preparations complete, she and Herman progressed into the corridor and checked the podium and guest registry.

Rowan decided to broach the other issue on her mind. "Did you ever know of my mother to behave erratically or in an unstable manner?"

He laughed. "Well, other than her running around chasing her dream, not really." The big man shrugged. He'd been a football player in high school and he still had the broad shoulders. "I mean, she was a little here and there and all over the place, but that was just Norah."

"How do you mean?" More of the worry that had become her constant companion twisted inside her.

"Well, she'd start something and then move on to something else. Seemed like she would forget all about the first thing she started. Then she'd look to you girls and accuse you of making the mess she made and lost interest in. A little scattered, I guess, is the best way to put it."

Fear pooled in the pit of Rowan's stomach. "Did she ever leave something on the stove? Forget to lock the door? Things like that."

Herman laughed. "All the time. She always swore she'd forget her head if it wasn't attached."

Why couldn't Rowan remember any of those things happening with her mother?

"She was a good momma, though," Herman assured her. "Just a little different, that's all."

"She was never ill? In the hospital or anything?"

He shrugged. "Only to have you girls. If she was ever in the hospital it was when she went off on one of her trips and didn't tell anyone."

And yet, as Anna Addington had stated, the FBI was in fact reviewing a patient file on Norah DuPont found among Julian's stored records. Dressler had informed Rowan that he could tell her nothing more regarding the file. Rowan had been so frustrated she'd ended the call without so much as a goodbye. Not exactly professional, but then, there was nothing professional about this case. It was entirely personal.

That much was very clear.

"Herman, do you remember the day Raven died? I mean, the details?"

"Every single minute," he confirmed. "As quick as I could I joined the search, like most everyone else in town."

"I was at home," Rowan said, her mind going back all those years. "In my room. Mad that Raven had been invited to that party and I hadn't. Mother was off somewhere."

"She said she was going to Tullahoma to the big bookstore. Some author was there speaking and signing books." Herman frowned. "I thought you went with her."

Rowan laughed. "Are you kidding? She didn't like Raven or me going with her when she was doing anything related to her books."

"Hmm. I guess I didn't realize you were in your room. I thought you were with her." Another deep frown furrowed his face. "You're right, though, 'cause when she joined your father to search for Raven, she was alone."

"Daddy was preparing Mrs. Rutherford," Rowan said, remembering the lady who had looked so old at the time, but she'd only been a few years older than Rowan was now. It was scary how fast time flew.

"He was." Herman nodded. "Then he got that phone call and had to rush out like a wild man. I was finishing up when he came back." He sighed. "Wasn't long after that he got the call about Raven and hurried out to join the search."

Rowan turned to him. "Are you saying my father left the funeral home that day before he received the call about Raven?"

Herman nodded. "He sure did." Then he frowned. "He never did say what happened. I just figured Norah had gotten herself into a fix and needed his help. He usually didn't say much when she did something odd. He was always respectful of her, even when she didn't really deserve it."

Herman talked on and on but Rowan didn't hear anymore. She couldn't get past the news that some part of her father's time was unaccounted for on the day Alisha Addington was murdered…on the day Raven died.

And there was the meeting Billy had told her about. Her chest tight with too much uneasiness already, she forced the words past her lips. "Did my father ever mention meeting with Julian in Nashville or here aside from when I introduced them years ago?"

Herman made a face. "He surely did not. He didn't like that man one little bit. No way he would have met him anywhere unless it was for you."

But he had… Billy had confirmed the meeting.

Herman was right, though. It probably had been for her.

Eighteen

Billy studied the reports spread over the small conference room table. He and Lincoln had been over these reports a dozen times and nothing had jumped out at them. Not one statement that led away from the idea that Raven DuPont had swum out into the water and disappeared. Reasons unknown. Her death had ultimately been ruled an accidental drowning.

The members of the search team who had gone through those woods to recover her body had prepared detailed reports. All four had been focused on getting to Raven.

"The kids were moved into the house," Lincoln said. "Mrs. Vining detailed the steps she took to usher the children inside and to do a head count. The only one missing was Raven. Everyone else was present and accounted for."

"But no one could confirm exactly how long she had been missing."

Lincoln shook his head. "One girl said she saw her talking to a boy, but when questioned further she realized the conversation she witnessed had been earlier in the day. Hours before anyone realized Raven was missing. Someone else said they saw her go into the house to use the bathroom and never saw her again after that."

"Did the witness who saw her go into the house recall the time?" Billy had to consider any potential opportunity for Raven to have left the party. His instincts were buzzing. He had a feeling she had left that party and it hadn't been via the water.

There was certainly the chance he was too close to this case and was seeing what he wanted to see versus what was really there, but he'd always trusted his instincts and he'd made it this far. Something was off with the events that occurred that long-ago July day. Granted, it was a hell of a lot easier to see the problem now with the other girl's bones found and plenty of time to consider different scenarios. He wasn't blaming Holcomb or anyone else for making the call they had made twenty-seven years ago. Billy just wanted to get this one solved and behind Rowan and the department once and for all.

"Let's go over the coroner's report again," Billy suggested.

Technically, there should have been an autopsy but everyone, including Burt, who had been the coroner back then as well, and Holcomb, the chief until Billy took over, hadn't wanted to put the child or the family through that trauma when her death looked so cut-and-dried. Billy would likely have made the same call.

"She had bruises and scratches," Lincoln said. "All were consistent with being caught in those limbs and bumping against the bank with the flow of the lake."

"What about her throat?" The other girl had been strangled. Maybe if the two had struggled there would have been indications.

Lincoln nodded. "A small amount of bruising." He frowned. "Look at this photo."

Billy accepted the eight-by-ten that had been taken of the body. He peered at the face identical to Rowan's. Only Raven's face had been bruised and bloated with death.

"See that thin line around her neck?"

Billy looked closer. "I see it."

"I've seen that before." Lincoln tapped his own neck. "My five-year-old jerked the chain with my St. Christopher medal right off my neck. Left a red mark for days."

"She was wearing a necklace earlier that day—the same or a similar necklace that was found with Alisha Addington's remains. The photo Ro gave me was taken while Raven was getting ready for the party."

"Let's look at the path of evidence," Lincoln said. "Raven was wearing the necklace. Then it was ripped from her throat. And now, all these years later, it's found with the remains of another young girl not a dozen yards away from where Raven was found."

Billy shook his head. "This was no accidental drowning." Adrenaline roared through him. "Alisha Addington was five years older. She was here on a mission. To get back at the woman who lured her daddy away." Billy was theorizing but he had a feeling he was on track. "Alisha killed Raven DuPont."

"But who killed Alisha?"

"I don't know." Billy grabbed his hat. "But I'm damned sure going to find out. Go over this report with Burt. See if he remembers anything else or if he had any conclusions that he decided not to include in the report. A hunch or what have you that he couldn't prove so he didn't annotate it. Everyone wanted to put that tragedy behind them."

Lincoln gathered the photos and the reports. "You going to see Holcomb?"

Billy nodded. "He should be back home by now. I recall that he took this case pretty hard. Maybe he'll remember the part that didn't fit with all the other pieces."

Lincoln hesitated. "All the evidence and witness statements line up to a point."

He was right, they damned sure did.

"And then," Billy said, "it all goes off in a dozen different directions and none of them feel exactly right."

"What we need," Lincoln offered, "is to show she left the Vining property alive."

Billy laughed, a dry sound filled with doubt. "Sounds easy enough." He exhaled a big breath. "Let's talk to the water rescue guys who found her, get their take on whether the swiftness of the current matched up with the time and distance we can't account for." Math had never been one of the former chief's strong points. "I'm thinking the current and the time were irrelevant. Raven DuPont wasn't even in the water until Alisha Addington pushed her under."

Luther Holcomb had been a good chief of police for more than three decades. From all reports he'd been a good husband and father, too. And then he'd decided to retire, and his first order of business had been to relieve himself of his wife. He'd run her off. She'd moved in with their grown daughter who was a registered nurse up in Manchester. Some said Luther was having a midlife crisis a little late and likely had a sweet young thing tucked away somewhere.

But that was not the truth.

Luther just wanted to be left alone. Billy decided all the cases over the years had gotten to him. Winchester was a small town but they still saw their share of unspeakable crimes. On top of that, Luther's wife was one ornery lady. She was spiteful and hurtful and flat-out didn't care about anyone but herself. She did what she wanted and Luther put up with it for years and then he put her on the road.

Or, actually, he'd hit the road. Many years back he'd built a fishing cabin off the grid and that was where he lived today. Like a mountain man living off the land and not caring if he saw another human being again.

Billy parked in front of the former chief's cabin and climbed out. Before he reached the steps Luther was at the door, rifle resting on his shoulder. A second later he recognized Billy. "Well, well, if it ain't the chief of police." He pushed the screen door outward and stepped onto the porch. Set his rifle butt down on the floor and propped the barrel against the wall. "What brings you up this way, Wild Bill?"

Luther Holcomb was the only person in the world who had ever gotten away with calling Billy "Wild Bill."

"I need to talk to you about an old case." Billy pushed his hat up his forehead. "You have a few minutes?"

"Sure do, and I got a new batch of shine."

Billy laughed. "Well, I guess a taste won't kill me."

Inside, the cabin was nothing more than two rooms. A living room–kitchen combination and a bedroom with a bath tucked into a corner. Not completely rustic, more like tiny living, cowboy-style.

Luther shuffled around in the kitchen and then came back with two pint jars half-full of moonshine. He set one on the table next to Billy. The other he cradled as he took his seat, the recliner he'd kept in his office.

"How was the fishing?"

"Not bad. It was better this time last year."

Luther took a sip of shine and Billy did the same. It burned like fire all the way to his gut. He shook himself. "That is powerful stuff." Whew!

"Keeps me warm on cool nights," Luther said with a knowing nod.

Billy imagined it did. "Let's talk about the day Raven DuPont drowned," he nudged. "What do you remember about that day?"

"Chaos." Luther shook his head. "Utter chaos. Kids were crying and arguing about who saw her last and which way she went in the water. It was like the fallout after a natural disaster but the only damage was one missing little girl—which was damned sure bad enough."

"A lot of panic and hysteria," Billy suggested.

"From the kids and grown-ups alike. The Vinings were torn all to pieces. Making that call to Edward to tell him Raven was missing and that we were starting a search was one of the hardest things I've ever done."

"Did anyone mention seeing a stranger at the party? Maybe a teenager who didn't belong or anyone they didn't recognize?" It wasn't in the reports, but if no one mentioned a stranger it couldn't have been there.

"No one mentioned seeing a stranger and I asked. Could have been some bastard casing the neighborhood or working in the area that took her. I looked at all avenues."

"Your reports didn't go into a lot of detail."

The older man's brows reared up his forehead. "If

anything was left out of my reports, it was an oversight. Trust me, Billy, I did my job."

Billy held up a hand. "I'm not questioning whether you did your job or not. I'm just going over the details."

The former chief relaxed again. "I heard you found some remains in the same general area Raven's body was found. ID'd her already, too, I hear."

Billy nodded. "A teenager from California, Alisha Addington."

"The daughter of the serial killer," he said as he took another swallow of shine. "The one who followed Rowan DuPont from Nashville."

"That's the one." Billy figured he'd better not take a second sip. The stuff had to be 200 proof. He needed to be able to walk out of here when the time came and to drive without the risk of harm to himself or anyone else.

"Like I said, no one saw anyone who wasn't supposed to be there," Luther said, restating the facts Billy had read in the reports. "But then, there were several blonde girls at the party, including Raven. If the Addington girl was there, she would have blended in well, don't you think? Hell, you know how teenagers are. Wishy-washy. Airheaded. You could ask them the same question a dozen times and get a dozen answers."

Billy hadn't considered the blonde scenario. He brought his former boss up to speed on what he'd learned about Alisha Addington from her mother. "If she crashed the party, mingled without really getting too close to anyone, she could have latched onto Raven and lured her into the woods and eventually to her death."

"Now that's a reasonable theory, Wild Bill. There used to be all sorts of paths in those woods. Not so much anymore. Are you thinking this was a murder rather than an accidental drowning? You have a motive in mind? Why would that girl come all the way from California to kill Raven?"

Billy nodded and gave him a condensed version of what he knew so far. "I think it's a strong possibility."

"Wouldn't have taken them long to get through the woods," Luther said, his forehead lined in thought. "Her body was found maybe a mile and a half or two as the crow flies from the Vining home. The distance was not so far but those woods were thick with underbrush and the water widened out and went in more than one direction. The two of 'em may have taken a path and then veered off into the less traveled area." He shook his head. "But Raven was no fool. She wouldn't have been lured away without the promise of something exciting—unless she had no choice."

Billy had considered as much. "Was there anything else about that day or about anyone who was there that stands out in your mind?"

"I will never forget—if I live a hundred years—the look on Edward DuPont's face when he and his wife arrived at the lake. I've never witnessed such anguish." Luther fell silent for a moment. "It was the most awful thing I've ever seen."

"You're certain they arrived together? In the same vehicle?"

Luther nodded. "He was right beside me during the search. I'm the one who tried to hold Edward back from going to his daughter before they could get her out of the water."

Billy grimaced. Though he hadn't taken his life the way his wife had, Edward had never recovered from that tragedy. Would anyone?

"Thank you, Luther. It was good to spend some time with you." Billy stood. "You should come into town a little more regularly. I miss our morning chats over coffee."

"I think the world of you, Billy, but I don't miss one damn thing from town."

"Be sure to call me if you think of anything else." It wasn't necessary for Billy to remind him, but he did anyway.

Luther followed him onto the porch. "You should talk to the Cardwell girl. She was closer to Raven than any of the others. She runs that bakery on the square. You're practically neighbors."

"Thanks, Luther." He didn't bother telling him he already had and he'd learned basically nothing—the same thing he'd learned from the other two girls who had been on Raven's friends list. "See you next time."

Billy climbed into his truck and started the engine.

With both Raven and Alisha dead, it was unlikely that anyone would ever know what transpired between the two in those woods on that hot, humid day.

The meeting between Edward and Addington was much the same. The only person who knew Edward DuPont well enough to possibly have heard he met with Julian Addington back in January was Herman Carter.

Unless Edward told Herman, he hadn't told anyone.

One thing was certain: whatever the two talked about, it was not the weather.

Nineteen

Geneva Phillips's daughter Patty waited in the lobby when Rowan returned from Charlic Hall's funeral service at the Baptist church. Mr. Hall was now buried in the family plot next door to the church and his family had said their final goodbyes.

"I received a call that my mom's body will be released on Monday. Can we go ahead and schedule visitation on Monday evening and the funeral in the chapel on Tuesday?"

Rowan smiled. "Sure. Let's go to my office and take care of that right now. Would you like a soft drink or coffee? Water?"

The other woman shook her head. "I'm fine. Thank you."

Since her mother had died—was murdered—only four days ago, Patty had every right to still be sad and upset, particularly considering the necessity of the autopsy. Still, she seemed even more troubled today than she had day before yesterday when she and Rowan last spoke. Maybe the reality was only now setting in. Delayed reactions weren't uncommon.

During the next few minutes they went over the schedule, and Rowan emailed the newspaper and the local radio station with the update, ensuring the wording was just as the sisters wanted. The obit had already been published. When all the details had been covered, Rowan moved around her desk and sat down next to her.

"Patty, I feel like there's something bothering you and I want you to know I'm happy to help any way I can." Often a funeral director had to provide a sympathetic ear. Maybe that was the underlying reason Rowan had decided to go into psychiatry. She had been watching her father do this her whole life before she met Julian Addington.

The other woman stared at Rowan in an odd sort of disbelief. "I didn't even want to come here but Jenn insisted. She said this was where momma and daddy made their predeath arrangements and we'd started here and people would expect her to be here and…and this is where we would finish."

Now Rowan was really confused. "I'm sorry, I'm not sure I understand. Is there some reason you didn't want to come back to DuPont?"

With any business there were issues from time to time, but her father always seemed to make them right when the occasional problem arose. Most often it was a misunderstanding with one or more family members—typically amid the family, but the funeral home was rarely left out of the equation. People in emotional distress often looked for someone else to blame—a tangible, safe place to lay their frustrations.

The tears were flowing when Patty met her gaze again. Rowan reached for the box of tissues on her desk and passed them to her. When she had dabbed at her eyes and collected herself, she took a deep breath and said, "Why would you refuse my mother's calls after my father's death? I understand your daddy had just died and you were going through the same thing." Her face pinched as if she might start crying again. "But momma only wanted to talk to you."

Rowan could not have been more shocked by the question. "I knew your mother when I was a young girl, and your father, as well. I have no idea what you mean, but I can tell you that if your mother had called me or dropped by whether I knew her or not, I would have gladly spoken to her. I have never received a call or a visit from your mother." She smiled as a memory surfaced. "I ran into her at the Piggly Wiggly one Thursday afternoon and she told me how sorry she was to hear about my daddy."

Patty looked away as if it hurt to hear the words.

Where was this coming from? Neither of the daughters had mentioned a problem between their mother and the funeral home in the other visits. It made no sense.

She stared at Rowan again. "I…I don't know." She scrubbed at her eyes with her hands. "Even after Jenn went back home—after we buried my father—I noticed momma seemed awfully upset. I thought it was just because she'd lost the love of her life." She smiled sadly. "That's what they always said. Daddy would insist Momma was the love of his life and she did exactly the same thing."

"Two very lucky people," Rowan acknowledged. Not everyone was so fortunate.

"But now I know that wasn't the only reason she was so upset."

Rowan frowned, waiting for her to go on.

Patty picked up her purse from the floor and fished

around inside. It looked exactly like Rowan's own hand-bag. Cluttered and full of things she might need—like a rubber band and a paper clip. She pulled out an envelope with her name on it and thrust it at Rowan.

"She wrote us both letters. She said something happened to daddy here—at the funeral home. She was waiting for it to be made right but that hadn't happened so far. She said she had called the funeral home a bunch of times and you were always busy and couldn't talk or you were out and then never called her back. She said she never wanted to have to tell us about it but she was worried that after Mr. DuPont died it might never be made right. She didn't want to worry us with it. She thought she could handle it and we'd never have to know but she wrote these letters just in case she died without it being resolved." Tears brimmed in her eyes once more and she shook her head. "I don't know what happened but I can't understand why you refused to talk to her."

Rowan felt stunned all over again as she read the letter that basically recapped all that Patty had just said. "I honestly have no idea what this is about. As I said, I have never received a call or a message from your mother. I return *all* calls. Always. I can assure you I will find out what this is about." She passed the letter back to Patty and placed a hand on hers. "Let's go over what you believe happened so I'm clear what we're looking for." Obviously Woody had taken the call, and Rowan barely restrained her fury over the idea that he'd failed to pass along the message.

Geneva's husband had died while Rowan's father was in Nashville visiting her. She'd thought she was protecting him by bringing him there, but what she did was bring him right to the killer's door. If she'd left him here he might still be alive. An ache pierced Rowan like a knife thrust deep into her chest.

No looking back. She could not change the past.

"Daddy was here for his visitation and funeral so his body was—" she cleared her throat "—prepared here. When Momma said her last goodbye to Daddy she opened up the casket so she could see all of him and something was wrong. She'd wanted a moment alone with him. That's why we weren't with her. She didn't say anything at the time, but I remember she was very upset. We never knew what happened. Like she said in the letter, she hadn't wanted to make a scene at his funeral. If we hadn't found these letters we would never have known. Chief Brannigan had us looking for anything that might be missing. That got us started going through her things and that's when we found the letters."

"I understand." Rowan nodded. "I wasn't here at the time. I was still in Nashville, but I am very sorry that after I came to Winchester, your mother was unable to speak with me. I will talk to Herman and Woody—they would have been here during that time—and I will find out what happened. I'll call you tomorrow with an update. You have my word. If anything that occurred at this funeral home was wrong, I will do all within my power to make it right."

"Thank you." Patty welled up again. "I just hate that she didn't tell us."

Rowan smiled. "She was trying to protect you from whatever it was. She was a very good mother and wife."

The grieving woman took a deep breath. "Well, I have to get back to work. I'll look forward to your call as soon as possible."

As they stood, Rowan assured her once more, "I will

call you tomorrow whether I have the answer or not, and I will call you every day after that until I do."

When Patty was gone, Rowan locked up the funeral home and drove straight to Herman's house. He had gone home after the Hall funeral service. He lived on High Street in one of the old bungalows Rowan used to pretend she would own when she grew up. She had decided in her child's mind that she would run the funeral home but she would not live there.

"Sometimes things just don't work out the way you plan," Rowan muttered.

Herman was sitting on the front porch in a rocking chair, sipping iced tea, when Rowan emerged from the car.

"Well, young lady, to what do I owe the pleasure of this visit?" He held up his glass as she climbed the steps. "Would you like a glass of my lovely wife's famous sweet tea?"

Rowan started to decline but changed her mind. "I would love a glass of sweet tea."

He placed his glass on the table between the two rocking chairs and pushed to his feet. "You sit down right here and I'll get it for you."

Herman hurried into the house, the screen door slapping against the frame behind him. Rowan set the rocking chair into motion and wondered if she would ever find the time to do this? When she lived in Nashville her life had been too hectic for taking a moment to do nothing but sit. Since her return to Winchester it had been equally busy. Burying her father and getting her legs under her with the funeral home and trying not to think of her father's killer being out there had been a hectic and troubling time.

She closed her eyes and pretended that the fresh air and sound of birds singing were the only things in this world that mattered at the moment. She didn't want to think about the police cruiser following her, parked a half a block down the street, or the bastard who had pretended to be her friend and then murdered her father and so many others and who was out there somewhere watching her.

"Here you go."

Her eyes fluttered open and Herman offered her the glass of tea.

"Thank you." She accepted the cool glass.

Herman settled back into his rocker. "What's on your mind, Ro? You look as tired as an old man coming out of retirement."

She smiled. "You know I appreciate that old man coming out of retirement."

He laughed and picked up his glass. "And I appreciate a little excitement in my life now and then. Keeps me young."

"Is Estelle home?" Rowan hadn't seen her in ages.

Herman snorted. "Are you kidding? She's over at the church helping with the food for the Hall family."

"That's kind of her." Rowan had completely forgotten that Herman and his wife were members of the Baptist church. "Tell her I said hello."

Herman set his rocker into motion. "I sure will."

Rowan sipped her tea for a time. Eventually, she said what she'd come here to say. "Tell me about Geneva Phillips's husband. Was there some sort of issue with the services we provided for him?"

Herman frowned. "I don't think so. But I can tell you that was the week I had the flu. Lord, I was as sick as a dog. Your daddy left me in charge and I fell down on the job. Woody had to take care of everything on his own. Lucky for him there were only two that week—Mr. Phillips and Mr. Werner."

Rowan thought about all Patty had said. "Apparently Mrs. Phillips was very upset by something she felt was wrong with the way her husband was prepared. She didn't elaborate in the letters she wrote to her daughters, but she insisted she tried calling me and I wouldn't return her calls."

Herman's jovial expression turned dark. "I don't like the sound of that. You better talk to Woody. He might be on the lazy side but I haven't ever known him to do anything poorly and sure enough nothing wrong, but you never really know what a person will do given the chance or out of necessity."

Herman was right. Rowan understood this better than most. You never really knew a person. Never.

She finished her tea and thanked Herman for his hospitality, and then she drove to Woody's house on North College Street. By the time she parked in the drive she was more than a little furious. He could be at work but she would rather confront him here than at Gardner's. Either way, she wasn't going home until she found him. Damn him. If he'd made some sort of mistake and then tried to cover it up she would see that he paid the price.

Deep breaths. She struggled to calm herself as she stalked up the steps to the front door of the small white house. He'd inherited the place from his mother, who had moved to a retirement home with her three best friends.

Rowan rapped on the door and chastised herself for thinking such a thing. There were far too many unknowns to judge the man. But she was most unhappy at the moment. It was impossible to provide a service to the public without having an issue crop up from time to time. The real value of the business was in how you handled those issues. Her father would never have allowed a customer to go home dissatisfied. He would have found a way to work things out. This behavior was not acceptable. No matter that Woody was no longer her employee, she intended to know exactly what had happened to upset Mrs. Phillips so badly and why he had taken calls and never passed the messages on to Rowan. He had allowed Geneva Phillips to believe Rowan didn't care about her feelings.

Fury swelled inside her again and she knocked a second time, a little harder. Maybe a lot harder.

Still no answer.

"Damn it." She stamped back down to her car and decided what the hell. She would find him even if it meant visiting the competition.

Gardner's Funeral Home was on the corner of South Jefferson and Third Avenue. The house wasn't historic and it wasn't nearly as large as DuPont's, but it was nice with its stately columns and the small balcony. Parking wasn't optimal but from what Rowan had heard, the services were handled well.

Rowan climbed out of her car and started for the entrance. She reached for the door and walked in. The lobby was small but reasonably impressive. The marble floor and angel murals on the walls were tastefully done. A table loaded with lovely fresh flowers sat in the center.

A woman appeared. The opening of the door likely set off a warning that she had company, or maybe they had one of those new high-tech camera systems. With all that had been happening lately, Rowan was glad the security company was coming to install a system for her. She should have done it weeks ago.

There was something to be said for doing things the old way, but not all things done the old way were best. Like that kitchen she needed to renovate.

"Good afternoon." The sixtyish woman smiled.

She looked vaguely familiar. Her black hair was peppered with gray. The gray dress and white pearls were elegant and understated.

"Hello." Rowan smiled. "I'm here to see one of your directors—Woody Holder."

The woman's eyebrows reared up in surprise. "Mr. Holder is not here at the moment. He's out on a call."

Which was code for he was picking up a body.

"Do you know when he might return?" All Rowan needed was five minutes and perhaps a pound of flesh.

"I'm sorry. I don't." She frowned. "Are you Rowan DuPont?"

Another smile automatically pushed into place. "I am."

"I'm Sandra Sturtevant. I was your fourth grade teacher."

Rowan's smile was genuine this time. "Mrs. Sturtevant, how nice to see you. I didn't recognize you. How are you doing?"

"I'm doing well. With the kids living halfway across the country now, I decided retirement wasn't for me, so I started working for Mr. Gardner last year." She glanced around and leaned close to Rowan to say, "I wanted to work for Edward but he didn't need anyone."

A laugh bubbled up in Rowan's throat despite her frustration at Woody. Now she remembered Mrs. Sturtevant. She'd been a widow since she was in her midthirties but she'd never remarried. She always said she had her teaching and her two daughters. Rowan's father had remarked once that since the Sturtevant daughters had moved away the widow was on the prowl for a new husband.

"You look great." Rowan noticed the big diamond on her left ring finger as well as a shiny band.

The woman noticed her looking. "Oh, you probably don't know. Randy Gardner and I married last fall. His wife died of emphysema the previous spring, poor thing."

"I'm so sorry to hear about his wife." She stretched a smile back across her face. "But congratulations to you."

"Thank you. We're very happy. Traveling every chance we get." The older woman put a hand to her chest. "I'm sorry, you're looking for Woody. Well, he's out picking up Lawrence Reed. He had a stroke a couple of days ago and, bless his heart, he didn't make it."

"That's just awful." The downside to operating a funeral home in a town this small was that you usually knew all your clients personally.

"I can have him call you," Mrs. Sturtevant offered.

"Oh, that's all right." Rowan waved a hand at the suggestion. "I'll find him." And she would. Damn him.

The former teacher stepped in close again. "Just one thing, Woody is a mortuary assistant. He is not a director."

Rowan nodded. "Sorry. I guess I heard wrong."

Sturtevant waggled a finger at her. "Now don't you go trying to steal him back. Randy will be most unhappy if that happens. He's been looking for a good full-time assistant for ages. He's tried to woo Woody away from you for a long time."

Rowan shook her head. "You tell Mr. Gardner he needn't worry. Woody is all his."

With a little waggle of her own fingers in goodbye, Rowan turned and strode out of the lobby. When she climbed into her car, she reminded herself to breathe again. She drove straight to the Reed home and waited until the Gardner's cargo van doors closed before slipping out of her car and hurrying up to the passenger side of the cab.

The driver slid into the seat behind the wheel but it wasn't Woody.

"Excuse me."

He jumped as if he'd been shot. He pressed a hand to his chest. "Jeez, you scared the daylights out of me."

"Sorry. I thought Woody Holder was picking up Mr. Reed."

The guy made a face. "He was supposed to but he called me at the last minute and begged me to take his place. He said some sort of emergency had come up."

Rowan faked a smile. "Thanks. I'll give him a call."

She walked back to her car and climbed in. Woody was avoiding her. He knew he was in serious trouble and he hoped to dodge her until she cooled off.

Not going to happen. She knew where he lived and where he worked. He couldn't evade her forever.

Twenty

Rowan sat up. Her heart pounded with the receding dream. Her sister had been floating facedown in the water. Then she'd lifted her head and stared at Rowan. *Come into the water, Rowan.*

Rowan blinked and took a long, deep breath. "God, I hate these damned dreams."

She threw the covers back and dropped her feet to the floor. Squinting, she peered at the time on her cell. Two a.m.

Freud's whimpering drew her attention across the room to the door. Had she closed the door? She didn't remember closing the door.

Shoving the hair out of her eyes, she stood. "Do you really have to go out at this hour?"

Maybe she'd forgotten to let him out after Billy dropped by. He'd gone over his thoughts with her about the case reports and his visit with Luther Holcomb as well as Raven's friends from school. He'd explained in-depth his and Detective Lincoln's conclusions on the photos taken of Raven's body.

Billy was convinced Raven hadn't accidentally drowned but had been murdered by Julian's daughter.

A cold fist twisted in Rowan's chest again. All these years it had been painful enough believing that her sister's death had been an accident…that somehow Rowan should have been there to help. Now, those feelings were amplified by the idea that someone had murdered her and Rowan had been at home stewing with jealousy. Did seventeen-year-old Alisha Addington's actions confirm her mother's claims that Norah and Julian were having an affair? Considering the father's psychopathic tendencies, it was possible his daughter had indeed inherited those same tendencies. Anna had admitted she thought as much.

Would Alisha have tried to lure Rowan to her death as well had she attended the party?

Had Julian known what his daughter had done when he took Rowan's case when she was a freshman in college? Was his motive some grotesque curiosity?

And why hadn't any of Raven's friends noticed that she disappeared from the party? All three had given the same story to Audrey Anderson. Giving the three grace, it was possible Raven had blown them off for the cool girl from LA.

There was a very good possibility that Rowan would never know the whole story.

Rowan pushed away the thoughts. She wasn't going to rehash those frustrating possibilities or solve that painful mystery now. She tucked on her glasses, stood and moved toward the door. "Okay, boy, if you need to go out that badly, let's get it over with."

Freud rushed for the stairs and disappeared down to the second floor. Rowan followed more slowly. As hard as she tried, she could not excise the turmoil of thoughts from her head. If this scenario she and Billy were piecing together proved true, did that explain why Norah had killed herself? Had she blamed Raven's death on her selfish actions? As much as Rowan wanted to believe that scenario versus the one she had believed most of her life, that her mother hadn't loved her enough, it was too early to conclude anything.

Rather than go to the door leading to the rear staircase as he usually did, Freud went to the front door of the living quarters. He sniffed at the door, made more of those whimpering sounds.

"What is wrong with you, boy?"

He pawed at the door and stared up at her expectantly.

"All right, then." Before unlocking the door, she hesitated, went back to her bedroom for her cell phone and handgun. If she was going outside she should have both with her. Billy would approve.

When she unlocked and opened the door, Freud barreled down the hall. Rowan moved considerably slower. She shoved a handful of hair behind her ear and toyed with the idea of visiting Tessa Cardwell in the morning to see if her story would be different when she wasn't being questioned by the chief of police or by a reporter. Tessa had insisted to Billy that she had no idea why Raven went into the water or if she did. She'd given the same story to Audrey. Apparently Raven and Tessa had a disagreement and spent the entire party not speaking to each other. Tessa claimed not to remember what they were arguing about that day. Some boy, she'd suggested.

Rowan would make it a point to speak to her. Maybe help prompt another…

For several seconds the object hanging from the

second-floor banister didn't register in Rowan's brain...
and then it abruptly did.

Rope. Wrapped around the banister and then knotted tightly to ensure it didn't pull loose. A noose hung
a few feet below the landing the same way it had when
she'd come home and found her mother suspended there.

In the lobby below, Freud stared up at the rope and
circled the space below it, growling and whimpering.

Her heart in her throat, Rowan hurried down the
stairs. Her fingers pawed at the dead bolt on the entrance door. Her heart suddenly dropped and thundered
so hard she couldn't capture a breath. She needed out
of here. *Now.*

When she was outside, she slammed the door behind
her and rushed across the parking lot, stood on the farthest edge and stared back at the house.

Freud remained at the door barking and snarling.

Hands trembling, Rowan called Billy from her cell
phone. As much as she didn't want to call him, particularly at this hour, this was far more than a mere misplaced object or unlocked door. This was the work of
someone who understood how deeply her mother's suicide had impacted her. Someone who knew her deepest, darkest secrets.

Julian, the son of a bitch, knew her too well.

The memory of one of his victims in Nashville wearing a noose exactly like that roared through her head like
a train rushing from a dark tunnel.

Billy answered on the second ring.

Rowan blurted the words. "He was here."

Billy didn't ask who, he just promised to come right
away. He stayed on the phone with her until, less than

half a minute later, one of the two officers on protection detail rushed into the parking lot, tires squealing.

"Are you all right, Dr. DuPont?"

She wanted to say no, that she wasn't all right at all. Instead, she bobbed her head up and down and hugged her arms around herself, her weapon still clutched in her right hand, her cell in the other. "You didn't see anyone go into the funeral home?"

He stared at her as if she'd lost her mind. Of course he hadn't seen anyone go inside. The entrance had been locked. She'd had to unlock the dead bolt to get out.

"I'm sorry, ma'am, I didn't see anyone."

"The side doors," she suggested.

"Why don't we check those?" he offered. "My partner is already checking the back door."

Numb, Rowan walked with him first to the east end and then the west end of the building. Both doors were secured.

"Do you want me to wait inside with you, ma'am?"

Rowan shook her head. "No. Thank you." She didn't want anyone to see what was inside. Billy would have to see it but no one else. Frankly, she couldn't bear the thought of anyone seeing what was in there. So she waited. In the middle of the parking lot, her arms tight around her body. The cool night air sending goose bumps over her bare legs.

Billy rolled into the parking lot a minute later. Rowan braced herself and waited for him to join them at the front entrance.

"You okay?"

All she could manage was a nod before she croaked, "We need to talk." She cleared her throat. "Inside."

"Thanks, Rogers," Billy said to the officer. "You can go back to your position now."

Rowan had no idea where the two officers were positioned. She had demanded they be out of sight and they had been. Was that the reason they hadn't seen the intruder enter the funeral home?

How could this be? No one else had a key—only she, Billy, Herman and Charlotte. Even the cleaning team had to go through one of them now. Herman would never, ever do anything like this. Nor would Charlotte. It had to be Julian. There was no other explanation. The question was, how?

Billy reached for the door, pulled it open and put a hand on her back as he ushered her inside. Her mind was whirling. Addington had been inside her house. Maybe not for the first time.

Why was he so intent on playing these disturbing games? Why not just tell her what it was he wanted to say?

Perhaps he was building up to some big climatic conclusion.

Rowan's gaze lifted to the banister and the air in her lungs vanished. The rope was gone. No noose...no nothing.

"Ro?"

Billy was looking at her now as if he feared she would shatter into a million pieces. She rushed up the stairs, ran her hand along the banister. "It was here."

Billy climbed the staircase and came to stand next to her. "Tell me what happened. What was here?"

"Freud woke me up. He wanted to go out...or something. He was whimpering and pawing at the door. So I got up to let him out, but he ran to this door." She gestured toward the living quarters. "He rushed into the lobby and barked and growled and just stared up at *it*."

"It?"

She moistened her lips and said what had to be said. "The rope with the noose hanging from this banister."

He stared at the banister now, ran his hand over the wood, smooth with age. There was no rope, much less a noose. "It was there," she argued. "I saw it."

He crouched down and visually inspected the banister more closely. "Oh yeah." He pointed to the wood. "You can see where something rubbed at the finish." He stood, his gaze coming to rest on hers. "Someone was in the house."

"Had to be. I know what I saw." She hugged herself tighter, felt the worry twisting harder inside her.

"You think Freud knew someone was downstairs before you woke up? Maybe that's why he was behaving strangely."

That was the only explanation that made sense. "I believe so, but he didn't bark so I can't be sure." She couldn't be sure of anything anymore. Her shoulders sagged in defeat.

Billy's arm went around her, and he ushered her toward the living quarters. "It's like you've said before, if it's someone he knows, he might not bark. Either way, we'll figure this out."

"It had to be him, Billy. It had to be someone who knew how that image would affect me." She explained about the victim in Nashville and how Julian had used a noose to taunt her then.

Julian wanted her to feel this way…uncertain and afraid.

Damn him!

When they were in her living room and Rowan felt reasonably calm again, she deposited her weapon and phone on the table by the sofa and turned to Billy. "What now?"

Billy was checking his cell. When he looked up he said, "I've got my officers checking the place from one end to the other. Windows and doors, all possible access points, for any indication of forced entry. We'll figure this out."

She scrubbed her hands up her arms. "We're going to need some caffeine for this. I'll put on a pot of coffee."

"Let's have a look around first, then we'll start the coffee."

Room by room, they went through the living quarters and then he led the way into the kitchen. Frustration tangled inside her. She had seen the rope and the noose. It could not have simply disappeared.

When she'd set the pot to brew she turned to him. "It was Julian. He's the only one who would understand how deeply Mother's suicide changed my life."

"You think he hired someone to do the job for him or do you think it was him? Is he physically capable?"

"He's a perfectionist, which prevents him from letting go of the things he wants to control. He's as physically fit as a man half his age. But it's possible he used someone to do the job." She shook her head then. "Either way, it's him. I know it's him."

"But does he have one of the new keys?"

"He managed to get one the last time we had the locks changed." Dear God, who else had he murdered for access to her? She shivered. "If he doesn't have a key, there has to be a window unlocked, something. He was here. No one else would know." Her pulse rate had begun to slow and still she felt as if she were running in a marathon.

"There wasn't a note or message left to you?"

She shook her head. "Not that I've found." Her gaze latched on to his. "You don't think I imagined this, do you?"

"You know me better than that, Ro. If you say it happened, it happened. I can see Addington playing those sorts of head games. Besides, there's evidence of something having rubbed against the surface of that wood banister. My evidence techs will check for prints or anything else they can find. But I need to know if anything else like this has happened? Maybe you thought it would be best not to tell me or you dismissed the situation."

"Nothing exactly like this, but…" She dropped her gaze for a moment. "I think I mentioned to you that I've been forgetting things. I turn around and things are in a different place than I remember placing them."

He reached out, tugged at an errant lock of her hair. "You've been under a lot of stress, Ro. Part of that is normal. I don't have to tell you this."

"It doesn't feel normal. It feels like I'm totally losing it but it's only when I'm at home." The realization dawned with such force that she shook with it. "I haven't forgotten a single thing or misplaced the first item when I'm away from home." She rubbed her arms with her hands. "He wants me off balance. He's trying to shatter my defenses a little piece at a time."

"I agree." Billy reached for his cell. "One moment." He answered and listened for a half a minute. The hard line of his jaw warned that this was not good news.

"Good job, Cooper. Thanks."

When he'd put his phone away, his gaze settled on Rowan's. "One of the basement windows was open."

Renewed fear spiked through her. "I never leave those windows unlocked, much less open."

"The evidence techs will find anything there is to find. Meanwhile, how about that coffee?"

She nodded and headed toward the kitchen. She'd almost made it there when she stalled. She whipped around to face Billy. "Where is Freud?"

Billy's look of confusion had worry zipping through her.

Rowan rushed downstairs and out of the funeral home, calling his name. Billy did the same. They walked the block, calling for him.

And then another block and another.

Freud was gone.

Twenty-One

The entire Winchester Police Department was keeping an eye out for Freud. Rowan had spent the predawn hours walking block after block around the funeral home. At daylight Billy had gone with Rowan from door to door.

No one had seen Freud.

Rowan was devastated.

Herman had joined the search, but when a client called, he had to go back to the funeral home to take care of business. Billy had enlisted the help of a friend at the local radio station who put out a call for assistance from the community. Audrey Anderson had called Rowan when she heard the news and posted an alert on the paper's online edition.

As difficult as it was to shift her attention from the search, Rowan still had to find Woody. The evidence techs were looking for anything left behind by the unknown perpetrator who had hung that rope on the second-story railing last night. Rowan had gone over the events before Freud disappeared a thousand times and she couldn't quite pinpoint the moment when she last saw him.

Whoever had left the rope and noose had known her well enough to understand she would be shocked by it and would react exactly as she did. Had Julian planned the whole event just so he could snatch Freud? He knew how much that dog meant to her. He hadn't hurt him last time. She hoped he wouldn't this time. But if he did…

"Son of a bitch," she muttered.

"Did you say something?" Billy shifted his attention from the road long enough to glance at her.

She shook her head and refocused her attention on the here and now. "It's possible, if Woody did something criminal, he may have cut and run."

"Or he could just be laying low until the heat dies down." Billy glanced at her again. "Are you thinking what I think you're thinking?"

She was too tired to smile or laugh, but the idea that they knew each other so well and thought so much alike even after all these years made her want to. "I'm fairly confident I am."

"If it's true—if he did something to Mr. Phillips's body—we only have a dead woman's word for it." Billy turned onto the street where Woody lived. "I guess we'll cross that bridge when we come to it. No point in upsetting the family unnecessarily with unsubstantiated theories."

"We're on the same page on that one." Exhaustion tugged at Rowan. She had only slept two or three hours last night and that had been littered with dreams. Not dreams. *Nightmares.* Everything about the past two months had been a nightmare. She glanced at Billy. Well, not everything.

The small white house where Woody lived looked as deserted as it had when Rowan came looking for him yesterday. The car he drove was not in the driveway. On a more optimistic note, someone had cut the grass since yesterday. When they climbed out of Billy's truck, she slid her cell phone into the back pocket of her jeans. The wind toyed with a wisp of her hair and reminded her that she should have worn a sweater.

"I doubt he's here." Rowan had not been this frustrated in a very long time. It felt as if every aspect of her life was coming apart at the seams and somehow Woody and Julian were the ones pulling the threads.

"We'll find him," Billy assured her. "You don't waste any time worrying about that. I will track his sorry ass down one way or another."

Rowan did smile then. "I want to be there when you find him."

Several knocks on the front door confirmed her conclusion. Woody was not home. "What now?"

"Now we go to his current place of employment." Billy indicated that she should precede him off the porch.

They had to keep looking until they found him. Geneva Phillips's daughters were counting on her and Billy to find the truth.

As Billy drove across town, Rowan stared out the window, her chest tight with worry about Freud. She should have been paying better attention.

"You know Freud is a smart dog."

She glanced at Billy. "He is. I'm hoping he's found his way home by now."

Herman would likely have called her, but she could still hope.

The parking lot at Gardner's Funeral Home was empty, just as it had been yesterday. Rowan and Billy got out and went inside. Like yesterday, Mrs. Sturtevant greeted them in the lobby.

"Good morning, Chief." She turned to Rowan. "To you, too, Rowan. I didn't expect to see you again so soon."

"I don't know if you heard," Rowan said, "but my German shepherd, Freud, is missing. I've been driving around town looking for him."

The other woman's eyebrows flew up. "I'm so sorry to hear about your dog. It's nice to have such a handsome chauffeur for your search."

Billy, his hat in his hands, smiled. Rowan moved on. "I wanted to talk to Woody to see if he might have any ideas on where else I can look for him." This, of course, was not why she wanted to talk to Woody, but she certainly wasn't going to tell this woman what she and Billy feared Woody had done.

Mrs. Sturtevant's flirty smile faded. "We had to fire Woody."

"Would you mind sharing the reason with us, ma'am?" Billy asked.

Rowan was glad he did. She felt confident the woman was more likely to answer that question from Billy than she was from Rowan. True to her long reputation, the lady liked to flirt.

"Well." She put hand to her throat. "To be quite frank, I'm not certain I should be talking about it."

Rowan kept quiet and let Billy do the placating and nudging.

"Ma'am, you can rest assured that anything you tell me will be held in the strictest of confidence."

"I'll just wait over by the door," Rowan offered.

This seemed to please the older lady. Billy's expression warned that he wasn't too happy about the suggestion, but he let her go. They both wanted to find Woody.

She stared out the door, soaking up the sunlight filtering in through the glass. All morning she hadn't been able to get warm. In her pocket her cell vibrated. She reached for it, saw Woody's name and tapped the screen to accept the call.

"Have you seen Freud?" she said rather than to demand the answer to the other questions she had. The question about her dog would likely put him off balance. She needed him confused and giving answers before he had the opportunity to think was a good way to start.

"No. Why would I know anything about your dog?"

"He ran away last night and I can't find him."

"Too bad about your dog but I really couldn't care less, Rowan. You got me fired."

She heard no indication in his voice that he was lying about Freud. Renewed worry seared through her. What if Julian had taken him? Clearing her head, she summoned as much fake interest as she could and asked, "How did I get you fired?"

"You went to Gardner's checking up on me and that old bitch got pissed so she fired me."

"I wouldn't have gone to Gardner's at all if you'd answered your phone, Woody. I need to know what happened with Howard Phillips. Mrs. Phillips's daughters are filing a complaint."

The last part wasn't exactly true—at least not yet—but he didn't know that.

"What the hell? The old hag was pissed because she said her husband's watch was missing. He wasn't wearing a watch when he got to the funeral home and she didn't bring one when she brought his suit. I don't know what the hell she was talking about. I'm telling you she was crazy."

Every word that came out of his mouth was a lie. From the slight quiver and the hesitation to the high-pitched adamancy.

"I'll need you to submit an official statement for my files."

"Sure. What the hell? I'm not taking the fall for whatever crazy shit that bitch hatched up."

Fear had crept into his voice. His anxiety was off the charts. Whatever he had done, he understood at this point that he was caught. "Can you come by and take care of the statement? Maybe we can discuss you coming back to work."

"You'd be willing to hire me back?"

Not in this life, mister. On some level he dared to hope. Later he would realize that he'd been foolish to do so. "Sure. Well-trained help is difficult to find."

"Good. Okay. I can come by after lunch."

"Great. I'll see you then." Before ending the call, for good measure she threw in, "Hey, if you see my dog, let me know."

"Yeah. Yeah. Sure."

The call ended and Rowan stared at the phone. Whatever Woody had done, it was beyond his usual boundaries of good and bad. He was afraid. The trepidation and distress had been heavy in his tone. Hopefully, her suggestion that she might rehire him and the worry about her dog had confused him about her real intent.

She intended to take Woody Holder all the way down for whatever the hell he had done.

Billy joined her, settled his hat into place and pushed the door open. They walked out together.

When the door had closed behind them, Rowan asked, "Why did she fire him?" She couldn't wait to hear the real reason.

"One of the other assistant directors found him groping one of their clients in refrigeration."

"Are you serious?"

"As a heart attack." Billy shook his head. "The woman, Marla Gifford, had recently undergone knee replacement surgery and her family wanted a full-view coffin with her wearing a minidress."

It wasn't unheard of. Families often wanted all possible steps taken to make a loved one look natural.

Billy reached for the passenger-side door of his truck. "So Woody was supposed to be covering the scar." He shrugged. "You know, doing the restoration thing to make it disappear. According to one of the other assistants, he was playing with her leg—not the one with the surgical scar."

Rowan waved her cell phone. "Well, that's not what he told me." As she settled into the seat, she recounted Woody's explanation for his firing and for Mrs. Phillips's complaint.

Billy walked around to the driver's side and got in. "You think he's lying about Phillips."

Rowan harrumphed. "He's lying about everything."

Billy reached into his pocket and retrieved his cell. "Brannigan."

He started the engine, listening to his caller. "I'll be there in ten."

He glanced at Rowan as he put his phone away. "I have to get to the scene of a drug operation. I won't be long. Will you be okay?"

She nodded. "Take me back to the funeral home and I'll catch up with Herman. I should be there anyway."

"We will find Freud," he promised her again. "And we'll find Woody. Trust me on that one."

Rowan didn't doubt him for a moment. "I have every confidence."

She was only too happy to step back and let Billy focus on finding Woody. He had told Rowan he would come by but she didn't believe him for a second. At any rate, she had something else on her mind just now...like finding out exactly what Woody had done.

Geneva Phillips's daughters had agreed to meet with Rowan at their mother's home. Rowan had considered the best way to approach her proposal, and there really was no easy way to ask, but she intended to give it her best shot. First, she gave them Woody's side of the story. The response was exactly what she'd expected.

"My father did not have a special watch," Patty argued.

Jenn shook her head. "He wore the same plain old watch he'd worn for as long as I can remember. To suggest he had been overly attached to it is ridiculous. He wore it but he wasn't attached to it like that and Mother certainly wasn't. In fact, she gave it to Patty's oldest. They wanted him to have it."

"That's right," Patty said as if she'd only just remembered. She made a face. "How could I have forgotten about that?"

"You've lost both your mother and your father in a very short time span. It's understandable that you would have difficulty remembering every detail of the past few weeks." Rowan felt their pain. It was not an easy transition at any age.

Tears welled and the sisters hugged. Regret tugged at Rowan. Even now she missed the close connection she and Raven once shared.

"I have a very difficult request, ladies." Rowan braced for protest.

The two looked at one another, then Jenn said, "We just want the truth."

Rowan nodded her understanding. "I believe the only way to be certain about any failing on the funeral home's part is to exhume your father's body at the funeral home's expense and to confirm any potential issues."

The two women stared at her for a long moment. Rowan was well aware that she was setting up her own funeral home for a potential lawsuit, but she would not allow this to go uninvestigated. If one or more services were not performed to standard, Rowan wanted to make it right. Geneva Phillips would never have written those letters had she not felt profoundly violated. This was more than some missing watch with mere sentimental value.

"You won't do anything…invasive?" Jenn asked. Worry lined her face.

"Absolutely not. We'll open the vault, bring up the casket and have it delivered back to the funeral home. The county coroner will visually inspect the body and I will evaluate the services performed here. As quickly as we have done so, we'll return the casket to the vault and restore the grave just as it was."

The two shared a look before Jenn asked, "Is this really necessary?"

Rowan shook her head. "No. Not at this time. We don't know that there was any impropriety or criminal act committed. We only know that your mother was disturbed by whatever happened. If it's your wish to let this matter go, then that's what we'll do. I would prefer that any wrongdoing be properly investigated and the appropriate steps taken, but I am looking at this from an objective place. I recognize this is not an easy decision for you."

Patty exhaled a big breath. "Momma was upset. We shouldn't leave this unresolved, especially considering whatever happened at his funeral may in some way be related to her death."

Jenn's eyes widened as if she hadn't thought of that possibility. "Oh my God, you're right." She turned back to Rowan. "We have to do it."

"We have to do it," Patty echoed.

"I'll talk to Chief Brannigan and get the request submitted. We'll try to get this taken care of quickly so that when your mother is laid to rest, her husband will be waiting for her."

There were more questions and Rowan was only too happy to answer each one to the best of her ability. As soon as she was outside she made the necessary calls. First to Burt so that he could be ready and then to Billy. Billy assured Rowan that he would get the order signed ASAP. He would give her a call when the exhumation was scheduled. She would meet him at the cemetery.

It was early. Their chance of getting the job done this afternoon was a good possibility. As the chief of police, Billy had the right connections to make things happen in a timely manner.

Rowan settled behind the steering wheel of her car.

She thought about Mr. Phillips and the woman Woody was accused of groping at Gardner's, Marla Gifford. The one thing besides Woody the two had in common was some sort of surgery before they died. Shoulder for Phillips, knee for Gifford. There was only one orthopedic clinic in Winchester. Ms. Gifford could have had her surgery done anywhere, but Mr. Phillips had his done right here in Winchester with Dr. Knowles.

The idea that she was onto something would not let go. A huge body brokering case in Nashville a few years back stuck in her head. A funeral home was literally salvaging body parts without consent from their clients and selling them on the black market. There was a huge demand for all sorts of parts as well as whole cadavers. Testing, training and numerous other uses. Of course, it wasn't necessary to have an orthopedist to remove the wanted parts. The funeral home in Nashville had been using everything from skill saws to reciprocating saws to chop up bodies.

Rowan shuddered at the idea. Hoped there wasn't anything like that going on in her hometown—in her funeral home.

Before driving away, she sent Billy a text.

Let's look at Knowles. He may be the connection between Gifford and Phillips.

Rowan hit Send and dropped her cell on the console. She started the car and pulled away from the curb. Her cell vibrated. She jumped.

"That was fast." She hadn't expected Billy to respond so quickly.

She braked for a traffic light and glanced at the screen.

Unknown Number. She tapped the screen to open the text message.

Meet me at the lake. You know where.

Her heart thumped. *Julian.* Who else would text her from an unknown number?

The light changed and she put on her signal and turned in a different direction. Her self-preservation instincts urged her to call Billy, but he would only insist on coming too and scaring Julian off. She glanced in the rearview mirror at the police cruiser right behind her. Maybe she could convince him that she needed to check something at the scene where Alisha Addington's remains had been found.

Whatever she decided, she had to make a quick stop at the funeral home first. She needed her weapon for this meeting.

Maybe she'd just save the judicial system the trouble of prosecuting the bastard.

Twenty-Two

Billy parked at the cemetery gate and climbed out of his truck. He glanced at the other vehicles gathered. The coroner's van was here. Herman had arrived with the DuPont Funeral Home hearse. He didn't see Rowan's car. Maybe she'd ridden with Herman.

He closed the door of his truck and surveyed the vehicles again. But if she was here, where was her protection detail? He pulled out his cell as he strode through the rows of headstones and put in a call to her. It went straight to voice mail. She'd sent him a text saying they needed to look into Dr. Knowles since he might be the connection between the two victims, Phillips and Gifford. Next, Billy put in a call to her protection detail. That call went to voice mail, as well. What the hell?

By the time he reached the huddle around Howard Phillips's grave, he was ready to go back to his truck and hunt Rowan down, but this exhumation was happening now. He couldn't just drive away.

The mound of freshly unearthed soil and the vault lid told him the crew had wasted no time arriving on-site and getting the job started. The groan of the lift that was already hauling up the casket reminded Billy that he was running behind. It had been that kind of day.

"You almost missed the party," Herman commented with a glance in Billy's direction.

Billy set his hands on his hips. "Those Crowder boys are cooking again."

Besides finding an abuse or murder victim, nothing riled Billy more than learning a methamphetamine operation had set up shop in his town. Lucky for him, most of those sorts of operations cropped up in the county. Sheriff Colt Tanner was on top of the drug business. He had taken a hard line with folks who dared to make, sell or buy drugs in his county. A few of those who had refused to give up the life had tried setting up shop in Billy's jurisdiction. Not happening on his watch. Not for long anyway.

"Those two never were no good for nothing," Herman grumbled. "Put their momma in an early grave, that's all."

"That no good son of a gun she was married to didn't help," Burt added.

"My daddy always said Axel Crowder wasn't worth shooting," Billy agreed.

"No, sir," Herman confirmed.

"Where's Rowan?" Billy asked since no one mentioned her and she still hadn't shown up or called him back.

"She told me she had to stop by the funeral home to pick up something and then she'd be right here," Herman said.

She hadn't mentioned stopping by the funeral home to Billy. "You'll be heading that way in what? Fifteen or twenty minutes?"

"Don't see why not," Burt said.

"I'll be there." He had a bad feeling. He wasn't waiting to hear from Rowan. He intended to find her. *Now.* His instincts were nudging him.

He walked back to his truck, pulled out his phone to call Rowan again and it rang. "Brannigan."

"Chief, this is Officer Trenton."

Trenton was one of the two officers assigned to Rowan today. Tension slid through Billy. "I tried calling you, Trenton. You still have eyes on Dr. DuPont?"

"Well, no. I thought I did but I was wrong."

Oh hell. "What does that mean, Trenton?"

"I followed her to the funeral home. She said she had to go inside and get something and she'd be right back, but she never came back. I went inside and she's gone. Just…gone."

"Then we've got a problem, Trenton. I'm going to need you to find her. Right now."

"Yes, sir, Chief. I'm working on it."

Billy ended the call and sent Rowan a text message.

Where the hell are you?

He waited…watched the screen. No answer came.

He drove to the funeral home and searched the place. As Trenton had said, she wasn't there. But her car was. That was the part that worried him the most. He checked in with the Phillips daughters. She wasn't at Patty's or with Jenn at her mother's home.

Maybe she was out looking for Freud again. He doubted she would give her protection detail the slip just to go look for her dog, particularly on foot. His gut tied into a thousand knots. This was about Addington.

"Damn it, Ro." He dug out his phone again and put through a call to Dressler as he drove from block to block, hoping against hope he would spot her. Once he'd briefed Dressler, he put Trenton and his partner on patrol looking for Rowan. While he was at it, he issued a BOLO on her just to be on the safe side.

His cell vibrated before he could get it back into his pocket. Burt Johnston's name appeared on the screen.

"Brannigan."

"Chief, you should get back over to the funeral home. We have a situation."

Worry twisted in his chest. "Is Rowan there?"

"She's still a no-show."

Damn it. Billy executed a U-turn. "I'm on my way. Did you find something when you opened the casket?"

"Yes and no," Burt said. "It's what we didn't find that's the real problem. Just get here as quick as you can."

Within ten minutes Billy was walking into the mortuary room. He looked from Herman to Burt. "What's missing?"

"His feet," Burt said. "Somebody took his feet from the ankles down."

Of all the things Billy had seen in his life growing up on a farm and then being a lawman for nearly a decade and a half, this had to be the strangest. He could damn sure see now why Woody Holder was avoiding Rowan. If the dumb ass had anything to do with this, he was neck-deep in serious trouble.

"What're your thoughts on what we're looking at here, Burt? Besides the obvious, of course." Billy had it figured for either some sort of bizarre fetish or black market body parts. With the internet, a person could pretty much buy anything. Selling stolen body parts would be a breeze.

"I'm leaning toward black market body parts. While we waited for you I did a Google search on feet, and a pair goes for several thousand dollars."

"You fellas forgive me for what I'm about to say—" Billy looked from one to the other "—but if you wanted to purchase a new pair of feet, why settle for an old man's feet? No offense."

Herman laughed. "I was thinking the same thing."

Burt angled his head and pursed his lips for a moment. "Bear in mind that the folks who buy this sort of thing have money. To a seventy-five or eighty-year-old man like me, Howard's sixty-five-year-old feet might look pretty damned good."

"I hadn't thought of that one." In reality, other than the various uses for cadaver bones, the parts from a dead body weren't transplantable, but there were numerous other uses like research and as teaching tools. If the seller had permission from the donor or the donor's family, there was nothing illegal about brokering body parts. Otherwise, it was stealing and abuse of a corpse.

Burt grunted a laugh and Billy shook his head. Graveyard humor, yeah.

Whatever else was going on, Billy had a bad, bad feeling in the pit of his stomach. "Herman, how long did Woody work here?"

Herman sighed. "Two years." He shook his head. "That's a lot of potential body parts."

Billy shook his head. "A whole lot. I need to find Holder before he tries to pull a disappearing act." If he hadn't already. "But first I need to find Ro." He was worried sick about her.

"I have a feeling," Herman said, his voice heavy with concern, "if you find Ro, you'll find Woody. He's backed into a corner now. No place to go."

Dread welled faster in Billy's gut. "You're right." He pulled out his cell. "I'll need a report with photos on all this, Burt. If anything else is missing, we need to know."

"Will do." Burt shook his head. "Poor bastard."

As Billy hustled up the stairs to the first floor he called Lincoln. He gave him a quick rundown on what they'd discovered, then said, "Let's get a warrant for Woody Holder's place. Find out where he worked before he started at DuPont. He may have been doing this for a while. And see if we can connect him to Dr. Jared Knowles."

Billy walked out into the afternoon sun. This would not go well for Rowan. Holder had been employed by her family's business. The lawsuits would stack up fast. He settled his hat into place. On top of everything else that had happened, she damned sure didn't need this. She felt things deeply. This would hurt her almost as much as it did the families of the victims. The fact that Winchester was such a small town where everyone knew everyone would only make the whole situation more difficult. The news would spark rumors and those would spread like wildfire.

Right now he just had to find her. He didn't want her hearing this news from anyone else. And he sure as hell didn't want Woody trying to resolve his dilemma by hurting Rowan.

When he pulled out of the parking lot, his cell vibrated on the console where he'd tossed it, the sound grating on his nerves and at the same time firing hope in his veins that it would be Rowan.

Lincoln again.

Billy tapped the screen. "Did I forget something or did you?"

"We have a situation."

Unease slid through Billy. "I'm listening."

"Patrol just found Woody Holder's car."

Knots of worry tightened in Billy's gut. "Where?"

"At the lake, near the scene where Alisha Addington's remains were found."

The worry swelled into fear. "I'm on my way there now. I want as much backup as you can send my way."

Billy ended the call and gunned the engine.

Twenty-Three

Rowan had been wrong about Woody.

He had shown up. In fact, he'd been waiting for her at the funeral home when she stopped to get her weapon before going to meet Julian. To her surprise he had at first claimed he wanted to discuss her offer to rehire him, but then he had jabbed a gun at her and ushered her out the back door and to his car. He'd parked in the alley behind the funeral home.

Ironically, he'd brought her to the lake. To the place where her sister's body had been found…where she had discovered Alisha Addington's remains. Yellow crime scene tape still fluttered from the bushes around the area. Those bones had set all this craziness in motion.

She couldn't resist surveying the woods around them, her gaze seeking any sign of Julian. If he was here somewhere—as she suspected—she wasn't sure how Woody's presence would complicate things.

Would Julian spot him and take off?

What she needed was to get rid of Woody Holder.

"You know they'll be looking for me by now." Rowan recognized that she should be afraid but she wasn't really, not yet. For the most part, she was mad as hell. She had survived a close encounter with the world's most prolific serial killer. She wasn't actually afraid of Woody Holder. She just wanted to kick his ass as best she could and then turn him over to Billy to finish the job.

But first she wanted him out of the way before Julian backed out on their meeting. And she was certain Julian was the one who sent the text.

Woody laughed and nudged her onward. "I'll be long gone before they think to look here and you…well, you'll be dead." He poked her in the back with the gun. "Those are my orders. You have to die."

She bit her lips together to prevent saying, *Far more ruthless killers than you have tried,* but she decided to keep that cold hard fact to herself. Perhaps it would give her an edge before this was done.

The underbrush tugged at her jeans, slashed across her hand, drawing blood. They were headed to the deep water's edge…closer than she had ever gone before. To the place where Raven's body had been tangled up in the limbs of a fallen tree. Her throat constricted ever so slightly but she refused to show her fear. He wanted her afraid. He wanted her to allow him complete control.

Woody Holder had likely never been in complete control in his entire life.

But today he had a gun and that made him feel brave and all-powerful. Strange how he was so easy to read now that that he'd shown a glimpse of his true colors.

"You really didn't have to kill Mrs. Phillips." Rowan shook her head. "You should have allowed her to talk to me. I could have cleared everything up."

"Oh yeah. I'm sure you would've been happy to explain how her husband's feet went missing." He pushed her forward.

She jerked back as her own feet sank into the muck at the water's edge. Her heart pitched and galloped. She thought of poor Mr. Phillips and what the idiot had done to him.

She faced him, barely restrained the urge to punch him, gun or no. "What the hell did you do?"

"I did what I had to do," he snarled. "Those who have everything always like to believe they're above doing anything wrong because they've never been pushed into a corner and left with no choice."

"There's always a choice, Woody. You didn't have to kill Mrs. Phillips any more than you had to steal her dead husband's feet." A person who would cannibalize the dead for their own selfish gain was the lowest of the low.

"Mr. Phillips didn't need his feet. I did." Woody stabbed himself in the chest with his thumb. "I considered picking up a few body parts now and then a fringe benefit of the crappy job."

Dear God, how long had he been doing this? Were his criminal activities restricted to his work at DuPont? Or had he been doing it at Gardner's, too? Where else had he worked? His psychopathy could go all the way back to his childhood.

"But then *he* found out what I'd been doing and everything changed."

Rowan stilled, grabbed at a sapling to steady herself. "Who is *he*?"

Woody laughed. "Oh, you wouldn't believe me if I told you. He's too perfect and too smart. No one would ever suspect him. No way. It's the have-nots like me that everyone suspects. No one would ever suspect him in a million years. Especially not you."

"Dr. Knowles?" Rowan suggested. "Is he the one who put you up to this? Is he the one who changed everything?"

More of that obscene laughter burst out of the piece of crap with the gun. "You are too funny, Ro. You don't know shit." He leveled the muzzle at her. "You should never have come back. Everything would have been fine if you hadn't come back. You complicated everything."

Rowan mentally scrambled for something to say. "You should have been more careful, Woody. When you steal from the dead, Karma is a bitch. Didn't anyone ever tell you that? What about your partner? Surely he has warned you not to be so careless."

"First, we're not talking about my partner. We're talking about you. Second, if you want to talk about Karma, how about the fact that you should have died when your friend the serial killer decided to come out of the shadows, but instead your dad bought the farm. How screwed up is that?"

Fury ignited so fiery hot in Rowan that she could barely restrain the urge to tear into him. "Why?" she demanded. "Why would you take advantage of people at their most vulnerable time? Wait." She threw up her hands as if an epiphany had struck. "Because you're a coward. A coward sneaks around behind closed doors to take advantage of others. That's what you are, Woody. You're a coward."

The muzzle bored into her chest now. "No, Rowan, I'm just a man who found an easy way to make a few bucks and got caught by the wrong asshole who wanted it all for himself. Besides, no one got hurt, they were already dead! If that crazy old bitch hadn't nosed around where she had no business she would never have known. I caught her in the refrigeration unit. I should have killed her then and stuffed her in the casket on top of her old man. No one would have been the wiser."

Rowan laughed despite the pain of the weapon boring into her sternum and the depravity of his words. "Who hired you to harvest body parts, Woody? We both know you aren't smart enough to put together a scheme like this on your own."

He sneered. "Maybe I'm not the smartest one in this partnership, but he couldn't do it without me. So he's stuck with me just like I'm stuck with him. It's you we have to get rid of!"

"You won't get away with it," she argued. "You won't. Billy will make sure."

"Even if you somehow walk out of here," he snarled, "no one will ever believe you. Because you're the undertaker's daughter. The only one who survived. Everyone knows how you used to talk to your dead sister and how you found your mother after she hanged herself. Then you got your father murdered. Anyone could have seen it coming if they bothered to look. No one will be surprised to find you floating facedown in the lake. Especially with you imagining all those things happening in your house."

The noose…the missing and moved items.

"It was you." Shock radiated through her. She had been convinced it was Julian.

He grinned. "Made you wonder if you were losing it, didn't we? Your daddy always talked about how bad what happened all those years ago hurt you. He worried about you. With him murdered and it being your fault and this new investigation into your mother and your sister, it's no wonder you threw yourself into the lake. We had it all planned."

"No one will believe I did this," Rowan warned. "Billy will never allow that to happen."

"Yeah, you're probably right. At this point, I don't really care. I'll be long gone. 'Cause what *he* doesn't know is that I'm not hanging around to see how this plays out. I am so out of here." He squared his shoulders. "Now let's finish this." He motioned toward the water with his gun. "Jump!"

"Just one question," Rowan countered. "Why did you wait so long to move Mrs. Phillips? That was your one mistake, you know."

He rolled his eyes. "I went over there to shut her up but when things got out of control and she ended up dead I got sick. I had to go across the street and puke so I wouldn't leave any evidence. I've watched every episode of CSI. I know my shit. The problem was, I never killed anyone before. When a neighbor came home, I panicked and left. Later that afternoon I realized I had to make it look like an accident. I wasn't worried about Burt figuring it out. He was never going to notice, and even if he had, I could have handled him." Woody's face twisted with anger. "But you had to get involved. Now, stop asking questions. I want to finish this."

Rowan shook her head. "You want to kill me? Then shoot me. I'm not jumping."

The muzzle gored into her chest. "Don't think I won't."

"Do it or go," she suggested. "Run while you have the chance."

He shook his head from side to side. "No way. You

know too much. Now jump or I will kill you where you stand. You see, that's another thing your daddy worried about—you can't swim."

Rowan stared straight into his eyes. "I'm not jumping."

"Stupid bitch." He jammed the weapon harder into her chest.

Hands suddenly grasped Woody's head and twisted violently. The snap of his neck echoed in the silence. Surprise captured his face, the gun slipped from his hand and then Woody Holder crumpled to the forest floor amid the decaying leaves and thick brush like a broken doll.

Julian stared at Rowan across the body of his newest victim. The air, the very movement of the earth seemed to stop. No matter that she had been expecting him, seeing him shook her. The gun Woody had dropped lay at her feet. She considered the chance of her being able to snatch it before Julian reached across the two or two-and-a-half feet between them and grabbed her.

Run, her mind screamed.

She couldn't.

Grab the gun.

She couldn't.

"It's good to see you, Rowan."

The sound of his voice seemed to send the world spiraling again and made her want to vomit. "I can't say the same about you, Julian."

He sighed. "However have we come to this place in our relationship, my dear Rowan?"

The peculiar combination of rage and regret and curiosity that roared inside her held her mute.

He nodded once as if he understood exactly what she felt. "You have questions about what happened."

He knew her far too well. "I do."

"My daughter was a brilliant young girl but, sadly, riddled with mental instability. Counseling, drugs, nothing seemed to help her. Then she heard about you and Raven, and Norah, of course. She was devastated and curious. She wanted to see what all the trouble between her mother and me amounted to. Even a rebellious teenager doesn't want her parents to split up. The need for unity is instinctive."

"So it's true, you and Norah were having an affair." It wasn't a question. She understood this now with complete certainty.

Julian smiled. "Are you certain you're prepared to hear the answer to that one?"

"Were you having an affair when you were her therapist?"

"Your mother needed many things. The comfort of physical pleasure was one of them."

"Was she really ill or did you make that part up to cover for your affair?"

"One day, perhaps you will know and understand. But not today, Rowan."

"Are you the reason she's dead?" Hatred and pain and a dozen other emotions whirled inside her like a hurricane.

"I suppose I am."

Another deep stab of anger burrowed into her. "Why did you kill my father? He had no idea who you were. He knew nothing about what you are. He was innocent in all this."

Julian continued to stare at her, said nothing.

Not taking her eyes from his, she lowered into a crouch and picked up the gun. To her surprise, he let her.

When she stood once more, he angled his head and searched her eyes. "Do you plan to kill me, Rowan?"

Was that what he wanted? Her to kill him? So she would carry that burden around with her for the rest of her life?

"Don't overanalyze the question, simply answer it," he said, irritation in his tone.

"I asked you why you killed my father." She wasn't going to do anything he told her to do. She wasn't that woman anymore. He had changed her life forever. Despite her best efforts, she trembled. Her fingers wrapped more tightly around the butt of the weapon.

Just kill him.

No. There was something she needed first. "I want to know the truth, Julian. Why my father? And what happened to my sister...to your daughter?"

For a moment he merely continued staring at her, then he finally spoke. "I've always tried to protect you, Rowan. First from my daughter. She was determined to destroy your mother, you and Raven. I followed her here, but by the time I arrived I was too late. She had drowned Raven right there." He pointed to the water. "And she was dead. There was nothing I could do for either of them, so I left. But that day—" he drew in a deep breath "—that very day I made a vow to always look after you, Rowan, and your mother. And I have. Always."

"I don't believe you." Her words were a feral growl. She wanted to watch him die more than she wanted to take her next breath. "What did you do to my mother? You obviously weren't looking after her or you would have known she was contemplating suicide."

"I tried. Sadly, I was unable to help her. But I have tried to protect you, Rowan. I prompted that bitch Juanita into telling me what Woody was doing. She was helping him in his efforts to unsettle you. It's a shame I had to torture her unsuspecting brother to make her talk."

Sheer hatred boiled up inside Rowan. "If you were trying to protect me, why did you kill Officer Miller? He was there to protect me!"

Julian laughed. "He was asleep on the job. He wasn't protecting you!"

She shook her head, steadied her aim at him. "What about my father? You had no reason to murder my father or the man who was protecting him. They were both innocent in all this. Innocent," she repeated.

When he didn't answer, she shook her head. "I already know the answer. You killed him because I loved him more than you." Her own words assaulted her, tore open all her most tender places. "How could you not have known that? He was my father." A single tear slipped past her valiant attempts to keep them in check. "Of course I loved him more than anyone else in the world."

She wanted to tear off his head. She wanted to gut him like a hog at the spring kill.

"Are *you* going to kill me now, Rowan?"

Her fingers tightened on the weapon. "There's a very good chance I will."

"Then I suppose you should know the truth." His own fury glinted in his eyes.

She waited, her entire being urging her to pull the damned trigger.

"In the event we run out of time, you should be aware that I left you a gift for the second time," he said, the anger suddenly gone from his eyes and his tone. "Perhaps one day you'll appreciate my kindness."

"Why did you kill my father?" she demanded, out of patience.

"Because he killed my daughter."

His words were like a sudden, swift blow. She shook with the impact, couldn't breathe for several seconds. "That's impossible."

"He had warned Alisha to stay away from his daughters, but she, of course, did not. When Raven called him from the party and told him all the things Alisha was saying and how devastated she was, Edward rushed to her. But Alisha stepped out of the woods before he reached the party. He stopped the car and demanded to know where Raven was and Alisha gladly showed him. My daughter had drowned his. It wasn't bad enough that I had taken his wife's love from him. Edward lost control—those are his words—he strangled Alisha and then he hid her body. For a time, he sat in the water holding his dead daughter. Finally, because he knew you still needed him, he went home as if nothing had happened."

Rowan shook her head. "I don't believe you."

"Believe what you wish. When your book was released I suppose it was my turn to lose control. I demanded a meeting with Edward. He confessed what he had done and dared to suggest that we were even. He wanted me to stay away from you, but that was never going to happen."

She'd heard enough. She refused to listen to any more of his lies.

"Put your hands up and get down on your knees." Killing him was too easy. He would pay for what he had done.

"Goodbye for now, Rowan."

When he turned his back, she aimed the weapon. "Julian! Stop or I will shoot!"

He kept walking.

"Julian!"

She squeezed the trigger. She saw his body jerk with the impact of the bullet. Then he disappeared into the trees.

The sound of backup tearing through the woods erupted seemingly all around her. The air sawing in and out of her lungs, Rowan scanned the woods. Where was Julian? She'd hit him.

Billy, followed by half a dozen other cops—including Clarence Lincoln—rushed toward her.

She pointed in the direction Julian had fled. "He disappeared in that direction. He's injured."

Everyone but Billy took off after Julian.

She found her voice. It felt weak and wobbly. "Woody was going to kill me. He intended to make it look as if I had killed myself." She took a breath. "Julian killed him."

Billy reached for the weapon in her hand. "You okay?"

"I think so." But she wasn't, not entirely. She wouldn't be okay until she knew she had stopped Julian.

Maybe not even then.

Twenty-Four

"Let's go over this one more time."

Weary of Dressler's questions, Rowan slumped her shoulders. "How many times do I need to tell you the same story?"

She knew the answer. Until he was satisfied that she was not holding anything back. She had told this same story to Billy twice, and then Dressler had blown into his office and demanded she start over, again and again and again.

Julian had disappeared. They'd found blood. She had definitely wounded him, but he had vanished.

"You received the text from an unknown number and you suspected it was Julian," Dressler prompted.

"Yes. Woody intercepted me when I stopped at the funeral home for my weapon. He took me to the lake so he could dispose of me since Chief Brannigan and I uncovered his body parts brokering ring. He and a still unidentified partner were salvaging parts from the dead and selling them. That's all I know at this point."

She had no idea how many bodies turned over to the care of DuPont Funeral Home had been abused in this manner. They had learned that he'd worked at Gardner's even longer, so some of the stolen body parts may have come from there. What they did know was that Dr. Jared Knowles was not his partner. Detective Lincoln had confirmed his innocence.

"Dr. Addington knew nothing of his daughter's murder," Dressler stated as if he still didn't believe what Rowan had told him three times already.

"He stated that he believed Alisha killed my sister but he has no idea what happened to her. Not that I would trust anything he told me." She turned her hands up. "I've told you everything I know. Surely, we're done."

She had told Dressler and Billy everything...except what Julian said about her father murdering Alisha. Rowan didn't believe him and she refused to taint her father's memory with the bastard's lies. Her father would never have walked away from Raven's body like that. Never. She also didn't tell Dressler or Billy about the gift Julian claimed to have left her. She needed to know what he was talking about before she disclosed that detail. Not that she wanted one damned thing from him but it could be a clue about her mother or the truth about how Alisha died.

"May I go home now?" she asked when Dressler simply sat on the other side of the interview table, staring at her.

"It's enough," Billy spoke up from his position propped against the wall by the door. "If you still have questions, you can talk to her tomorrow."

Dressler threw up his hands. "Fine." He glared at Rowan for a moment. "But I'm not convinced you've been completely forthcoming, Dr. DuPont."

Rowan pushed to her feet. "So charge me with something."

When Dressler simply shook his head, Billy escorted her out of the interview room.

"Thank you," she murmured.

"I don't like that guy anyway," he whispered.

Rowan almost smiled. *Almost.*

The walk through the police station was oddly quiet. Everyone was out in the field searching for a man they would never find. Billy had ordered his officers to keep the news about Woody's death quiet until he had a handle on exactly what the man had been up to.

Outside, they loaded into his truck and headed for the funeral home. Rowan sank into the seat, exhaustion bearing down on her.

They'd barely reached the street when he said, "Tell me the part you're keeping from me, Ro."

She stared straight ahead. "I've repeated exactly what happened several times."

At the end of the first block beyond the station, Billy whipped to the curb. He turned in his seat and set his dark gaze against hers. "Don't do this to me, Ro. We've known each other for a long time. We're friends and I've always been here for you and I always will be, but I need to be able to count on the same from you. I know you wouldn't keep anything from me without a good reason and I respect your feelings, but you're not thinking straight on this one. No matter how strongly you feel about this case, I need you to trust me, Ro."

He was right, she couldn't do this to him—at least not all of it. "He said he left me a gift. I'm assuming it's at the funeral home."

The disappointment in Billy's eyes pierced her. She

shouldn't have kept that from him, not even for a minute. The other—well, that was for another time… She couldn't do that to her father. "I'm sorry. I don't know what I was thinking."

He made a few calls, and by the time they arrived at the funeral home, three other official vehicles—including Dressler's—were there. Billy unlocked the lobby door and passed the keys to Detective Lincoln, who hustled around to the rear door.

"Stay out here," Billy ordered her, "until I give the all clear."

There were a million things Rowan wanted to say to him, like the fact that there could be anything inside. "You shouldn't be the first one in, Billy."

The chief of police was not the right man to go in first.

He looked to the officer standing closest to Rowan. "Don't let her out of your sight."

She wanted to be angry, but she had a feeling the energy would be wasted. She'd held out on him and now he was going to override her warning. Just like when they were kids.

But they weren't kids anymore and this wasn't as simple as who could ride his or her bicycle the fastest.

This was life and death.

He ignored her plea and walked inside, weapon drawn.

For fifteen minutes Rowan hardly managed a breath. She remained braced for gunfire or an explosion. Terrified of what could happen beyond those walls.

Finally, the door opened again and Freud burst out.

Rowan's knees gave way and she barely caught herself. She dropped into a crouch and hugged the animal. She murmured softly to him while he sniffed and licked at her. Then she realized what Julian had meant about leaving her a gift for the second time. He'd left Freud alive in her home in Nashville when he'd murdered her father and the police officer assigned to his security detail.

Billy walked out and handed her a plastic evidence bag. "He left you a note."

Hands shaking in spite of her best efforts, she accepted the bag and stared at Julian's bold, elegant strokes on the piece of funeral home stationery.

Holder intended to kill Freud when he was finished with you. I've never had any tolerance for anyone who abuses animals. J

Strange coming from a serial killer. Rowan passed the bag back to Billy. "We're not going to find Julian. We're wasting time and resources. We should leave that to Dressler." She said this knowing the agent was striding toward her. "Woody wasn't smart enough or ambitious enough to run a black market body parts operation on his own. He had an accomplice. We need to find his partner. That should be our focus."

Billy said nothing. He was still angry with her.

Dressler stopped next to Billy and held out his hand. "I'll take that, Chief."

His gaze still glued to hers, Billy handed the agent the evidence bag. "You can take the search for Addington from here, Dressler. I have my own cases to solve."

Rowan had never appreciated Billy's alliance more than she did at that moment.

While Dressler and his team searched every inch of

the funeral home, Rowan sat on a bench outside and showered Freud with attention.

Her phone vibrated in her back pocket. They'd found it in Woody's car. Clarence Lincoln had tossed it back to her rather than putting it into evidence. Rowan was grateful. She owed the man one.

Rowan didn't recognize the number but it was a local one, so she answered.

"Rowan, this is Patty. My sister and I found a document and we thought it might be important to learning the truth about what happened to our father."

"What sort of document?" Rowan's full attention shifted to the conversation.

"It's some sort of authorization saying that my father's body was being donated for research. But that can't be right. Mother would never have permitted that even if my father had told her to, and I don't think he would have."

"Your mother's signature is on the document?" Based on what Patty and Jennifer had told her, that couldn't be right.

"Yes, but it's not her signature. It's forged."

Rowan was familiar with the type of document to which Patty referred. "Did a representative from Du-Pont sign it?"

"It has your father's signature on it."

"Can you take a photo of the document and text it to me?"

"I'll do that right now."

"Thank you, Patty. I assure you we'll have the whole story soon." That was as much as she could share, but she had promised to keep the sisters informed and she'd needed to give them some sort of update.

The call ended and Rowan's phone vibrated with an

incoming text. She enlarged the photo. Rowan's heart dropped to her shoes. The signature wasn't her father's, but she recognized it immediately.

Billy parked in front of the house and Rowan stared at it, her heart breaking.

"You sure you want to be part of this, Ro?"

She nodded. "I have to be."

She and Billy climbed out of his truck and started up the walk. The man she had adored like an uncle her entire life sat on the porch, a glass of tea in his hand.

He didn't speak, just sipped his tea while they climbed the steps and then sat down on the porch with him. Rowan felt as if her heart was being ripped from her chest.

She moistened her lips and managed to utter one word: "Why?"

Herman's mouth worked a bit before the words came out. "Well, it's a sort of long story."

Billy held up a hand. "Before you start, Herman, I need to advise you of your rights."

Rowan felt as if she were falling into a hole, and the hum of Billy's voice was all around her, reciting the words she knew all too well to the man she had loved her whole life.

"When Estelle was diagnosed with cancer," Herman said, "there was nothing they could do for her except this experimental treatment that the insurance company wouldn't pay for." He turned up his tea and took a swallow before meeting Rowan's gaze. "I know you're disappointed in me, but I would have done anything to keep her alive. Anything at all. And, God forgive me, I would do it again." He nodded in emphasis of his words. "I found out completely by accident what Woody was up to over at Gardner's and I made him cut me in on it. But I never let him do it at DuPont's." He shook his head adamantly. "Nope. I wouldn't do that to your daddy. What he did to Mr. Phillips was behind my back. When Geneva came to me, right here at this house, I told her I'd get to the bottom of it. When I went to Woody and demanded to know what the hell he had been thinking, I had no idea what he planned to do to make the problem go away."

Herman fell silent for a long moment. "I wanted to kill him, but I knew if I did, I'd have no way to fund Estelle's treatments." He stared at his hands and the half-empty glass. "I told myself it wasn't hurting anyone but I was wrong." He met Rowan's gaze again. "Now who's going to take care of her? I wasn't honest with you before. The truth is, the cancer is back, more aggressive than ever. And now this. I've told her everything. She ran me out of the house, won't even talk to me."

Rowan drew in a sharp breath. It jammed in her throat for a moment, but somehow she managed to get the words out. "I will. You have my word. I will always take care of Estelle."

They both cried then. Rowan wanted to hug him but she couldn't. What Herman had done was wrong. Unforgivable. On top of their grievous crimes, he had allowed Woody to come into her home and to do things to make her feel unbalanced and uncertain of herself at an already vulnerable time.

Billy arrested him and escorted him to the cruiser that pulled to the curb in front of the house. He didn't put Herman in cuffs and Rowan was glad he hadn't. She didn't want to humiliate the man no matter that he had hurt her.

She went into the house to explain everything to Estelle but she was already gone. Judging by the empty bottle of painkillers and the empty, overturned water glass, she had decided to take her life. With the cancer back and after her husband confessed to her Rowan could only imagine how devastated the poor woman had been.

Of course Rowan couldn't be sure of exactly what had taken place. That was for a medical examiner to determine.

But it was over now…for both of them.

Twenty-Five

Sunday, May 12

Mother's Day hadn't been anything special for Rowan in a very long time. As a child, she and her father always journeyed to the cemetery and placed flowers on her mother's grave on this day each year. The first year Rowan had cried. After that one, she felt numb. Her only thought had been, what sort of mother chose to leave her child in such a selfish, uncaring way?

Eventually she had stopped wondering why and she'd gone on with her life. She no longer paid the slightest attention to Mother's Day. It was just another one of those holidays that were irrelevant to her intensely focused career mind.

Herman had told Rowan that all the way up to the last year of his life, her father had taken flowers to Norah's grave each Mother's Day and to Raven's grave on her birthday. Rowan intended to carry on those traditions because her father would have wanted her to do so. It was the right thing to do, she supposed.

This morning she had overseen the graveside service for Estelle Carter. Billy had allowed Herman to attend. Rowan would miss them both. But right now she intended to enjoy dinner with Billy and his family. Billy's mother, Dottie, and his father, Wyatt, were amazing people. She wouldn't allow all that had happened to spoil this day for them.

Rowan stood on the back porch of the house where Billy had grown up. The pastures spread out for as far as the eye could see. Horses grazed on the left and a few cows on the right. Chickens chattered around the backyard. Nellie, their old bluetick hound, lay on the porch. Once in a while she swiped her tail back and forth, reminding anyone who might be watching that she was still alive. Freud lay beside Nellie. Rowan had worried he would chase the chickens but so far he only watched in avid curiosity. Still, when she went inside she would be taking Freud in with her.

Billy had insisted she come to dinner with him and his family. They didn't want her to be alone. They had no idea that she had been alone for a very long time, even before her father's death.

Her father had done all in his power to make her happy and to make up for the losses they had suffered that awful year so long ago, but he couldn't possibly. Rowan appreciated his efforts. He had been a very special man. A smile tugged at her lips. She missed him so much. Losing him had left a gaping hole in her life.

She would never believe Julian's twisted story about her father. More likely he had murdered Alisha himself.

If Julian hadn't shown that day at the lake, it was possible Woody would have shot her. She certainly had intended to fight him every step of the way but he had been the one with the gun. Apparently Julian had been watching her. He hadn't sent anyone else to do the job for him. The idea that he would take such a risk still stunned her.

Was he that convinced that he could outmaneuver law enforcement? Of course he was. Julian would be the first to admit his arrogance. A man couldn't be as brilliant as he was without knowing as much.

Would he still be watching?

Rowan doubted he would be quite so obvious. Though he clearly had some bizarre obsession with Rowan, he was not a fool.

The screen door behind her opened, and Rowan glanced over her shoulder. Billy walked out, a beer in each hand.

"Dinner's almost ready," he announced as he handed her a beer.

"Thanks." Rowan sipped the cold beer, savored the taste and enjoyed the feel of the sweating bottle in her hand. "I needed a moment."

Billy leaned against the railing that encircled the porch. "You're at home here, Ro. You don't need to explain needing a minute alone."

"Your mom and dad are still as kind as ever."

After Norah had died, Billy's mom had tried so hard to make Rowan feel mothered every chance she got. She'd taken her for her first manicure and several other firsts that only a woman could handle properly. Rowan would always be thankful for how Dottie had stepped in to help.

"They love you like a daughter." Billy smiled. "Momma always wanted a daughter."

Rowan studied her friend for a long moment. "You should get married, Billy, and give her one."

He looked away, focused on gulping down half his

beer. Then he swiped his mouth and chuckled. "Well, that isn't exactly a simple thing, Ro."

She propped a shoulder against the porch post next to him and stared at him in defiance. "Why not? You're an attractive, intelligent man with a powerful position in the community. Women should be lining up to be Mrs. Billy Brannigan."

His gaze shifted again and another gulp of beer disappeared from his bottle.

Rowan shook her head. "I'm sorry. I shouldn't have made such a cavalier statement. I'm fully aware it's not as simple as that. You're more like me than I realized. We're so focused on our work, there's hardly time left for anything else."

He nodded, still not meeting her gaze. "Work is my significant other."

"You know," she ventured, "you can't afford to keep two of your officers watching me 24/7 for God knows how long. Moving forward, we have to face the fact that I'm going to take care of myself."

His dark eyes held hers for a long moment. "You know he'll be back. He won't stop coming until he has what he wants."

He was right. If that wasn't bad enough, Anna Addington apparently did intend to stay in Winchester until she had the answers she sought. Not to mention there was Detective Barton. And Agent Dressler. All eyes were on Rowan. If the world was lucky, Julian would come after her again soon, and Billy or Dressler or Barton would capture him.

Except she wasn't so sure he could be caught.

Rowan bit her lips together and nodded. "I just have to be prepared for him next time, that's all. I really can take care of myself, Billy." She met his gaze, hoped he saw the certainty in her own. "You've trained me well. I did wound him, you know."

Billy nodded. "You damned sure did. I'm proud of you, Ro."

This surprised her. "Then you agree that I can take care of myself?"

He inclined his head and studied her. "Maybe, but you have to promise me that you'll be extra careful, always watchful, and you'll carry your weapon at all times. And come to the firing range with me twice every month."

"I can do that."

Billy made a face. "That was way easier than I expected."

"I don't intend to make whatever Julian has in mind easy." She had no desire to end up another of his victims.

"We can start with a refresher course tomorrow if you like," Billy suggested.

"You're on."

Dottie appeared at the door. "Enough shop talk, you two. Dinner's ready."

Rowan's heart felt light as she and Billy followed his mother inside. He pulled out her chair and then settled beside her at the big family dining table. Mr. Brannigan did the same for his wife. They laughed and talked and ate and Rowan felt normal for the first time in a very long time.

Who knew how long that would last.

* * * * *

*Dr. Rowan DuPont is back in
the next installment of The Undertaker's Daughter
coming in October from Debra Webb and
MIRA Books. The heart-pounding twists will have you
rushing to turn the page! Julian Addington isn't the
only serial killer watching Rowan and following her
home...*

THE UNDERTAKER'S DAUGHTER

Twelve hours earlier...

Her chest threatened to explode but she couldn't stop. She had to keep running.

He was coming.

It was dark…so dark. Her head felt thick and foggy. Couldn't think. Mouth was dry. She tried to swallow. Impossible.

Where was she?

Didn't matter…didn't matter.

She was dead if he caught her. She understood this with complete certainty. He would kill her and that was all that mattered. The fact that she didn't know him was inconsequential. That she was a good person was equally irrelevant. She had never purposely hurt anyone. She obeyed the law. Went to work. Was kind to her neighbors. Patient with kids and old people.

None of that mattered. He was going to kill her and she didn't even know why.

Run.

Faster.

Her legs felt so heavy. Running in sand. Like on the beach. She remembered running on the beach. *Vacation.* A smile tugged at her lips. Just last summer. A long overdue week away from work…away from all the crap in her life. She could go back there this summer… or maybe she'd just go now.

All she had to do was close her eyes and float away.

She felt herself falling, falling. She went down on one knee, then collapsed onto the ground. Her eyes were too heavy to open. Her body would no longer cooperate no matter that she told herself to get up…to keep running.

Too hard.

The sand…

Her hand lay splayed across the ground. Not sand… not dirt. *Carpet*, or a rug. She was in a building…it was a house…something.

Her mind suddenly rocketed back to the here and now.

Her eyes still refused to cooperate with her brain. A new rush of fear fired through her veins.

She couldn't move…could not escape.

Footsteps came nearer and nearer.

He was here. Standing over her.

She'd come to his home willingly. Images flashed in slow motion inside her head. She'd trusted him. Wanted him. He wasn't like all the jerks her age.

Her heart thumped hard. *No.* He was worse.

He was a killer.

And now she was going to die.

One

"**O**ur killer chooses his victims and ends their lives basically by euthanizing them. He then meticulously prepares their bodies specifically for your discovery, Detectives."

Rowan DuPont surveyed the group of homicide detectives seated around the small conference table. "Beyond the fear they suffer upon capture and during the hours before he fatally sedates them, they experience no true physical discomfort. These are soft kills, not intended for the gore or the violence."

"You're certain the perp is a *he*, Dr. DuPont?" Lieutenant April Jones, the only female detective in the room, asked. "We've found no evidence of sexual assault. With this sort of soft kill, in my experience this is a method most often utilized by a female killer."

Rowan crossed her arms over her chest and considered the barrage of crime scene photos lining the story-board. "The reason we can safely assume the unknown subject is male is, in part, based on the way he dresses his victims, the abundance of flowers he uses around the bodies. It's almost like a courtship, but not. It's more a 'look at this—see what I'm doing.' None of this careful staging is about these two women." She gestured to the diagram of evidence she had arranged for this morning's briefing. "Because neither of these women is his true victim—the one he really wants to take from this life."

Frowns and grumbles worked through the team. No one wanted to hear that particular conclusion. But Rowan could only call it the way she saw it. Her instincts would not allow her to see these murders any other way. They were too clean, too *soft*. The unsub had gained no pleasure from these acts, shown no real passion.

Almost a decade ago while serving as an adviser on a case with the Metropolitan Nashville Police Department, she realized this was what she wanted to do when she completed her residency. Having graduated at the top of her class at Vanderbilt and spent four years of residency at the largest psychiatric hospital in Nashville and then an additional two-year fellowship in forensic psychiatry, Rowan had been handpicked for Metro's new, elite Special Crimes Unit. Now, six years later, though she neither possessed a gold shield nor carried a weapon, she felt as much a pivotal part of the department and this unit as any of the detectives waiting expectantly for her to continue.

"I'm not sure I follow," Jones admitted.

Jones was the senior detective in SCU. She was one of the first female detectives allowed into the formerly all-male territory of the worst crimes one human could commit against another. There had been a time when female cops were considered too weak and too emotional for homicide. No more. Detectives like April Jones and her peers had long ago disproved that theory. Still, their male counterparts outnumbered them. But that was changing. It was no longer a boy's club by any means.

"We'll get back to that in a moment," Rowan assured Jones.

Another thing Rowan had learned well was that when she presented a more unusual aspect to an investigation, she needed to make her case first. The folks in this room were the cream of the crop at Metro—experienced and decorated. They knew how to conduct an investigation into the truly bizarre with one eye closed and one hand tied behind his or her back. When someone stood in front of this elite team and announced that their usual way of doing things wouldn't work, there had to be solid reasoning behind the theory.

"You list his goal as revenge," Detective Tom Bennett noted. "Revenge for what?"

"That, Detective Bennett—" Rowan moved toward the end of the board where she'd outlined her conclusions on this killer's story "—is the sixty-four-million-dollar question to which we all want the answer."

"Sixty-four-thousand-dollar question," Lieutenant Jones corrected.

Though fifteen years Rowan's senior, Jones likely wasn't old enough to remember the 1940s radio quiz show or the television show that came later but most everyone knew the idiom. "Inflation, Detective, inflation."

The older woman chuckled and gave her a nod of acquiescence.

Rowan turned back to her storyboard. "Our killer has a goal. And, yes, I believe the motive for that goal is revenge. He wants to make someone pay and these murders are a way of paving the path toward accomplishing that goal. His dilemma is simple—how does he achieve his ultimate goal without getting caught?" She turned once more to the avid listeners gathered in the room. "He has made it abundantly clear that he does not wish to be caught. We know this because he hasn't left a single clue. Not one shred of evidence."

"What makes you so certain," Bennett pushed, "that our two vics aren't just the type of women he likes to kill? Doing it softly or not, maybe murdering gorgeous blondes is the only way he can get off."

The others, all but Jones, laughed. Jones glared at Bennett. No matter that she was older than any of those present and outranked the whole lot, Jones no doubt considered them dirty old men. Rowan certainly did. Bennett wanted an answer to the question Jones had asked moments ago and he hoped rephrasing the query and bullying it back into the conversation would force Rowan to alter the course she'd chosen to take. Patience was running out. In a homicide investigation every minute counted and Rowan had used up too many of those precious minutes. Sometimes she had to remind herself that not all on the team appreciated her *long way* of getting around to things. First, however, she intended to put the arrogant detective in his place.

"Detective Bennett, every man in this room has a penis," Rowan said in answer to his comment, "does that mean they're all dicks like you?"

The heat of humiliation spread across his face. "Yeah, yeah. Point taken."

"Things are not always as they seem." Rowan studied first one crime scene photo and then the next, mentally reviewing the art and language of the killer's work. The way he'd poised the bodies was undeniably a work of art.

Two beautiful women in their late thirties had been carefully selected. Sandy Tyler and Karen Ross. Both had long blond hair and blue eyes. Each had a slim build and was medium height. These were well-educated women with enviable careers. Unmarried. No children. Upscale downtown apartments.

The epitome of the hip, sophisticated, urban woman.

Once their unsub had chosen his victim, he abducted her or lured her from a place she frequented, suggesting he'd familiarized himself with her routine. This took days or weeks and endless patience, unwavering determination. Within forty-eight to sixty hours after the abduction her body was discovered in a public place, staged as if she'd been prepared for burial. The meticulous attention to detail and the sheer intricacy of his staging required a great deal of planning. Compared with the short time he kept his victims, the timing was more solid proof that he had no desire to linger, to enjoy his work or any pleasures the victim's presence might offer. These two women were a means to an end and nothing more. Not special or important to him in any way beyond making some sadistic statement only he understood at this point.

"He dresses his victims in simple cotton gowns," Jones said, "arranges their hair over their shoulders, crosses their arms over their breasts and then surrounds their bodies with red rose petals. What's the significance of the gowns? Purity? And the rose petals—blood?"

"The cotton gowns are plain, simple, that's true," Rowan agreed as she turned back to Jones and the others, "but that doesn't mean the choice to use those particular gowns was a simple one. I believe these organic gowns were chosen for their quick decomposition rate. The cotton would decay fairly quickly."

"I've narrowed down the orders that shipped to Nashville in the past six months," Detective Lex Keaton, the newest member of the team, offered. "We're still looking at forty buyers who walk into the shops that carry these particular ones. I'm whittling away at that list."

"Why bother with a swift decomp rate if he wanted the bodies found quickly, which he obviously did?" Bennett remained unconvinced of Rowan's working theory.

"He wants us to know that he could have masked that clue if he'd chosen to do so. If the bodies hadn't been found for several months, we wouldn't have a way to narrow down the type of gown worn by the victims or who bought them because that clue would have disintegrated."

"I thought you said he doesn't want to be caught," Bennett countered, that smugness creeping back into his tone.

"He doesn't," Rowan reiterated. "Those forty buyers are purchasing the product from one of six shops in the greater Nashville area. If a customer walks into one of those shops and pays with cash, tracking him down is virtually impossible. He could be anyone, anywhere in this city. Our unsub knows this. He's playing with us. Building up our hopes only to let us down."

"The flowers," Jones said, moving on to the second part of her question. "What is the significance of the flowers?"

"The flowers are fresh." Rowan thought of the pungent scent of the roses at each of the crime scenes. The killer had chosen the type carefully—as he did all other details. He selected a rose with a strong scent.

"These are not petals bought in bulk, though there is a vast amount left with each body." Yet another aspect of the killer's need to play games. Rowan sensed his seemingly contradictory decisions were perhaps even intended as an insult to their intelligence. "We believe the roses are grown locally. The lack of preservatives and fertilizers found by the lab suggests a responsible grower. Someone who cares for the environment as well as the beauty and fragrance of the plant. Yet another aspect of his work designed to give us a glimmer of hope that we'll be able to track him down, only to find it's another dead end."

"So do they represent blood?" David Wells asked.

Wells was the youngest of the four detectives assigned to the case. Rowan felt confident there was a reason—probably nepotism since he was related to the chief of police—he'd made detective so quickly and slipped right into the Special Crimes Unit. None of the others had complained since the young man carried his weight, but that pass would only last until he made his first misstep.

"Our killer carefully washes the bodies before dressing them and placing the flowers around them, even sprinkling a good number on top of the bodies. It's my opinion," Rowan said in answer to the question, "that he uses the flowers because the bodies are not embalmed."

"To camouflage the stink," Bennett said in his usual, coarse manner.

"Very good, Detective." Rowan wished she had a gold star to stick on his nose. "Before the process of embalming came into widespread use, it was a common practice to surround the dead with flowers and other plants with strong fragrances to help mask the odor of the rotting corpse. By surrounding and sprinkling his victims with the rose petals, he's depicting a burial scene. He wants us to recognize that he's honoring the sacrifice of his victims. They've given their lives for him—to help him achieve his goal."

"Honoring?" Jones questioned. "How do you figure that? He kills them. How is that honoring a person by any stretch of the imagination?"

"He regrets their sacrifices were necessary, a pleasant disposal ritual is the least he can do. Most killers simply dump the bodies of their victims. Our unsub is killing two birds with one stone, assuaging his conscience and giving us something to ponder."

"He sure as hell isn't giving us any usable evidence," Bennett muttered.

"It's true that he leaves no evidence to help us identify him or to narrow down where he commits these heinous acts, but there are some things that are out of his control," Rowan reminded all present, particularly Bennett. "The human body tells us many things. Above all else it provides a distinct road map—a story, if you will—of the life lived, the bumps along the way. Injury, disease. It reveals how it was treated by the environment, the home or the lack thereof, in which it lived and by those taking care of it like spouses, children, caregivers."

"The Language of Death," Wells said with a grin. "I read your book, Dr. DuPont. You read the bodies like a story. The story helps you build a character sketch of the killer. You use that story to figure out his motivation and the conflicts involved with attaining his goal."

Rowan was impressed. This was the first case for Wells as a member of this unit. He'd done his homework. Always a good sign. "Very good, Detective. Now you know my secret."

It wasn't rocket science or a part of the psychic realm. It was simply paying attention to what the body told her. Every victim had a voice that had been silenced, but the body still told the story loudly and, on occasion, quite clearly. Warmth spread through Rowan's chest as she considered that her father had taught her this. As a fourth generation funeral home director and mortician, her father knew a thing or two about death. He swore by the adage that a person's body at death told the story of their life. One only needed to pay attention. If that wasn't enough, she'd grown infatuated with the psychopathy of serial killers when she chose her first topic for the pursuit of academic publication. It was that publication in a medical journal that first put her on Metro's radar.

"Wait a minute," Bennett said, his gaze narrowing. "I just had an epiphany, Doc." He stood and swaggered up to the storyboard. "Every time our guy kills one of these gorgeous blue-eyed blondes—" he gestured to the photos of the victims "—he's killing *you*."

Rowan stared at the photos provided by the families—photos taken before the women were murdered. Unfortunately, Detective Bennett had a valid point. She was the perfect example of the killer's preferred victim. Like the others in the room, it wouldn't be the first time she had been some sort of target if that were the case. Her work with Metro was widely publicized, particularly during a case like this one. The release of her first book three months ago had put her face on television screens more than once in recent weeks. It was certainly possible she had inadvertently awakened this beast.

Uneasiness slid through her. Maybe *she* was the intended victim.

All the more reason to find him quickly.

Two

Rowan ignored her salad and stared out at the lake that bordered the hotel property. She couldn't shake the comment Detective Bennett had made.

...he's killing you.

Obviously, she had considered the idea. With her blond hair and blue eyes and the ages of the victims, of course she had. She wasn't oblivious to the possibility. Beyond those similarities there was absolutely no reason to believe this case had anything to do with her. Until the detectives discovered some piece of evidence that linked her personally to the murders, she had no intention of borrowing trouble.

She'd done enough of that for one lifetime before she was twenty.

"This case is getting under your skin, Dr. DuPont."

She blinked away this nagging thought and focused on the man across the table. Dr. Julian Addington, her longtime friend and a renowned psychiatrist with multiple critically acclaimed publications to his credit, had invited her to lunch. A much-needed distraction. It was rude of her to ignore him or the lovely restaurant he'd chosen. The view, the atmosphere and the company were pleasant. She had no excuse save her inability to fully extract herself from the case—an ongoing problem lately.

"I'm sorry." She picked up her fork and stabbed a lettuce leaf. "I keep thinking about the way he prepares the bodies as if he is well versed in the steps of a funeral preparation."

"His efforts are that detailed?" Julian searched her face, a frown marring the familiar features of his.

Like her, he was a natural blond though his hair was more a grayish white than blond these days. His eyes were a darker shade of blue. Even at sixty-six, he remained quite handsome and most distinguished looking. Like her father, he was tall and lean, though unlike her father, Julian worked out religiously. He believed a strong body was part of maintaining a strong mind. The man still ran in marathons. More important than all those things, he was a good and caring friend. He was the one to turn her life around at a particularly dark moment.

"His work is very detailed," she confirmed. "The soap and shampoo are common ones utilized by funeral homes across the country. Rather than suture, he uses superglue for the eyes and lips—many morticians do the same. Even the cotton he selects to fill the various orifices is a common trade brand. He wants us to understand that he knows what he's doing. For some reason, he feels that knowledge is relevant to achieving his goal."

"It's as if he is speaking directly to *you*."

Funny how that theme appeared determined to echo today.

"Yes." The confession made breathing marginally

easier. She'd picked at the idea like an irritating scab that wouldn't heal for the past two days. Part of her had wanted to put the theory out there for the detectives to debate, but another part of her wanted to ignore the signs.

"That said," she qualified, "I'm not prepared to conclude that these murders are about me—not at this time anyway. The unsub has made no contact with me directly and he's left no tangible suggestion that I'm his intended target. Frankly, there are far too many other, more viable avenues to explore first."

No matter how rational her declaration sounded and how solid the reasoning behind it, the words still felt hollow. *Too early to go there.* Not enough evidence. If she repeated the crucial phrase enough times, perhaps it would sink in and stick. Though she was not a detective, she was still a part of the investigative team. Making a case personal was never a good thing…unless the unknown subject left no choice. As she just told Julian, the unsub had not communicated directly with her or addressed any communication to or about her. Arriving at that conclusion was simply premature.

"The book has made you an even more high-profile figure." Julian sipped his tea, then settled the delicate bone china cup onto its saucer. "Growing up in a funeral home, the daughter of an undertaker, as well as the painful loss of both your mother and your twin sister have now been shared with the world. It's possible you have an admirer. Someone who commiserates with you, who feels as if he knows you better than you know yourself and he wants you to feel whatever he's feeling. Perhaps the victims are a gift—part of a courtship ritual, of sorts—to get your attention."

Rowan drew in a deep, cleansing breath and admitted—

to herself if to no one else—that her old friend had a valid point. One she'd already made to the team, leaving out the idea that she may be the target of the unsub's devotion. "He's not looking for attention, he wants some sort revenge. The victims are nothing more than a catalyst. With all due respect, I can't see this as any kind of courtship ritual in the usual sense. He's courting the end game, preparing his target for what's coming. Trying to get her attention."

Though she had used that same term loosely in today's briefing, the context had been completely different.

"You know as well as I," Julian countered, "that anger—the need for revenge or to punish—goes hand in hand with passion. The worst one human can do to another is often done by the spouse or the lover of a victim."

Rowan laughed in spite of the dire subject. "Well, then, we can eliminate me as a potential end game victim. I have no significant other, much less a spouse and I'm afraid my work is my lover."

Despite the concern furrowing his brow, Julian's lips quirked the tiniest bit. "What about any other aspects of the murders? The drug he uses? Is there anything else about the cause or manner of the deaths that relates to your life?"

A quick mental review of the autopsy and lab results sent ice slipping into her veins. "He used a similar drug to the one…I took all those years ago."

Julian's eyebrows lifted. "But not the same one."

"Not the same name, but the same effects. It works quickly and basically renders the victim incapacitated."

She'd swallowed a handful of a similar drug her freshman year in college. Her throat tightened. Since it wasn't the same one, she really hadn't given any weight to the drug in terms of a personal connection. Had she purposely been blocking a similarity that hit too close to home? It was completely unlike her to allow her objectivity to slip so badly. "There was water in the first victim's lungs. Not a significant amount, but some."

"Again, the same as what was found in yours," Julian suggested. "Except you survived."

She nodded, the move jerky. The doctors had said Rowan was extremely lucky. Her hair had been soaking wet when she was found in that tub. After the sedative had done its work, she had slipped under the water. Somehow, she'd beaten the odds and risen back to the surface before it was too late. Her father had insisted she'd had a guardian angel watching over her. Maybe her mother or her sister had reached down from heaven and saved Rowan. But Rowan hadn't believed in angels—still didn't.

"Or perhaps," Julian went on, "he only wanted the lab to find enough water in her lungs to remind you of the sister you lost."

Images and voices whispered through Rowan's mind. Before she could respond, he continued, "And what about the wounds on her wrists? They were slashed and then sutured, another common denominator between you and the victims. Perhaps his interest is more focused on you than you are prepared to concede."

Her fingers instinctively tugged at her sleeves to ensure her own scars were covered. She hadn't shared that aspect of her past with the team, but like the rest of the world they had likely read about it in her book. Frankly, she didn't want to see any of this, didn't want to have to face the fact that her being the target was a viable possibility. She felt suddenly uncomfortable, even with her old friend. Her careful focus on her work generally grounded her. If she were completely honest with herself, her work was her life. To have any aspect of work complicated with her personal life was not something with which she was prepared to deal.

And yet she had bared herself in the book. That decision would haunt her the rest of her days, she feared. Why oh why had she allowed her editor to lure her into that tell-all trap?

Baring one's soul sells books, Rowan.

Rather than confess the gale of uncertainty currently spiraling inside her, she produced a sad smile for her dear friend. "I'm afraid that most people would have trouble finding me interesting by any distortion of the definition. Besides, these are not particularly unique characteristics amid the population of a metropolitan area the size of Nashville."

This was statistically accurate no matter that her instincts were sounding off warning bells—the same ones she had been purposely ignoring for approximately two days.

Of all people, you know better than to ignore your instincts, Rowan.

"But those are characteristics unique to you." Julian leaned forward and put his hand over hers. "The time for plausible deniability is over, Rowan. You cannot allow your need to save professional face any level of priority over your personal safety."

His words haunted her the rest of the afternoon.

North Avenue, 11:10 p.m.

Clad in her robe, her feet bare, Rowan padded down to the front door to check the locks a second time. The expansive windows that made up her mostly glass-and-steel home had captivated her at first. She had loved the straight lines and gleaming surfaces…the feeling of infiniteness. Of late, all that openness—especially like now, to the dark night—had become imprisoning. More and more she found herself hiding in areas of the house that had walls impenetrable to the eyes of the night.

The case. *This case.* The one the detectives in the SCU had dubbed the Undertaker was getting to her. She shook her head. Even when the team had given the case that moniker, she'd ignored the correlation to her history.

Freud, her German Shepherd, had faithfully followed her down the stairs. When she was home, he stayed close. His need to do so had crowded her at first; now she appreciated his nearness. Freud was a good and loyal companion with few demands. Like her, he had a past that had left him damaged and broken beneath the surface where no one else could see. That same past had permitted a bond between them—the kind of bond she rarely allowed in her life.

She checked the double set of dead bolts she'd had installed on the front door in addition to the door's locking handle, then leaned forward to peer at the keypad to verify that she'd set the alarm. She'd left her glasses upstairs on the bedside table. The aging body's growing dependency on things like prescription eyewear was subtlety terrifying. Thank God for contacts. At least the rest of the world didn't have to be privy to her weaknesses. It was as if the closer she drew to forty, the more she fell apart.

Eight months to go until the big four-oh. She groaned and hugged herself as she stared out at the darkness. Streetlamps fought valiantly to light the night but failed miserably beyond a pale circle of gold around their bases. She'd been so excited when the contemporary home that could only be called a masterpiece of progressive architecture came on the market. The West End location was mere steps from coffee shops and restaurants and Centennial Park. West End Avenue provided a major transit corridor for easy access to anywhere in or beyond the city.

What more could a single, unburdened with children woman ask for? A hip neighborhood as well as the perfect home for someone who wanted to bring the outside in and who had nothing to hide.

Except she had lied to herself and recently those lies had started to fester, and now they were erupting to the surface.

The scars on her wrists stung as if the wounds had only been inflicted yesterday instead of when she was thirteen and certain she wanted to die—to be with her mother and her sister who had died the year before.

Not just her sister, her *twin*. She and Raven had been mirror images, best friends. They had done everything together. Or at least they had until their twelfth summer. Raven was suddenly popular with the other kids while Rowan remained the outcast. The more popular her sister became, the more condescending her attitude had become. Suddenly, Raven was one of the in girls, the snobbish, mean girls. The invitations came to Raven—like the one to the party at the lake house of one of the wealthy families in town—but not to Rowan. Rowan had begged her sister not to go. Not just for purely selfish reasons, either. She'd felt a suffocating dread; a panic that had bordered on hysteria.

Raven went anyway and, for a very long while, Rowan had hated her for it.

Three hours later the phone rang with devastating news, but Rowan had known her sister was gone before the call came. Her father stoically identified Raven at the morgue, yet when the body was brought to the funeral home for final disposition her father had been inconsolable. He had refused to allow anyone to touch her, and insisted on preparing her himself.

Rowan vividly recalled hovering at the door of the preparation room, her own devastation barely contained and survivor's guilt eating her alive. She had watched as her father attempted to do what he must, the steps as familiar to her as breathing. She and Raven had been assisting their father since they were seven years old. Four generations of DuPonts had owned and operated the funeral home, each one passing the business down to the son or sons in the family.

Without any sons, Edward taught the family business to his daughters. By twelve, they were well versed in the family business. She and Raven knew the steps by heart even if they weren't physically strong enough to complete certain ones that involved lifting the bodies. That day, the day Raven died, Rowan went to her father's side when he broke down completely and helped him to prepare her sister. It was the least she could do. It was the last time she would touch the sister who was as much a part of her as the heart beating in her own chest.

The circumstances of her birth and her childhood ensured that Rowan was intimately acquainted with death from the very beginning of her life. Her grandfather DuPont had died the day before she and Raven came into the world. Edward insisted on taking a family photo before his father was buried. The twins were ensconced in the deceased DuPont's lap, with their mother and father on either side. It was the way of things during her formative years. Living had always been far more mysterious and fearful to her than death.

Not quite six months after Raven's death, their mother, Norah, hanged herself. More guilt piled onto Rowan's shoulders. If she had been the adoring daughter Raven had been, perhaps her mother would have wanted to stay rather than to follow the daughter she'd lost to death.

Rowan forced away the painful memories and drifted up the spiral staircase to her loft bedroom. Despite the teasing from the other children at school and in the neighborhood, growing up in the house that was also a funeral home never bothered her—not until Raven and then their mother died. Everything changed then. Rowan no longer felt whole. She became more withdrawn. Two attempts to commit suicide before she was twenty only added to the tragic history of her family. Looking back, she deeply regretted the hurt she had caused her father.

But those painful years were far behind her now. She had chosen a path in life that made her feel whole. She loved her work. Felt purposeful and productive.

Rowan climbed between the sheets and forced her eyes closed. Freud curled up on his own bed right next to hers. She refused to consider for another second the idea that this case was personal. Until she had evidence to support the theory that the unsub had targeted her, she would not waste time and resources acting upon the scenario.

Odds of this being about her or her book were remote at best.

Slowly, she slipped into a fitful sleep, dreams of

her sister and of walking the halls in the house where she grew up streamed through her restless mind. By 2:00 a.m. she was wide-awake, her childhood still rambling through her brain. The second and third stories of the massive Victorian-style house where she'd grown up served as the living quarters while the public part of the funeral home was on the first floor. In the mid 1950s a chapel was added, extending the first floor out from the west side of the house. For symmetry, a portico was built on the west side, allowing for more expansive covered parking for the hearses and family limousines.

The mortuary was in the basement. Her father had completely renovated that space and added the latest, state-of-the-art equipment when Rowan was a teenager. On the first floor the hardwood had been refinished, new paint and wallpaper. New, more welcoming and comfortable furnishings.

Only the best for the families who chose DuPont Funeral Home for their deceased loved ones. The renovations had no doubt been in part prompted by the upgrades done at Gardner's, the only other funeral home in town. Edward DuPont was nothing if not a savvy businessman.

Rowan tossed and turned until four, her eyes closing for the last time as the digital numbers slipped to 4:01. Images of the house and the meticulously manicured grounds that had been her childhood home slipped from her dreams only to be replaced by vivid color imageries of Raven. She and Raven had often stood face-to-face, staring at each other as if peering into a mirror. After her sister's death, Rowan continued to talk to her reflection for years. Talking to her sister as if she were still there had been a useful coping mechanism at first. But then the nightmares began.

In those heart-pounding dreams, Rowan would find herself on the banks of that lake—the one where her sister had drowned. The dark water would lure her like a beacon. Raven would beg her to come into the water.

Raven's cold, lifeless arms reached for Rowan. Her pale face looked sad, her eyes pleading. "Come into the water, Rowan. Come and play."

The voice echoed through Rowan's soul, had her fighting to withdraw from sleep. She told herself to wake up but the dream refused to let go.

"Hurry, Rowan! Come into the water with me. *Daddy's coming soon.*"

Three

Rowan couldn't shake the unsettling dreams that had invaded her sleep last night. Hard as she tried pouring herself into work, the images and voices just wouldn't let go.

"Dr. DuPont?"

Rowan pushed away the troubling thoughts and met the lieutenant's gaze. "I'm sorry, what did you say?"

April Jones set aside the interview reports the two of them had been reviewing. "Are you certain you're all right? You don't seem like yourself today. Usually you're laser focused on whatever we're working on, but it feels like you're not even in the room."

"I'm sorry. You're right. I'm distracted." Rowan reached for the next report, the one from the interview of Karen Ross's mother. "I didn't sleep well last night."

"It's the comment Bennett made, isn't it?"

Rowan could play off the question, but that would be futile if in fact this unsub chose another victim who looked like her and with whom she shared a similar background. Frankly, to continue ignoring the concept would not only be foolish it would be counterproductive.

"Yes," Rowan admitted. "I'm weighing the possibility that his suggestion carries more merit than perhaps I first believed. I wouldn't want anyone else to lose their life because we hadn't assessed all possible avenues."

Took you long enough to say the words out loud.

"Your book may have tripped some degenerate's trigger," Jones suggested. "He may be trying to prove you're not as brilliant as we all know you are. Or maybe he wants you to himself. Either way, the sooner we acknowledge it's a possibility, the sooner we can properly protect you."

This was exactly what Rowan did not want. "I appreciate your concern, but I'm perfectly capable of taking care of myself, Lieutenant. I carry pepper spray. At home I have the best security system currently available and I have a big dog. I am always careful. I don't need a protection detail. It would be a waste of valuable resources. Resources that need to be focused elsewhere."

Jones raised her eyebrows. "We've gone over these interviews half a dozen times." She gestured to the stack of papers. "We haven't found anyone new in the victims' lives. No enemies. No recent falling-out with anyone. No trouble at work or at home. No financial issues. You hit the nail on the head with your conclusions about these women, Doctor. They're not who our guy has his sights set on. They're only foreplay for the big finale. I didn't sleep last night, either. My gut is telling me that he wants *you* to know he's coming. You are the big finale and we need to be prepared for that move."

There it was—the conclusion Rowan could no longer

deny. "I should take a break and check on my father. I need some fresh air anyway."

She stood. Jones didn't look very happy that Rowan had backed out of the conversation at such a pivotal juncture.

"I've already spoken to Captain Doyle," the detective plunged onward before Rowan could escape. "He's in agreement with the rest of us. We have to take this threat to you seriously, Dr. DuPont. We've danced all around it for days now. It's time to stop pretending this isn't about you. There are necessary steps that need to be taken."

Rowan wanted to be angry that Jones and probably Bennett had gone behind her back with this theory, but she wasn't a fool. "Give me a few minutes and we'll discuss the situation."

"Just make sure you go to the smokers' cage," Jones said, "otherwise, if you're going outside, I should go with you."

With a resigned sigh, Rowan assured her, "I'll be in the cage."

She couldn't exit the room fast enough. Rowan's chest felt exceedingly tight. Drawing in a breath was next to impossible. She needed five minutes out of this office—out of this building. Checking in on her father was a good excuse. Far too often, she found herself so caught up in a case that time slipped away. Her father—her only remaining family—was generally the one on the losing end of that scenario.

Fortunately, the elevator was deserted. She reached the lobby and hurried toward the west corridor, purposely avoiding eye contact. She fisted her cell and pushed through the exit that led to the only place on city property where the smokers were allowed to indulge their habit. The *cage*. The small area was closed in with steel mesh on all sides, and there was a roof along with four overhead fans to help circulate the air. Rowan imagined the winters were rather unpleasant but at least this space prevented folks from having to loiter in the parking lot as was the case when smoking was first abolished in any of the buildings. The enclosure as well as the cameras—she instinctively glanced toward the two well-placed dark domes—provided a measure of security and some degree of protection from the elements.

Luck was on her side once more—the cage was empty. Relieved, Rowan drew in a deep breath, her olfactory senses protesting the stench of stale cigarette butts in the receptacles made for their disposal. She could tolerate the unpleasant odor for a few minutes. God knew she had smelled far worse at the numerous crime scenes she'd studied over the past six years. Right now, she needed the trees and the sky and simply being outside the confining walls of her office and that damned conference room.

Daddy's coming soon.

The last words Raven had said to her in one of last night's fractured dreams shook her even now, in the glaring light of day. She should have called her father days ago. He had been the first thing on her mind this morning, but she'd been running late. She didn't call him often enough, certainly didn't visit like a daughter should.

She put through the call and the instant she heard his voice she relaxed the tiniest bit. "Hey, Daddy."

"Ro, sweetheart, what a pleasant surprise."

They chatted casually, playing catch up for a few minutes, before she moved to the heart of the matter. "Daddy, are you feeling okay? When was the last time you saw Dr. Lombardo?"

"Had a complete physical last week. Doc says I'm as healthy as a horse. You don't need to worry about me, little girl."

"That's great." Another flash of relief rushed through Rowan, making her knees weak. Her father had turned seventy his last birthday. She wanted to have him around for as long as possible even if she was far too negligent in her calls and visits.

"Why do you ask? Is everything all right with you?"

The note of worry in his voice made her feel even guiltier. In her thirty-nine years she'd given her father far more reason to worry than he would ever give her if he lived to be a thousand. She really had not been a very good daughter.

Exiling the painful thoughts, she said, "I'm fine. Everything okay with the business? Busy as usual, I guess."

"Don't you know it, little girl. If there's one thing in this life we can count on it's death. Won't ever be a shortage of the dying."

Her father had used that cold, hard fact to try and persuade her to follow in his footsteps in the family business. *You'll never lack for job security. There's something to be said for that, Ro. It's a respectable, reliable way to earn a living.* Choosing not to go into the family business was the other way she'd hurt her father. He'd been devastated for a time. So much so they hadn't spoken for an entire year after she'd shared her decision. But that had been a very long time ago. Since that unbearable time she'd tried hard to make up for their lost year.

"Can't argue with that," Rowan agreed with his assessment, more of that tight band of tension around her skull loosening, if only marginally.

"I was thinking about you this morning," he said. "I meant to call you on my lunch break."

She could picture her father peering down at whatever body he had stretched out on the prep table at present. One glove on, one off to answer the phone as blood and other bodily fluids drained away in preparation for being replaced by preserving chemicals.

"I was thinking of you, too." She smiled, deciding not to mention why. He would not be happy to hear that Raven still haunted her dreams twenty-six years after her death. Rowan had decided that some connections transcended death. She'd done extensive research on the bond between twins. She and her sister would be a part of each other as long as one of them continued breathing.

"I wanted to call and tell you that a friend of yours from up there in the big city stopped by yesterday," Edward announced. "Said he wanted to see the place where you grew up. I gave him the grand tour. He went on and on about what a big star you are with Metro."

Rowan frowned. She hoped it wasn't some reporter digging for information to be used in a scathing article related to her book. Though she was grateful her book was doing so well, she had not anticipated the more unpleasant aspects of success. With the admiration and respect shown by most of her readers came hostility and condemnation from a few others.

"Really? What was his name?"

"Name was Tyler Ross. The way he went on, I thought for sure you'd been holding out on me. Especially since he's an undertaker, too."

Her father kept talking, but Rowan stuck on the name—Tyler Ross. Sandy *Tyler*… Karen *Ross*. It was a combination of surnames from the victims. The two victims who looked like her. Coincidence? Not even remotely possible.

Which meant only one thing: the murders were undeniably connected to her.

Worse, the killer had reached out to her father.

North Avenue, 6:30 p.m.

"I really appreciate you coming all this way to bring my dad."

Winchester Chief of Police Billy Brannigan was a cowboy, heart and soul. Like Rowan, he'd grown up in Winchester. Unlike Rowan, Billy had been one of the most popular kids in school. A hometown hero during high school and college. The big football star who never failed to make time for fund-raising rodeos in the summer. Folks swore Billy was born wearing a Stetson and cowboy boots. He was a year older than Rowan but he'd made it his mission to take her under his wing, so to speak, after Raven's death. Though they had always been friends, he had gone above and beyond the call after that tragic summer. Rowan had been lost, Billy had watched over her, threatening to pound anyone who wasn't nice to her.

He was the sole reason she had survived high school.

Tall, broad shouldered and impossibly charming, he grinned down at her before hauling her into another bear hug. "You know I would do anything for you and your daddy."

Yes, she did know this. He was a faithful friend. When he let her go, she stood back and assessed him from those well-worn boots to the top of his handsome head. "Well, I can tell you one thing, Billy Brannigan, forty definitely looks good on you."

He took off his Stetson and ran his fingers through his dark hair. A smile tugged at her lips as she considered how many times as a starry-eyed teenager she'd dreamed of running her fingers through his hair. He had dark brown eyes, a classic straight nose and a perfect square jaw, not to mention those movie star lips. She had fantasized about kissing those lips since she was fourteen years old. But she never had. Just foolish adolescent girl fantasies. She'd outgrown those years ago.

Rowan and Billy were friends. Truth be told, he was her best friend even if they rarely laid eyes on one another. Back home he remained the most eligible bachelor in Franklin County. Like her, he'd never married or had kids. Rowan was well aware of her own reasons. She did not have the time to devote to that kind of relationship. As for kids, frankly, she didn't quite trust herself to be completely responsible, 24/7, for another human. Work sucked her in like a junkie to her drug of choice. She wasn't sure what kept Billy from the altar. Too many choices to choose only one, she imagined.

"Well, now," he said in that slow, easy drawl of his, "if we're going down that road, look at you, Ro." His gaze swept over her. "You look amazing, just like always."

She decided to enjoy the compliment instead of arguing the validity of it the way she generally did. "I hope you'll stay for dinner."

He smiled and she felt more relaxed than she had in days. It was so good to see him—circumstances notwithstanding. "Since I almost never get to see you anymore, yes, ma'am, I can stay for a little while before I head back."

Little being the operative word. She understood completely. The return trip to Winchester was close to two hours. She took his hat. "Make yourself at home and I'll round up Daddy."

"You got it."

She placed the Stetson on the sideboard in the entry hall and crossed the room. The first floor portion of her home was one expansive open space with only the staircase interrupting the flow. The entry hall flowed into the living room, which flowed into the dining room and around the staircase into the kitchen. A door from the kitchen led into a small hall where the powder room was on the left and the laundry room on the right. At the end of that small hall was the door to the two-car garage. A floor plan made for entertaining, not that she entertained often. Sometimes Julian joined her for dinner. Once in a great while she had April Jones over for lunch. Beyond the annual department Christmas party and the occasional birthday party, baby shower or wedding, that was about the extent of her entertainment calendar.

Who had time for a social life anyway?

Her father had taken Freud into the backyard. Rowan suspected he'd wanted to give her and Billy some alone time. Edward DuPont had always hoped she and Billy would become a couple. To her father's way of thinking if they had, Rowan would have stayed in Winchester and taken over the family business. He might have been able to retire by now and spend his days taking his grandsons fishing or his granddaughters to the ice cream parlor.

Despite her father's hopes and the occasional speculation among the Winchester gossip grapevine, Rowan and Billy had never been anything but friends and there would likely never be any DuPont grandchildren. A fleeting sense of sadness accompanied the realization. Generally, her unmarried, childless state didn't bother her. Maybe seeing Billy had resurrected those foolish adolescent daydreams.

Well, you are only human, Rowan—though Bennett and some of the other detectives might debate that deduction.

Outside, her father tossed a battered Frisbee into the darkness of the backyard. Freud dashed after it. "Daddy," she called from the deck. "Come inside. Billy can't stay long. We should have dinner before he heads back home."

Freud raced up onto the deck like a dog half his age. He'd turned eight this year. He'd spent the first three years of his life being abused by his drug trafficking owner. The thug had murdered at least four people but it took the SCU some time to prove it. When the animal's owner was arrested Rowan seized the opportunity to rescue the dog. The two of them had been good for each other. She'd learned some measure of responsibility to something besides her work and Freud had gained a life without fear or pain.

Edward DuPont climbed the final step and put an arm around her. "I sure am glad to see you, Ro, but I don't think all this fuss is really necessary. You know your old man can take care of himself. Besides, that fella seemed completely harmless to me."

"Most people considered Ted Bundy quite charming and certainly harmless until they learned about his dark side." His pained expression told her she'd made her point. "I'll feel better with you here until we figure this out."

He didn't argue any further so they walked inside where Billy waited, propped against the island like he owned the place. Unlike all the other kids in school, Billy had always been completely comfortable hanging around the funeral home. Not that he had done so that often—he was a popular guy, after all—but when he did, he had been as at home as Rowan. He was a good guy, then and now.

What was wrong with the women back home?

"I guess a little vacation is good for the soul." Her father kissed her on the cheek. "But I can't leave Herman for too long or he'll start to believe he can run things just as well as me."

Herman Carter was her father's longtime assistant director. Until he retired two years ago, Herman had been with the family business for as long as Rowan could remember. After Herman retired, her father had hired Woody Holder to take his place. Even after two years of working together her father wouldn't dare leave Woody in charge. As always, Herman was happy to step up to the plate. He and her father had been friends their whole lives.

Rowan was grateful her father had a friend like Herman. Both loved playing cards about as much as they did breathing. Back home their weekly card games were legendary. Rowan remembered sneaking downstairs to watch her father and his friends drink whiskey, smoke cigars and play cards. It was the closest thing to a social life besides church on Sunday the man had. Many times she had wondered if her father had chosen to remain alone because of her. He'd poured his entire life into raising his only remaining child and running the funeral home.

Then she'd deserted him.

More of that guilt settled onto her chest, bearing down

on her heart. He'd forgiven her, she knew this without doubt. Maybe it was time she forgave herself. Her gaze shifted from her father to Billy. Then again, perhaps her decision to leave her past behind had been a bigger misstep than she'd comprehended at the time.

A lifetime ago. No point looking back now.

With the dinner she'd had delivered warming in the microwave and filling the house with mouthwatering aromas, she and Billy set the table. He teased her about having a state-of-the-art kitchen she never used and she ribbed him about his longtime peanut butter sandwich fetish. When they'd gathered around the table, Billy caught her up on all the hometown gossip. Her dad put in his two cents' worth now and then, making Rowan laugh more than she had in ages. The easy banter refreshed her soul. It had been a long time since so much laughter had filled her home. Most of her time at home was spent poring over transcripts or police reports and evidence photos from heinous crimes.

Tonight there was no talk of murder. Rowan relaxed and enjoyed the company of her two favorite men.

Tomorrow would be soon enough to dig back into the mind of the killer currently haunting her waking hours.

Four

Metropolitan Nashville Police Department
Wednesday, March 13, 10:00 a.m.

"I really don't want to be any trouble, Ro."

Edward DuPont didn't like being the center of attention any more than Rowan did. They both preferred to simply do their work without any bustle or fuss. Life was easier that way. It was a shame she hadn't considered how the publication of a book would change things, perhaps for both of them. Frankly, she'd been certain a handful of copies would sell and that would be the end of it.

"Now, Daddy, I explained everything last night. This will only be for a few days. Just until we figure out what's going on with the man who showed up asking questions about me. You promised to be a good sport about it."

Her father had been happy to see her last evening, but this was another day and he was accustomed to getting on with his work in the privacy of his home. No matter that he had given a detailed description to the sketch artist, the man who'd shown up at his door remained an unknown subject. Jones and Keaton were sending the sketch to funeral homes all over Tennessee and to the tri-state area. Hopefully, if he was or had been employed by a funeral home nearby they would soon have a name. Beyond the fact that he'd called himself an undertaker, the conclusion that he was in the business was an easy one to make since he used all the right products— assuming he was their unsub in the homicide case.

Still, he could simply be taking advantage of the moniker that had ended up splashed all over the headlines and in the news.

"It's you I'm worried about," her father said, his face as well as his tone heavy with unease.

Rowan braced her hip on the edge of her desk, grateful they were in her office rather than in the task force meeting room. The last thing she wanted was for any of the detectives to hear the uncertainty in her father's voice. Worry and doubt had a way of igniting like a match to dry leaves.

"Why would you be worried about me? I have an entire department of law enforcement officers looking out for my welfare." She, of course, knew the answer. He had worried about her—far more than necessary— since the day her sister died. What parent wouldn't? As much as she wanted to consider otherwise, her father had more reason than most. Those infernal scars on her wrists burned. Automatically, her fingers tugged at her cuffs to ensure the scars were covered.

His gaze followed the subtle move. "I know you're a strong woman, Ro. I'm not questioning that or your mental stability."

Here it comes. Struggling for patience, she reminded herself that she rarely spent time with her father, the least she could do was hear him out while they were together whether it was for a day or for a week.

"But when a person has gone down *that* path," he said, dropping his gaze to the floor, "sometimes it's easier to find themselves back on that same road. When life gets difficult, I mean."

"It's been twenty years, Dad."

He met her gaze once more and the hurt there tugged at her heart. Rowan understood his feelings. Losing a child was the greatest pain a parent could suffer. To have a child attempt suicide came with the added agony of knowing that child no longer wanted to live—that, as a parent, perhaps you had somehow failed. She had done that to her father when she made the choice not once but twice. There were no adequate words to explain or to defend her choice in a way that would make him fully understand or would lessen the pain he still felt at the memories. Or even to diminish the fear he suffered at the mere idea that it could happen again.

"I know," he said, his face clouded with the regret he felt at dredging up the subject he knew would cause her discomfort.

"There have been numerous studies and most concur that the likelihood of a person attempting suicide again after such an extended period is minimal." She doubted a more clinical response would make a difference, but she had to try. "And I have no reason to feel that level of defeat, disillusionment or pain. I'm happy, Daddy. Very happy. I love my work. My book is—" she turned up her hands "—more successful than I expected. You never have to worry about me going down that path again. I promise."

Her father pushed out of the chair in front of her desk.

He shoved his hands into his pockets as if he wasn't sure what to do with them. "You're all I've got in this world, Ro. I don't want to lose you. It's not right for a child to die before a parent. I can't go through that again."

She went to her daddy and put her arms around him, laid her cheek against his chest. "I will never hurt you that way again, Daddy. You have my word."

As a teenager, she hadn't stopped to think how her actions would hurt her father—her only family. She'd only been thinking of herself and how badly she wanted to escape the pain and emptiness.

"So." He gave her a final squeeze and drew back. "That Billy sure seemed happy to see you."

Rowan laughed. She reached up and patted her father's too-thin cheek. "Don't you go trying to play matchmaker, Daddy. Billy and I are both happy just being friends."

His frail frame shook with his laughter. "I've been trying for close to twenty-five years. How can you expect me to stop cold turkey now?"

This was true. "Just don't be disappointed if all your efforts are for naught."

"A man can dream, little girl."

He kissed her forehead, and Rowan studied her father closely for the first time in a very long time. He looked so old. An ache pierced her. How could so much time have passed without her paying attention? His gray hair was thinning. He'd lost weight since the last time she saw him. She doubted he weighed more than one forty-five or one fifty. At six feet tall that was razor thin. His color was good, that was something. He'd always had that olive skin from his French ancestors. Rowan and her sister, on the other hand, had inherited their mother's Scottish coloring, blond hair, blue eyes and fair skin. Attempts at suntans had always resulted in sunburns.

"I think you're the one who needs a girlfriend." She patted his flat belly. "Preferably one who can cook."

Another of those deep laughs echoed from him. "I want you to know I work very hard to keep this lean physique."

A rap on the door drew Rowan's attention there as it opened and Lieutenant Jones stepped in. "I apologize for the interruption, Dr. DuPont, but we need to take a ride."

The look in the other woman's eyes told Rowan all she needed to know. "Daddy, have a seat. We'll be back in no time." She hurried around her desk and grabbed her purse. "If you need anything at all you let the officer in the hall know." She gestured to the television hanging on the wall. "Feel free to make yourself at home."

"I'll be right here waiting for you," he assured her as he reached for the remote on her desk.

When she and Jones were in the corridor outside her office Rowan asked, "We have another victim?"

Jones nodded. "Her boyfriend claims he hasn't talked to her in two days. He was out of town on business until this morning. They last spoke late Monday night. She hasn't been answering her cell since then. When he arrived at her apartment this morning she wasn't home. Her phone and purse were there, but not her. He called her office, she hasn't been to work at the accounting firm where she's a partner since Monday, either."

Rowan's heart sank. "Does she fit the profile?"

Jones nodded. "She could be your twin sister."

Except her twin sister was dead.

Rowan prayed they would find this woman before she ended up dead, too.

South 5th Street, 11:50 a.m.

"Mr. Jenner, let's review the timeline once more."

While Jones and Bennett questioned the distraught boyfriend of Dharma Collette, Rowan wandered through the missing woman's apartment. The apartment was nestled into a nice complex only steps from Frederick Douglass Park and mere minutes from downtown. Though she and her boyfriend, Peter Jenner, had dated for three years, they had not decided to move in together as of yet. Collette had never been married and had no children—exactly like the other two vics.

Exactly like Rowan.

Jenner was sincerely worried about his girlfriend. Rowan had watched him carefully during the first portion of the interview. She didn't spot a single tell to suggest he was being less than truthful. He traveled frequently for his work so his absence this week was not unusual. The home screen on his phone was a Titans football logo and he held a sweating can of beer in his right hand as they talked. It was the third one he'd had since they arrived. Collette apparently kept a good stock of his favorite brew.

The apartment was tidy and well kept. Nothing to suggest forced entry or that there had been a struggle. Keaton was reviewing security footage to see if Collette had been visited by anyone in the week prior to her disappearance. Her cell phone records had already been ordered to ensure there were no deleted calls or texts. The missing woman had walked out of the building at nine on Monday night to go for her usual run—which was why she hadn't taken her purse. According to Jenner she generally took her cell phone with her on runs. He admitted that he had known her to forget it from time to time.

No numbers had called her cell that weren't in her contacts list. No strangers entered the building and went to her floor. To her boyfriend's knowledge she was not having trouble with her family or her work. Her sister, two brothers and parents had been contacted. No one had seen or heard from her. Collette had no history of mental illness or other issues that might send her into hiding or prompt her to run away.

Detective Wells was running down any financial transactions on her credit or debit cards. Rowan was confident they would find nothing useful. Dharma Collette hadn't run away or gone into hiding. She had been taken by a man who knew how to pluck her from her life without leaving the first clue.

Rowan wandered through Dharma's bedroom once more, careful not to get in the way of the two forensic techs searching for any sort of evidence that might give their investigation some sense of direction. Unless the unknown subject made his first misstep, that wasn't likely. The apartment only had one bedroom, but the living area was quite large. Collette's car was still in her designated parking spot. The boyfriend had confirmed that her running shoes weren't in her closet. The security footage showed her leaving the building on Monday night wearing those running shoes and a lime-green running suit.

If the same man who took the other two women in the Undertaker case had taken Collette, they would find her body within the next twenty-four to thirty hours.

And another woman would be dead for no other apparent reason than to get Rowan's attention.

Five

"Number twenty," Jones said as they parked at the curb in front of the final funeral home on their list.

Rowan surveyed the one-story 1960s-era building. She and Lieutenant Jones had been to nineteen others so far, many of which were very much like this one. The facade of some were more upscale than others but none had any real character. "You know, these places just don't look and feel like funeral homes."

Jones turned to her, her hand on the door. "I guess you would know better than most."

Rowan allowed her thoughts to wander back to her childhood—something she rarely did. "Winchester was a small town. Still is. As a kid I went to funerals at the only other funeral home in town but it was very similar to ours—a big old historic house that served as both business and home to the owner. Picking a funeral home in a small town was sort of a big deal in those days. Ours or Gardner's. Some folks only took their loved ones to

Gardner's, some only came to us. It was generally based on the one their parents and grandparents had chosen."

"I know what you mean," Jones said. "I grew up in a little hole in the wall all the way over near Knoxville. If you were black, there was only one funeral home you used—the one for the black people." She shrugged, her hand still resting on the door handle. "It wasn't that folks couldn't choose wherever they wanted to go, especially in recent decades, it just became a habit. Black folks operate the place, black folks give them their business."

"If we ever had one like that," Rowan said, "it was before my time and no one talked about it."

Jones laughed. "Of course not. The world's too PC to talk about the truth."

Rowan wondered if it was really the concept of political correctness or if more folks had simply become blind to color. She didn't see black when she looked at April Jones. She saw detective, female, wife, mother, friend—pretty much in that order. But then, her father had been a strong influence about color and differences in general. He had raised his children to love and respect all people. Maybe she was naive to believe more people felt that way these days, but she could always hope.

"Just another reason to turn off the news." Rowan rarely watched television, the news in particular.

"You got that right," Jones agreed. They emerged from the car and across the roof of the car she said, "We get a firsthand look at the news every day without some fool on the air twisting it around to suit his or her own agenda."

Rowan smiled. "Human nature can get ugly sometimes."

The lieutenant's phone buzzed as they walked up the

sidewalk. Jones checked the screen to read the text she'd received. "Collette's phone records and credit cards gave us nothing." Visibly disgusted, she shoved the phone back onto her belt.

Rowan hadn't really expected anything useful. Their unsub had proved too clever for a mistake that elementary. But, in time, they all made mistakes. No matter the intelligence level or the years of experience, a killer was still only human. The trouble was they didn't have the luxury of time.

Collette would be dead by morning, if she wasn't already.

A media blitz about the missing woman—Dharma Collette—was running on the news and all other social venues. Traffic cops were distributing posters of Collette's photo everywhere. The department was doing everything within its power to find the missing woman. God only knew if it would be enough. Although, sketches of the possible funeral home employee who had visited her father had been sent wide, the response, especially locally, had been minimal. After dropping by the search at Collette's office, she and Jones had decided to knock on doors, starting with the local funeral homes.

Inside Kendrick Funeral Services Jones made the introductions, as was par for the course. Rowan showed her credentials when the director looked from Jones's badge to her. They went through the steps, showed him the sketch of the man who had visited her father. When he studied the sketch for longer than expected, Rowan and Jones exchanged a cautiously hopeful look.

"Do you recognize him?" Jones asked.

"Well—" Kendrick bit his lips together for a moment "—he dang sure looks like one of the assistants who worked here before I took over. But I can't be positive." He handed the sketch back to Jones.

"We'll need his name and address—any info you have," Jones said.

As a rule, Rowan allowed the detectives to do the talking so she could watch the responses. Later they would compare notes. In her opinion, this man was telling the truth.

"I wish I could help you but my wife is out of town. She won't be back until tomorrow. Our daughter is having our first grandchild. I'd be there, too, but my deputy director is out sick and I had two passings arrive."

"Congratulations," Rowan offered, "about the grandchild, I mean." This was another understood step between Rowan and the detectives. She always played the "good" cop part. "Boy or girl?"

Kendrick grinned, his face beaming. "Boy. Gonna be named William Albert after his granddaddy."

"You can't pull his file?" Jones asked as she dragged her cell free of her waist, her patience thinning. She always checked her phone repeatedly when she was running out of patience. The time on the screen reminding her that more precious minutes were slipping away.

"Afraid not. There was a fire not a week after we bought the place. All the files were destroyed."

Rowan's hopes fell. Just their luck this would be the one and there were no personnel files available. "What about the previous owner?"

"He passed away, but my wife can tell you anything you want to know." He tapped his temple. "Got a mind like a steel trap. She looked over all the files when we bought the place. She'll remember everyone who worked here. If he did, she'll know his name and whatever else was in the file about him."

"Perhaps you could call her." Rowan smiled. "Check on your daughter's progress."

Jones offered, "I'll snap a pic of the sketch and text it to you. You can send it to your wife and have her look at it that way."

He frowned. "I'm afraid I don't know how to do any of that. My wife is the one who has all the gadget smarts."

"Lieutenant Jones can do it for you," Rowan urged. "She's our resident gadget guru." That wasn't entirely true, but of the three of them Jones would certainly be the guru.

He handed over his phone without hesitation. "Happy to help anyway I can."

Thankfully, his cell was a smartphone. Jones snapped a pic and sent it in a text to Mrs. Kendrick's contact number in under a minute. "Can you call her and explain what we need?"

Rowan looked from the lieutenant to the man, hoping he would continue to be agreeable.

"Sure. Can't guarantee she'll answer since cell phones aren't allowed beyond a certain point. She could be in the delivery room this very minute, for all I know. But if she doesn't, I can leave a message and the minute I hear from her I'll call you."

"We appreciate your cooperation," Jones assured him as she returned his phone.

"All right." Kendrick made the call and, as he'd predicted, he had to leave a message.

When he'd finished, Jones gave him a card. "When you hear from her, call me. I don't care what time it is. Day or night. This is very important, Mr. Kendrick."

Before they were back in the car the cell attached to the lieutenant's waist sounded off. "Jones."

Rowan listened, hoping to pick up on something the caller was saying. The voice sounded like Bennett but she couldn't make out the words. As Jones listened, she started the car and rolled away from the final funeral home on their list. She grunted a couple of uh-huhs before ending the call.

"That was Bennett. He's with Anna Stein."

"Collette's best friend according to Jenner." Rowan's pulse rate started to climb. "Does she know anything?"

"She won't talk to Bennett." Jones braked for a traffic signal that turned red. "She says she's only talking to a female detective."

"Maybe we'll catch a break."

Even as Rowan made the statement she doubted that would be the case. There had been no relationship issues with the other two victims, she doubted the killer would change his MO at this point. More often than not, when a woman refused to speak to a male detective it was generally related to sex and/or cheating. The woman counted on another woman being less likely to judge or to tell the man involved.

"Catch a break?" Jones grunted again. "I ain't holding my breath."

Rowan decided not to mention she'd had the same thought. The situation was dismal enough without echoing the idea over and over.

19th Avenue South, 6:00 p.m.

Anna Stein lived in a studio apartment two blocks from Music Row. She worked at the same accounting firm as Dharma Collette but she wasn't a partner as Collette was. Also unlike Collette, Stein looked more like a party girl. She had the dark circles under her eyes from lack of sleep, the empty overturned vodka bottle on the counter and an ashtray full of cigarette butts on the coffee table. Her nails were chewed down to nubs and the red polish she'd applied a week or so ago was chipped. Tight leggings left nothing to the imagination, while a midriff-length T showed off her flat belly. More telling, the woman couldn't sit still for a minute.

"She was seeing someone," Stein announced after beating around the bush for fifteen minutes. She chewed at a thumbnail, her right leg bouncing. "I don't know his name or what he looks like, but he's older. She said he was older and smart. Really smart." She pulled her legs beneath her, probably to keep them still. "Maybe you noticed that Peter isn't so bright."

Rowan had pegged him as average intelligence. Perhaps Ms. Stein had confused a lower intelligence with his good old boy, laid-back mentality. Peter Jenner was a football fan. Tailgating was likely his favorite way to party. Rowan doubted he liked dancing, more likely he preferred throwing back the beers and watching others sway around the dance floor. But that didn't mean he wasn't plenty intelligent any more than her lifestyle meant she wasn't a nice woman.

"So she and Peter were having trouble?" Jones nudged. "Have you witnessed them fighting or did Dharma tell you about the trouble they were having?"

Stein shook her head. "Are you kidding? Peter is far too laid-back to work up the energy to fight. He's the kind of guy who just waits out the trouble. He lacks passion. He has a good thing with Dharma so he isn't going to rock the boat."

"Is that your assessment," Rowan asked, "or Dharma's?"

"That's what Dharma said and she's right. He's just happy no matter what. I used to think he was on Prozac or something but I met his father at a Fourth of July barbecue and he's exactly the same. I guess the men in that family are just light on testosterone and heavy on the serotonin."

"You're not aware of any trouble at home or at work that Dharma was having?" Jones prodded. "Except for the possible affair with this unknown older man."

"She *is* having an affair," Stein stated. "She told me this older guy was utterly intellectual and so sophisticated. He made her feel important."

"She told you nothing about him other than how he made her feel?" Jones stayed after her about the description. "Not even a first name or a nickname?"

They needed something, anything.

Stein shook her head. "Handsome. Distinguished. That's all she told me."

"Where did she meet this handsome, distinguished man?" Rowan asked. "At work? On a run? Maybe at the gym?"

Stein sat back, her hands stilled as if she'd just remembered something. Rowan's anticipation sent her heart beating a little faster.

"She met him in the park where she runs."

"Frederick Douglass Park?" Jones confirmed.

"Yeah. She runs there, like, every night." Stein shook her head. "I don't see the appeal but I guess you have to love running to bother. She even runs when it's raining or snowing."

"Peter doesn't run?" Rowan asked. He'd said he didn't but there was always the chance he'd lied. Though she hadn't picked up on any tells, considering his overly laid-back way, he might be one of the few who could lie without the first tic. Still, he had been out of town. His alibi checked out.

"No way. The only running he does is to the store for another six-pack."

Jones passed the woman a card. "Call me if you think of anything else. This is very important, Ms. Stein. Every minute counts."

The woman's face fell. "She's going to die, isn't she? Just like the others."

Jones stood, Rowan followed suit.

"Not if we can help it," the lieutenant assured Stein. "But we can't do this alone. Talk to her other trusted friends. See if you can learn anything about this new man in her life or anything else that's new or out of the ordinary."

Collette was the first victim to have a new man in her life. The other victims had nothing new going on—at least not as far as any of their friends and family were aware. Unfortunately, the vague description of older and distinguished did not match the man who had visited Rowan's father.

One step forward, two steps back.

"I will." Stein nodded adamantly. "I'll talk to everyone I can think of." She frowned. "Is that why the cops were in her office today?" She glanced at Rowan. "You were there, too."

"Sometimes people leave notes or emails that might help," Rowan offered.

Stein shook her head. "Not Dharma. When she's at work, it's all about work. Her personal life never enters the building. She doesn't even talk personal stuff until we're at lunch. She's tenacious like that."

Something else Rowan had in common with the victims…they were all workaholics.

Six

"**Y**ou didn't have to go to all that trouble, Daddy."
Rowan pushed her plate away and slumped in her chair.
She was stuffed. More often than not she came home
from work and went straight back to work. Dinner rarely
entered the equation. Now all she wanted to do was curl
up in bed and watch mindless TV—something she never
took the time to do.

She almost smiled. Having her father around had her
regressing to her childhood days when there was always
someone taking care of her. Images of her father preparing her hot chocolate on a cold night or fresh lemonade
on a hot summer day flashed through her mind. How
had she not realized how lucky she was even after losing
her sister and her mother? She had always had her dad.

"It's not often I get to cook my favorite girl a meal."
He stood and gathered their plates.

"Let me do that." She pushed her chair back and got
to her feet. "You did the cooking."

He drew the plates out of her reach. "You worked a twelve-hour day. You've done enough."

He headed to the kitchen. Rowan grabbed their water glasses and trailed after him. When Raven died, her daddy had done all the cooking. Norah—her mother—had been too depressed and withdrawn. Sometimes Rowan thought her mother had purposely tuned out so she could put emotional distance between her and the people she loved. Rowan was convinced that deep down Norah had planned her escape from the moment Raven's body was pulled from that wretched lake. She could not—would not—continue living and risk that kind of pain again. It was easier for Rowan to believe that was the case than to believe her mother loved Raven more than her. In truth, she would never know.

Those very thoughts were another of the many, many things Rowan had felt guilty about after Raven died.

That's the past, Ro. This is now.

When she and her father finally made it home an hour ago, she had gone straight to her room to shower. She'd needed the hot water to relax her tense muscles. She'd stayed under the spray of water longer than she'd intended. By the time she'd dragged on lounge pants and a T her father had pulled together a dinner of tuna mac and cheese and a salad. It was a miracle the salad fixings were still edible. Rowan usually ate out or had something delivered the way she had last night. If she'd been thinking clearly she would have ordered something before she hit the shower. Ignoring her own body's needs was typical behavior, but she should have realized her father would need to eat.

"I'm sorry I didn't think to stop at a drive-through or to order delivery, Daddy. I'm a terrible hostess."

He turned off the faucet and settled his hands on the counter. She'd never noticed all the age spots before. Her heart squeezed. How had she allowed so much time to slip away without spending more of it with him? He looked so frail. He looked so *old*.

"I have a feeling food isn't one of your priorities, little girl." He bent his head to one side and studied her. "I worry about you."

Rowan set the glasses aside and hugged her arms around his thin waist. "You do not have to worry about me. I promise." She set her chin against his chest and stared up at him. "I worry about *you*."

A frown furrowed its way across his craggy face. "Now why in the world would you worry about me?"

"You've been alone for a very long time."

"Here we go again." Her father unwrapped her arms from his waist and shooed her aside so he could access the sink. He turned the faucet back on and resumed rinsing their plates and then he placed each in the dishwasher. "I don't need a wife, I have Herman."

Rowan laughed, couldn't help herself. Her father had always said Herman was like an old woman, always hovering over him, feeding him and urging him to go to the doctor for every ache and pain.

"Forgive me," she teased, "I forget you have Herman."

When the plates, silverware and glasses were in the dishwasher, he dried his hands. "I am not lonely, Rowan. Beyond the fact that I miss you every day, I'm fine. I have the families and I have Herman."

"How is Estelle?" The last her father had mentioned, Herman's wife was battling cancer. Rowan hoped it was a good sign that she hadn't heard more.

"She's doing great." He nodded slowly. "It was touch

and go at first, but Herman found her one of those new experimental treatments and she's doing great."

Rowan smiled. "I'm so glad to hear she's responding well." Not all experimental treatments worked for the approved participants.

Though her father had never been very outgoing—like her—when it came to social events, he gave himself completely over to the families whose loved ones were brought to his funeral home. He became their friend, their confidant, their therapist and often their minister. Rowan suspected it was his utter dedication that set the mold for her career-oriented mind-set. God knew Norah could never focus on anything for too long. If Rowan had a dollar for every book her mother had started and never finished, she would be rich. More of that Southern girl guilt heaped onto her shoulders. It wasn't her mother's fault no publisher was ever interested enough in her work to want to publish it. Determination—that had been her mother's strongest asset. She'd researched and written her stories—at least the beginnings—for as long as Rowan could remember. Images of late nights and empty wine bottles filtered through her head. Frequent weekends away...all in the name of research.

Norah DuPont had been so different from Edward. How had the two ever ended up together? And why would a woman so determined and seemingly devoted to her family suddenly give up and end her life?

It still made no sense to Rowan...and yet, she had acted out in a similar manner. She had no right to judge her mother when she had attempted the same.

Don't even go there.

"You know..." Rowan hesitated. Julian had told her that if she ever made this confession to her father it would only give him false hope. She searched her father's face. Did she dare say the words? *Now or never, Ro.* "I have…often regretted not going back home…to you and to the funeral home."

There, she'd said it. The world hadn't ended but the surprise in her father's expression tugged at her emotions, making her eyes burn with the need to cry. The surprise shifted to something else, something unreadable and unsettling.

It felt like forever before he spoke. "You made the right choice."

Her breath caught with her own surprise. "But I thought—"

He nodded. "I know. I always hoped you would take over for me. DuPonts have operated that funeral home for more than a 150 years. But many of them, like us, paid a heavy price. All I want is for you to be happy, Ro. If this—" he glanced around her home "—is what makes you happy, that's all that matters to me. The business will be yours to do with as you please when I'm gone."

Reeling from the exchange, Rowan grappled for balance. Of course she knew her father wanted her to be happy, but she hadn't realized how at peace he was with her decision. Julian was wrong. They should have had this conversation years ago.

"Would you like a glass of wine, Daddy?" She didn't have anything stronger to offer. She hoped he said yes because she very badly needed a glass after their respective revelations.

He gave a nod. "A glass of wine would be nice."

Relieved, she said, "You go on and have a seat. I'll be right there with the wine."

He hesitated.

"Go on. I'll be right there."

Her father drifted over to the sofa and settled in. She searched for a bottle of her favorite blush and opened it. As she snagged two stemmed glasses all she could think was how she couldn't wait to tell Julian.

She'd made the right decision. She wished she had been honest with her father years ago. Then again, perhaps Julian had been right about not rushing into such a conversation. Timing was everything. Maybe last year or even five years ago would have been too soon.

When she'd settled on the sofa next to her father, she poured the wine. She handed him a glass and forged ahead with the questions she had wanted to ask since she was a teenager. Now that she'd opened the door to that part of their past, there was so much more she wanted to know. "Did Mother ever talk about ending her life... *before*? Had she tried before?"

Edward drank from the glass until he'd emptied it. Rowan poured him another. They both needed a little bracing for this particular conversation.

"She never mentioned anything of the sort, ever. If she had ever tried before I never knew. I really don't think she had." He moved his shoulders up and down. "I can only assume she was so devastated by Raven's death that she couldn't go on."

Rowan sipped her wine, considered the kindest way to frame her next question. There really was no way to do so. "Did she ever love me the way she loved Raven?"

Her father set his glass aside and turned to her, his knees bumping hers. "Your mother loved you just as much as she loved Raven." His forehead creased in thought. "I believe she would have done exactly the same thing if it had been you who drowned. Her inability to go on was about losing a child—not which child."

Rowan understood this, for the most part. She was a psychiatrist for God's sake. And she had told herself the same thing repeatedly. But to a twelve-year-old who had just lost the other half of herself, her mother's withdrawal and subsequent suicide had been devastating. The idea that she'd tried to do the same thing to her father twisted like barbed wire deep inside her.

"I realize what I did hurt you deeply." She met his eyes. "I did the same thing to you that Mom did to me. I'm so very sorry, Daddy."

He took her hand in his. "As much as losing Raven and Norah hurt me, those losses hurt you far more. You were devastated and confused. You made a mistake. It took time for you to find your way again. I'm just glad you did—even if it brought you here, away from me."

"I swear I'm going to visit more often, Daddy." She squeezed his hand, blinking rapidly to hold back the infernal tears she didn't want him to see. The last thing she wanted was to have him worrying more than he already did. "I know I've said this before, but this time I will back up my words with action."

Her father tugged his hand free of hers and gently placed his arm around her shoulders. "You do the best you can, little girl, and I'll be the happiest daddy on earth."

Rowan leaned into him, thankful she'd had the courage to have this conversation. As soon as she went to bed she was going to text Julian and tell him she'd done it. Julian would be happy for her, if a little surprised.

"You know that Billy brags about you all the time."

Oh lord. Her father would likely go to his grave trying to pair her with Billy Brannigan. "He probably brags on his truck and his dog, too."

Speaking of dogs, Freud was curled up at her father's feet. Whenever she visited her dad or he came here, Freud stuck to him like glue. Funny, she realized, he'd taken up with Billy, too.

Or maybe Freud had simply smelled the scent of his daddy's bluetick hound on Billy. He'd mentioned dropping by their house before coming to Nashville.

"You'll see," her father argued. "One of these days the two of you will end up together. If I'm not around, you just remember I said it first."

"So you're psychic now, are you?" she teased.

"On some things." He stood his ground.

"I know one thing for certain." She peered up at him. "You're the best dad any little girl could ever hope for. Even when I didn't show it, I have always been aware of how lucky I am. I really will visit more often from now on. I promise."

He smiled and quickly turned away. No matter that he tried to cover up the move, she saw him dab at his eyes. She wasn't the only one feeling sentimental tonight.

Before she could stop herself she thought of the Collette family. No amount of promises would give them any comfort tonight.

Rowan dreamed of her sister. Raven always came to her in the water. Rowan had gone many times to the lake where her sister drowned. She would stand on the bank and peer into the water. The last time she'd visited her father she'd gone back to that same place—not the backyard of the home where the party had taken place, but the bank in the wooded area where they'd found

Raven's body snagged on a tree that had fallen into the water years before.

Rowan stood on that bank now. It was only a dream, her brain understood this, but it felt entirely real. The water was dark. Beneath the water, in the places where the lake was the deepest, there were old cars and no telling how many bodies. The lake was actually part of a reservoir and a damn. Parts of it had been used over the course of its fifty-plus-year history for a dumping ground. But it wasn't those other bodies floating toward her in this dream.

Deep in the water she could see her twin sister reaching for her, always reaching. *"Come into the water with me, Rowan. I miss you."*

Rowan gasped and sat straight up in her bed. She pushed back the covers tangled around her body and fought to slow her frantic breathing. No other dreams were as vivid as the ones she had of her sister. Strange that she'd never dreamed of her mother. Julian told her from the beginning that some losses were too deep and too painful even to dream of. Rowan supposed he was right. Maybe that was why she'd never once dreamed of her mother.

Her cell hummed, the plastic case vibrating against her bedside table. She picked it up and squinted at the too bright screen. Wouldn't be work. They would call.

It was Julian.

You always were headstrong.

She looked at the time. 1:55 a.m.

What was he doing awake at this hour? She'd sent him the text about the conversation with her father hours ago.

Maybe he'd been jarred from sleep by a bad dream, as well. He'd told her often that he struggled with unpleasant dreams of his own. One would think with all their training they would never suffer such discomforts.

Not true at all.

She tapped a quick response. LOL we should both be sleeping.

His answering text said: Dictating case notes. Sleep well.

Rowan turned her cell facedown on the bedside table. The chances of her sleeping well were slim but she had to try.

Dharma Collette was counting on the entire department—including Rowan—to find her before it was too late.

If it wasn't too late already.

Two hours earlier...

Dharma told her eyes to open but they refused.

He'd put her into a bathtub. Washed her body...her hair. She'd lain there unable to move like someone paralyzed.

Why wouldn't her eyes open?

The drug. She wasn't sure what kind, but he'd kept her disabled since bringing her here. She'd bumped into him after her run on Monday night. He'd smiled and suggested they get coffee. She'd been only too happy to climb into his car. She liked him, felt comfortable with him. Wanted something better in her life.

Why had she trusted him?

He'd seemed so nice. Peter had been out of town again and she'd needed someone. This man understood how to talk to a woman. They'd never even kissed, yet he made her yearn to have his strong arms around her...to feel his lips on her body.

Didn't matter that he was far older than her...he made her feel things she had stopped feeling for Peter months ago.

She should have known he was too good to be true. Men like that didn't exist anymore outside romance novels. His kindness and attentiveness were only about luring in the next victim.

She was the next victim. She was going to die.

Tears seared down her skin. Though she couldn't open her eyes or move a single part of her body, she could cry. Lying on her back, the hot, salty drops slid down her skin, disappearing into her freshly washed hair.

"Now, now," he murmured as he wiped the tears away with a soft cloth, "no need to cry. It will be over soon."

Open! Her mind screamed but her eyes refused to obey. *Move!* She ordered her right arm to move but it would not. Then her left. Still nothing.

He lifted her head and placed something around her neck. She felt the rough texture press into the soft skin at her throat. Her brain struggled to identify the texture. Rug? Burlap? *Rope.*

The realization formed in her foggy brain at the same time she felt the rope tighten around her throat.

She told herself to struggle. She could not. Tried her best to suck more air into her lungs. Didn't work. Then she felt herself being pulled upward.

Tighter...tighter...the rope cut into her skin. Higher and higher, it pulled her upward until her feet dangled in the air.

Until she could not breathe at all.

She was dying.

Seven

Dharma Collette wore the same type of white cotton gown the other victims had worn. Red rose petals encircled her position in the grass beneath a copse of trees. Petals had fallen like crimson snowflakes over her posed body. Rowan concurred with the medical examiner's estimation that she had been dead approximately ten hours.

There was one glaring difference between Dharma and the others: she wore a noose fashioned from a braided rope around her neck. Lying alongside her was the length, approximately six feet, of the rope. Just enough for the killer to loop over some object or structure and then to pull her into a hanging position. Based on the bruising beneath the noose and the subconjunctival hemorrhage in the eyes, the cause of death was unquestionably asphyxiation.

Memories of finding her mother hanging from her neck at the funeral home, followed immediately by the long-buried images of the photos Rowan had discovered in a drawer in her father's closet streamed through her brain like binge-watching a horror series. Her mother had been hanging from a rope that had been secured to the second-story banister. The detective who'd investigated her death had taken photos of every angle before allowing her body to be lowered from its dangling position. Blood had pooled in her feet and legs. The expression on her face had been twisted and grotesque.

Rowan banished the terrible memories. She fought back the uncharacteristic emotions suddenly clawing at her. She never had this problem on the job, but this time the case was personal. This woman—like the other two—was dead because of her.

Frustration, misery and anger coiled into one, tightening inside her as forcefully as the rope that had killed Dharma Collette.

"She didn't struggle," Rowan said, strong-arming her attention back to her work. These women were counting on her to help find their killer. "The only bruise I see, beyond those around her neck and the ligature marks on her wrists and ankles where she was restrained at least part of the time, is one bruise on her left knee. It looks fairly old. At least three days. She may have fallen on her run Monday night. Nails are clean." With a gloved hand, she inspected Collette's fingers one by one. "She died in an upright position." Rowan leaned closer to get a look at her neck and throat. "The rope isn't only for show, he definitely hanged her."

Like your mother.

The words echoed through her, sending the cold seeping deep into her bones.

Jones crouched next to her. "If you need to step away from this," she offered, "we'll all understand."

Of course everyone knew her mother had died this way.

The damned book. Fury roared through Rowan, the heat and fire of it chasing away the cold, obliterating any calm she had managed. She should never have discussed her private life that way. All she had accomplished was to hand this bastard fodder for his sick imagination.

Pull it together, Rowan. Anger won't help find this unsub.

"It's important that I do this." Forcing all the certainty she possessed into her eyes she urged the other woman to see how desperately she needed to be a part of finding this killer.

"All right." Jones turned her attention back to the body. "What else do you see?"

"He must have kept her drugged since there's no indication she struggled to free herself. He held her approximately seventy-two hours before he killed her. Keeping her drugged is the only way she wouldn't have fought her bindings and him. The marks around her wrists and ankles would be far more pronounced if she had struggled." These victims were too much like Rowan to have given up without a fight.

The killer knew this.

Dear God. She had given him everything he needed in that damned book.

All her secrets.

Well, almost all of them. There were some things she could never tell anyone except Julian.

"Jones."

At the sound of the detective answering her cell Rowan blinked away the disturbing thoughts. She could not allow her emotions to keep getting in the way. She focused on Dharma Collette. He'd hanged Collette and then he'd had to move her here but he'd waited to ensure lividity would confirm she'd been hanged by the neck.

He wanted me to know...

After being placed in this park on her back some amount of blood had shifted into the new position from the sheer pull of gravity, but it was paler and the amount was hardly significant. Collette died in an upright position, hanging from that noose.

Just like Rowan's mother.

Rowan stepped away from the body. The medical examiner would confirm her conclusions but she didn't need confirmation. What she needed was to find this bastard before another woman disappeared.

As they drove away from the crime scene, reporters waited outside the perimeter. They closed in on the car to try and get a usable shot of the people inside.

"Someone leaked the theory that these murders are related to you." Jones glanced at Rowan as she eased through the throng of reporters.

Rowan turned her head away from the intrusions, ignoring the shouted questions. Her throat felt bone dry. "When did this happen? I haven't seen anything on the news. There were no reporters at my house this morning or at headquarters."

"That was the call I got a few minutes ago. The chief is not a happy camper."

If he pulled her off the case... "He has to let me finish this."

Jones nodded as she sped away from the crowd that had finally been contained by the uniforms attempting to protect the perimeter. "Captain Doyle told him that you're essential to this investigation. He's given us forty-eight hours to get this case solved." She glanced at Rowan. "He doesn't want to see your face on the news at any point during that time."

"He's not the only one."

Rowan thought of Julian. She had acknowledged his hard work in her book. He could be in danger, if nothing else from being hounded by reporters. Good lord, she should have thought of that already. "I need to make a stop."

Jones sent her a sidelong glance. "Your father is safe at headquarters."

Rowan shook her head. "Dr. Addington is mentioned in the book. I should make sure he's okay."

"What's his address?"

Rowan provided Julian's home/office address and Jones assigned a one-man security detail to Julian as they drove in his direction. Rowan was immensely grateful.

Too many innocent people had died because of her already.

Rosa L. Parks Boulevard, 12:45 p.m.

Rows of Victorian town houses once lined what was now Nashville's Central Business District. Dr. Julian Addington lived and worked in one of the few survivors of late-twentieth-century progress. He had inherited the impressive residence with its equally prestigious address from his grandmother. He'd received numerous offers on the property over the years but he refused to sell. Instead, he'd set up his practice on the ground floor more than thirty years ago and renovated the upstairs to his taste. During college this was where Rowan had come each week for her session with him. Though she hadn't been his official patient for more than a decade, they were friends. Good friends.

Julian's home had been and still was like a second home to her.

"I'll just be a minute."

Jones nodded. "I'll check in with Kendrick, see if he's heard from his wife. That daughter of his should have had her baby by now. We need a damned break."

"A break would be a nice change of pace."

The detective's cell phone rang as Rowan emerged from the car. Maybe that was Kendrick or, better yet, one of the other detectives in SCU with a lead that would help them find this killer before he took another victim. All they needed was one significant clue…just one thing, dammit!

Fury swirled through Rowan. If the unsub wanted her, why didn't he come after her in the first place? As if she didn't know the answer.

Games. Sick, disgusting games.

Frustration dogging her every step, she made her way to the front entrance and reached for the door. It was locked.

Frowning, she checked the time on her cell. Maybe Julian had taken a late lunch. No problem. She'd go on in and leave him a note. She walked across the postage-stamp-sized front lawn and went around to the back of the house. Under his favorite wrought-iron chair he kept one of those small metal key boxes folks often tucked into a wheel well on their vehicle. She crouched down and felt around under the chair. No key box. A frown pulling at her forehead, she moved the cushions to make sure he hadn't relocated it on the chair. Then she checked the other three chairs that sat around the table.

No key box. A quick look under the smoker's station—
something he provided for his patients who smoked—
and no luck. She searched the patio until there was no
place left to examine.

Maybe he'd decided the key box was too much of a
risk. The only thing the key had unlocked was the front
entrance and this door from the back patio that led into
the lobby. His office door and the door to the stairs that
led into his private residence had separate locks—the
kind with codes for locking and unlocking. It was possible there had been an incident he hadn't told her about
and he'd felt it necessary to remove the emergency key.

She pulled out her phone and called him. The call
went directly to voice mail. Now she was fairly convinced there had been an emergency with a patient.
"Hey, Julian. I hope you're okay. I stopped by but you're
not home. Call me. I need to know you're okay." She
drew in a sharp breath. "The bastard left another victim."

She ended the call and tucked her phone away. Another victim…another woman dead because of her.

Squaring her shoulders in spite of the worry and guilt
crashing down on her, she walked back around front
to find Jones rushing up the sidewalk. Rowan's heart
started to pound. Surely there wasn't another missing
woman this early. Was it possible their killer had finally
made a mistake and some useful piece of evidence had
been found?

It would never be that easy.

"Kendrick's daughter had her baby. I spoke to the
wife. She gave us a name. Greg Ames." The detective's
lips quivered into a smile. "This could be the break we've
been looking for."

Rowan hurried to keep up with her as they moved back toward the car. "Do we have an address?"

"Got it. He worked at the funeral home the Kendricks bought until the previous owner died." Before climbing into the car, she jerked her head to her right. "Got that security detail in place."

Rowan spotted the Metro PD cruiser. "Good."

When Jones had settled behind the wheel and Rowan had pulled on her seat belt in the passenger seat, she asked, "Did Mrs. Kendrick remember anything else about him?"

Jones hesitated a moment before easing away from the curb. "Only that he left under a cloud of suspicion that he'd been messing around with some of the…ah… bodies."

"Jesus. No charges were filed?"

Jones shook her head as she moved into the flow of traffic. "The previous owner's wife couldn't make the charges stick. It was her word against his and her husband was dead—heart attack—so he couldn't back her up."

Rowan took a breath. "I almost hate to ask this question, but did he have a specific type?"

Jones glanced at her, a cold certainty in her eyes. "Blondes. He liked blondes."

Eight

The small bungalow left a lot to be desired in terms of curb appeal. The roof had been patched multiple times, always with shingles that didn't quite match the existing ones. The siding was in desperate need of a fresh coat of paint. Shrubs were overgrown, the grass hadn't been cut in weeks and a pile of newspapers rotted on the sidewalk near the front steps.

A decade-old sedan sat in the driveway. Jones ran the plate to confirm the vehicle belonged to Greg Ames. The Kendricks had bought the funeral home a year ago. Ames could have moved or died since then.

"The car is his." She turned her cell screen toward Rowan, displaying the DMV photo of Ames.

Rowan's tension shifted to the next level. He was a perfect match to the sketch artist's rendering of the man who had visited her father. "If we're lucky, he isn't aware we've gotten so close."

"If we're lucky," Jones echoed.

Rowan shifted her attention back to the house. "Blinds

are closed tight. It's possible he's holed up in there, maybe taking a nap after his latest kill."

Some killers stayed high on the act for hours or days after a fresh kill. Others crawled into their safe place and crashed. On the other hand, if Ames was their unsub, it was possible he'd merely gotten up and gone to work this morning as if it were any other day. So far they hadn't located a new employer. Tracking down what he'd been up to for the past year would take time.

"I'm thinking the same thing," Jones agreed. "Let's knock on the door and see if he's interested in playing nice."

On the drive over, Rowan had contemplated the potential motives for the unsub's actions. Without any additional details she could only conclude that he'd grown obsessed with her somehow—perhaps through the book—and that had led him to go to such extreme measures to draw her attention.

Still, the fact that he'd made no move to contact her directly niggled at her. She should have at least received an anonymous letter or a phone call. Something to indicate he was building toward this level of violence. Slipping over that edge was rarely done without some impetus. He would want a reaction—some sort of feedback to fuel his ego.

Beyond the occasional impulse kill, murder rarely happened without a motive and some amount of planning—even if it was only the decision to pull the proverbial trigger. The unsub who had abducted and murdered three victims so meticulously so as not to leave a single shred of evidence had planned his work down to the last detail had a complex motive driving him.

Jones called in their location and requested backup as

they exited the vehicle. Rowan glanced around the yard as they climbed the steps to the porch. The killer had been exacting in his work. Precise. Careful. Nothing on the surface of Greg Ames's existence could be defined by any of those terms.

Jones banged on the door with the side of her fist. The silence beyond the front door had Rowan's heart sinking. No one was home. It was too quiet.

"Mr. Ames." Jones pounded again. "This is Metro PD. We need to speak with you, sir. It's urgent."

Still not a sound inside.

Rowan's hopes deflated completely. "If he's in there, he's not coming to the door."

Jones reached for the knob, her gaze latching on to Rowan's. "Does this door look ajar to you?"

The door was unlocked, and sure enough when she turned the knob it opened a fraction. "It does. Very strange that he would leave it open like this."

"Wait." Jones frowned. "Did you hear something?"

Rowan narrowed her gaze. "I think I did. Someone calling for help, maybe."

Jones readied her weapon and gave a nod. "I'm going in, Doc. Step back and wait for backup. They're right behind us."

Rowan backed up, braced against the wall to the right of the door while Jones called out to Ames and cautiously entered his residence.

With three women murdered so close together, it stood to reason that he could have another one in there...*if* he was their guy. However, without exigent circumstances what they were doing was illegal—if anyone found out.

As Jones moved deeper into the house, calling out to

Ames with each step, Rowan ventured across the threshold, careful to maintain a proper distance.

The interior of the house needed as much TLC as the exterior. Big box television, well-worn sofa and a coffee table. Typical single male furnishings but completely lacking in the obsessive details associated with their unsub's work. A small table with only one chair was tucked into the space that ninety-degreed from the living room into the kitchen. Cabinets were mostly bare. Fridge was stocked with beer and bologna and little else.

"Dr. DuPont!"

Rowan moved back through the main living area and into the hall that led to the bedrooms and bathroom. Jones stood in the hall, staring into the open door on the left. Judging by the look on her face, what she'd found was not what they had hoped for.

As Rowan approached Jones called in the address and the code for a body. Holy hell. They were too late.

Jones stepped aside for Rowan to see into what turned out to be the bathroom where a nude male—presumably Greg Ames—lay in the claw-foot tub, his right arm dangling from the side. Blood pooled on the dingy white tile floor. A message had been left in blood on the white-tiled wall that surrounded the tub: *This is the way you should have done it in the first place.*

Her heart pounding, Rowan tugged gloves and shoe covers from her bag and slipped them on. The painted parts of the walls in the room were a grimy white, the same as the tile. A single window with a yellowed shade overlooked the tub from the wall behind it. A pedestal sink was cluttered with deodorant, a razor, toothpaste and brush. The toilet lid was closed as if he'd intended to lay a towel there but had forgotten or changed his mind.

Or perhaps he'd sat down for a moment before climbing into the tub.

His left arm lay in the crimson-tinged water next to him. His knees were bent since the tub was only about four and a half feet long and he was at least six feet. His head lay back on the porcelain rim. Skin was ashen. Mouth and eyes open. Based on his DMV photo, it was definitely Greg Ames. And the same man who had visited her father.

Considering the coagulation of the blood on the floor and the state of lividity, Ames had been dead more than twelve hours, perhaps as much as twenty-four. Taking care not to step in the blood, Rowan went down on hands and knees to look under the tub. Right away she spotted what she was looking for: the straight razor he'd apparently used to end his life. Blood smeared the stainless steel blade and handle.

Then she shifted into a crouching position and studied the injury to his right arm. A horizontal slash had been made across the wrist, but the one that likely helped him to bleed out sufficiently for his heart to stop beating was the vertical slash that cut even deeper into his flesh. The right arm had without question suffered serious damage to important anatomical structures. With an injury that deep, there was scarcely any doubt. Rowan tried to visually evaluate as much of the other wrist as possible but the blood-tinged water prevented her from seeing well enough to determine if both slashes were present on that one, as well.

She stared at the cross Ames had made with the two intersecting slashes and a memory rammed hard into her brain.

During college, before she'd gone for the handful of

sleeping pills, she'd considered doing exactly this. Except she knew that once she slashed one wrist this way, the ability to slash the other would be taken from her. The damage to nerves and tendons often left the hand non-functional. Without help, it was nearly impossible to do the job right. If the injuries to his left arm were equally severe, she doubted he had done this alone.

Was it conceivable there was a second killer? A partner?

There were cases, of course, where two or more killers worked together, but this didn't feel like that kind of kill.

She reread the message. Beyond the puddle of blood that had dripped from his right arm the floor was clean of blood, suggesting Ames hadn't written those words himself. He would surely have left blood drops and smears everywhere while attempting to write the words.

"Crime scene folks and the ME are en route," Jones said.

Rowan blinked. She pushed to her feet and faced the detective. "Where are his clothes?"

Jones glanced around the room, her eyebrows arched upward. "Good question."

They moved from room to room, picked through the dead man's meager belongings but they didn't find any discarded clothes, not even a laundry hamper with whatever clothes he'd worn since the last time he did laundry. There was no washer and dryer in the house and none of the clothes in the closet or bureau appeared to have been worn. Jones even checked his car.

More importantly, they didn't find anything related to the other three victims. In fact, what they found was evidence of a lonely, unhappy life lived by a man still drawing unemployment and using a government food card. There were no photos of family or friends, and no cell phone.

"Whoever helped him do this and left that message took his phone in addition to his clothes," Rowan announced as official vehicles piled up in front of the house.

Jones waved a card—a gift card or credit card—she'd found in the bedside table. "He would have used this on one of those pay-as-you-go phones. I'm calling the carrier now."

During the next hour and a half the evidence techs searched the house, tore apart the sofa and anything else that might conceal evidence.

"Got an appointment card," one of the techs announced.

He passed it to Jones, who sent Rowan a surprised look. "Apparently, Ames was a patient of your friend Addington."

Rowan moved to the detective's side and had a look at the card. There had been an appointment with Julian yesterday.

"You think there's any chance you can get your friend to talk?"

"Probably not without a warrant."

"The guy is dead," Jones reminded her.

Though that was of little consequence, Rowan said, "I'll see what I can do."

Jones tucked the card into an evidence bag. "I'll go with you."

Rowan waved her hands in protest. "I should do this alone. If he's willing to talk, he's more likely to talk to me alone."

Jones tossed her fob to Rowan. "Take my car. I'll

catch a ride with one of these guys. I want that security detail watching Addington's office following you."

Rowan started to argue but she wasn't a fool. She put in a call to Julian and this time he answered. He wasn't home. He'd decided to spend the weekend at his lake house and urged her to join him. Since Hendersonville was only a half hour away, she agreed. Her father was safe. Ames was the only lead they had in the case; anything Julian was willing to share could prove useful.

She had nothing to lose.

Rowan gave Jones the address and promised, "I'll let you know what I find out."

She called her father as she pulled away from the crime scene. Maybe it was foolish but she just needed to hear his voice and to let him know she would be home in time for dinner...hopefully.

Rhoades Lane, Hendersonville, 4:35 p.m.

The chalet sat on the very edge of the lake in a private wooded setting that was breathtaking anytime of year. Rowan had been here a few times over the years. Julian often held small, intimate parties at his lake house. Everyone loved the place. On first look the rustic logs and aged rock of the facade suggested old and rugged but that couldn't be further from the truth. The home had towering windows overlooking the water and every imaginable amenity. The distance from the city—from civilization in general—assured peace and quiet.

Rowan parked in the drive, immediately noting the security detail parking on the street a dozen or so yards away. She waved to him as she walked toward the house. When she left she intended to instruct him to stay behind. If Jones was intent on assigning Rowan a personal security detail she would need to call in someone else.

Julian met her at the door and gave her a hug. That was the moment when she realized how very tired she was. This week had been far too long.

"I'm so glad you came." He closed the door behind her. "Did your father return to Winchester?"

"No, he's still at the office."

She left her bag and her shoes at the bench near the front door. Julian firmly believed that one brought into their home whatever they'd encountered each day, physically and spiritually speaking. Rowan had no desire to bring the bad vibes from a crime scene into her friend's home.

A frown marred Julian's smooth brow. "Oh. I thought perhaps he'd gone home since you found time to visit me."

"I can only stay a little while." Rowan made a face. "I'm sorry. This has been a really tough week."

"You need a drink."

She started to decline but decided one couldn't hurt. "That would be lovely."

Rather than follow him to the bar, she wandered to the wall of windows that overlooked the lake and the setting sun. It was so peaceful here. Everyone should have an escape like this.

"Any news on the case?" He brought the gin and tonic to her. She hadn't realized what a refreshing drink it was until Julian introduced her.

She savored a long swallow, hoping to make the answer a bit more palatable. "Not really."

"I saw your face and name splashed all over the news."

She sighed. "I suppose they'll torture me that way until this case is closed."

"You're a strong woman." He smiled and tapped his glass to hers. "You can handle it."

"I like to think so." She might as well get this part out of the way first. Julian did not tolerate secrets well. "I forgot to mention that I was worried about you so I asked Lieutenant Jones to assign a security detail to keep an eye on you. I hope that was okay."

He smiled, the expression as caring as that of any father. "It warms my heart that you worry about me. Though I have to say, I haven't noticed one."

"He was waiting at your office." She shook her head. "I didn't know where you were until I called again a few minutes ago." It hadn't occurred to her until just then that Julian hadn't returned her call from earlier. She shook it off. Perhaps he hadn't gotten around to checking his voice mail.

Another substantial swallow of her drink and she dared to broach the actual subject that had brought her here. "What can you tell me about Greg Ames?"

The whole drive over she kept thinking of the way the man's arms had been mutilated—in that cross-like pattern. As a college freshman determined to end her misery, she remembered thinking that if she had done it right the second time, she would have been left with a cross on each wrist. Not that it would have mattered since she would have been dead. Rather than take the chance of not being able to finish the job she had opted to swallow the sleeping pills. It was far more painless and didn't require anyone's assistance. Certainly didn't leave such a mess.

Still, the message on the wall at the Ames crime scene could have been written for her.

This is the way you should have done it in the first place.

She had not mentioned anything about considering that route for her departure from this life in the book. It was one of the few things, despite her editor's urging, she had decided was too personal. She supposed the message could be coincidence, but so much of these four murders appeared related to her past—to the damned book—she doubted that was the case.

"He's a patient," Julian said slowly, "which, as you know, limits what I can tell you."

His words brought Rowan back to the here and now. "True, but at this point you can choose to disclose under exceptional circumstances. Your patient is dead and he may hold the key to answers related to three murders. Frankly, there's a possibility his own death was a homicide."

They hadn't found a single piece of evidence at the Ames home linking him to the three murders or anything concrete to suggest he hadn't committed suicide. Except the idea that it was highly improbable that he'd written that message and then cleaned up the mess or that he'd disposed of his clothes while bleeding to death. Ultimately, he could be just another lead that turned out to be a dead end—no pun intended…except he didn't feel like a dead end. The message felt like an even more solid link…to *her*. Something he shared with Julian could seem completely unrelated but might ultimately break the case.

"He was a very confused and depressed man. It's a shame he had to die."

Rowan gave herself a mental shake and shifted her attention back to the conversation. "I'm sorry." She turned to Julian, had trouble bringing his face into focus. She really was far more exhausted than she realized. This case was taking a heavy toll. No—her responsibility in these murders was taking the toll. "What did you say?"

"I put him out of his misery late yesterday. In any event, he was no longer needed. He wanted to die—he'd told me so on numerous occasions. I simply helped him do what he had wanted to do for years. Since you've obviously been in his home, I'm sure you saw what a pathetic life he lived. The most important task he ever performed was a simple job for me."

The glass fell from Rowan's hand. She blinked, comprehension dawning in her fuzzy brain. Oh God. He'd drugged her.

Part of her wanted to deny the assertion. Wanted to chalk this entire encounter up to total exhaustion, a mental breakdown with hallucinations. But she was here—in Julian's home—looking at him, listening to his voice.

This was real and it was happening now.

Stay calm, she told herself. Ask the expected questions. "I must have missed something. Why would you kill him?"

"Because he had served his purpose just as the others had."

"Wait." She pressed her hand against the glass wall in front of her to steady herself. This couldn't be right. None of it made sense. "What do you mean the *others*?"

"Dharma, Sandy and Karen, of course. Who else would I mean?"

Her knees gave out, but he grabbed her before she hit the floor. Her arms wouldn't work…she couldn't fight him. He carried her to the sofa and placed her helpless body there.

"Greg played an award-winning role when he visited your father. Just as the others did in foreshadowing what was coming for you, Rowan."

"I...don't...understand." She couldn't make her mouth work right anymore. She needed to get up. To fight. ...couldn't...

"Now, we have to finish this. It's time."

"Julian...what're you...doing?" Her eyelids kept drifting closed. She could not go to sleep. Had to stay awake! Her heart pounded, adrenaline rushed through her veins...but it would never be enough to help her resist the effects of the drug.

"You chose Edward over me. Dedicated your book to him. Dared to tell me you regretted not having gone home to take over the family business like he'd wanted. All these years, all my work." He shook his head, fury radiating in every word. "You threw *us* away. You have always cared more for him. That's clear."

"He's...he's...my father." The words came out slurred, but he understood. She saw the understanding in his eyes. "You and I...we're...just friends."

"Oh, Rowan, we are so much more than friends." He exhaled a big breath. "But you destroyed that. Now, when I'm done, you will finish what you started all those years ago. After all, no one knows you better than me. I've always been able to anticipate your every move just as I knew you would come to me when you found Ames."

He sat down on the edge of the sofa, swept the hair from her eyes. "I know you, Rowan. I know you better than you know yourself. You couldn't please your mother so she left you. You couldn't please your father, you let him down. Those other women are weighing heavy on your conscience. I assure you, when I'm done, you will want to end the agony of living with all that guilt."

His words so closely mirrored her feelings...so many times she had felt exactly that way. Sadly, all that he said was true.

But she did not want to die. She wanted to be there for her father. She'd only just recently begun to see that what she really wanted was to give him what he'd always wished for.

"No." The word warbled but came out strong. "This time...you're wrong about me, Julian."

Her eyes closed again, taking the image of his face with her into the darkness.

"You'll see. Goodbye, Rowan."

Nine

Wake up, Rowan!

She was still asleep. Or maybe she was dead. Her mother stood in front of her. She still looked thirty-six. And why wouldn't she? That was her age when she'd died.

You left me.

Rowan didn't say the words, she thought them. How could she speak? She was unconscious or dead.

Her mother smiled. Her blond hair, her blue eyes looked so alive, so real. How could a dream be so vivid? Maybe Rowan was dead.

I couldn't stay...

Her mother faded away, leaving Rowan standing on the second-story landing of her childhood home, right next to the banister her mother had used to hang herself. Maybe Rowan was dead and this was hell.

Except she didn't believe in hell any more than she believed in angels.

I'll never understand. Rowan looked around. She was alone. Where was her father?

"She's waking up!"

"Rowan! Dr. DuPont, can you open your eyes?"

Rowan tried to open her eyes. She could hear the voice—Lieutenant April Jones. Why was she in Rowan's dream?

"Open your eyes, Dr. DuPont!"

Rowan didn't recognize the male voice, but her body instinctively reacted to the command. Her eyes fluttered open.

Faces came into focus. One was a man, young, brown hair cut short, dark watchful eyes, she didn't recognize him but the uniform was familiar. *Paramedic.* So maybe she was alive.

Jones smiled down at her. "You gave me a hell of a scare, Doc."

Rowan struggled to sit up. Her body still wasn't responding properly. Her muscles felt too lax, as if they no longer belonged to her.

"Your vitals are stable, Dr. DuPont," the paramedic explained. "It'll take some time for the drug he gave you to wear off, so let's take it easy for a bit."

He. Julian.

"Where is he? Dr. Addington! Where is he?" And why was she still alive?

"We're not sure," Jones confessed. "We're just damned glad he didn't—"

Shouting jerked the lieutenant's attention from Rowan. "Hold on."

She didn't have to finish her statement for Rowan to know what she'd meant. Julian hadn't given her a lethal dose of the drug. The real question was why? Why hadn't he killed her as he had the others?

Jones disappeared and the sound of running footsteps filled the room.

"What's happening?" Rowan demanded of the young man still watching her closely as if he feared she would slip back into that unconscious state from which he'd chemically hauled her.

The paramedic shrugged.

Was Julian still here? Had he been hiding?

"Help me up," Rowan ordered.

"Sorry, ma'am, it's better if you take it easy for a few more minutes."

Rowan hoped the glare she arrowed at him was fierce enough. "Help me up and take me to wherever Lieutenant Jones went or I will let your superior know how you refused to follow my directive."

He weighed the words for a moment, the concept that she was a doctor likely proving the deciding factor. "Have it your way, then."

He helped her to her feet, supported most of her weight. Her legs were rubbery but she managed to move along beside him. The progress up the stairs was frustratingly slow. Halfway up, he stopped, picked her up and bounded up the rest of the way.

When she was on her feet once more, she nodded. "Thank you."

He grunted something that sounded vaguely like "yeah" and ushered her toward a door at the end of the hall. Rowan still didn't quite trust her bearings but if she recalled correctly the other end of this corridor was the guest wing of the upstairs. Three bedrooms, each with its own bath. The end that appeared to be their destination was the owner's suite. They entered the double doors that led into a large sitting area with a small bar and an incredible view of the lake. Another set of double doors led into Julian's bedroom. It was decorated as exquisitely as she would have expected. Yet another set of doors opened to the en suite. The far wall was glass and offered another spectacular view of the lake and the forest that surrounded it.

"This way."

The paramedic steered her toward the low murmur of voices. They walked through a single door and into a massive closet. Elegant suit jackets and matching trousers hung in strict rows. Ties were flawlessly folded and showcased by color behind glass doors. Shoes polished to a high sheen were displayed along the lower shelves of the generous closet. The room smelled of silk and cashmere, the finest wools and Julian.

At the far end of the extravagant space was what appeared to be a vault door but it stood partially open.

Rowan moved forward when her escort had stopped. "I can make it from here."

He nodded. "I'll be in the bedroom if you need me."

The paramedic understood that whatever was beyond that odd door, he didn't need to see it unless told otherwise.

Rowan moved slowly, hanging on to the edge of a shelf. When she paused in the opening, she spotted Jones, Wells and a forensic tech standing in the middle of the large room. Like a vault, the space was climate-controlled and all walls, ceiling and floor were lined with a dark material—rubber maybe—that served as a noise reducer or perhaps additional insulation. White shelves wrapped around the walls. She counted three small safes, doors closed, which meant they needed to find the combinations or the keys.

Each shelf was filled with glass or plastic cubes, organized by size and shape. Some cubes contained what appeared to be pieces of female lingerie. Some had jewelry or a playing card from a card game deck or a lock of what appeared to be hair. Others contained driver's licenses.

"What is this?" The question came from Rowan. All in the room turned to look at her except Wells.

Wells frowned at the screen of his cell phone before meeting her gaze. "I don't know about the rest of this stuff, but at least two of the driver's licenses belong to homicide victims."

"Jesus Christ." Jones surveyed the hundreds of carefully curated items. "Doc, I think your friend is a serial killer."

Unable to properly process the comment, Rowan asked, "Where is he?"

Jones shook her head. "We don't know. He was gone when we got here. He took the car I lent you." She looked away a moment. "He left Jackson, the security detail assigned to him, for dead. We got here in the nick of time. He's in surgery in critical condition, but he has a chance."

Rowan braced herself against the door frame, any strength she had regained draining out of her. "He killed Ames and the others. To get back at me for…"

Her voice faded as another wave of weakness overwhelmed her.

"Let's get you into a chair, Doc." Jones pulled Rowan against her and ushered her back into Julian's bedroom and into a chair. The detective settled into the chair on the opposite side of the small side table. A nod to the paramedic whose name Rowan still didn't know sent him out of the room.

"We've issued a BOLO for Addington and the car he's driving, though he's probably abandoned it by this point. We've got people looking for him at the airport, train and bus stations. Everywhere. He's not going to get away," Jones promised.

Rowan shook her head. The urge to vomit hovered at the back of her throat. "I can't believe I didn't see any of this."

"Let's not worry about that right now," Jones urged. "I'll have plenty of questions for you when you feel up to it."

"I'm fine." Fury erupted inside Rowan. "Ask me whatever you like. I want him caught as badly as you do. Maybe more," she confessed.

Jones reached for the cell phone on her belt. "Hold on a minute."

Rowan hadn't heard the phone ring. Most likely Jones had silenced it when they approached the house. Standard operating procedure.

Rowan wished she had a bottle of water. Her mouth was so dry. She should call her father. He was still at headquarters and probably wondering when she was coming back. She didn't even know what time it was. He would not be happy about her close encounter with... Dear God, if Julian had killed all those people...

"Doc."

Rowan shifted her gaze to Jones. She hadn't realized the call had ended. She was still too groggy. "Sorry, I was just thinking that I needed to get back to headquarters."

"That was Detective Keaton. The car Addington was driving has been found."

"Julian?" Her heart started that frantic pounding again and suddenly her head was doing the same. She needed water. And, unfortunately, time.

Jones shook her head. "Addington is gone, but..."

Her hesitation had a new kind of dread expanding inside Rowan. "What?"

The older woman moistened her lips and took a big breath. "They located the car at your home, Doc. Addington drove it there and then used your cell phone to text Vasquez."

Officer Vasquez was the uniform assigned to her father today. A thick blackness wound around Rowan, tightening like a vise, threatening to drag her back into the darkness of unconsciousness.

She would not hear this. Would not listen. She shook her head. "No."

"Vasquez believed it was you telling him that you were home so he drove there as per the message. When he arrived he saw the official vehicle—the one you and I often use—so he accompanied your father into your home. Addington was already there."

"No. No. No." Rowan surged to her feet. The room tilted.

Jones stood, pulled her against her chest, held her tight. "Vasquez and your father are dead. I am so very sorry, honey."

Rowan tried to scream but she was too weak. Tears streamed from her eyes. She would have collapsed into a heap but Jones held her closer, tighter and murmured softly to her.

Julian's words reverberated in Rowan's head.

...when I'm done, you will want to end the agony...

Ten

Lieutenant Jones and the rest from SCU had come to her father's funeral. Rowan appreciated the gesture. Jones had actually arrived before the funeral and insisted on taking Rowan to lunch where she proceeded to try to talk her into changing her mind about the decision she'd made.

Rowan couldn't do that. Her decision was the right one.

Julian Addington had seemingly fallen off the face of the earth. Of course he had the resources to disappear. Rowan imagined he had overseas bank accounts and perhaps a home in some country that didn't share an extradition treaty with the United States. She doubted he would ever be found.

Her entire adult life she had prided herself on reading people, alive or dead, and forming a reasonably accurate assessment of who they were and how they fit into this world. But Julian had completely fooled her. She had no idea why he had bothered to go to such trouble for her.

Oh, Rowan, we are so much more than friends.

He'd said those words to her and she still had no idea what he'd meant. They'd never shared anything beyond a doctor-patient relationship that years later had developed into a friendship. Absolutely nothing more. Like many things about him that would likely remain a mystery, too.

So far Metro, with the aid of the FBI, had a preliminary estimate of more than a hundred victims to Julian Addington's credit. Not only had he kept souvenirs of all his kills, he kept an appointment book—the victims' pertinent personal information and the final disposition were included on the date he carried out the kill. The case had thrown the FBI for a loop. Addington was different from any serial killer they'd encountered. He chose an MO and killed a series of victims, whether two or three or ten or twelve. Then, he changed his MO completely. It was as if he changed his preferred victim and mode of operation often so as not to become bored. Or perhaps because he became someone else—a different personality who killed for a different reason. He had killed all over the country.

Addington would change the way the world looked at serial killers.

Special Agent Lancaster from Quantico's Behavioral Analysis Unit had refused to believe that Rowan had been so completely fooled. Her education and training should have allowed her to see what Julian Addington was…but she had not. Her colleagues at Metro had stood behind her, but the investigation was far from over. Rowan suspected she would remain a person of interest until the bitter end.

She bent down and took one of the beautiful white roses from the blanket on her father's grave. She would press this one into the family bible. There was a pressed rose from Raven's funeral as well as her mother's already there.

Rowan was the only one left.

...when I'm done, you will want to end the agony...

No. Rowan's lips tightened. She would not give that bastard the pleasure of accomplishing his ultimate goal. He had murdered at least four people to get her attention, to make her feel the guilt and then he'd killed her father and the man protecting him to tip her over the edge. She would not give Julian Addington what he wanted.

If he wanted to see her give up he would have to come back here and do the job himself.

"It'll be dark soon."

Rowan turned at the sound of Billy's voice. She managed a weak smile. As the crowd had drifted away from the cemetery, she had returned to her father's grave. "I forgot to take one of the roses for the family bible." She showed him the rose in her hand.

He nodded. "Why don't you let me take you to my place, Ro? You don't have to go back to the funeral home and go through all that. Herman has everything under control."

He was right. It was almost dark. Everyone who had come to the graveside service was gone now, headed back to the funeral home for the gathering in her father's honor. The cemetery was deserted. She'd told Woody to drive the hearse back to the funeral home. She'd ridden to the cemetery in the hearse with her father. Her heart sank all over again. He was gone. Dead and buried.

Two days ago when she'd arrived in Winchester and told her father's assistant director that she would be taking care of the preparation of his body personally, Woody had not been happy, but it was the DuPont way. Woody didn't know or understand. Herman had come to the funeral home and insisted on helping. Rowan hadn't argued. She had let him. He and her father had been best friends their whole lives. It was only right that he be a part of her father's final moments before being interred.

Hundreds of people had come to her father's funeral and then many more had filled the cemetery. He had been a beloved fixture in the community all of his adult life, just like his father, grandfather and great-grandfather before him. Though her heart remained heavy, her chest had filled with pride as the crowd gathered to show their respects.

Once the flowers were all arranged around the grave and there was nothing left to do, Rowan had thought everyone was gone but she should have known better. Billy wouldn't have left without her. She wasn't sure how long he had watched and waited for her to feel ready to go.

"I should be there." She could walk—the funeral home wasn't far—but it was cold. She'd only just become aware of how cold.

She looked from her parents' wide granite headstone to her sister's smaller one. A gulf of emptiness widened inside her. She pushed it away. She had Billy and Herman. Billy offered his arm and she wrapped hers around his, so grateful for his steady presence.

"I could take you to my place, let you relax while I go to the funeral home and help Herman," he offered as they walked through the maze of headstones with the shadows of night descending rapidly.

"Thank you, but you know I have to do this."

He sighed. "I know." He opened the passenger door of his truck and held her hand while she settled into the seat.

A gathering with family was expected after a loved

one's passing. Her father would have been the first to suggest good food and companionship after his funeral. Though, like her, he had never been a socialite generally speaking, he believed in going the distance for the passing of a loved one. He had loved his work and he had done it well.

Silence enveloped Rowan and Billy as they drove through the small town that had changed little since she was a child. She was home. Somehow, no matter how long she had lived in Nashville, *this* was still home.

Rowan's lips lifted slightly when Billy parked in front of the funeral home. She could see Freud waiting beyond the beveled glass of the front entrance, tail wagging. No matter that there were likely dozens of people milling about inside the lobby, he watched for her arrival. She still had Freud, too. They would get through this together. Whatever Julian's—the bastard—reason for sending Freud into the backyard rather than killing him, too, Rowan was grateful.

"What happens now, Ro?"

She turned to the man behind the wheel, the dim glow from the dash highlighting his worried face. For a few seconds she couldn't think how to answer the question.

"Are you heading back to Nashville?" he asked when she didn't answer his first question.

"No." Deep breath. Besides April Jones, she had not shared her plans with anyone. It was time to do that now. "I'm staying."

He nodded slowly. "Sorry. I didn't think of that. You have to take care of your father's estate. I guess you'll be selling the funeral home."

She shook her head. "No. I'm staying, Billy. I'm taking over the business the way Daddy wanted."

"Ro." He reached out, took her hand in his. "Your daddy understood you didn't want that life. He wouldn't want you to stay now out of any misplaced guilt or sense of obligation. All he ever wanted was for you to be happy—wherever that might be."

She nodded. "I know, but this is what I want. It's what I was born to do."

A grin spread across his lips. "Well, in that case, let me be the first to officially welcome you home." He reached across the console and gave her a hug. "I'm glad you're back, Ro."

"Thank you." She smiled, the first in many days. "I'm counting on you and Herman to bring me up to speed on all I've missed."

Billy gave her a nod. "I'll do my best."

She knew he would. Billy was a good man and so was Herman. She was in great hands.

Billy was at her door by the time she unfastened her seat belt. They strolled up the walk to the front entrance of the DuPont Funeral Home, and Rowan felt genuinely at peace with her decision.

She looked up at the old Victorian mansion backdropped by the full moon. She was home and this time she intended to stay.

As the undertaker's daughter, this was her destiny.

* * * * *